Gatsby's LAST RESORT

A Telluride Murder Mystery

R. J. Rubadeau

Beacon Hill Publishers, Telluride

A NOVEL

Gatsby's LAST RESORT

A Telluride Murder Mystery

R. J. Rubadeau

First edition published by Beacon Hill Publishers a Sirius Publications
Company. November 1, 2010

Beacon Hill Publishers
P. O. Box 3836
Telluride, Colorado 81435
publisher@BeaconHillPublishers.com

Beacon Hill Publishers
Books That Matter

Printed in the United States of America on acid free paper.

ISBN 978-0-9817313-5-3
LCCN2010937869

Book Cover Design by www.KarrieRoss.com
Interior Design by Gwen Gades www.beapurplepenguin.com
Cover Art Work by Roger Mason www.rogermason.net

ACKNOWLEDGEMENTS

A book never gets finished without a lot of help. I had the colorful community of Telluride in my corner. As Will Rodgers, the 20th Century dean of hilarious observation, was fond of saying that it's easy to be funny, wry, and cynical when he had the whole damn Congress working everyday writing the material. My hometown does the same for me. Thank you Telluride.

Thanks: to Jim Kolar who was a constant source of procedural wisdom and support, to ace mystery writer Randall Peffer for offering guidance in the early drafts, to Amy Canon for being a tireless reader and mentor, to author John Heckler for early story twists and a collaborative nature. A special appreciation to my peer readers Susan Saint James, Clint Viebrock, Sharon Shuteran, Bob Trenary, and Shauna Palmer . Kudos to my editor Regan Tuttle. A very special thanks to iconic Telluride (& the world) painting talent Roger Mason for the cover art.

I want to thank the Telluride Writers Guild and Amy Canon, the Wilkinson Public Library and Scott Doser, Between the Covers Bookstore and Stuart and Joanna Brown, and Susan and Clint Viebrock of *Telluride Inside... and Out* webzine for sponsoring the inaugural Community Publishing 101 program in Telluride. This unique partnership provided the platform for this book to launch itself to the publishing process and set the bar for other volumes under the Preserving America's Regional Voices Achievement Award guidelines.

Books by R. J. Rubadeau

Novels
Gatsby's Last Resort
The Fat Man
The Big Snooze

Non-fiction
Bound For Roque Island: Sailing Maine and the World

Poetry
offshore
(collected poems 1968-2010)

For Mary, always

"What I cut out of *The Great Gatsby* both physically and emotionally would make another novel!"

F. Scott Fitzgerald, 1934

One

The Right Word Is Dead

Kissing a dead man is not as glamorous as it sounds. The blue lips feel cold as a frog's belly. The taste is a mix of despair, mucous and table salt. The smell is a funeral without the flowers. If given a choice, I wouldn't do it before breakfast. I didn't have a choice.

"Move it Buster, or I'll put the thumbscrews to you." My ten-year-old daughter, who responds to the name of Cody, smiled her pearly whites, reached across from the passenger seat, and hammered the horn.

I jumped and strangled a startled squeak.

"Button your yap," I said.

Following the horn scramble, I settle back into my slow gallows shuffle in the general direction of the bank. I have a favor to ask at the Telluride Savings and Loan, and with the way my life is going, I expect a negative answer. My future is hinged on a single word. The favor I need concerns an ancient Mustang convertible that needs one or more of everything. I feel both its pain, and a long-standing moral obligation to put it out of its misery. I need something that starts quicker than I do in the mornings, but my business account balance is about twenty bucks away from lap dancing for pesos at a Mexican truck stop. The list of tapped out creditors must include the entire town, or else I'm as poor a private detective as most folks believe. People illegally cross the street holding their wallets when I approach. I am shameless and harry them like a bucolic sheep dog.

Mark Twain explains that the difference between the right word and the almost right word for a writer is the difference between lightning and a lightning bug. I take Twain's advice seriously. If you want to be a real writer, you have to be cold, wet, scared and out running naked in the thunderstorm with a kite in order to find the right words. This deep immersion method of literary research I apply with fervor. My passion embarrasses my whole family.

"If you were going any slower, you'd be backing up."

"Stow it, sister," I said and turned back towards the rust and red Mustang with a raised fist. "You better pull your mouth in, or you'll get a goog, and I'll pop a tooth out of it."

"Good one," Cody said, admiring my pre-breakfast choice of other people's words. The young lady isn't worried over her dental work. Cody is the brains of our lopsided partnership. We share an addiction for books written before either of us were born, and annoy anyone within earshot by quoting from them as often as possible.

"If I'm not back in ten minutes pump the place full of hot lead," I said, pausing at the door. Cody winked. "And get your butt off to school. You'll be late."

As a Western Slope Ute with a dark Irish humor, I try not to be surprised when warned in ancient mystical ways of events about to happen. Foretelling the future is actually a cinch. It helps to be a born pessimist. If things aren't getting worse, they're a pleasant surprise. For no apparent reason, on this particular bright day, a shadow passed over me from the cloudless sky. Occasionally, once in a bright blue moon, aboriginal mysticism collides with the laws of probability. Sixty seconds later I twisted the knob on a major problem.

~

The limp body of the white and black spotted cow hit the polished wooden floor with a splat as I opened the door to the bank president's inner sanctum of the Telluride Savings and Loan. Two pounds of painted leather and plastic beans made a loyal thud; then it was the sound of a breeze rustling through Aspen leaves as the rush of air from the opening door vibrated the loose folds of the plastic shopping bag.

"Sorry to bother you," I said to the silhouette behind the desk.

My eyes adjusted from the bright morning sun in the lobby to the shuttered bank president's office. Designer fabric blinds hid the trio of floor to ceiling windows and gave the twenty-foot square room a sickly greenish glow. The room smelled of peppermint.

"Help," I said. It was barely a whisper as I finally saw the details of the body hunched forward in the high-backed leather chair.

A white, translucent plastic bag was wrapped tightly around the head of the man seated behind the mahogany desk. An overlapping wrap of wide gray duct tape held the lethal cowl tight to the thin neck above the tidy Windsor knot of his tie. The nameplate I swept aside as I launched myself across the polished empty desktop read: "Stewart Lambis, Esquire."

"Help." My yell echoed through the half-open door. The already quiet bank went mute.

I tore my fingers through the thin plastic. The face exposed was a mottled blue; lips stretched rigid white. His pale brown eyes were open, glazed over and unfocused. I tried to yank him from the swivel chair to put him on the floor, but came up short. Handcuffs pin his arms behind his back. A short steel chain looped through a chair spring bound the wrists.

"Hey," a voice said. "What are you doing?"

I quickly straddled the body in the chair and tried my best to pinch his nose, pull down his chin, tilt back his head and open his air passage. I started mouth-to-mouth resuscitation.

He tasted dead.

"Stop!" An astonished male voice from the doorway made the exclamation point sound like an embarrassing question.

After a dozen more deep exhales and some hard handed pushing on the heart cavity trying to fill the man's lungs with no response. I felt for a heart beat. I gave up, released his nose and pulled my face away from his. I felt a last settling in his chest and a slow release of shallow, stale breath against my cheek.

"Let him alone." A feeble female voice tried to sound forceful and failed.

"Please." The polite one added a cough at the end.

I finally let the dead man's head fall back over the chair to stare at the ceiling. I looked over my shoulder. The doorway was full of faces. None dared to enter the dimly lit room. I wondered at their shocked and puzzled expressions until I suddenly realized what I must look like. I awkwardly got off the man's lap, feeling my face turn red as I regained my feet.

I shuffle once, then raise my hand and carefully closed the dead man's eyes. I began to pull the plastic bag back up to cover his face then stopped. What was I doing? I stepped back and let my arm drop to my side. The silence from the doorway meant everyone was focused on my every twitch.

I opened my mouth to try and explain. I shut it again. What was I going to say? Up until a few minutes ago, Stewart Lambis and I had just been nodding acquaintances on the streets of our little mountain ski town. Now we were caught in the final act of his death rattle with my lips on his. I couldn't for the life of me remember why I had even come into the bank.

"Call nine-eleven," I said. I wiped my mouth with the back of my hand. No one in the doorway moved as they stared at their boss, expecting him to suddenly wake up and explain it all to them.

"Call an ambulance." Somebody finally contradicted me when the strained silence wore tissue thin. It was obvious I was the only one who knew a stiff when he saw one.

"Call the cops," I said.

The "Oh, my, God" and "What happened" murmurs began as I bent over and picked up the miniature cow that had likely slipped from the dead man's fingers with his last breath. It was toy size, fit snugly in my hand, made of soft black and white spotted leather, and stuffed full of beans. One like it rests on nearly every local business man's desk to remind us all of the peculiar essence of our beautiful hamlet that is only protected from over crowded "Aspen-ization" by the eight-hundred green acres of undeveloped Valley Floor to the west. The pastoral prize extends along the only road into and out of town.

I set the cow gently back on the desk, wondering about the handcuffs, the grocery bag, and the nagging certainty that Stewart Lambis might have a bovine secret he wasn't going to get a chance to tell. I resigned myself to wait for the police, remembering suddenly that a used car loan was my reason for being at the wrong place at the wrong time. Chances were lousy I was going to get an answer today.

Although Deputy Officer Darryl tried to come up with a solid reason to keep me at the jail until he could prove I had somehow killed Stewart Lambis by sucking the breath out of him, I was finally let go when it is confirmed by everyone else at the bank that I had simply found the body. The salacious lip attack I was obviously guilty of came after he was probably already dead.

≈

I needed a hard drink and a place to collect my thoughts. I could still taste the cold insides of the dead man's mouth after two iced tumblers of Bushmills. My name, coming from the table across the room, as I sat alone on a corner stool at the New Sheridan Bar, riveted what was left of my attention.

"Did he really kiss a dead body?"

"It's what they said."

"Jeese Loueese." A giggle broke into the gap.

"Wit Thorpe has nothing, wants nothing, is a nothing," said a raspy female voice. "A waste of prime mountain air."

"Do you think he really killed him?"

"Well, he beat the rap the last time."

A lot of reckless hair did a wave around the table as they all agreed with the blindness of justice.

"Is he crazy?"

"You could say his inner child pretty much runs things inside that little ol' head of his."

"Did you see the Indie Film Fest premier of his latest half-finished work in progress last month?"

"It was just his amateur, blurry video bloopers of people screwing."

"No." A now familiar voice contradicted the statement with a smoker's laugh. "It was badly focused evidence of other people screwing other people's spouses."

"Imagine that being your job?"

That ushered in a liquid moment of silence for the victims.

"Someone said you could tell who they were even though their faces and privates were spotted out." It was a stage whisper.

"Sweetheart, I recognized most of those men, and I didn't need their faces to do it."

"Patsy Susie." The voices howled in chorus.

"He calls himself a writer, but I hear he couldn't write his name in the dirt with a stick, some phobia about finishing things or something."

"His wife is such a saint." Another female voice picked up the pause. "Is she going to be embarrassed when they charge him with … what ever?"

"Is kissing a dead person a crime?"

A pause allowed all the time needed to consider the facts and take another long pull of alcohol. Digger was working on the next round in a hurry.

"He can't seem to hold a job. He's been fired all over town. The only thing he can do is sneak around and get the goods on wayward husbands, and choral society partners."

I could imagine pursed lips wrapped around these words.

"Would you put up with it?"

"Not me," Patsy Susie said. "Even if he was good under the sheets. Got to admit that he fills out his jeans. Maybe his wife isn't so saintly after all."

"Patsy Susie." The squealer repeated her first chide with a staged horselaugh and a snort. "You're always aiming at the crotch."

"He is kind of sinister," the other said. "Foreign, dark and sleek, a hunk, like those old movie stars. Antonio Bandaras on steroids maybe?"

"A mostly drunk lightening rod for trouble and a liability for the town." The first voice out of the gates added. "I pity the kids."

"Two little girls, right?"

"My mother always said, 'if it has wheels or testicles you're going to have trouble with it.' Given the choice, I want to own a nice set of wheels and have a bundle of money. I'd take a new Mercedes over having any man in the damn universe. You can always get laid. An expensive ride impresses the young meat in this town to death." Patsy Susie brought them all to laughter again.

"Isn't that the truth." They all agree, clinking their empty glasses together.

I've got more experience with disappointing women than anybody else I know. Retreat was the only course of action that made any sense. I slunk out, with a subtle wave to Digger as he nearly lost control of the tray of drinks. I did it without drawing attention. I can do that. Slinking is an art that can't be taught, only learned by becoming invisible of necessity when your fat is in the fire. I had studied the science since being "re-fired" from the local ski mountain and just about every other job I've ever had. It seems I have trouble taking orders from those foolhardy people who dare to employ me. I am now trying to be self-employed, but find I can't take orders from myself either. Slinking around and videotaping the unwary for money is now my indentured profession. Most days it isn't really as much fun as you might imagine.

Two

Rose's Problem

I was being watched, and I knew it. The skin on the back of my neck crawled with fire ants. Walking into Rose's, Telluride's default grocery store for its fifteen hundred residents, I feel as though I am facing a hangman's noose. I owe someone a favor, and the bill is due. My day is predictably going from bad to worse.

Rose had recently installed a two-way mirror in her closet sized office to watch the cashiers. She would have preferred to be out front, watching each exchange from the drawers, doing random spot tallies, but the health conscious customers and local town statutes in Telluride wouldn't let her chain smoke in her own grocery store.

Rose Laphorn, born and raised in Rifle, Colorado, hated any infringement on her God given rights to free range grazing, ancestral water allotments, packing an assault rifle if she wanted, and doing whatever she damn well pleased on any property she owned. "Hell, let them shop someplace else," she said to anyone who would listen and cheated on the odious clean air ordinance every day. The world is simple and sharp for Rose, divided into two categories of people: those who are trying to cheat her out of her just profits, and those who haven't tried yet.

I gag quietly when I let myself into the cubicle following the gruff response to my knock. She stamped out a nub into a full ashtray and shook another slender white cylinder from the pack on her desk. A noisy, dusty, stained green smoke-eater whirs impotently in the corner. People in the store file silently past the two-way, blue tinted window behind her back.

"How they hangin'?"

It was meant to be an affectionate greeting. To her I am just another kid she had hired before, and is now back looking for a job.

I wait, nervous, just as I had twenty years ago when I had applied to be a bagger and stocker. I remembered sitting upright in the same chair, inhaling the second-hand smoke from unfiltered Camels, and feeling intimidated.

"Thorpe, I want you to catch the rotten bastard now." Rose paused, the lighter an inch from the end of the new cigarette. She lights up and blows a rolling wall of billowing smoke in my direction. "Catch him and kill him."

"Kill who?"

"The raping son of a bitch."

"Rape?"

"Every other goddamn day this month." Rose stuck her face forward across the desk. The aging folds of pasty smoker's skin framed the glinting gray irises that floated in a soured yellow cream. Her brows were plucked randomly and penciled as unevenly as a haiku poem. Her seldom washed silver hair lay askew in sagging tendrils with a long number 2 pencil stuck behind her ear. She was daring me to ask another question. I kept the yapper shut.

"You owe me," she said with a belligerent look.

I agreed. She had once hired a half-breed juvenile delinquent who needed a job to stay out of jail when no one else would. I owed her a lot. I would likely still be a delinquent if she hadn't given me a shot. The fact I still behave like a juvenile is my own doing.

"This is more than just about money," she said as she handed me an invoice from the pile on her desk. The bill was from Baked In Telluride and listed a bread delivery of ninety-three loaves of various shapes and grains. The bottom line was seventy-eight dollars and nine cents.

"I want the lousy little shit on molesting, rape, sodomy, and willful destruction of private property."

"Who?"

"How the hell should I know?" Rose coughs up some phlegm, chews, and then swallows it again. "You're the private detective."

I was. Silence became my best defense from the obvious facts. She sucked deeply and stared at me with mongoose eyes, the kind of cruel gape reserved for a wounded snake.

"How did he taste?" she finally asks.

"What?"

"The dead bank guy." Rose wheezed up into a laugh, unable to contain herself at my expense. "The whole town is glad you're out of the closet so now we can keep an eye on you, mister twinkle toes."

"I don't have any problem with gay people."

"Obviously, *Chico.*"

"You do?"

"No problem, as long as they pay cash."

I gave her my coldest stare, and she blew more smoke at me. My options were minimal. I could throw a hissy fit and leave because she was questioning my manhood, but that would be throwing gasoline on an already roaring fire. My other option was to stay, take the abuse and do exactly what I will have to do anyway. I was astonished at the clarity of my thoughts, as the mounting nicotine ingestion began making my heart thump and my head hurt.

After finding out the rest of what Rose wanted me to know, I left the store in a stumbling hurry. In the clear mountain air outside, I took a flurry of deep breaths and resigned myself to the fact that I will have to do exactly what Rose asks or leave town. I think about my kids, my wife, my house mortgage, my whole sorry life, and blow out of town ten minutes later on a random tip about another case that, for want of a better term, I was working.

Three

Paradox

Can I drown a brunette in this?" I ask. My morning was only almost over, and another drink was the worst idea in the world except for all the rest.

"How tall is she?" Mick, the one-eyed bartender, responded with feigned interest.

"Five-eight, nine." I cut the air above my head with a flat hand. I was seated on a wobbly round stool at the bar and barely caught the foot rail with my cowboy boot as I tried to regain my balance.

"Here," he said, pouring another inch of Bushmills into my glass. Mick owes me. I had driven to hell and back to get here to the Town of Paradox; all for nothing.

The adage reads: "good bartenders, like Irish mothers, may not always be right, but they are never wrong." So much for adages. Mick had been dead wrong. It was a recurring flaw of mine that I trusted bartenders more than Irish mothers. This *camarera* had destroyed my misplaced trust once again. Mick was also Yugoslavian with a heavy accent and not a twig Irish, which helps explain the bitter disappointment I had in myself for believing in this particular tooth fairy. First Rose's bread rapist, and now this. I sighed loudly. Mick took it wrong.

"Don't guilt me, man," Mick said. I detected a whine in his voice.

"Guilt isn't a verb," I said, taking a sip of the whiskey, confident in my usage.

"It is when you do it," he said and poured another inch in my glass before I could set it down.

The dust lay thick in the shadows of the bar. Harsh slivers of sunlight from the windows exposed the old tables and mismatched wooden chairs scattered about the undulating riprap of the scarred and battered, pastel-tinted linoleum. Hot, high plains desert waited just outside the heavy metal door. Melancholy was not exactly the right word to describe my mood. I searched for a substitute. Pride in my vocabulary was one of my many faults. Glum might be the word I was searching for.

"Troubles?" Mick seemed intent on making conversation as part of his ongoing apology, but he defensively put the square bottle back on the shelf behind the bar.

"The DA is breaking my balls." I grumbled and drain the extra dollop of amber liquid. I grit my teeth as my jaw muscles spasm from the assault.

"Vise-grips," I said, wiping the ice sweat from my upper lip with the back of the hand that held the glass.

"Ouch." Mick adds a painful expression for color, and grabs his crotch for protection and sympathy. He paused in that position. It put a crimp on follow-up conversation.

I usually confine my afternoon on the job drinking to a couple of beers, but this has already been a day I intend to forget quickly. Dead bodies before breakfast have a knack of changing the daily routine.

I had already wasted the better part of the morning on the road to nowhere. Paradox's name comes from the fact that it is a very distinctive high-sided valley that runs straight as an arrow for a couple of dozen miles. The one river that flows into and out of the valley does so at a ninety degree angle to the valley floor, cutting a deep canyon through sheer cliffs on both sides. It is a place for strange sightings. The brand new silver Mercedes Z3 that Mick thought he saw at a friend's trailer had turned, on further inspection, into a few decades old silver and gray-primer spotted, Honda Accord. I was fairly certain a little homemade crystal meth had something to do with this case of mistaken identity.

It is hard making a living as a mostly honest private investigator on the western slopes of the Colorado Rocky Mountains. Trusting Mick and running afoul of the hard-assed female prosecutor for San Miguel County, known by everyone as "The Iron Maiden," is no way to increase my income.

The Assistant District Attorney has been on my case for years, and now wanted my gun permit revoked for "reckless endangerment of a minor." I was, of course, guilty, despite my continuing protests to the contrary.

"On second thought, I think she's at least six-foot tall in those stiletto heels," I said with a husky voice of justification. I motioned for Mick to re-fill the glass. He was happy to oblige. We were alone in the bar. I had an ongoing problem. Mick had the solution.

~

Idiot is my middle name. Wilfred I. Thorpe was the birth record legacy handed down from my long departed father. The DNA donor was an idiot too, and had vanished "for the coast" as soon as he found my mother pregnant. Mom never knew what the "I" stood for. Her family speculated and settled on the obvious. Most people liked the joke behind the lonely "I," and put it prominently between my other two initials. I was called Wit. It still enrages the bigots in the Four Corners area that a half-breed Ute would carry a moniker that suggests he is ironic and funny at the same time. Enraging bigots is the second best thing I do.

The short version of the crime that put me on the ADA's shit list was anything but circumstantial. It seems that after a long and sleep deprived weekend of chasing the horny little jackrabbit in the silver Z3 all over the San Juan Mountains, I stumbled exhausted into my own bed. I had left the snub nosed thirty-eight caliber Smith and Wesson in its leather hip-clip holster, unloaded, on the nightstand.

Unfortunately, it was also the Iron Maiden's nightstand. Our three-year-old daughter, Katie, had been poking at the barrel with one of the shells, using the pudgy fingers of her perfectly beautiful little hand when we woke up to her presence this very morning. Busted, tried, convicted and sentenced before coffee.

As Mick the one-eyed bartender did what he did best, I pulled out my cell phone and called home. With my new priority for today firmly established at seeing how quickly I can drown my problems, I wasn't going to make it back in time to pick up Cody from school. I am hoping Angelina, my cousin and sometimes nanny, was in a benevolent mood and would do the chore for me.

No answer, no luck, *es mi problemo*. I look at the sweating glass of whiskey and ice longingly. I shake myself like a wet dog, throw a twenty on the bar alongside my business card. It read: Last Resort Detective Agency; Telluride, Colorado. A Literate and Discreet Investigative Service.

"Is this a joke?" Mick said, finally fully engaged. He held the card up to his black eye patch.

"Call me if you spot that bald headed, over-sexed bowling ball or his silver Z3 ever again," I said.

Mick saluted me with a ham-sized karate chop to his forehead. It was lucky he didn't knock himself out with the blow, trying to make it snappy and worth the huge tip. He staggered backwards holding his hairline. I wondered if his middle initial was "I".

"Always there for you, man," Mick said with a groan as the iron door slammed shut, pulled sharply by a heavy sash on a frayed clothesline rope.

I walked out into the harsh high desert sunlight heading for the 1972 Mustang. It wasn't vintage, just a rusting, falling apart wreck. It was the reason I needed a loan for a new secondhand car from a dead man. I had seventy five miles of winding Rocky Mountain road back to Telluride and twenty minutes to do it in. Success was about as probable as anything else in my life turning out the way I wanted today.

four

Victimized By Sheep Herders

The look in those cold green eyes was venomous enough to wilt a ten-foot Sequoia Cactus. I should be used to it by now. I had known her all her life. Familiarity does not lesson the "I'm in for it" feeling as the angry intent in those peepers washes over me like a bucket of glacier water. She slammed the car door and kept herself from meeting my stare after that first breathtaking visual assault.

"Cody, I got hung up," I said. It sounded lame. "I tried to call. The school office wouldn't answer. I left messages."

Silence speaking volumes did not do the absence of a response justice. She pinched her lips together tightly until they were only a razor slit. She balanced her briefcase on her lap and waited for me to die a gruesomely horrible death. Obliging her would have probably let me off the hook too easy.

"If I had a cell phone," she said, dragging on the last word for a full five seconds. "I could have got the message."

I tried to adopt a calm, resigned fatherly tone. "We've talked about the cell phone thing. No can do, Frodo. Your mom would have a fit." Then, remembering that I shouldn't blame the other parent, I added, "I would too."

She snickered, crossed her arms and glared at the windshield in front of her. It was her mother's look, and it meant business. Waiting for the windshield to crack from the intense pressure, I swallowed nervously without letting her know. She knew. It was also obvious she hadn't heard about bank guy Lambis and the kissing part of my day, or I would be forced to detail the event. That chore would happen soon enough. No rush on my side.

"How was school?"

"I hate it," she said, finally buckling her seat belt across her lap.

"What's to hate in fifth grade?"

I was given the Look again. "Everything," she said, putting an end to the subject.

We drove away from the now empty front stairs of the red brick Telluride Elementary School. The principal waved down from her office window with a lukewarm smile and an expression of resigned disappointment over my normal late arrival. The Look again. Is it part of the Y chromosome? I felt that I needed and deserved detention every time any woman's eye passed a fleeting judgment.

"No friends?" I asked. I knew the feeling.

"Please."

"What?"

"They're sheep," she said.

"Soft and cuddly?"

"Brainless," she said, "and victimized by sheep herders."

"And you're...?"

"Fat. P-H-A-T," she said. Spelling it out with an emphasis on the last letter.

"Is that, like, really cool?"

"It stands for Pretty Hot And Tempting," she said with no apparent emotion. "And that's me." Her thumbs on both hands hit her sternum in a coordinated jab.

I hesitated with an embarrassing lurch of a slippery clutch at the stop sign and looked over at this miniature of her mother. She was brushing imaginary crumbs from her lap. The briefcase was now down in the foot-well of the front seat. How had she gone from nine years old to twenty overnight? I know girls are smarter, but this is ridiculous.

"Who are you?" I ask. "And what have you done with my daughter?"

I got a crack of a smile and figured I was forgiven and we had an understanding. It was a blood bond among equals; the dad to daughter understanding. She would let me know what that understanding was at the appropriate time on her agenda.

"Well," I said, trying to head off the warning bells in my head that screamed I was being set up. "What have you got for me, Watson?"

Her silence stretched into a full minute as we rolled slowly out onto Colorado Avenue at the town's official speed limit of fifteen miles per hour. I could see the body language had taken a definite turn for the better as her mind started to spin with the important facts of her day.

"I'm Sherlock," she finally said. "You're Watson."

"Whatever," I said, ignoring an old argument. "What you got?"

"What's it worth to you?" She asked. Her forearms were now loosely crossed over her stomach. Her eyes were again predatory slits as they gazed at me from profile. The perfect little nose swung up in a delicate nub, just like her mother's.

"Depends on the goods." I played along in our usual negotiation ritual. It was going to cost me. No getting around it. I had been late. I had nothing positive to report from a wasted day. And, I only had one thin twenty left in my pocket. I was in trouble.

"Two cases you're already working on have new twists," she said with only a slight lisp as she studied her nails at full arm's length. "And," she said, loading on the added enthusiasm, "a really, really rich woman wants to hire someone to throw her husband's new boyfriend out of her father's house."

"Who owns the house?" I blurted, unable to resist the bait, and instantly forfeited any bargaining position I might have had. The munchkin was getting good at this. I wasn't going to save any of that twenty.

"Want to talk turkey?" she said, twiddling her little pink thumbs in her lap. I nodded. She did most of the talking.

I admit to the casual observer that it might seem a bit unethical to pump your fifth grader for gossip. But kids say the dandiest things to each other about what they overhear at home. It is amazing what Cody can pick up during those few minutes at school when the kids finally get to talk among themselves. My justification is that if you don't want the juicy stuff to get out and around town, don't talk about it in front of your kids.

Third-hand gossip from children has proven to be my best source of much needed firsthand information and potential income. Sure, I have been known to use teachers and even school administrators when they need the extra cash, but my best stuff, came from the juicy gossip with the truth tucked inside. The best conduit for intimate information, right up there alongside bartenders, hairdressers and barbers, has always been the parroting of their parents' conversations that flows like a spring stream from the kids. Besides, it is definitely cheaper. Teachers won't give it up for a sawbuck anymore. They want beers, lunch, and a fifty to ease their guilt at being a gossiping snitch.

I ended up minus the twenty and the use of my cell phone at the rate of a dollar a minute. I had to pay for each needed word out of her sweet little cherub mouth. The whole deal took four blocks. One of us was getting really good at what they did.

"It was worth it," I said, trying to save face, as we slapped a low five on the deal.

I now knew where my wandering husband in the Z3 goes for whoopee during these long afternoons. It was also in my best interest to get my bill quickly to the attorney of yet another doubtful wife because she and the hubby are sleeping together again on the sly from their kids. And finally, she had a solid lead on making some potentially easy money, persuading a gay couple to simply copulate elsewhere.

"The day is finally looking up," I said to myself. I always make that mistake.

Cody was busy calling her friends and giving them her new cell phone number as I came back into awareness of what really was happening in my world. I could feel the vise-grips getting ready for another painful squeeze.

This morning, on top of the gun thing with Katie, Cody had debated at the top of her lungs for a full ten minutes with her mother and me for letting our "oldest" daughter be the only one without a "personal emergency cell phone" in her whole fifth grade. The fact we didn't scoff at her proclamation was a sure-fire litmus test that we lived in Telluride, a privileged Colorado ski resort and festival town, which is way off the scale in high rollers.

"Mom can't know," I said, sounding pathetic.

She stared at me, phone to her ear waiting to be connected. This pitying look underlined the sad conclusion that I was a moron as well as an idiot. She would not even attempt an answer. How could her mother not know? She was going to be on her phone from now until sometime next week. I had been had, good. I felt my stomach clench at the thought of dinner that evening with my harem at 416 Hollyhock Lane.

five

A Full Time Ladies Man From New Orleans

I took the coward's way out and dropped Cody off at home. I received a cold stare from our reluctant nanny Angelina and a smacking wet kiss from Katie with my announcement that I had to stop back down at my office. I could smell the graham crackers and milk on my cheek as I park the car in the alley behind the Croswell Building. My office was on the third and top floor, up four switch back flights of creaky narrow stairs, and cantilevered out over East Colorado Avenue in a single dormer. And, I mean the whole office.

Stepping over the shin biting wooden bench that almost blocked shut the inward opening door; I descended the two short steps to the closet sized, thirty square-feet, half-octagon of the room. The major redeeming features of the hovel were the ten foot tall, divided, oversized windows. The knee to ceiling panes of glass hid behind pulled paper shades. They formed four walls. The door and the guest bench were the other.

Two scarred and worn desks were pushed up against the opposing braces of a tandem of windowsills. Each small desk was crowded with a computer monitor and teetering piles of yellowing copy paper filling to overflow the available horizontal surface. The two old wooden swivel chairs touched each other back to back. Unoccupied floor space without a stack of file folders or musty old books with paper page markers galore was nil. Squeezing two live bodies in here usually took a shoehorn.

Vladimir Nabokov, who wrote *Lolita* and loved to hunt the butterfly in Telluride, once said that all the rest of the world's books "seem to be all by the same writer who is not even the shadow to my shadow." I wanted to feel like that about my writing just once. I had recently pledged to write only when my emotions boil over and the itch drives me crazy. I wanted Lolita in my writing. I always got a few shades less.

Flopping into the hard wooden seat, I pulled myself up to the desk. A finger to the keyboard space bar sent the Wes Studi's Magua screen saver into the ozone and a document window opened. Arial font, 12 point, square margins set at an inch, with no fancy formatting, ever, gradually appeared before my eyes. It read simply "Short Story," centered and underlined. The empty space that followed filled me with a sickening dread. What to say? Who is it all about? When should I begin?

Hemmingway once said about beginnings, "Not too soon, but not too damn much after." What the hell did that mean?

My newest, and probably last, attempt at becoming a real writer hinged on tapping into a raging blizzard of emotional chaos, to ride the ragged edge, and bring the words on the page to life. I swallowed hard, feeling as low as quail crap, half as animated as a dissected frog. Using three fingers on each hand, hunting and pecking, I began to type. All I could think of as the fingers moved on the keyboard was how much I wanted life to be caught up in a mystery, and as easy to appreciate, understand, and predict in retrospect as the surprise endings of my favorite books had always been. I bit the nip of my tongue and let it go.

~

The man she called Gatsby slid into the rich red leather driver's seat of the 1922 Packard Coupe with a menacing look. She was spent, slouching in the saddle soft upholstery against the passenger door.

"You've got to tell me, everything, now," he said with an implied and very real threat, slamming the door shut with a compression of air that hurt her ears. "People are talking about you, and now me, deary. The parties are dying, stale. They don't want us around anymore. If I didn't bring the booze, they wouldn't have us. Tell me why, you worthless southern bitch."

The woman took a gold cigarette case from her patent leather hand bag, offered the open box to his icy stare and then slowly extracted a long thin custom rolled Galoise Vixen from among a half-dozen others. She studied the Long Island fog swirling in the pale light from the shoreline security lamp. Waves crashed in a dying hiss just out of sight against the breakwater of the private yacht club's parking lot. A foghorn moaned. The smell of damp seaweed at the waters edge was sharp, iodine, rotten, unmistakable.

Gatsby was chewing the inside of his lip and was suddenly mesmerized by her fingers as she tapped the end of the white cigarette against the flat gold top of the closed case three times at each end. His eyes then followed the cigarette to her rosebud full red lips. Without a tremble, she flicked the flint wheel of the thin gold lighter, and bluish smoke billowed towards the dash and windshield. He stared at her mouth and the perfect oval it formed around the smoke. Her little finger dabbed at a minute bit of tobacco on her pink tongue, drawing it out. She avoided his eyes.

"It's just about me and the hospital," she said.

"It isn't a hospital."

"I can't help it."

"You aren't sick."

"I am already dead."

The bootlegger reached across the space between them and slapped her soundly. The impact echoed a gunshot in the tight quarters of her car.

She smiled around the pain. "I really can't stop it."

He slapped her again. The cigarette dropped from her fingers. She bravely tried to smile still, but the tears in her eyes and the taste of blood in her mouth made it look like a lewd suggestion. She fought the necessity of it, but finally swung her eyes around to look directly at him.

Gatsby grabbed her by the lapels of her full length Cashmere coat and pulled her face close. He stopped, shaking her. Their noses were an inch apart. He scanned her fear with his hard blue eyes. She could smell the whiskey on his breath. His face suddenly collided with hers. A rigid tongue smashed against her closed teeth and finally parted them to swim inside. He tasted her blood too. It spurred him on.

She sighed with resignation into his greedy mouth and felt her legs part, falling open on the soft red leather seat...

It was fully dark when I realized that I had been writing for nearly three hours. The stress in my neck was evidence of the unobserved passage of time. I hit "save" and took a deep breath. I reached past the screen and pulled the cord on the shade. It rolled quickly up, all the way to the top and over with a rumbling flapping sound I always loved, but dreaded having to set right. The cool yellow glow of the streetlights below filled the office as I shut off the overhead fluorescent lights. Out the window, across the rooftops on the other side of the street, the lights of the ski area's gondola terminal building, high up on the mountain, glittered against the vanishing definition between the peaked ridges and the coal black sky.

How had that trance happened? Gatsby? Where did that new story tangent come from? Who the hell was the woman? And why was this Gatsby character slapping her around? The first four aborted drafts had been simply a character sketch of a 1920's bootlegger: cute, wordy, and horrible. They were a slow meandering tale of an obsessive compulsive partier and adrenaline junky who stumbles towards his own demise. This new thing was the best writing I had done in years. Time was actually suspended. The story flew. Just like a real writer.

I forced myself to shut the computer down without rereading a single word. Let it cook overnight in its own juices. Don't worry it to death like a starving dog with a butcher's bone; at least not right away. Give it time to ferment. Patience was a hard new lesson my barber was trying to teach me. He said it was something real writers had. I wasn't sure what he meant.

I pulled the shade back down. Standing up on the desk to grab the fabric-covered ring on a string, I saw the town sheriff's white Bronco slowly ease down Colorado Avenue. I was glad I had shut off the office light. He was probably already rolling right along on my case, taking charge personally. The *putz* definitely wanted to be the one to take my gun permit. He had a thing for my wife. It was puppy-ish, self indulgent, embarrassing, and publicly recognized by everyone in town.

The Sheriff also had a different kind of thing for me. He thought I was capable of murder. I couldn't disagree. In two years of the private eye business, I had already been on trial for one murder I didn't commit and had now stumbled over another dead body with more questions than answers.

I decided right then that Sheriff Bueller would have to wait until I was ready to make this particular collar that would make his day. Bueller would likely view this particular duty as a part of his career highlight reel. To him, I was an amateur, a cop wannabe, a fraud. The Last Resort Detective Agency was riding a brief bureaucratic window of opportunity that allowed anyone in the State of Colorado with the inclination to hang out a Private Investigator shingle the prefect right to do so.

I was, by my own account, an unpublished writer playing at being the people I was trying to write about. I still hadn't been able to complete my first book that was half-finished two years ago. I finally burned the old carcass and took to reading F. Scott Fitzgerald's magazine submissions from the 1920s and am now working hard at writing a readable short story. So far I was still waiting for the words to magically appear on the page.

Feeling sorry for myself, I decided to make a few calls. It was important I find a paying customer before the next round of threats from my creditors arrived.

My finger punched the number for Mrs. Agnes Singer into the desk phone. I had no trouble reading my daughter's perfectly formed, rounded numerals on a scrap of lined writing paper. I waited for the ringing to start. I expected an answering machine and wasn't disappointed. I left an introduction, a heart felt endorsement for my services, and hung up.

Ernie Sampesee called from the open door as the phone hit the cradle. His baritone voice projected into the dust filled cervices of the office.

"Wit, my boy, you're in deep, deep trouble," he said. The smile that accompanied the pronouncement beamed, and I knew he was right. "But I certainly envy you the audacity to blow your own horn like that."

"What trouble?" I asked, ignoring his admission of eavesdropping.

Ernie laughed and the sound forced me to breathe deeply to deal with my increasing anxiety. I can always gauge the exact level of truth in what my barber says by an assessment of how much he is enjoying my pain. It was another thing the self-help books said: "real writers always enjoy the pain of others." If that was truly the test, maybe Ernie was the closest thing to a real writer I knew.

"That's what I like most about you, Wit, old cod. You don't even see trouble when it's smacking you in the forehead. People in town are describing you as that guy from the Li'l Abner cartoons with the black cloud over his head."

"The one with all the consonants and not a vowel in sight?"

"Exactly," Ernie said, helping me into my old wool coat one arm at a time.

"Did you hear I was caught in an act of endearment with a corpse?"

"Absolutely," he said. "It's the talk of the town."

"What are people saying?"

"They are now calling you 'The Kiss of Death Kid.'"

"Is that all?"

"I only listen to the polite conversation," Ernie said.

"Are you keeping something from me?"

"Almost daily," he said.

"What can I do about this?"

"Give them something else to talk about."

"You mean do something stupider than I did today."

"Exactly."

"I feel like a third-rate schmuck."

"No, my boy, you are an absolute first-rate schmuck."

"Just once in my life I want to be referred to by the gossips as a sometimes pimp and full time ladies man from New Orleans,'" I said as I closed the door to my office.

"You aren't from New Orleans."

"Details," I said.

We ambled arm in arm, loudly and awkwardly down the narrow stairs.

Six

A Worthless Contest

Ernie Sampesee is the only son of two successful Wall Street lawyers and was guided into corporate tax law at Ivy League schools. He settled a billion dollar claim against the government on behalf of a Texas oil company and retired with a cool eight figures in the bank. He fit hand in glove into Telluride.

I would guess that our small community's unearned income, averaged on a per capita basis, would outstrip Brunei as the richest place on earth. The difference between a Colorado mountain town's disgustingly rich residents and the rest of the world's allotment of the breed is simply a matter of scale and tone.

The normal Telluride "trust funder" drives a five-year-old SUV, has a smallish, cozy house to die for, and walks their kids to school wearing baggy polar fleece and funny Alpaca wool hats. The conscious effort is to appear as if you were somehow getting by on your own. It is a difficult role to put forward when your personal checking account balance fluctuates upwards, sometimes over six figures, depending on when the inherited premiums and dividends are electronically transferred.

Ernie, however, does not prescribe to this Spartan, low-key, code of inconspicuous wealth. He dresses well, drives a Bentley, has a three million dollar rooftop dwelling on Colorado Avenue, and sends his wife on extended shopping trips and relative visits that last for months. My well-to-do barber looks like Vincent Price, is nearly as tall as my six feet two inches and weighs about fifty pounds less. Ernie is in his mid-sixties and looks it in a comfortably worn, eccentric way.

"Pity about the long drive to nowhere," Ernie said as we continued to sit at the bar in the New Sheridan Hotel. The local riff-raff was giving us some elbowroom to conduct our business in private. Monday nights are slow, especially in a relic of old school stodginess like this one. No flat screen televisions and over a thousand glistening bottles backed the bar. Cut glass mirrors doubled the effect.

"I gotta get the goods on that Z3. Cody gave me a solid lead, and I'm desperate. The insurance is due on my car. I already spent the retainer, and the wife in question is beginning to think I'm not even trying," I said.

"You got trouble? A dark cloud rules my enjoyment of life. I've got to get over this morally bankrupt vision of myself as a filthy rich barber. I am obsessed with a vain effort to see people who have to actually work for a living as noble."

"Noble?"

"As a Codfish. I long for the mantel of the lowly blue collar."

"We aren't noble. We're envious." My second wish of the day was that I should have Ernie's problem.

"To our ongoing worthless competition," Ernie toasted to make me feel better.

We both sipped our cheap well scotch trying to make it single malt and taste eighteen years old. This old palace of a drinking establishment had steadily gone downhill in the arena of intelligent conversation and clientele since William Jennings Bryan delivered the Cross of Gold speech here in 1889. The passing of time was lately a recurring theme in my thoughts.

"How long we been at it?" Ernie asked.

"At what?"

"Racing to see who can do the least with the remainder of their lives."

"A long time," I said.

"But, at least, we two proudly display the grit and gentlemanly stamina to see it through to the end." Ernie's baritone voice projected around the bar.

"Probably," I said and sipped my drink. We would surely be the only non-family mourners at each other's funeral. A thousand bad questions formed in my head.

"Why me, Ernie?"

"Why you what?"

"Why waste your time being worthless with me?" I was approaching pathetic and feeling worse.

Ernie pushed back his chair, swiveled towards me, and gave me a long hard look. "You make me laugh. Hanging out with you is like being with Job. You're never sure when the other shoe is going to drop, but odds are it will surely happen before sundown." A sip passes his lips.

"You find a steaming pile of trouble everywhere you step, my friend. I enjoy watching."

"So, I have entertainment value?"

"For the whole town, my boy, the whole town."

Ernie smiled with that warm confidence and good cheer that unnerved those around him. "You try to come across as some hard bitten detective from an old movie and the story always ends up with you getting the wrong end of the deal and being a pushover for some woman with perky attributes, a hard luck story, and a gun in her purse."

"I am pathetic."

"Indeed," he agreed.

"Who do you figure killed Lambis?" I asked.

"Not suicide?"

"Hadn't thought that angle," I said. My face flushed with embarrassment.

"Wasn't he a little light in the loafers?" asked Ernie.

"Maybe," I yawned, "not confirmed, but that's not a problem in this town, or with me; or with you as far as I know. In fact, it's expected for any single middle-aged man who isn't out chasing everything hot and hollow in stretch pants. Take the Choral Society?"

"We are civilized, aren't we?" Ernie mused into his glass and called for two more. "Lovers? Money problems, blackmail, depression? Ideas?"

I shrugged trying to pretend the answer wasn't going to bother me until I found out. It wouldn't go away until I did something about finding out what happened in that office. Lambis was the first dead guy I had ever tasted. Why didn't suicide seem the right answer? Had I seen something that ruled it out? Or was I too stupid to see the obvious?

"Rooted out any federal spies lately," I asked, wanting to change the subject from my worthless life, the kiss of a dead man, and my ongoing money problems.

"Found a real sharper at the photo shop the other day." Ernie confided in a hushed tone. "He followed me in, and I cornered him, demanding that he report immediately back to the IRS that I had unmasked him, and did not appreciate their unscrupulous and underhanded schemes to hound my life."

"It made my day," he said after a chuckle.

"Was he really a spy?"

"How should I know? He seemed genuinely contrite," Ernie said, dismissing the thought that he could have been mistaken. My barber was sure the IRS wanted revenge for his victory over them in a corporate tax court a decade ago. "Regardless, the story will get back to the feds that I am still on guard."

"And crazy," I said. I visualized the hawk-faced barber cowering some poor innocent tourist into a verbal corner with false accusations and feigned fury.

"That too," he said.

"Any new detective gossip come spewing up out of the barber chair?" I asked hoping the answer was no, so I wouldn't have to pick up the bar bill.

"The only open case I have current is the Schnauzer disappearance. She has yet to turn up. Been what, six weeks? I helped you put up flyers in every bar in town. That was an unforgettable pub crawl, was it not? The coyotes probably had her for a snack, but I have my ears on, hoping for a break. Maybe she'll call in."

"Good man," I said and smiled at the logic.

We were quite the pair, all right. I was postponing the inevitable meeting with the Assistant District Attorney. Another full amber colored glass appeared magically at my napkin. My best intentions for facing the music and taking it like a man are often waylaid by a stiff drink. It was happening more often lately.

Patsy Susie Blaze, real estate broker, and by far the most successful one in town, sat in the farthest corner of the bar with two men. I noticed through a growing scotch haze that the tall bearded one wore black leather and the short fat one an expensive Italian cut silk suit. She listened intently to what her guests were saying, but watched Ernie and me with a bemused expression. Her smile was fixed, her eyes hungry. She was ready to close the deal, any deal, but the vivacious broker knew that everything happens in its own good time. She ascribed to "Telluride Style." Life could follow its own simple rules as long as she got her six-percent commission. She was still there watching when I got unsteadily to my feet for the lonely stagger home.

Seven

Gone De Sade

W it Thorpe," I said into the intercom. "I have an appointment."

I was cautiously optimistic the next morning, after a lonely night on the couch, as I cleared the first hurdle of security to enter the lobby of the Franz Klammer Lodge and Resort. The name Thorpe must have been recently purged from the undesirable's list. It hadn't always been the case, and it wasn't ever my fault. Scandal, digging it up and documenting it on videotape, is more like a hand grenade than laser surgery when approaching an upcoming divorce. Collateral damage is inevitable, and I always got the blame. Stirring the pot from the bottom up was my business; getting some on you is unavoidable. I try to accept that creating emotional chaos is an unavoidable byproduct in my line of work. Regrettably, I often smile because of it. I find karma amusing.

Robert Forrest Singer had, by his wife's rigid moral standards, suddenly gone "De Sade." A case could be made that this was not entirely true. Forrest had simply decided his mid-life crisis was going to involve exploring his sexuality with other people, including men. According to the wife, he had gone off one weekend to an exclusive men's only retreat in Sodoma, Arizona to explore the art of the male mystique with a guru. He had heard about the religious spa through an article in *Forbes Magazine*. Amidst the giant sculpted penises and red river canyons he learned to masturbate in a circle with others, open his arms and emotions to other sensitive men, and find his true bi-sexual, free-Id self.

His wife, Mrs. Robert Forrest Singer was not amused when "Sandy," as he was known, demanded that their Telluride home become a satellite campus for the new sexual revolution amongst enlightened males. She had moved into a friend's two million dollar time share condo in Mountain Village; roughing it while beginning divorce proceedings. Mrs. Singer and I sat, staring out at the dark brown lift terminals and the green lower slopes of Misty Maiden. We were having tea served by a square faced Ute woman from La Paz who often served as itinerant domestic help for the well-to-do residents. The woman, Wilma Mankiller, had helped me out once by locating a bail bond skipper when I needed it. She was also a second cousin. We wouldn't let our eyes meet. We were afraid we might laugh out loud. It was funny to her that a fellow refugee from the Ute reservation would be sitting, sipping tea from delicate china cups, and making small talk with a shriveled old white woman, as if any of it mattered.

"And you want my agency to evict him from your house?"

"Is there a problem?"

"He may have some rights to be there," I said. I have usually assumed correctly that spouses generally exhibit unsupported and naive beliefs of property ownership during divorce proceedings. That's why, says my barber, the realist lawyer, it is important to get a retainer up front. Often a client is the last to know that a divorce is a no win financial mess with only the lawyers getting their fair share of the loot. I soon learned I was talking to a divorce expert.

"The house is in a trust, set up by my father three husbands ago. It is not now, nor ever was, communal property. Robert Forrest Singer, the preening fagot, my current husband, and his frilly friends are squatting at West Egg and basically trespassing on my dear father's memorial vacation home. I want them gone," she said. Her voice a viper's litany of sibilant sounds. My neck hairs came to attention.

"We usually don't become involved in property settlement issues unless the court has already made a ruling," I said. "It just gets very sticky." I tried a seventy-watt smile.

She squinted disgust in my direction.

"Sometimes," I said.

"Listen here, boy. That little weasel hasn't a pot to piss in. He was broke when I married him. He hasn't worked a day since. And I have a pre-nuptial agreement solid enough to ram a big fat zero up his ass when the time is right." Spittle flecked at the corners of her ribbon thin, pearl colored and slightly rouged lips.

"I don't need another 'do nothing' lawyer type in my life. I'm looking for a problem solver, and I got all the money I need to find one. Is that clear enough? I want him and his swishy little friends out of my father's house, now. You're a big strong guy, figure it out."

Agnes was a spare no expense, well preserved, dried up and mean, seventy years ornery. The fact she had a sailor's vocabulary was disconcerting. I admitted to myself without engaging in another conciliatory smile that she would eat most men alive. I was most men.

"Gotcha," I said.

Her smile sent a shiver through me. This woman's heart would be a transplant bargain; it appeared unused.

"Friends?" I said. It was the first I had heard about a crowd.

"Fellow inmates from the Arizona church that turned my husband into a queer." Her back got straighter as she perched forward on the chair. "Deviants."

"How many friends?" It was an important question, knowing from experience that sexual orientation has nothing to do with being tough to handle.

Her glare degraded my manhood.

"Do you have the balls I need for this simple little assignment?" she said. Her eyebrows lifted in subtle challenge above the cosmetically altered to perfection face.

"I can ask them to leave," I said. Strong-arming is not one of the services listed on the agency flyer, but who was I to quibble? I needed the money.

"Perfect," she said, taking my hand in both of hers and sealing the deal with a cold pressure. I immediately hoped she was more merciful than my nine year old when it came to discussing my fee. It seems I have an admitted problem negotiating with strong willed women of any age. I was soon shown out the door before a check changed hands.

～

My 1972 Mustang's blown muffler rumbled loudly in 3rd gear as I left the Mountain Village turnoff and started down into the deep canyon that forms the backdrop of Telluride. I have never taken this view for granted. I reckon no place on earth nearly two miles high is more conducive to living than right here.

I turned right at Society Corner and headed into the box canyon towards the tiny town three miles away. The valley cows grazed to my right in black and white formal wear, spreading themselves conspicuously along the millions of dollars of Valley Floor real estate that simply grew green grass to feed their cuds. I thought about the toy cow in Lambis' hand when he died. Had he been trying to leave a clue to his killer?

The public radio station KOTO was playing a jazz set by Etta James. In spite of the Blues, I still wasn't allowing myself to think about my troubles at home, there were plenty. I had stumbled to Hollyhock Lane after midnight last evening, and I was barely drunk enough to think I could sneak in. The only thing worse than being a coward is being caught red handed in the act.

If I can't hold my own with Cody, then I am at a total loss when it comes to my wife. The words from her beautiful full lips tumbled down on me in my stupor. I couldn't disagree with anything that was said. It was not a discussion. No ultimatums, no mention of firearms, just a severe level of disappointment at my less than stellar decision making during the last forty-eight hours. And now I was mixed up in another mess involving a mysterious death.

"But we talked all this out the last time when it wasn't my fault. It's the same."

"We didn't talk it out," she said. "You defended yourself over every crazy act of idiocy, and I got over it."

I finally stopped being pigheaded and promised to do gooder. I would try to reverse the downward spiral of my life. She had my word. She took it for what it was worth and closed the door to our bedroom.

I don't often have these moments in real life when I feel like I am even partially being understood. My big problem is that any positive reinforcement for my odd and self-destructive actions in real life usually comes from reading the clear and clever motivations of fictional heroes in someone else's books. Usually my random moments of revelation come from those great writers who are now long gone and dead. I envied them the clarity of their simple declarative sentences.

A real writer like F. Scott Fitzgerald seemed to have had it all. Scotty lived a life full of characters that would leap onto the page without a lot of thought. He had lived in Paris and its rich soil of lust, greed, love and sacrifice. Why couldn't I have the same luck? It must have been a snap for Fitzgerald. I consciously ignored, absolutely, the writer's nightmarish emotional anguish with his muse, the drinking, the madness, the bi-polar personalities, and the tragic early death just like any other fan. I think inconsolable was a good word for my mood.

Eight

Bowling

Remember the old fairy tale about the man who was granted three wishes? He first tested the genie by wishing for a nice pot of black pudding. His wife berated him vehemently for being so stupid to waste a wish that he lost his temper. He shouted, "I wish the black pudding was on the end of your nose." It took his last wish to get the pudding off her nose. I treat this parable as one of life's primary lessons. The message is to be cautious with what you wish for, because you almost always get it, and it's always black pudding.

I was hoping to meet the woman in the Packard Coupe and the mysterious bootlegger Gatsby again in my office that afternoon, so I stopped in for a haircut and a shave. Barber Ernie's, as it is now known, was one of the oldest storefronts on Colorado Avenue and located conveniently right below my own office in the same building. The barber was also my landlord. He owned the whole block.

"My favorite private dick," Ernie said as I sat down in the ancient swivel chair.

"That's what your wife said last night too," I said. The stale rejoinder was for the three seated customers. It was our old shtick, and they pointedly ignored us. Ernie's wife had been out of town for the last three months with no return date in sight.

"Take my wife," he said, "Please."

Droopy Drawers Hal and Frank laughed, just as they did every morning.

I told him to cut my hair so I looked like Robert Mitchum playing the detective Philip Marlow.

"Won't do any good."

I shrugged knowing he was right.

"You're the Tony Danza kind of haircut. Everybody says you look like him only taller, bigger, and meaner. I personally don't see it."

"Everyone?"

"Except the Sheriff. He thinks you look like Ted Bundy."

"He just wants my wife," I said.

"Who doesn't?" he said. "She's PHAT."

I had to admit Ernie was right.

Ernie's smile turned to a frown, remembering something important, "Oh yeah, the Sheriff himself was looking for you this morning, might still be waiting upstairs in your office."

"When were you going to tell me?"

"I didn't want to be the one to spoil your day."

I offered Ernie my neck, and he shaved it for me with a long straight razor. He repeatedly stropped the shining blade on the leather strap hanging at the back of the barber chair. When Ernie retired after winning all that money, he candidly admitted to his shocked wife that he had always wanted to spend the rest of his life being a barber like his grandfather.

The Sampesee moved here to Telluride ten years ago, and Ernie claims he has doubled his life expectancy by opening up this shop. Somebody was always stopping by, mostly to talk. Ernie was not a great barber; he was a great talker. Only the brave or hopeless chose Ernie's over the other hair salons in town. I was the only one who trusted him with a razor. Fast healing was an attribute I always banked on.

My hair was hopeless. Ernie cut my head the way he always cut it, each tuft having its own length. I looked the same in the wall mirrors after he had done his best. At least the shave was close, too close, but I loved it. It was so old school. Ernie's shave was one of the highlights of my morning.

I also reasoned that if I survived the barber's chair first thing, nothing else in the day would be as dangerous.

"At least you told me."

"Yeah, you could say that."

"Tell me more. What's the scoop on a Mr. Robert Forrest Singer up at West Egg in Mountain Village?" I asked Ernie for a little *quid pro quo* as I paid my twenty dollars for the cut and shave. I was personally putting his nephew through St. Lawrence University in upstate New York on the installment plan.

"Is that the monster of a house just down from Twister?" Ernie mentioned the ski run that makes some trophy homes "ski-in, ski-out" and worth double the price.

"Probably. Twenty-five-thousand square feet or something."

"Gotta be," said Ernie. "He doesn't come in here. Goes over to The New Wave and gets his hair 'dressed.' Folks call him Sandy."

"Anybody know him?" I said, eyeing the disappearing twenty in Ernie's hand.

"Seen him a couple of times with the dead bank guy at Rusticos Restaurant." Ernie opened his 1870's register with a pull down lever like a one armed bandit and deposited the money in a lonely wooden slot.

"Real friendly like, old cod." Ernie said.

"You gonna' go all jealous now 'Mister Kiss of Death?'" he asked with a wink at the posse.

"You don't mean Stewart Lambis?" Hal asked.

I looked at Ernie. Ernie nodded at Droopy Drawers Hal who sat in a chair waiting for dinnertime. It was barely 9 a.m. Hal was a regular. He had only let Ernie cut his hair once, so he was considered a smart regular. He was here every morning and afternoon since retiring last year from the Colorado Supreme Court as their Chief Justice.

"That's the guy. Did you know that just before you kissed him to death he just bought some million dollar shack in town?" Hal said. "Driving the rest of us out. It was that damn Patsy Susie that sold it to him too. Boy, I'd like to have her dough."

Hal, a curmudgeon by nature, was just another victim of the mountain town belief that anyone who had come to Telluride a day after you was a no good "second home owner" looking to screw things up for "us" locals.

"Any new gossip about who killed him?" I asked.

"Rumor is his boyfriend was all broken up that you wouldn't leave Stewart alone. You were his new 'bum boy' and the other guy got jealous," Hal said. He stood up and hitched his pants up to his non-existent hips for effect. Ernie and Frank had a big laugh at that one. I wore a frown and tried to be offended by the political incorrectness of the remark. The posse rode me hard until I left the room.

~

I assumed the Sheriff with a warrant for my gun permit was still upstairs, so I went back outside to the Mustang and thought I would get out of town and keep my schoolyard manhood for a couple of more hours. I liked the reassuring weight clipped on my waistband in the small of the back. It made me feel like an apprentice adult and an honest-to-God, real hard-assed detective, like my fictional mentors.

I drove up Fox Farm Road and onto Ophir Crest Loop heading for the garish stone entrance to West Egg. The holed muffler was going to make a surprise attack impossible. I pulled past the huge stonework entrance. A massive beam arch over the tall granite pillars supported a grotesque bronze sculpture of a bald eagle ripping apart a lamb that it held to the ground beneath huge talons. You could almost hear the bleating of the poor doomed sheep.

I tried the garage door style remote that Mrs. Singer had given me and was not surprised that the code had been changed. The heavy wooden gate remained locked across the winding entrance road that led upwards into the tall aspens. The house, where I could just see the red gabled roof, was just over the knoll and directly along the ski run.

I tried to gently ease the clutch and keep the growl of the exhaust to a low roar, as I pulled past the gate and continued upwards on Ophir Crest Loop towards the dirt track to Magic Meadow, another ski run that, after leaving the car behind, would take me further up the mountain.

A few minutes walking brought me within view of the massive combination of buildings that comprised West Egg. I squatted down in the tall grass and focused my daughter's pastel blue bird watching binoculars on the grounds. The size of the house was staggering. It was shaped like a horseshoe surrounding a huge car plaza the size of a professional basketball court. The wing to my left was built above four huge double door garages. The main portal was a vaulted roof rising sixty feet or more across a hundred feet of frontage, full glass panels supported by a set of four matching pillars made of intricately stacked rock layers. In front of the main entryway appeared six matching solid granite bunkers, like tank traps on Normandy Beach. Each was capped with an incongruous, delicate, black-iron light fixture. The remaining wing to the right was a long glass hallway extending from the main house, ending in a separate guest cottage of more modest mansion-sized proportions. This last structure was made entirely from huge red-stained round logs.

I whistled softly.

On the third floor balcony, seated around the steaming hot tub were seven men and a solitary woman in different stages of relaxation. I noticed the one I took to be Mrs. Singer's husband reclining in a heavy wooden cabana chair. She had given me a crumpled picture from an old newspaper. It matched. He looked like any one of a couple of dozen fifty to seventy year old men in Telluride who were trim, fit, perpetually tanned and smelled like money. You would see two or three on every walk through town, often with a trophy blonde, a third their age, in their clutches. I always waved and said "howdy," envying them the blondes.

I watched Patsy Susie Blaze sit down next to Singer and begin to rub oil into the soft, wispy hair of his chest. She wore a bathing suit and her frisky breasts rubbed against Singer's arm. The young man massaging Singer's temples, standing behind the cabana chair, was shirtless, with long dirty blonde hair that hung in his eyes, shiny black leather motorcycle pants hanging on his hips, and a huge silver dollar sized ring pierced his left nipple. I whistled softly again.

Didn't that hurt?

I should have been more careful, seeing that I had already taken notice of the half dozen Harley Davidson motorcycles parked around a matching set of white Mercedes sedans in the parking plaza. A vest with colors hung from a handlebar. It read: "Sodom's Devils."

The cold steel of the illegally shortened double-barreled shotgun pressed against the side of my neck and my jawbone. A placement sure to draw a quick shiver. I became as still as a rabbit.

"Nosey bastard," a deep baritone voice said calmly behind me. This was good. Talk was better than an explosion.

"Curiosity killed the cat," said another voice. This was not so good.

I slowly started to raise my arms in a standard surrender position when the world erupted and the lights went out.

They brought me around with an ammonia ampoule under my nose. I was in a bowling alley.

"The 'peeping tom' lives," A blurry figure emerged from the pain between my eyes. The man sat forward in my field of vision and swatted me on the forehead with a chicken drumstick. I nearly blacked out again. The gristly chicken part drew back away and disappeared into a bearded mouth with bright white teeth. I watched him chew, noting his above average dental work, trying through a haze to find my present location in Wonderland.

"What are we gonna do with him?"

"Who the fuck cares?"

"Sandy maybe?"

"Naw, he said he didn't know this jackass. Some local private dick from town. We was to shoot him dead if we ever saw him again. You hear that, asshole?" I was given a shake. "Shoot you dead."

"So what do you want to do with him?"

"Fuck if I know."

"We're in the bowling alley," someone said, "let's bowl."

"Good idea."

I was grabbed under both arms and jerked to my feet. I felt the bile come up in my throat as my ankles were yanked back, and I floated perpendicular, face down, looking at the polished parquet floor of the bowling lane. A few trial swings, for good luck,

"Careful," I heard a voice from a distant canyon say and a hand squeezed my ass. It then removed my clip holster and gun. "Wouldn't want any of us to get hurt by accident, now would we?"

I was run and then launched down the single alley towards the ten duckbills. I was a strike. My last thought before I lost both breakfast and consciousness was, "Who the hell puts a bowling alley in a ski house?"

Nine

Hammie Over Miami

I sat in my office with a bag of frozen peas held against the lumps on my head. My scalp felt as dumplinged as a mogul field. That little reconnoiter hadn't turned out exactly as I had planned. The office phone rang. It hurt. I picked it up without thinking.

"Yeah."

"Wilfred?"

"Sheriff," I said.

"I thought I'd swing on by." It wasn't a question.

"Won't do you any good."

"No?" I could feel the excitement in his voice. Confrontation and physical violence would be the icing on the cake for the Sheriff in making this revocation of my right to a concealed weapon. I stifled a groan.

"I lost it. The gun."

"Lost it?"

"Yup."

"How's that?"

"Up on Twister somewhere, must'a fallen out of my jacket or something." I said, "The Good Lord eighty-sixed the thirty-eight, so I don't need your damn permit, because I haven't got a gun."

"That right?"

"Yup."

"Why don't I just swing on by anyway," the Sheriff said. Again, it wasn't a question. "We can talk about it."

"Sure thing," I said and was up and out the door before the phone knew it was hung up. I took the frozen peas with me, hung the "be back in five minutes" sign on the knob and taped my concealed weapon permit onto the glass, right under my name. Even Bueller couldn't miss it.

≈

"Give it up, Sherlock," I said to Cody as she slammed the car door. My head thumped like a bass drum.

"You're late," she said.

"Only five minutes," I said trying to steady the pea bag on my head so I could shift, steer, and hold my palm out for the phone in between activities.

"That's like being early," I said.

"Like, whatever," she said flipping open her cell phone and concentrating her little face with the nub of a tongue peeking out between almost closed pearl white teeth.

"I need the phone," I said. I had to call Ernie and get a gun, a big gun. I was going back to West Egg and set some things right, waste some trash, wreck some bikers. She punched up the speed dial.

"Bailey?" she said into the phone, ignoring me. "You won't believe..."

I removed the phone from her ear.

"Bailey? She'll call you back." I said calmly.

"Listen young lady," I began as I disconnected Bailey, "This is a business phone. Important business and your dad needs it to make a living."

"A living?" Cody's smirking retort was dry and ironic, so unbecoming a tone for an almost ten year old.

The phone suddenly started playing Yankee Doodle Dandy. I glared at my daughter, knowing I wouldn't be able to figure out how to reprogram a normal ring. I looked at the caller ID screen. It was the Sheriff's office. I knew the number by heart.

"On second thought, squirt," I said with a grand flourish, "you keep it." Yankee Doodle went to voice mail as I handed the phone back to her.

"Bailey?" She lost no time reaching out. "What?"

I looked down at her legs see-sawing in the front seat. I turned my attention back to driving and thought of Gatsby and the mysterious lady.

"No, that was no boy toy," Cody playfully screamed into the phone to head off a wild rumor that was sure to run rampant at the elementary school tomorrow morning. "That was only my dad."

Going back to West Egg would only cause me trouble. It was a stupid, macho, testosterone-laden decision that was disappointingly true to form. I struggled with thinking of something different, something novel like my fictional heroes, to remedy the situation.

Why was Sandy Singer hanging out with a motorcycle gang? Were they just protection? Why did he need protection? Were they all gay like Agnes Singer said? What had any of this to do with Lambis and his murder? Gunless, phoneless, on the run, beat up physically and psychologically, confused; I knew it was time to try and write. I needed to piss out the venom in my churning guts with words, and drive a steaming hole of art through the bottom of the urinal.

$\approx$

The soapsuds swirled around the firm mounds of her breasts as she let the warm water slosh in the high backed tub in her penthouse room at the Algonquin Hotel. He snored loudly in the next room, tangled in satin sheets, satiated and smug.

She tried to relax and let the water wash away the doubts. She gently touched the bruised and tender lips between her legs. He had been rough. Dismissing her cries of pain as passion. She felt violated, raped. Why did he have to be that way? She sighed, wishing it all could be over and done with. Why didn't he just leave her? They all did, eventually. With all that was at stake, why did she risk coming back to his bed night after night?

She was no fortune teller, but the sequence of betrayal, revenge, ownership had played itself out again and again He would grow tired of her, start to look for the spark of a new flame. She could only guess when the signs would make it necessary for her to do what must be done. She stared at the cold steel blue metal of the German Luger pressing into the plush folds of the white bath towel on the slender black-iron stand beside the tub.

If only she had stayed in the car at the club with Gatsby, told him everything, begged for mercy, sanctuary. She could have saved a life; maybe her's too. Maybe she still could. Her eyes closed and she felt Gatsby's strong hand groping at her throat. His tongue in her mouth. Her uterus shuddered without warning. She gasped.

Death could never be so sweet.

~

With the lights off in my office, hiding from the law, nerves on edge, I had tried to re-establish contact with the story. Erotic images kept getting in the way. I struggled with what the mysterious woman had to say. It was frustrating, awkward, futile. I finally pushed back from the keyboard and slapped the side of the computer monitor with an open palm. It stung, and I held the numb fingers against my chest resisting the urge to put the tips in my mouth like a sissy.

I checked the message machine, having shut down the ringer and let everything go directly to the box. Six messages and five of them from the Sheriff's office demanding that I come talk to them and file a report on the missing firearm at once. These five messages were the good news.

I dialed the number from the fifth message with dread. I find that advancing age is a tool for buffering down every emotion except fear.

"Rose, this is Wit," I said loud enough to be heard over the blaring television at the other end of the line. "Our boy at it again?"

"Wit, I had your word," she started raising her voice. "I've got your bill for two-hundred and fifty dollars."

"Rose..."

"I want his thumbs broken or something. Isn't that what you tough guys are supposed to do?" I could hear her suck heavily on a cigarette as the applause from a game show spilled through the speaker. Is that your final answer?

"Rose," I tried again. "He's just a bread squeezer, not a serial killer."

"Shoot the bastard," She said.

"Rose? Rose!"

Click.

I had solved the case this morning by simply pointing a video camera at the bread racks, hidden behind a Pepsi display, and letting it run for four hours. Jeffrey Breene, billionaire, and ironically the same errant husband with the Z3, was also a bread mutilator. He had done eleven loaves of French bread in about forty-five minutes.

Rose, I knew sadly, was most likely to soon be another victim of the legal system. The most she could file in court was a personal property claim. It would cost Rose close to twelve-hundred bucks, at two-fifty an hour, for the lawyer to prove that Breene was entering her grocery store and squeezing loaves of fresh bread until no one else would buy them.

The judge might even rule in Rose's favor, but would probably refuse to reimburse court costs, including my fee, figuring the whole thing was overkill and should be part of Rose's own cost of doing business to deal with vandals and not muddy the waters of the court with trivial lawsuits over a few loaves of bread. We would prove our case and be laughed out of court.

The bread squeezer held all the cards. All I had was a tape of him doing the deed. I had called and talked to him about it. He wasn't the least bit embarrassed and told me to mind my own business. He also hung up on me when I called back. He then changed his number. It was unlisted. I had gone just about as far as I could with it.

Rose felt she had hired me to put a stop to it. I told her I was hired to find the perpetrator, period. I had informed him he was no longer welcomed at the store and had finished my job. I was not honor-bound to see to punishment.

I knew I would have to do something. I hadn't wanted to be the bully. This was turning into another colorful, lose-lose, image reaffirming case. Unfortunately, I reminded myself, doing crap like this paid the bills. It was a fat chance I was ever gonna get paid for this gig unless I did the rest. I was being played by a no-nonsense, willful woman once more.

<hr/>

Katie had been making asleep noises for five minutes but I read on, whispering, sitting with my back against her headboard, turning the large pages with the colorful pictures and short nonsense verses. I just loved Dr. Suess' *Green Eggs and Ham*. At the end, I managed to slide off the bed and tiptoe out the door without even waking the cat, Topper, which lay curled up on the foot of Katie's bed. I noted proudly that I walked like an Indian. Makes sense, because I am an Indian.

The cat jumped down, thinking I was on the way to the kitchen with the express mission to get him a late night snack, and Katie, fully awake in an instant, called from her room.

"Night-o daddio, ham-what-am." She was not sparing my feelings. "Hammie-over-Miami."

I threatened her with worse than death. She giggled and snuggled deeper under her covers.

My wife was at her office working with a prosecutor in from Montrose and getting ready to try a case before "Hang 'em High" Judge Annie Cromwell in the morning at the local courthouse. I passed Cody's room and saw through the door that she was doing homework and talking on the cell phone. All's well within my small world of certainties.

I poured myself a half-tumbler of Jameson's neat and went out onto the porch. I couldn't get that damn woman out of my mind. Her breasts rose above the suds in the tub every time I closed my eyes. What was the gun for? Was she going to shoot Gatsby? Why? Who was this other man at the Algonquin Hotel who bruised and violated her? Who?

The lights of Telluride spread out below the porch on Hollyhock Lane. The house was built on the side of the steep mountain that hems in the mining town from the north. Our cars had to be parked above the house on the seasonal jeep road to Imogene Pass. We walk down sixty-seven steps from the road to the house. Sure, it was the low-rent district; average market value on our block was only a half million, "Ka-ka" by local realtors' skewed perspectives. We had bought it from my wife's uncle who sold it to us, as a wedding present, for what he had purchased it for fifteen years before. We were over-housed, by Telluride standards for working stiffs, but we could make ends meet, barely.

I felt the warm glow of the whiskey taking hold before I allowed myself to think about what to do concerning West Egg and Mr. Singer. It was hard swallowing the sudden swelling of anger over the manhandling I had suffered at the hands of the motorcycle jocks. Touching the knob on my head under my hair, I fought down those graphic images of revenge. Nothing was going to be enough once I started down that road and I knew it. Dig two graves was the Sicilian warning, but, it was my *modus operandi*, and it never fails to get me in deep trouble.

"Think," I said roughly. "Think." I was shaking, holding the railing, trying desperately to put a lid on a steaming vent of anger. My imagination ran wild as I throttled each biker to near death.

"Good idea, Shamus" she said, slipping up behind me. "You think," she paused to underscore the joke, "I'll do the rest."

Her arms circled my waist and her breasts pressed against the small of my back. I felt her lips through my heavy cotton denim shirt. She bit my skin and laughed a low sensuous chuckle, tugging at the shirt fabric with her closed teeth. Her hands began to slide my buckled belt open. She slid her hand inside the loosened front waistband of my pants.

I closed my eyes and saw her breast with its rigid nipple emerge from the white suds in the tub. An erection pressed with increasing determination against the leg of my jeans. My tongue caught in my throat.

Who?

I turned, and the hallucination was gone. What the hell? The erection lingered to see what was what. Why wouldn't this strange fictional redhead leave me alone?

Did I want to be left alone?

"Jesus H. Christ, of course I do," I said.

I drained the rest of the whiskey and walked slowly back towards the kitchen, hitching my pants and arranging myself as I went.

I needed reinforcements, liquid and other, and I suddenly had an idea where I might find them. Unfortunately, Ernie and I had an appointment before getting anywhere near that solution tonight, and I was late. We were teaming up and going after the bread squeezer. I called Angelina. She swore at me in both Spanish and Ute, arriving by cab in ten minutes for an extra twenty. It was a good thing she was my cousin and her kids needed new shoes.

Ten

The Bread Squeezer

We drove towards Mountain Village. My barber and I were in agreement that moneyed madness had always given me the willies. For Ernie, it was simply the way things were. I was jumpy and nervous as we attempted to close the loop on Rose's grocery store criminal. The evidence of the crime was on the videotape resting in Ernie's lap.

Fondling bread in public is not something you expect from a really rich guy. It just doesn't make sense in the worlds I experience. As F. Scott Fitzgerald said, "Life is much more successfully looked at from a single window." I thought I knew what that meant. It didn't mean that I had to accept other folks' strange behavior as normal. I just had to accept their actions as their actions.

"Jeffrey Oswald Breene made his money the good old fashioned way." Ernie continued his update. "He married it."

"Nice work if you can get it," I said taking the turn past the Peak's Golf and Racquet Club.

"His wife is heiress to, among other things, Occidental Petroleum. She is also the only child of only children, just like me. Old Jeffrey has squandered tens of millions of dollars in bad business deals and dead-end investments."

"Sharp as stump?"

"The bumbler's net worth keeps rising by leaps and bounds each time one of her relatives dies. Go figure."

"How do I find a wife like that?"

"You did, old cod, you did."

"I forgot," I said as I tried to locate the entrance to Single Tree Lane.

Having more money than me wasn't hard; most homeless people would qualify. I had married my wife before I knew her family was bound to make her stinking rich some day. I was pretty sure it would never affect my bottom line, and it was still hard for us to make the mortgage payments each month on her salary and my paltry retainers. We would never be on the financial level of Ernie or Jeffrey Breene.

Ernie had known Jeffrey since his own Princeton days where they battled it out at the Eating Club's Open Whiskey Drinking contest from freshmen year on. Sampesee was an Ivy man; Breene was Cottage. He was stiff competition, yet neither ever won the coveted title. A cad named Reginald Akers III, known fondly as "Aker Turd," won the blasted thing four years in a row. A feat unequaled, according to Ernie, in the two hundred and thirty years since the founding of that grand institution. No, not even F. Scott Fitzgerald, my current literary hero and Old Nassau's most illustrious partying grad, attained a similar high water mark of notoriety.

I turned the Bentley in a long graceful curve into the courtyard of the only house on Single Tree Lane.

Ernie told me he had met Jeffrey a few times since their college days. Didn't much like the fellow. Jeffrey had gotten sober and stayed that way. He took himself and his "business interests" much too seriously. But, the obscene amount of money he had accrued through marrying well and the grim reaper had come with a price. I was at least glad of that. Nobody's life should be perfect.

His wife, according to my barber, was a fifth generation arrogant shrew, addicted at an early age to preserving the rarefied air of New England money, and thought sex was way beneath her station. She was, according to Ernie, a "paper thin, mean spirited bitch who hated Telluride and everything in it." She stayed in Palm Springs, Biarritz, and Newport Beach eleven and a half months a year.

Ernie said, "The only thing I really envy Jeffrey is his dirt on the assorted players in our little town. I hear the old boy shovels it around at cocktail parties and fund raisers like a barber."

I hadn't quite been able to tell Ernie about Jeffrey Breene's wife hiring me to find him in the sack with someone other than her. I had just gotten another advance by electronic deposit today, promising I would have the goods in a day or two. Now that I knew Jeffrey's destination for his liaisons with his paramour, it was only a matter of time.

I watched Ernie fingering the five folded twenties of my recent advance in his pocket to recompense him for his troubles and to help pay my rent. Our plan was that he was going to talk with Jeffrey and get him to stop fondling loaves of bread in public places. It was an unpleasant situation, made worse by the fact that, to protect the less than crystal reputation of my little firm, it had to be done before Rose got violent. The clock was ticking.

Jeffrey Breene answered the deep-throated chimes and swung open the huge wooden doorway. Corpulent was the word I was searching for. He hadn't seen his shoes on his feet, except in a full-length mirror, for a decade or more.

"Still a dapper," Jeffrey wheezed from the exertion of extending his arm in Ernie's direction. Ernie was dressed to the nines in tweed and Egyptian cotton. Over it all he wore a long cashmere duster. Jeffrey ignored me with a shifty eye.

"Jeffrey, my good man, great to see you," Ernie said as we entered the huge foyer.

"You're looking wealthy," Ernie said to the back of the figure that waddled ahead towards the interior of the house wearing the first smoking jacket with black velvet lapels I had ever seen outside of a 1930's movie.

"Yeah," he said over his shoulder with a laughing gurgle. "The inheritance fairy struck again. Babs' father kicked. I finally hit the ten-figure mark. A billion. Not bad for poor white trash, eh?"

Jeffrey's parents according to Ernie had been upper middle class in Larchmont, New York. To hear him tell it now, he had grown up the son of a sharecropper in the Gobi desert.

"Babs well?" Ernie asked.

"Peachy," he dismissed the reference to the source of his fortune with a wave of his pudgy hand. "What's this all about? What's he doing here?"

"Mr. Thorpe is my driver tonight, and he has a favor to ask after we have our talk."

"I won't kiss him," Jeffrey barely contained his enjoyment at his joke. "No offense."

"I wouldn't either," Ernie said.

I kept my mouth shut, glared at the two of them and hoped for the best.

Ernie had phoned Jeffrey at 7 p.m. and lied. I was only a small part of the lie. We were supposedly here on town business.

Public service is part of Ernie's own enjoyment of Telluride, and over the years he has joined a number of organizations to beautify this and protect that. One of these volunteer groups had evolved into the perfect bait for a man like Jeffrey. The San Miguel County Historic Preservation Commission is exclusive, powerful, and its decisions are law, literally.

The Commission, by virtue of its role as a planning and zoning advisory board, has the sole authority to pass its judgment on the "historic nature" of all new construction of every single-family home in the region. The succulent thrill of telling someone that they must say, "please, may I," as they design a seven-million dollar home to put on their two-million dollar piece of property is heady work indeed. Membership is similar to an Ivy League private club or the British House of Lords.

"During the annual early fall 'Bicker,'" Ernie said after drink orders had been exchanged with the maid, "Or the real world's version of our beloved Princeton tradition, 'many are proposed, few are entertained' for a spot on the Commission. It's a very shallow ethnic and socially driven pool to fill vacated seats for life."

Ernie was chairman emeritus of the group.

"The Commission is looking for a few good men," Ernie said to Jeffrey lifting his glass again and toasting in his chum's general direction. "A Cottage and Princeton man might be just the ticket."

Jeffrey was fat, not dumb, and he eyed us suspiciously.

"Why me?" he asked, and his piggish eyes drilled through my chin before he shifted back to Ernie.

"I need a gentleman to stand alongside me, Jeffrey, old Maud." My partner's manner was toady. "There are so few of us left."

Jeffrey tried to hide a piggish smile as he dragged the cup to his lips. Ah, Ernie, you still have it, I thought. The rest of the rent was almost in our hands.

"We come from a long lineage of stalwart fellows, Jeffrey. We are the very people the masses get to make fun of in their movies and tabloids as they go about their humdrum lives. You and I stand a breed apart. Privileged, moneyed, educated, connected in ways the rest could not understand," Ernie winked conspiratorially, purposely excluding me, probably afraid I was about to giggle. "We are by breeding, eccentric. Those delightful little foibles each of us have that make such great gossip. Don't you just love having the luxury of texture when the rest are such milque-toast? It drives the mob crazy."

Ernie cleared his throat affectedly.

"The problem sometimes is finding just the right deviant behavior, proper for a gentleman's pursuits, without pushing the wrong buttons," said Ernie.

Jeffrey squirmed in his seat, finally seeing where this was going. He frowned.

"I, personally, have always found the title 'Commissioner' to be just the right amount of honor and homage due a gentleman. Distinguished, but unpretentious, especially here in Telluride," Ernie started again.

I listened as the night wore on, finally resigning myself to the long haul and figured that by the time my partner was done convincing this bread squeezing miscreant of his duties as a gentleman, we would be lucky to be making minimum wage.

—≈—

Things had slowly gone from bad to worse at the house on Single Tree Lane. Jeffrey had started drinking, Ernie and I hadn't stopped. The living room with its eight-foot tall fireplace and its grand piano was behaving like an ocean liner in a storm. Jeffrey clapped his porgy hands and called for another song.

"Seventeen months," he slurred. "Sober seventeen goddamn months 'till tonight. Ofts' the wagon. Oh, boy."

"Don't fret Jeffrey," Ernie caught his attention with a single E-sharp. "Welcome back to the fold. Your sins are forgiven. Gentlemen should never be morose." He hit a full G-chord with both hands. "Or sober."

Ernie launched into an old parody of Cole Porter's "It's Too Darn Hot." The story is often told that his embryonic entertainment skills as a freshman at Princeton had matured and developed into a full-scale musical comedy routine by graduation. He always brought down the house. The student body loved him, at least according to Ernie.

"Ernie," Jeffrey motioned him back to the table at the rousing finale.

"I felt like I was just warming up. But, alas, I see a morning is just over the horizon." Ernie addressed us in clipped New England tones. "My drinking partners are in their cups. It is time to sing Happy Trails." Ernie closed down the grand piano. "I spare you all the humiliation."

"We's gentlemen," Jeffrey said profoundly.

"Yes we is," I said simply, noting as a literate drunk the grammatical error. "Commissioner Breene?" I added, "Promise me something?"

"Any-sing."

"Stay away from the breadline at Rose's."

Jeffrey tried to focus and couldn't. His lips wouldn't work. He grinned, raised a sausage-sized index finger and tapped it alongside his nose.

"It ain't the bread." He whispered as one conspirator to another.

"Not the bread?" I said.

"You'll see." He tapped his nose again and winked. "S'tommorrow, you'll see. We's gentlemen."

I had an eerie premonition. This wasn't going to turn out well. I just hoped it had nothing to do with plying soft white dough in some prison kitchen. Ernie and I left to the rattle of Jeffrey Breene's snoring in a chair, sounding like a chainsaw among the leaves of his two-story indoor plants.

Eleven

Rose On The Warpath

We gentlemen had agreed to meet at Rose's Market at 10 a.m. As I drove Ernie and the Bentley into the dirt lot, I spotted the conspicuous Z3 parked in a handicapped space near the front doors. I pulled to the furthest point possible, away from the entrance, and Jeffrey Breene walked back to where I parked and slid into the back seat of the Bentley. He had on a conspicuous black trench coat with the collar turned up.

My fashionable barber wore soft wool pants of dark herringbone, a white linen shirt, probably Croatian, and a long tan camel hair coat with a thick wide belt and deep pockets. He had no idea how to dress to go to a supermarket. His wife or his servants handled these things for him.

"Great disguise, old boy," Ernie said to Jeffrey Breene and I was startled that our minds were in the same place. "I thought you were banned from Rose's and her immediate environs for the duration."

"Fuck you," he said in return. The words pained him.

"We are with you, my boy," Ernie said from the passenger seat. "It's just the first hangover of a new life. I understand the unaccustomed pain, not the sobriety that led up to it."

Jeffrey certainly looked the worse for wear. He hadn't shaved, and he smelled of the vestiges of clammato juice, horseradish, and vodka. The eyes that stared back at me when I turned around had lost their focus and were filled with disdain.

"I don't know why I'm doing this," Jeffrey said.

"It's the gentlemanly thing to do?" Ernie sniffed.

"You've got to promise me..." Jeffrey started and then stopped. He buried his aching head in his hands. "I need a drink."

"Excellent idea chum, let's repair to a couple of cozy stools at the Sheridan and re-think our assault on the bread," Ernie said, turning to me with hope in his voice.

"No," I said, "We have to get this over and done with. Rose is on the warpath."

Jeffrey smiled in a sardonic manner. It intrigued me, and I urged him to speak with a wiggling index finger. He finally, reluctantly, began to spill the beans, and the tale he told, in lurid detail, was the Promised Land for a small town detective. Ernie and I would have to go on alone from here. We were struck with the same mystical awe Woodward and Bernstein experienced when "Deep Throat" gave them a jingle. It was so simple. All we had to do was not get caught.

≈

"You know the woman district attorney? Her husband? Wit Thorpe, the fired head of the Ski Patrol on the mountain, you remember? The Thorpe running that private detective agency. Did you hear that he is a homophobic porno producer? First, the X-rated film festival thing, kissing a dead body, and now harassing gay men up on the mountain. I kid you not."

"Doing what?" the second woman's voice was startled into paying closer attention to what the first woman was saying.

"The Sheriff has had a complaint filed by a gay couple up on the mountain. What a Neanderthal, I swear."

Their voices were low enough to be just above whispers, but the words carried through the racks of bread with perfect clarity. Ernie and I were unnoticed, hidden behind the slanted floor to ceiling wooden bins from the combination coffee stand and gourmet deli section. The smell of warm bread assaulted my nose. My ears were perked for the next conversation as the women moved on towards the cereal aisle, their voices fading.

During the last thirty minutes I had heard gossip on everything imaginable. The latest Valley Floor land development rumor, dirt that a certain blonde real estate tigress was flopping around with a married man, and that the Mayor's teenage daughter was seen smoking a joint with a certain local septuagenarian hippie in front of the Steaming Bean, to name only a few of the choicest tidbits.

Often times the women who had just shared their secrets came around the racks and pushed their carts right past us. Overdressed and nervous as to proper procedure, Ernie would pick up a loaf of fresh bread and examine it carefully as they passed.

The next duo of town criers had arrived.

"Ernie who?"

"Ernie Sampesee, you know, the guy worth all that money, drives a big fancy car? Talks funny."

"Oh yeah, the Dandy."

"The what?"

"Dandy, you know, like the old days. Someone who drinks martinis and dances with Ginger Rodgers."

"Yeah, that's the guy. What about him?"

"He's gay."

Ernie's fingers dug into the soft bread flute in terror. He bit his lip to keep himself from protesting the charge.

"No. Really?"

"Absolutely."

"How do you know?"

"It's all over town."

The loaf slid out of the waxed paper in Ernie's hands and hit the floor.

"What about his wife?"

"Camouflage. Eye candy for the locals to throw us off the track. Why do you think she is gone all the time? He and that porno filming friend of his, Wit Thorpe, are quite a pair."

A pause.

"He was kissing a dead body the other day. Right? Wasn't that banker gay too?"

"Do you think?"

"No, couldn't be," she said. "Could it?"

"A couple?"

There was giggling.

In shock, we both started to leave at the same time. Ernie was placing the mutilated carcass of the Italian style loaf back into its bin without its wrapper attached when he spotted her. A charging rhino would have been less obvious. Rose, a lit cigarette dangling from the corner of her hard-set mouth, pointed the finger of doom at him.

"You fucking bread squeezer," she said in a bellow at the top of her gravel-based voice.

Ernie backed away in panic and crashed into the shopping cart of the two women we had just heard discussing us through the bread stacks. One of them was Patsy Susie Blaze. She looked amused at Ernie's dilemma and eyed me with the look of a hungry, but patient bobcat. Ernie panicked, pushed the cart out of his way and sprinted quickly down the aisle. I followed. Rose bellowed again and hustled off in hot pursuit, her accusations, spiced with smoke filled epithets, following at our heels out of the crowded store.

We let ourselves quickly into the Bentley. Locking the doors as the crazed old woman closed on the vehicle. Rose was running behind us and kicking the right rear panel as I left the rutted parking lot at the sedate pace demanded of the antique town car. A crowd had gathered at the doors to watch the debacle. It was much more than a retreat. The town criers would later call it a full rout.

Another successful case put to bed by the Last Resort Detective Agency. A few more jobs like this, and I'll check myself into the loony bin. Right after I get out of the poor house.

Twelve

The Kiss Of Death Kid

After calling in nearly every favor both Ernie and I had outstanding, and telling the story about how I had experienced a good old-fashioned butt kicking in minute detail to each new recruit, I arrived, at high noon, in front of the locked gate to West Egg.

"That's right, my name is Wit Thorpe," I said, putting theatrical menace in my voice, barking into the speaker of the gate intercom, continuing to make my point with the security guard up at the house. "I have Marshall Earp here with me and we are acting under specific written instructions from the owner of this property."

Virgil Cuthbert, AKA Marshall Earp, tried to cover my mouth with his callused hand.

"You don't want to deny us access. We only want to show Mr. Singer what his wife, the house's rightful owner, would like him to see," I said.

I slapped Virgil's hand back and made the shushing sign in his face. The gate finally buzzed, clanked and swung inwards, opening up the drive to the house. I pulled Cuthbert's F-350 crew-cab Ford dual wheel pick-up and specialized trailer through and watched the gate swing shut behind us.

"That's false info, buckaroo," Virgil said. "I ain't impersonating no police officer. Earp's my competition name and that's all. Don't ever do that again. Got it?"

"Sorry," I said. I wouldn't do it again. Unless I really needed to.

"You sure this is kosher?"

"As a rabbi's ass," I said.

"And these guys are a little light in the manhood department?"

"No," I said. "They simply have a different sexual orientation than the rest of us."

"Orientation?" Virgil said. "Is that some big college word us cowpokes don't understand?"

Cuthbert had graduated from Stanford with a PhD in Physics and had been a mathematics professor at MIT for thirty years before he moved west and became a cowboy. I shook my head and listened to the round of snickers in the back seat.

"You better tell us again, there, sonny," Virgil said in his practiced cowboy drawl. "Tell us how this bunch of sexually oriented lightweights kicked your Native American ass so completely that you had to come to us old fart cowpokes to bail you out."

"Let us re-live every colorful moment again so we have the right ornery attitude when we're shooting their eyes out," said another old cowboy from the back seat.

"Wasn't you just caught kissing some guy in town to death?"

"That's right partner," said Sue, "Isn't your new moniker: The Kiss of Death Kid?"

Drygulch Slim, Judge Roy Bean, and Snake Eyes Sue sat shoulder to shoulder in the rear seat, their wide Stetson hats touching brims. They, like Earp, were dressed entirely in period costume of an 1860's cowboy, right down to chaps, latigo, and shiny spurs. Each was long and lean, nearer seventy than sixty and had the worn and wrinkled faces of the open range. Their eyes were wide, wary and bright, as if to stand in sharp contrast to the weathering of the years. "*Duro*" was the closest word in Spanish; roughly translated it meant leathery and tough.

Each of the quintet wore a wide gun belt with a hip high pistol on their favored hand side and a second identical weapon on a cross-over holster that hid their respective belt buckles. A bandoleer hung across each chest with rows of shotgun shells and thirty-eight caliber light load carbine bullets. Straddled between their knees were the antique weapons to make use of the long gun ammunition.

"I do like the bowling part best, deary," Snake Eyes Sue said in her soft, Lauren Hutton voice.

"Naw, tell me again how they cold cocked you up in the meadow," said the Judge with an expulsion of snuff juice into a hand spittoon he always carried, "that's the stupid part I like best."

"Stupider than kissing a dead man?" Earp laughed again.

"He says he didn't know the poke was dead until he started in upon kissin' him," Sue added.

"Seems like he could have asked the feller if it was all right to plant a lip lock. Don't you?" Judge Bean weighed in with his two bits.

"Young ones got no manners no more," Earp said and twirled the ends of his mustache.

I ignored them.

How could they be so calm? I was as nervous as a cat in a dog pound. I convinced myself that we had the element of surprise and that counted for a lot. The cowboys and Sue continued to bate me with the punch lines from my assault. They laughed and laughed all the way up the mountain. My head hurt.

≈

I stood at the door to the main house alone. I had laid on the doorbell for a few minutes and was just about to raise the twenty pound knocker to pound on the bronze eagle head mugging me in full shriek, when the door opened and I looked into the face of the bearded biker man, sans drum stick. I gulped, he smiled, showing sharp white canines. He was younger than I had thought, or I was older; either way, he moved on pneumatic springs like a linebacker.

"Come in," he said politely. Posing as a trained detective, I also noticed that my powerful young friend had shed the biking leathers and was dressed in an expensive suit that must have cost more than I made, ever. A Rolex, if I wasn't mistaken, peaked out right below the cuff of the nappy dark coat.

"Follow me," he again spoke as a host directing me to the dinner table.

I obeyed, following him into the huge main foyer. It seemed the size of a cathedral. A tooled leather floor made me want to walk lightly. I thought better of it. That was the kind of twinkle toes could get me gang raped by Sodom's Devils. A snicker escaped my lips at the thought. It was a sleeper joke, fuel added by the fact I wasn't the least bit homophobic; gay men hiding in the bushes to ambush straights is the joke that found my funny bone. I snickered again. It must have been the password. The bearded one never looked back. We walked on towards the fleet of decks on the second floor of the main house.

Forrest Singer again sat in the same cabana chair outside at the edge of the huge hot tub. The blonde boy from the day before sat at his side in leather pants and no shirt. The young man's body was sculpted and lean, his mouth was small and held in a feral rage, a shadow of a beard smudged his cheeks with sad hooded eyes peaking out under a tangle of unwashed bangs.

Singer was the only other figure on the porch not in formal business attire. He wore a cotton boat necked shirt and a pair of white tennis shorts. It appeared to be a convention of Wall Street lawyers advising a wealthy client on vacation.

"What the hell is going on?" I said. "You filed a complaint?"

"I beg your pardon, Wit? It is Wit Thorpe, hapless private detective, is it not?" Singer said, not getting up, or offering to shake hands. "Have you come to apologize for being drunk and disorderly? Showing up uninvited and crashing my private retreat with my business colleagues?"

I stared.

"I believe there was the matter of the, ahem, vomit on my bowling alley?"

A ripple of laughter erupted from the nine of them. The bearded doorman, who was nearest me, put a heavy hand to my shoulder. It was a mistake.

The devil made my left hand swing quickly backward over my shoulder. The flat callused knuckles catching the ridge of his nose. I turned on the balls of my feet, dropping my back foot, and sent a leveraged power punch with my open right hand to the sternum. I stayed fit sparing at Benny Hanna's Dojo. I was now as slow as a bull when in competition, but I could still punch a ton. The bearded man staggered in reverse, collapsing into two of his friends and then sat down hard on the wooden deck gasping for air.

It was a suicide move, kid's movie stuff, just plain stupid. I felt the thrill rush of satisfaction, expecting the roof to cave in.

The bearded one simply held a finger aloft and the pack ceased their simultaneous quick movements in my direction.

"Maybe Walter and the bowling team had that coming," Singer said. "But I wouldn't advise you to underestimate my friends and what they are capable of."

"Me, either." I tried to lower my voice an octave, but it still sounded squeaky and defensive.

Singer gave me a quizzical look that evaporated into raised eyebrows that said clearly I must have gone to school on the short bus.

"Where the hell is my gun?" I said calmly.

"I don't know what you're talking about. I have no business with guns. So messy." Singer stood. He was tall, almost fit in a soft health club way, had a lisping "s", and oozed money. Both effected attributes reminded me of his wife.

"What the hell does my wife want you to show to me? Incriminating pictures?" He seemed about to call our little chat over. "Walter?" he said, with a raised eyebrow that insinuated I be shown the door.

The well-dressed goons laughed, even the bearded one named Walter, who was struggling to his feet, yet to fully catch his breath. I guess they were way past being embarrassed about their sexual orientation. That put the kibosh on plan "B".

"Why did you kill Stewart Lambis?" I asked the first question that popped into my head.

Everybody stiffened. I had struck a sore spot.

"How would we know who killed Mr. Lambis?" Walter growled as he reached for my arm.

"You and he were seen to be real chummy," I said to Singer. "Could be the police might want to know that?"

"Are you threatening me?" Singer had regained his arrogance of control.

My realistic chances of winning any points with threats and intimidation in this audience were nil. Being a bully was about the entire gamut of my detective skills. What was I going to do now, frisk 'em for my gun and then pistol-whip them all into leaving the house? Best to stick with plan "A" and figure out the nuances later. My job was to get them all outside into the courtyard for the sharpshooters. How that was going to happen had me pretty much stumped.

"How about we step outside?" I offered off the cuff not knowing what else to say. "What your wife really wants me to show you is in the courtyard."

Singer smiled a frozen smile, thought a minute while we all waited, and finally opened his palm towards the doors to the deck.

"Okay," he said. "I'll bite."

"Man, was that tricky," I thought as I led the way down the flights of stairs back towards the front door. Walter's heavy hand again rested on my shoulder.

≈

The custom trailer had been placed in the far corner of the paved acre of driveway, away from the entrances to the house. It now resembled a lawn-storage-shed sized jail. It even said "Jail" in big red Edwardian letters on the sign above the double swinging doors.

Four identical sets of stands and targets stood two to a side forming the wings of a stage. Ten plate-sized metal swing targets on six-foot tall stands, five full-sized male cutouts, and eight crouching cowboys with hats in silhouette were propped on breakaway tripods behind scattered hay bales. Each collection of targets was set a bit differently but the total number of options were the same for all four. The black outlined figures, guns drawn and pointed, looked like a full posse of deadly two-dimensional hombres.

"What is this, a wild west show?" Singer laughed and folded his arms. All of his colleagues did the same. It was ridiculous. They were posed in a group like a Blue's Brothers impersonation club, eyes hidden behind similar aviator style Ray-Bans.

The Jail blew open and Snake Eyes Sue was the first through the doors. With a movement as quick as a rattler, she drew her six-shooter and opened fire.

Arms left their folded positions in a hurry, and half of the group hit the ground. The other half crouched reaching under their jackets for empty air. Variations of slang swear words rang out.

Live ammunition began striking home on the heavy armor plates, spinning bull's-eyes. Five shots and she holstered the pistol like a tongue flicking back into a reptile's mouth. The other gun was immediately in the empty hand, and five more shots rang out. Five more heavy metal targets echoed with the deadly compression of lead against iron and started spinning.

Two more desperadoes suddenly burst through the door. They did full forward somersault rolls on the courtyard bricks, coming up blazing. Sue had holstered her other pistol, and a lever action carbine came forward from a buckskin-fringed scabbard on her back. The rifle sounds were loud above the pistol fire from the other men. Plates were spinning and silhouettes were dropping like flies. Virgil was firing with both hands.

By the time it took Sue to empty her rifle and pull a double barreled shotgun into her hands, approximately six-point-eight seconds, the cowboys had both slapped leather twice, picked up rifles and were leveling their profiled targets as well with shell casings ejecting everywhere.

With practiced movement Sue fired two shotgun blasts, broke the gun ejecting the shells and shoved two more home. In the time it takes to answer a phone, the barrage of bullets was over. Ninety-two targets had been gunned down. Ninety-two bullets had been fired.

Singer and the rest of the cowering audience were in various stages of shock. Their ears ringing from the barrage of gunfire. Each tried to recover from their instinctive reaction with as much dignity as possible. Most of them were brushing at the parts of their pricey suits that had come in contact with the dusty plaza bricks when they had scrambled for cover. One was lamenting a ripped knee.

Singer stepped forward. His tanned face was beet red. I thought he might explode. Anger and hate had replaced fear in an instant.

"World Champions," I said. "Each and every one is a Cowboy Action Shooter. And they don't take kindly to people putting guns in my back. Your wife wants you out of her father's house. I wanted to show you I could get guns too. Don't make this a battle you can't win."

Singer tried to slap me. It was so slow a move, I debated if I should let him do it. I finally brushed the hand away with a sweeping side block. He grabbed his wrist from the contact.

"I'll kill you, you bastard," he said. Tears welled up in his eyes and he turned, still holding his forearm and stomped off into the house. Walter stepped forward. Virgil appeared instantly at my shoulder, efficiently shoving new cartridges into the side-loader of the carbine. Walter stepped back and stuck an index finger out at me from ten feet away.

"We'll meet again, Wilfred" he said in a normal tone of voice. "Count on it."

He followed Singer towards the house; the rest of the well-dressed goons fell in behind, some backing up, guarding their flanks; so much testosterone, so little reason. What the hell was going on here?

~

I should have been prepared for jail, but it always comes as a surprise. At least the Sheriff had let the rest of the posse go. I already owed Virgil and the Over-The-Hill-Gang Cowboy Action Shooters more than a few favors without getting them thrown in the Hoosegow. I paid them for the demonstration, and they went their way.

The Sheriff had been leaning expectantly against his Bronco when I turned back away from the house after the smoke cleared. It quickly dawned on me why the guests at West Egg had not been armed. As law abiding citizens, Singer had called in the law to evict a chronic trespasser. I was being charged with harassment. The Sheriff also claimed later that he saw me assault Mr. Singer.

I sat alone in a plush cell. The holding facility in Illium Valley had been nicknamed "Sheriff Bueller's Bed and Breakfast." It was an upscale confinement area with video camera surveillance, intercoms to the guards' station, and a down comforter on the single bed. Progressive, but still a cell.

I couldn't ask my wife to bail me out. She had helped the judge set the bail. My one call had gone to Ernie's answering machine. So I cooled my heels and felt sorry for myself.

I finally buzzed the intercom and asked if I could have some paper and a pen. They asked what for. I told them I wanted to write down my confession in lurid detail. They said they would check with the Sheriff. Twenty minutes later, I had a legal pad and a Bic. I wrote from behind bars in a state of deep, resentful depression.

~

The Gatsby had followed her. Keeping the Packard well back in traffic in the darkness. The radio was tuned to the *Amateur Hour.* Vibrating chimes led to a commercial as he pulled into the vacant space the cab had just left. She was already inside the revolving front doors of the Algonquin Hotel. The doorman approached the Packard from the sidewalk and Gatsby waved him off with a menacing backhand. He watched her cross the lobby, striding towards the elevator.

She moved on ball bearings. Every motion fluid and leading to a concentration of attention on her hips. The long straight lines of the dress showed a sinew of calf and a turn of delicate ankles in high-heeled shoes. Gatsby's mouth went dry. An erection began to form in his pants.

Clutched under her bare arm was her valise-sized strapless purse. She stared straight ahead, oblivious to the eyes that followed her across the polished slate floor. Newspapers dropped, arms crossed, conversations lagged as sexual fantasies flicked about the room with the speed of Tinkerbelle.

She disappeared into the elevator and was gone. The huge clock arm above the doors slowly swung through the numbers until it could go no further. It was the penthouse noted Gatsby. He then pulled across the street to the parking lot and found a spot where he could watch the entrance to the hotel and made himself comfortable, dropping the rakish brim of the brown fedora lower on his forehead. His eyes narrowed. He smoked a cigarette, through a cracked side vent, and waited.

Four minutes later he noticed a burst of commotion in the lobby. She ran from the elevator in a panic and stumbled to her knees, her purse spinning across the polished stone. A dark object separated itself from the purse, a woman screamed.

Gatsby watched the pantomime through the wide windows in the bright lobby as he started the engine and gunned the car forward, out of the lot, over the curb and into traffic. Cars slammed on brakes and squealing tires were drowned out by the sharp blaring of horns. Gatsby's headlights swept in an arc across the lobby of the hotel.

She scrambled forward on her knees as the crowds' attention was captured by the Packard, crunching tin, and the angry horns. She picked up the gun and held it out at arm's length. She got to her feet and scooped up her purse. Threatening a gentleman who had only stepped forward, unable to contain himself, trying to help a beautiful lady to her feet.

She backed into the revolving doors and out onto the lamplight shadows of the street. The Packard's passenger door flew open. She lunged head first towards its safety. Sliding onto the red leather seat she slammed the door behind her.

Gatsby and the woman locked eyes. A crackle of possession, ownership flashed between them. A cynical smile creased his lips. The face of a killer, just like hers. She exhaled, sadness sweeping over her body. It weighed her down and pressed her hard into the seat.

She ground her teeth and growled low in her chest, quickly raised the German Luger pointed it towards his stomach and ordered him to drive.

≈

The last gate swung open and let me out of the jail, with the peeling laughter of the Deputy Sheriffs echoing behind me. I walked over to Ernie's cream-colored Bentley and let myself in the rear door.

"I don't want to talk about it," I said in warning as I slid into the back seat. "Damn Jackbooted Pleistocene mugwumps."

"Your vocabulary impugns an Ivy League education," Ernie said, hoping to make me feel better.

The only ivy I had ever gotten close to made me itch.

"They kept what I was writing before they released me," I said. "Can they do that?"

"I wouldn't be surprised," said Ernie.

"Damn fine lawyer you turned out to be," I said.

Without another word my barber pulled away from the jail and headed for the nearest watering hole.

I was in no mood. And now Gatsby was in trouble? Kidnapped? Dead? What? He was the only clue I had to the mystery woman. And now my writing was in the hands of the law. Damn it all to hell anyway. Could anything else possibly go wrong today?

"Rose left a message on the machine and wants you to pay her back the two hundred and fifty dollars," Ernie said, getting right to the point.

"Huh?"

"She says if that's what you charge to find a bread rapist, that's what she's owed for finding one herself."

"We didn't take care of Breene?"

"Well, yes, my boy, the new commissioner will no longer be torturing the Wonder Bread."

"So what's wrong with Rose?"

"Me."

"You?"

"I'm the new bread squeezer," Ernie confessed the obvious with enthusiasm and a lopsided, scotch induced smile. "You're to break my thumbs, old codfish. And she wants her money back by tomorrow."

"She hasn't paid me anything."

"Irrelevant," Ernie said, and I knew he was right.

I didn't tempt fate by asking any more rhetorical questions about possible wrongs. I guess hope is the feeling we have that the feeling we already have is not permanent.

Thirteen

The Redhead In The Penthouse

Mom was in court, you were in jail," Cody said. "I called a cab."

"Ever think about walking the four blocks home?" I asked, knowing I was riding a dead horse.

"Please."

"Your mother's daughter," I said into the phone. "Katie okay?"

"Angel took her down to the park."

"You okay?"

"Yeah, sure," she said. "Dad, what exactly is a pervert?"

"Does this have something to do with me?" I said.

"Does it?" she said. "I looked it up." She was warning me that I had better not try to lie.

"Where is this coming from?"

"One of my informants tells me that the Sheriff's Department has proof that you write porn, are a peeping tom, and anti-gay." The last was the worst accusation by far according to the tone of voice from my fifth grader. "Its all over town."

"I got to go."

"Don't be homophobic. Dad, it's not a life style choice but biological sexual orientation, and a purely natural way of life for loads of great people."

"Bye," I said.

"People have the right to choose."

"Tah."

"Denial is more than just a river in Egypt, Dad."

"Toodles..."

"Get help, Dad." She got in the last word before I could hang up. Eavesdropping, extortion, thievery and greed were all in my daughter's playbook. I smiled in pride for my offspring. And, she was already defending personal liberties against all comers. I figured she had her head screwed on pretty straight.

≈

I followed the perp to the Wyndham Peaks Hotel in Mountain Village. Jeffrey Breene had parked his car back in town in an underground spot under Spiral Stairs condos that belonged to a friend and rode the gondola up and over the mountain to Mountain Village. Telluride has the only public transportation system in the country that offers a gondola as part of its free municipal bus service. It was fifteen minutes in the air and saved a half hour drive. The gondola was a local's daily routine. It was so obvious I had missed it thinking the guy had to be out of town. His silver Z3 was a hard ride to miss.

Cody broke the secret with a Twinkie. A second grader spilled the beans over lunch. It cost me four hours of cell phone time.

Staying far enough behind my target so that I wouldn't be noticed was second nature to a private detective.

"Hey Wit," the valet parking attendant yelled in a booming voice from a hundred yards away. We had played beer-laced ultimate Frisbee once or twice. The moron reasoned this gave him the right to blow my cover.

Jeffrey Breene turned, saw me, recognized who I was and what I wanted in an instant. He quickly pushed open the huge wooden doors, scuttling across the lobby on short stumpy legs. He was well and truly gone when I finally got inside the door. Three hundred and fifty rooms, all with doors and dead bolts to lock me out.

I went back into the sunlight ready to take my frustrations out on the carhop. In the middle of his being frightened and my being angry, we stumbled on how he could make it up to me. All I had to do was park cars while he did the deed. I took his baseball cap and red Peaks Resort Staff jacket as a disguise. He took the ice bucket, champagne, and long stemmed glasses from the trunk of my car and headed for the room service door to the kitchen. He'd get a waiter's coat and deliver the complimentary champagne to the newly checked in couple. It was the off-season and, with a ten percent occupancy rate, finding the right room would not be too difficult even if Breene used an alias.

I just hoped the valet remembered what I said about how to aim and activate the video camera hidden in the base of the silver tureen. The trick was to simply point the bucket's Sampesee Family crest towards the bed. Don't get it backwards. Nothing is worse than expecting some pay-the-bills raunchy sex to prove philandering and ending up with awesome sound effects and a beige wall for two hours.

Life always has a way of throwing you curve balls when you least expect it. The redheaded mystery woman from my story walked out of a white Mercedes sedan on the arm of Robert Forrest Singer. He tossed me the keys as he went past and glided her with a hand to the small of her back towards the Peaks' lobby, never giving me a second glance.

"The Penthouse," he said over his shoulder. The arrogant prick was oblivious to who I was. It was all I could do to not go after the man who had bowled me, had me arrested, and had made my life miserable and unproductive for the last couple of days.

The woman recognized me at once with a startled expression. I was sure of it. Her green eyes flashing behind the curtain of glossy red hair were troubled, vulnerable, hypnotic, and dead certain I was likely in league with the devil. She moved away from me in a hurry.

I, on the other hand, was stunned, frozen, holding Singer's still warm keys in my hand. The Penthouse? Singer and my mystery woman? What the hell? Was I going crazy?

I left quickly when my reluctant operative returned, having accomplished the first part of his mission. The cheap bubbly was now fueling adulterated lust.

Two hours later I was back at the Peaks. The white Mercedes was gone. With a twenty-dollar bill and forgiveness, I retrieved my champagne bucket and most likely had the goods on the lover boy copulating with a certain real estate broker. The carhop was now a full fledge operative for the Last Resort Detective Agency, just like a hundred and fifty other minimum wage professionals in Telluride. He seemed proud of it.

Trying desperately to generate some modicum of enthusiasm for monitoring the content and quality of the taped proof of spousal infidelity, I drove back to the office. Not much in the detective business is worse than watching two aging, pudgy and mismatched bodies going through the ABC's of banal carnality. Somebody's old mom and dad going through all the required positions, learned from watching hard-core porn on their DVD players at home. It gave me the shivers.

The sudden apparition of a character from my story was also giving me the quakes. She was by far the most real thing I had ever created on paper and now she was also alive, breathing in the flesh. That woman knew things I couldn't even dream about. You could just tell. I needed to find out everything about her.

I knew, of course, that she couldn't be Gatsby's mystery woman, and that a composite collage of imaginary faces had suddenly become specific when I saw her this afternoon. But, she knew me. I don't usually get that deer in headlights reaction because of my good looks. Maybe I was going crazy. Seeing fictional characters might qualify me for a loony. What was going on? What was she doing with Singer in the Penthouse?

"Like, duh," I said aloud to myself. The thought and image of her naked, on top of him, riding hard produced a tremor and I sat down at my computer in a stew of conflicting emotions.

Was I jealous? Good. Maybe this was the jolt I needed. It was time again to write. I felt like my head was about to explode.

≈

She steadied the Luger in her lap and stared straight at him, ignoring the road ahead. Gatsby turned frequent corners at high speed, splashing puddles across the empty sidewalks. Off in the night, sirens wailed. They hadn't spoken. He drove towards the docks, entering off Harborview and dropping into a long section of empty storage warehouses. He turned into the first one with an open door, shut off the car and doused the headlights. The gun on her thigh never wavered.

"Here we are again," he said.

"Yes."

"Did you use that thing back there? In the Penthouse?"

Her face was backlit and dark in the dim light from the dock floods. She nodded.

"Is he gone? Is it over?"

She nodded.

"Can't you tell me what this is all about?"

She shook her head. Her hair shifted loudly against the satin collar of her dress.

"Can't or won't?"

"Won't."

"Can you tell me who he was?"

"No."

"Can't or won't."

"Neither." Her voice was a whisper. "I don't know who he was. One of you." Her head shook again. She sniffed softly. She was crying.

Gatsby felt the prickle of standing hairs at the back of his neck. This wasn't going well. She was going to shoot him. Sadly but certainly he knew it to be true. Regrets were something this lady lived with while those around her died. Sweat rolled in cold tracks down his ribs.

He reached across for her with a slow determined arc of his left arm. She placed her free hand in his to make him keep his distance. The barrel of the gun rising menacingly to aim at the center of his throat. He carefully guided the offered hand back to his lap. They sat for a few seconds fingers entwined. Gatsby felt the wetness of tears on the soft skin at the back of her hand. Was there a chance, even yet?

He tugged gently, turning his hand over on top of hers and pulled at it again, insistently edging her palm towards his crotch. A sigh rushed from her mouth, ending in a low primal moan, and her shoulders suddenly sagged. She allowed him her hand to guide. The bright red nails and her long delicate fingers closed along the erection that was expanding down the inseam of his pressed and pleated breasted wool slacks. The gun never wavered as her fist and shoulders began a slow rhythmic pumping. Her hair swished lightly on satin. He immediately forgot he was probably going to die.

She bit her lip, turning so he could see her profile. Her breath began to catch in her throat, he was thrusting forward now, rising off the seat, and she felt a sudden release of her own seminal juices seconds before Gatsby joined her. He growled like an animal as he came. The gun came out of the shadows quickly and pushed against his temple as her hand continued to milk the semen from him.

"Again," she hissed her mouth moist at his ear. "Again." She urged him on to complete himself.

A single loud report sent the seagulls on the docks aloft. They soon circled and daintily resumed their respective perches in the pecking order of the moment. Each bird knew its place without pausing. They looked ahead not seeing anything but the future.

So like people, she thought as she walked away from the car down towards the docks. Her shoulders sagging under the weight of all she had done in the past two weeks. She clutched the purse under her arm tightly. Her head hung on her chest. If only things could be different. One more act of betrayal and it would be all over. The whole sorry mess of her life would finally be dead and buried.

≈

My wife's office called my office and officially informed me that in the matter regarding the legal pad from the jail; I could certainly have a photocopy of the writing I had done while in custody at thirty-five cents a sheet. Since I had declared it a "confession," the originals would stay in their hands, hers and Sheriff Bueller's, until the charges had been answered. Who knew the vagaries of the criminal mind?

I fumed, I seethed, I just about blew a gasket feeling I was being denied a gazillion amendment rights, but I simply said thanks and hung up. I was in enough trouble at home without giving a rash of attitude to my wife's priggish prima donna secretary. Her name was Audrey, and she deserved the name and everything that went with it.

I gazed down at the computer screen. A single loud report? What was that? Gatsby jacked off and dead?

I felt the world shift. The old muse was definitely missing something here. Gatsby wasn't supposed to die. He is, was, the main character. Main characters don't die in the middle of stories. They only die at the end. It's a goddamn rule, I'm sure of it. I ran my hands through my tufts of hair. What was I going to do now?

The phone rang. I picked it up. It was her, she, whatever. The mystery woman come to life.

Fourteen

Call Me Randy

"Mr. Thorpe?" I knew as soon as she spoke that the voice and the face were one and the same. I just knew.

"Wit Thorpe," I said.

"My name is Miranda Sterling. Wit? May I call you Wit? Wonderful. I am presently working for Mr. Singer and Meyer Wolfscheim on a documentary about their struggles to free men from themselves."

"Do these men know they're prisoners?"

"Don't you?" she said.

What could I say?

"My film crew would like to come by and interview you at your convenience. Would now be okay? We wouldn't trouble you for long." Her voice was full and rich; her manner engaging, professional. She was good. The warning bells were just now going off.

"Ms. Sterling..." I said.

"Miranda," she said.

"Miranda then." I knew she could hear my smile through the phone. "Why in God's name would you want to interview me?"

"The other side's point of view," she said.

"Other side of what?"

"Doctor Meyer Wolfscheim."

"*Gezundheit.*"

She laughed. The sound was Aspen leaves in a summer breeze.

"I don't know from any refugee doctor," I said in my best Mexican-Ute accent hoping she'd like the comedian.

"And you didn't try to lead a bunch of local vigilantes to intimidate Dr. Wolfscheim and Mr. Singer from pursuing their attempt to set up a mission here in Telluride? Firing guns at them?"

"Hell, no," I said, feeling the sweat pores in my armpits begin to run.

"Is it because they preach a more open world regarding men's sexuality?"

"How's that?"

"Does it repulse you to think of men having sex together?"

"That's the other side?" I said.

"Are you part of a conspiracy to keep the message of bi-sexuality out of Telluride?"

"That's the message?"

"Bi-sexuality is natural, instinctive, and part of humanity," she said. "You have a problem with people being bi?"

"Hell, I'll go you one better."

"Pardon?"

"I'm way past bi. I'm basically tri-sexual," I said. "I'll try anything."

No one laughed.

"But the assault..."

"Listen Miranda. I'm just a working stiff. Hired by a homeowner to make some unwanted house guests disappear. I got no dog in any other fight but that. I don't care who Singer wants to diddle. I just want him to leave my client's house while he does it, so I can get paid."

"That's it!" Miranda was excited and encouraging.

"That's what?"

"That would be great in the documentary."

I couldn't think of anything to say. I exhaled loudly.

"You're angry."

"No I'm not."

"See? You'd be great." Her voice was like honey. "We can discuss the questions beforehand."

I paused, knowing I was being led like a bull to slaughter. Should I plod on and accept my fate? I decided instead to throw the dice. After all, this was my mystery woman, and I knew she would bite.

"Have a drink with me. Just you, alone, dump the crew," I said. "I'll let you try and convince me."

The sound of her sigh rasping in my ear sent chills up my spine. I could almost see her legs fall open on the red leather seat of the Packard coupe.

She agreed immediately. We would meet me at the Excelsior in twenty minutes. I was up and out the door in a heartbeat. Ernie's kind attention to a cut and shave would help the time pass and calm my banging heart. My watch said 5:47 p.m.

≈

The streetlights had banged on along Colorado Avenue as the cold shadows from the mountain closed in over Telluride. As soon as I entered the warm interior of the Excelsior I saw her. How could you miss a woman dressed like a woman amongst the jeans, khakis, and shapeless polar fleece vests of mountain town fashion? She was a vision of pulchritude.

She sat on a high stool at the bar. Her long trim legs crossed, showing a lot of shimmering sheer nylon with a spiked high heel hooked in the footrest. A bright rich green sleeveless blouse exposed toned and tan arms the color of toffee. It's a fact that mumps, measles, and puppy love are all worse after thirty.

She smiled with a Cheshire cat certainty. I felt as if I had been clubbed between the eyes. It was her, goddamn it; the red hair, the perfect cheekbones, the patrician nose, a wide sensuous mouth, the sharp teeth. Dangerous eyes.

"Wit?"

"Miranda."

Her eyes were on mine as I closed the ten feet from the door to the bar. I couldn't let it go, although I wasn't trying very hard. I knew this woman. I created her, gave her whole, as a slowly nurtured personal fantasy, to that asshole Gatsby. Now she was back, only real. She was so familiar. I felt possessive, needing to rush in and establish ownership.

I edged in amongst the crowd, leaned over the bar without removing my leather coat. My thigh brushed against her nearly naked knee, and she pushed back. The lines at the corners of her beautiful green eyes joined the smile on her mouth. Her eyes would not break from mine.

"Do I know you?" she said.

I just stared into her eyes as the sharp edges of conversations drowned out the silky blues coming from the sound system. She sipped her white wine, licking the last bit with the tip of her tongue at the edge of the glass.

"What are we doing here?" I said, leaning in so just she could hear.

"Meeting again for the first time?" Her voice was like chimes above the din.

"You feel it too?" I asked with a slight hesitation.

"Maybe," she dropped her eyes.

"What are we doing here?" I asked again.

"Wasting time," she said, her eyes daring me to keep the innuendoes going. Leaning in closer, she rubbed her cheek against mine. The charge was electric.

"Am I?" I asked in a husky voice. "Wasting time?"

"We'll have to see," she said. "Any ideas? We could get the business talk over with first? I can be very convincing. Some place more private?"

My throat was coated in cotton.

"Any ideas?" she asked finishing her wine.

"Your place, or, your place," I said hoarsely.

"Call me Randy." She said with a cough that sounded like laughter in my ear.

"I'm excited too."

"No, really..."

"Yes, really," I said failing to note the descending coldness around her delicious green eyes before it was too late.

"No..."

"You be randy, I'll be kinky, and we'll get along fine," I said, breathlessly, leaning closer and whispering in her ear, feeling myself getting hard. "I promise you'll forget..." I stopped, almost adding the name Gatsby, finally managing, "...everything."

She jerked back and gave me a heart stopping cold quizzical stare.

"I said call me Randy, R-A-N-D-Y," she said, embarrassed. "Miranda, Randa, Randy..." Her voice trailed off. "Jeez." She cleared her throat, sliding quickly from the stool and standing up, all business, taking great care not to come in contact with me again.

"Oh," I tumbled back to reality, realizing finally how out-of-line I was. We were on different pages. She obviously wanted me on tape, not in the sack.

Her eyes would no longer meet mine. She backed a full step away in disgust, and I was saved from further humiliation in that particular direction by having Yankee Doodle Dandy start playing loudly from the cell phone in my coat pocket.

"Yeah," I answered the phone, drawing added and unwanted attention from our tightly packed neighbors at the bar.

"Will you talk with your daughter?" Cody yelled in an exasperated voice in my ear. "Talk some sense into her."

Cody passed the phone to Katie who was screaming at the top of her lungs, "Hamie-over-Miami, Hamie-over-Miami, Hamie..."

I could hear Cody trying to drown her out with a litany of "Shut-up, shut-up, shut-up..."

I could picture Angelina cursing in Spanish under her breath, calling these two, "*enfants brujo*", devil children.

"Please, sweetheart, stop yelling, I'll be right home." I said it loudly so that Katie could hear me. Everybody in the bar could hear me too.

I hung up. The restaurant chatter was gone. All eyes were on me. Things were veering out of control. Hollyhock Lane was simply one small item added to the list of places I didn't want to be.

The force of the open handed slap rocked my head all the way to my shoulder. It stopped conversation throughout the entire restaurant dead in its tracks.

"You two-timing deviant," she slapped me again with the other hand. I nearly went down. She opened up a nosebleed. Those arms were more than toned. She spun me around and shoved me towards the door. It opened, saving me a painful face plant on the etched glass. I was suddenly supported in the arms of Jeffrey Breene, bread-squeezing billionaire. His face blanched and he almost dropped me.

"Leave me alone," he leaned down and screamed into my face. "Can't you people just leave me alone?" He dropped me to the sidewalk, turned and scrambled away into the shadows on the dark side street. The door to the Excelsior tried to swing shut, but my legs were in its way. I couldn't buy a break.

"I wouldn't give you a glass of water if you were dying of thirst in the desert. Go home to your wife." Miranda continued to play at high volume on center stage. "Go fuck yourself. You...you misogynist cretin." She gave a good broken-arm *fazoo*. The entire bar and restaurant applauded and cheered. She smiled that megawatt smile, turned to her audience and bowed with a flourish of her tanned and toned arms and her magnificent red hair.

I got to my feet, dusted myself off and left the front of the building behind, hearing the laughter and applause for blocks, heading towards home. It was 6:32 p.m., and I was mighty confused.

≈

My wife had come in over an hour ago, but I sat in Katie's bed with my back against the headboard and Dr. Seuss in my lap. I was thinking. Found out I was way out of practice in that department.

All of the logical explanations didn't add up. Was I really some kind of deviant? This woman meant nothing but trouble. Was that whole thing my fault? I replayed the scene, and it didn't look good for me. I was such an idiot. Like a hound dog chasing a car. What would I have done if I had dug my teeth into that delicious tire? Dropped away in a dead faint, probably.

I was hopeless. A failure at everything including being a simple bread and butter detective. Maybe they would hire me back on the mountain as an EMT and ski patrolman. I should just tell Mrs. Singer, and the rest of my dysfunctional clients, to get themselves another boy. Give it all to Ernie. I should hit delete on my computer and send Gatsby and the mystery woman back to the nether world where they came from. It would all be over. Wouldn't it?

On tip toes I left Topper the cat and Katie snoring.

I knocked lightly on the closed door to our room. Pausing a beat, girding myself, I pushed gently on the door and opened it to her standing in the way.

"Who is she, Wit?" My wife asked calmly, elbow on the door jam blocking my attempt to slip by.

"No one."

"Oh, she's some one all right," She said. "Half the town watched her slap you around in some little lover's spat a couple of hours ago."

How to explain? I simply held my hands up in the classic question pose.

"It's nothing," I said.

"It's something, and I think I deserve to know what."

"I don't even know her," I said. "Honestly. I'm a victim of circumstances."

"I've heard it before," said the ADA without a trace of compassion.

"Give me a break?" I tried a shy smile, the one she loved. The Iron Maiden didn't crack an inch.

"Sheriff Bueller called, wants to talk with you," my wife said as she fought back the tears. "The woman filed sexual harassment and verbal assault charges."

I leaned forward in disbelief.

"Is she the redhead in the story?" My wife asked.

I nodded, confused.

"You know that..." Her voice finally lost its calmness. "You know that much about her. How she likes her sex? Her groans and moans? Is that right?"

"Screw you, buster," she said quietly

She slammed the door and I went to the couch in the living room. It was 10:22 p.m., and I was alone with no alibi.

fifteen

A Trunkload of Trouble

The radio was playing at better than half volume. Other family noises were also coming from the kitchen as I rolled over, forgetting where I was, and continued rolling right off the couch. I landed hard in a tangle with the single thin blanket. Katie giggled. I propped an eye open to my darling three-year-old daughter. She was smeared cheek to jowl with peanut butter and held a soggy, half-licked bagel towards my face.

"Bite it horse," she demanded. I did and grabbed her around her pudgy middle and tumbled her to the floor to give her my swiveling head to her stomach, a real nuggy. She screamed a long torrent. I finally let her up, and she snatched the soggy bagel back from my teeth and ran back into the kitchen. I smoothed the peanut butter leftovers from her hands into the tufts of my hair.

I was still in the rumpled clothes from last night as I shuffled into the kitchen in dreadful need of a cup of coffee. I brushed at the front of my denim shirt. It still held the dark spatters from my nosebleed of last night. The look I received from my wife was not the one I expected. No scorned woman here. It was the cold, calculating stare of a prosecuting attorney. She held a dark brown file folder in her hands. She spun around and picked up the phone with the coldest shoulder possible. The number was punched home from memory.

"Sheriff Bueller," she said, "this is District Attorney Thorpe. Concerning the investigation into the death of Mr. Singer? Yes, that's right. I want Wilfred Thorpe picked up for questioning. Contact me when you have him in custody. I'll be talking to the judge."

I stared, blinking to shut down the dream and wake up.

"Yes, I know you had probably already planned on it, but I didn't want any misunderstandings about where my office is coming down on this thing."

She listened. Her eyes closed to the world.

"Thank you," she said, "I appreciate that very much." A pause. "Yes, as a matter of fact he is right here."

She passed the cordless phone to me. With a last withering look she turned, swinging the file folder at the end of her arm. She went straight to the bedroom to dress.

I watched her walk away.

"Thorpe?" Sheriff Bueller wanted to know.

"Sheriff."

"You heard the lady."

I refrained from the obvious rejoinder. "How do you want to do this?" I asked.

"I could come right by," he said

And take me away in handcuffs, I finished silently for him. "Got to take the kid to school. I'll stop by your office this morning."

"Wilfred?" he said.

"What?"

"Don't you forget, now?" He sounded as if he hoped I would.

≈

I knocked on Cody's door and opened it. She lay on her already made-up bed, head on the pillow. Fully dressed for school, in a knee length plaid skirt and a fuzzy blue turtleneck sweater, perfect, right down to frilly white ankle socks and shiny black buckled shoes, she twiddled her thumbs.

"Sherlock?" I said in a bit of a panic.

"From now on I'm Bond, Jane Bond. On her majesty's secret service."

"What's going on?" I said.

"Simple change in names "Q."" She patiently started to explain.

"Not that," I said, "the Singer thing."

"You can call me Ought-ought-seven."

"Cody."

"Okay, okay," she sat up on the bed. I came in and closed the door quietly. "Singer's dead. Shot and stuffed into the trunk of your car. You left the wreck parked in the alley behind your office."

"Shot where?"

"One to the noggin," she said as if dead people were always part of our daily discussion. "They found him this morning when a worker showed up at Maggie's to start the dough. The trunk was wired shut, but you must have missed stuffing a hand in, and the baker saw it."

"How do you know this?"

"I read the file."

"No."

"Yup."

"No possible chance you...you..." I was afraid to ask.

"Yup," she said. "Got some pretty good copies off the phone fax machine in the hall."

I gulped.

"What are they worth to you?" My daughter smiled brightly as I sat down on the edge of the bed. She looked to all the world as innocent as the average almost ten-year old. I remembered an old saw about books and covers.

≈

"Ernie?"

A low groan escaped my partner's lips.

"I'm in deep trouble."

Another groan.

"I need your help." Silence followed. "I'll be by in ten minutes."

The phone at Sampesee's hung up.

A Sheriff's Patrol Bronco cruiser followed a courteous distance behind as I dropped the girls at school and headed for Ernie's. When I parked, he parked. He waved. I didn't wave back. I guess Bueller considered me a flight risk, the asshole.

~

Singer's body had been found by Lois Miller of Norwood. She was one of two bakers who do the morning shift at Maggie's. The police were called at 5:30 a.m. this morning.

I scanned log reports from the first officers on the scene. As the documents had arrived at my wife's door at 7:45 a.m., they were still sketchy. The crime unit's report and the Medical Examiner's first cut would be done by noon.

I passed each page across the table to a tousle haired Ernie as he tried to ingest sufficient caffeine to jump start his heart.

"They don't have the weapon," Ernie said. "It sounds like it could be your missing thirty-eight though." He slurped loudly in the shallow antique china cup and tilted the polished silver pot on a spit to fill the void with Brazilian Breakfast Blend.

"Says here the blood in the trunk is minimal, and you must have shot Singer somewhere else and tried to hide the body."

I moaned and washed my face with my hands.

"They list it as a possible hate crime because Singer's wallet and pockets were not rifled, and a recent history of actions by Mr. Singer to protect himself from you for trespass and intimidation for his sexual preference were well documented in the Sheriff's Office."

"They are already building a case against me?" A strident whine was in my voice.

"Being paranoid is so annoying." Ernie was waking up to his many opinions. "But, you're probably right. Bueller would love to have another chance to call you a murderer."

"What am I going to do?"

"You don't have many options when it comes to murder." Ernie tried to focus his bleary, hung-over eyes in my direction.

I stared blankly back.

"You do it?" Ernie said.

"No matter," he added quickly, "I don't want to know. The obvious and most productive thing now is to act like you didn't shoot the codfish."

"I didn't."

"Fine, my boy, whatever."

"I'll prove it," I said.

"No doubt." Ernie's sleep ravaged face was intense and sincere. "More Sampesee juice?" he said reaching for my coffee cup.

I was even failing to convince my barber that I was innocent. But he was right, it didn't matter what he thought. This particular Sampesee would not abandon the ship. At least not this early in the game. He liked to watch my pain.

"I have to borrow the Bentley Friday night."

"What ever for?"

"Dinner and a movie for my daughter and six of her most loyal friends. I'm the chauffeur."

"I'll have to remember that when I am in need of good livery," Ernie yawned and scratched his head. "You're such a good father."

"Yeah," I said taking all the credit possible for my latest required payment to a brilliant master extortionist.

≈

I called Judge Roy Bean from my phone at home. The Judge, also known in non-cowboy life as Doctor Emile Zoloff, was the former chief of forensic pathology at the University of Colorado Medical Center in Denver. He had heard about the body from the half-awake DJ on KOTO radio. He wanted to be filled in. The Sheriff had already called the Zoloff residence this morning and wanted him to stop by the office to take another statement about the discharge of weapons at West Egg. He laughed nervously.

"I reckon they want us to confess," he said.

The Judge listened silently as I ran down the facts of what I knew. I didn't ask for a favor, and he didn't offer to do anything else.

Twenty minutes later the fax machine in the hallway hummed and clicked and slowly rolled out the complete San Miguel County Medical Examiner's confidential first cut at the autopsy, final notes due by 5 p.m. the next day. The body was to be released for shipment back to Hartford, Connecticut for internment in the family plot. Random and widely different sentences in the five page report were boldly circled by the Judge.

"Cause of death was a gunshot wound to the head. Head trauma was extensive. Death was immediate. Manner consistent with a bullet wound at short range. Powder residue and muzzle burns on victim's skin and hair"

"The bullet entered the right temple and exited 1 cm behind and 2 cm below the lobe of the left ear. The bullet was not recovered on the scene. The wound appears to be the product of a medium-sized caliber bullet. The pistol was fired at point blank range."

"Blood accumulation on the clothes and rug in the trunk from the wound appeared minimal. Pooling from the exit wound at the collar and shoulder could also be called minimal. Indications are that the victim may have been placed in the trunk an hour or more after death."

"The victim's hands were recently cleaned and smelled strongly of a disinfectant, possibly an alcohol-based hand wipe."

"Scraping of the skin, but no bruising, at the waist was observed."

"Towel fibers, white sun cotton, were found deeply embedded (3-4 cm) in the wound.

"The victim wore no clothes."

The last circled segment made my head swim. The words lost focus and I had to read them three times before they made sense.

"The residue of semen accumulation of .06 grams was found in the shaft of the penis, an amount consistent with the victim ejaculating within the hours prior to death."

I could almost hear the swishing of her red hair against the velvet collar of her dress as she milked the semen from him. Her husky voice pleading, "Again...again," in a harsh sexual whisper. Gatsby's mysterious woman strikes again.

~

"You're a little late," Ernie said when I saw him later on that morning. I looked at my watch. It was just after ten a.m.

"You've done your daily quota of shaves?" I asked, confused.

"Not me, you," he said and pointed out the store front window at two uniformed sheriff deputies, each walking across Colorado Avenue with a hard drive tucked under his arm. One was also carrying my phone message machine in his free hand.

"Can they do that?" I asked Ernie.

"Yes, they can," he said solemnly. "They have a warrant."

"Damn."

I bounded up the stairs and was breathing hard when I unlocked the door, ripping the search warrant cover sheet from where they had taped it to the glass. I barely glanced at the inventory confiscated reminding myself to set Cody loose on obtaining the entire search document, which would outline the prosecutor's game plan for investigating the murder. The office was even messier than before. The huge gaping holes on my desk had become avalanches of paper. I panicked thinking of the redheaded woman and the story. I would never find out what happens.

I dropped to my knees and grabbed the wastebasket, pulling from it the scribbled on and badly edited printout of the crucial latest pages of the story. Relief swept over me, and only then I fully realized that I was behaving very strangely for someone who hasn't a thing to hide.

Sixteen

The Delicious Itch

Sheriff Harley Bueller had tidied up the interrogation room at the jail since I had been in yesterday. Murder suspects get all the perks. The used, recycled paper coffee cups had been removed from every horizontal surface. The tabletop even smelled like lemon furniture wax. I'm sure a new tape was also in the video camera behind the window in the observation room. My wife was probably sitting there too. Waiting for me to crack, I suppose. Bueller interrupted my reverie with another question.

"No one in your home can collaborate your alibi that you claimed to be sleeping on the couch and were present on Hollyhock Lane between 10:30 p.m. and 6: 10 a.m."

"Was that a question?"

"Would you like to tell us why you were sleeping on the couch?"

"No."

"Is there anyone else who could tell us where you were last night?"

I stared at his square, dimpled chin.

"A redhead maybe?" A smile creased his lips. It was out of place. I saw his eyes flicker towards the two-way mirror.

"Fuck you, Bueller."

The unmeasured response to my expletive from the Sheriff was a sudden snake strike. "We have motive, opportunity, the bad blood between you and the deceased, witnessed threats, and a copious amount of means, right down to the body being in your car."

"Like I said."

"Also, while we don't have the gun, we do have the bullet wound to indicate a thirty-eight could have been used. Your gun was the murder weapon, right?" Bueller was almost breathless.

"I reported it lost," I said.

"How convenient," he said.

"We also have a crime scene scenario, written by you that describes in detail how you are going to commit the murder. That's premeditated murder, first friggin' degree, life without parole, or maybe even the death penalty."

I stared him in the eyes. He was all the way back to enjoying himself.

"I'm lobbying hard to add some rape and kidnapping too. You sexual deviant, you."

I labored to keep my mouth shut. I stared at the mirror. My own reflection seemed distorted.

"Fuck you, Bueller." I said softly.

"This is the witty comebacks department? Not very quick for a big, bad writer are we?" His eyes wandered to the mirror once again. I wondered how much damage I could do before they stormed in here and beat me unconscious with riot clubs. Bueller was big and beefy, close to being in-shape, in an offensive lineman sort of way. I honestly couldn't do enough harm to make it worth it, and I sighed, letting my shoulders sag.

"I think you ought to lawyer up, Wilfred." Bueller said with a gleam in his eye. "Seems we got enough to charge you with a capital offense. *Deja Vu* all over again, ain't it?"

A sharp rap landed on the mirror. I imagined it was my wife's wedding ring. Bueller did not acknowledge the interruption, except to gather his stack of reports and legal pads together. He stood to his full height of six-four and tugged up his black mesh belt over his almost flat stomach.

"Who says lightening doesn't strike twice in the same place. This time you ain't gonna' walk." Bueller smiled, turned on his heels and left the room. The reference to the last time he had tried to pin a murder rap on me was unwarranted and unwanted. I glared at the closed door for the benefit of my anonymous audience and refrained from giving the appropriate physical gesture that would indicate Bueller's number of human parents.

My wife had removed herself from the case and a young, earnest newcomer to the District Attorney's Office of the neighboring county took my statement. I was now busy killing time until they decided to let me go or charge me with murder. I had called Ernie, and he was on the way.

When I asked Ernie's professional guestimate on how long I would be here in jail, he had said, "anywhere from ten minutes until forever." The statement had eased my mind. That kind of double speak probably indicated a fairly competent lawyer.

I was again running over the list of people I thought should be questioned about Singer's untimely demise. Walter, the motorcycle goon, was probably, certainly, capable of murder. Agnes, the wife, would have castrated Singer first with a serrated knife, but maybe she was showing restraint to throw me off the scent. The sex guru from Arizona might know something that would help. The blonde haired male lover of Singer occupied the inside track for fifty percent of all murder motives. Anyone else in the motorcycle gang might be guilty, and a hundred people in Telluride I didn't know who might have had a thing for trophy home owners.

And, of course, Miranda Sterling, my mysterious redhead, who had been in the Peak's penthouse with the man not thirty-six hours ago. She assuredly deserved a once over. Once over? I felt the hairs on the back of my neck tingle and jump to attention. The nipple from the soapy bath flooded into my wide screen imagination. I began to wander down the threads of that old familiar fantasy.

Things were going downhill quickly from strange to weird. I had to admit if I were Bueller, I would think I had a good suspect: trespassing, unlawful entry, sexual harassment, intimidation with firearms, threats, assault, and a long history of erratic behavior that had recently caused the authorities to yank my gun permit.

Add a complete graphic description of the murder, including a one-in-a-million sexual twist with the victim, all conveniently saved on my computer hard drive in a file that pre-dates the event.

My Assistant District Attorney wife claiming a conflict of interest was no boon to my game plan. A moron could make this case stick.

I had a headache. Thinking about my certain future was causing my brain to fry. I picked up the yellow paper and pen. The young Assistant District Attorney had given me strange looks as I confiscated his legal pad and received his assurance that I could leave the jail with it. I could see him making a mental note to add something to his own report on my statement. It was probably the single word: paranoid.

I was in abject despair when I wrote:

~

Another place, another town imprisoned her as a soon to be extinct cable car clattered by, empty. It was night; a fog of bad air hung along the wet streets at knee level. Pages of newspapers were splattered flat by a recent downpour on the wide downtown sidewalks. Functioning street lamps were few and dim. The collar of her trench coat was turned up against the damp, and the pillbox hat with a rolling wave of lattice was low on her forehead. The red hair spilled out in torrents, up and over the collar of the coat.

Her steps were forced, random, as her high heels scrapped and clicked on the deserted street corner. She seemed to have no desire to get to her destination. She stepped off the curb and crossed the cobblestones. The heavy weight of the Luger inside the clutch purse banged against her legs.

An unlit staircase led from the street up to the second floor. She leaned despondently on the banister as if exhausted as she mounted the stairs. The door to the apartment was open. Shaded lamps cast bright pools of light inside. She entered and closed the door behind her.

"Aren't you supposed to say something like 'Honey, I'm home?'" His voice, harsh and deep, came from the dark corner and the recliner chair.

"Honey, I'm home."

"Don't get smart with me, sweetheart." It was a threat.

She unbuckled her coat and let it slip off her shoulders to the floor. She swept away her hat and sent it spinning to the couch. She walked towards him, her face featureless. She tucked her purse up under her arm.

"Is it done?"

She nodded.

"Dead?"

Again, she nodded.

"I'll be damned," he said softly. "So, how does it feel?"

She reached out into the darkness to let the back of her fingers come in contact with the rough five-o'clock shadow on his cheek. She sighed when the expected physical shock wiggled up her arm and down to the pit of her stomach. The delicious itch began between her legs.

He took the arm roughly in his huge hand and bent it towards her chest forcing her painfully down to her knees on the carpet next to the chair. He grabbed a handful of thick hair at the nape of her neck and bent her towards him.

"How does it feel?" His breath smelled of Turkish cigarettes. He barred his yellow teeth in a snarl.

She couldn't speak. Her mouth opened, but the words couldn't come. She breathed in gasps of remorse, fighting to hold back the pain. How does she feel? Having just eliminated from her life the only man who could have rescued her from what was to come? The single person who could save her soul? She was incapable of describing her complete despair. Her mouth felt full of dirt. The man shook her roughly, making her hair fly and tangle. He demanded again.

"You bitch," he said, "tell me how killing off that rotten two-timing, boot-legging bastard made you feel. Did you fuck him first?"

She licked her lips, knowing words were not necessary, and slowly but surely pulled against the pressure of his hand in her hair and brought her face to his lap. She tugged at the material of a tucked pleat in his dress pants with her teeth and moaned. She set down her purse and her hands deftly sought out the front vent buttons of his Seville Row tailored trousers and began to peel them back one by one.

He raised her head with a quick jerk of his arm and held her rigid while his left hand slapped her roughly across the open mouth. Her wide sensitive lips were bruised. She licked them. He was breathing heavily.

"You'll answer me later, I swear you will." His spittle flecked her cheek that burned bright with the force of the slap.

He shoved her face back down as his manhood sprang free of its cloth confines to greet the prodigal return of his loving wife. A car horn peeled from the street below. He grunted and threw his head back in the chair as she took him fully into her mouth with a greedy gulp.

Her other hand slipped silently and unnoticed into her purse.

Seventeen

Running True To Form

I was free this morning on bail. The kind of bail only Ernie Sampesee could afford. I had been charged with murder one, released after a night in jail, and told not to leave the city limits of Telluride and Mountain Village. The office was the only place I felt the least bit comfortable so far. The whole town was buzzing and waiting to get a look at me. I was, after all, an accused murderer. The first in almost two years and I was the previous one too. Excluding me, you had to go back to 1962 before you found another murder trial. I was a hot celebrity commodity even by Telluride's jaded standards.

My calls to Agnes Singer's number at the Franz Klammer Lodge had gone to a generic voice mail. On a wild guess, I looked up the number for West Egg in my notes and her maid picked up on the second ring.

"Yes, Mrs. Singer was in. No, she could not be disturbed; yes, I will give the lady of the house the message that you had called." I wanted to prolong the conversation just to listen to the sweet British accent of the woman. I found her voice soothing. She hung up.

How was I going to get myself out of this mess?

All that came to mind as an answer to the main question was to start at the beginning. Solving a crime and writing about it have got to be pretty close to the same thing. Find the clues, eliminate the suspects, work the chronology, don't get sidetracked, and get to the truth. It was a simple formula made difficult only by the unexpected, the unknown, and the obvious. This was the best advice I had come up with after those long hours in the slammer? I admitted to myself, I was not the sharpest tool in the shed.

Agnes Singer had started it all by bringing me into this. She had hired me to be a junk yard dog. Was my getting involved an elaborate set up for her to get rid of her husband? Was the outcome that predictable? I thought honestly about any other scenario that could be considered plausible. I searched for an alternate conclusion that took into account my well known *macho* bullshit and the Sodom's Devils' aggressive natures. None jumped out at me.

Avoiding Ernie's barber chair like the plague, I went down the back fire stairs and climbed into the Mustang. The whole block knew when I started it up. The wreck belched black smoke as the clogged choke threatened to cough the engine into silence. I backed out and lurched down the deep red dirt ruts in the alley as the clutch did its usual stutter step.

The sun was bright, warm; the sky was blue without a cloud to mar its color; one of three hundred such remarkable days each year in Telluride. I was just starting to let my shoulders relax, concentrating on the tasks at hand, when I spotted the Sheriff's Department white Bronco two cars back. I drove past the Valley Floor towards Society Corner at a sedate thirty-five. The tension came back in a sudden knot as I tried to plan my next caper.

I knew full well I wasn't supposed to mess with potential witnesses. Bueller, my wife, and the shiny new ADA from Dolores had all made that very clear. Ernie the lawyer had agreed. I could be thrown back into jail without the benefit of bail if I tromped on the "people's right to establish their case." Yet, Agnes Singer was a big part of the story. She had answers I didn't even have questions for. Talking to her was priority one. Not getting caught doing the deed was a close second.

I turned around at Brown's Homestead barely a mile out on the road from town and headed back in a cloud of black smoke for Hollyhock

Lane. The Valley cows were packed in a tight herd watching in silent judgment the pollution I belched into their clean air. The Deputy Sheriff waved as I passed him. I saw his yellow turn blinker go on as I dropped down the low rise pushing the speed limit at 35 mph. Daryl, the deputy, was in no hurry to follow. A high speed pursuit was ridiculous when you have a box canyon blocking every other exit from Telluride but this single two lane road. I had decided I needed some climbing gear from the garage at home and a big hug from my daughter Katie. It had been a tough couple of days.

Starting at the beginning was taking a circuitous route.

≈

I was almost afraid to pick up Cody from school. What if I saw in her eyes that she thought I really did murder Singer? I wasn't sure how I would handle that loss of faith. The thought chilled me. I was fifteen minutes early at the elementary steps.

The passenger door creaked open. My pen stopped without a single word having hit the yellow pad. I looked up, and Cody smiled. In that single, untroubled look I knew she was with me. I had seldom been more thankful in my life. Tears welled up in my eyes and I had to cough and look away. It would be okay. I couldn't let her down, or totally let myself down. I would somehow find out what the hell was going on.

"Guess what?" she yelled and my eardrums rang.

"What?"

"Denver Manz asked me out."

"Wow."

"Yeah, wow."

"Like a real date?" I asked, believing this date, in my naive fatherly way, to be her first.

"Like, dinner and a movie."

"You mean the big event is this Friday?"

"Sharp as a stump." My daughter used my wife's standard retort for a rhetorical question.

"Let me get this straight. I drive, I pay the check, I disappear when it's time to hold hands under the table. And this is something my daughter gets asked to? A date for the other guy? This boy's dating gig is brilliant."

"And the townies say you are all brawn and no brain." She mimicked her mother once again. It stung just a bit. I loved her for trying.

I chuckled, resigned at the circumspect way of things, pausing at the stop sign on Columbia and Aspen.

"Oh," Cody said, "Denver isn't a boy."

The clutch slipped, and the Mustang stopped dead.

Eighteen

Meticulously Waxed Armpits

The Telluride to Mountain Village Gondola is actually two separate rides. The cable threads over twenty-six poles to the top of the ridge, where, at the huge midway-station and restaurant, skiers can off-load to access the Eastern slopes of the mountain. The ride also spans fourteen poles back down the other side of the mountain to the terminal in the middle of Mountain Village, with access from there to the fifty or so mountainous trails fed by a feeder system of high speed quad chairs. Some of the poles that suspend the Gondola cars and chair lifts are over a hundred feet high.

My plan was simple. I would get on the Gondola in town and not get off at any of the scheduled stops. The Deputy Sheriff would not be able to follow me unless he could fly. Everything was going according to plan except the eyewitnesses. I had a middle-aged couple on vacation from Detroit with me inside the Gondola car. I was forced to hop aboard after they loaded, in order to stay a step ahead of the law. I balanced my mountain pack on my knees and watched the Deputy Sheriff join three people in the car behind as we pulled, with a powerful swing, out of the base terminal and started up the mountain.

"I just can't believe this, Marvin." The woman said as she thumbed through a free real estate magazine highlighting the latest dwellings available in the Telluride region. She raised her voice an octave as we rumbled over the first tower guide wheels.

"What's that, Sweets?"

"One-point-two-three acres for two-point-six-seven-million." She held out Patsy Susie Blaze's full page add. The one with the tanned and blonde broker riding the wooden rail fence, cowboy hat held aloft. I cringed.

"No way."

"And that's without a house."

"No way."

"You live here?" she made it an accusation.

I nodded.

"How do you afford it? What do you do that you can afford this?" She rattled the paper in her hands.

"I write."

"No way," he said.

"What's your name? What have you written?"

I stared at her eyelashes laden with heavy mascara, under penciled in eyebrows. The ferret like quickness of her darting eyes gave me the shivers.

"I read everything." She dared me to doubt her. "You embarrassed? Give me a name."

I was frozen in a lie like a deer in headlights.

"You write porn? Kid's books? What?"

"Cussler," I said for spite. "Clive Cussler."

"Dirk Pitt?" she asked, skeptical. "NUMA?"

"No way," he said, equally nonplused.

"Would you excuse me?" I said and smacked the nylon backpack open on the floor, emptying out a 150 meter climbing rope, my climbing harness, carabineers, and a pouch of chalk. I had planned to make my exit a little further up the ridge, but I'd pull the plug now. I stuck my legs through the webbing of the climbing harness seat, pulled straps tight against my thighs and clipped two carabineers to the front ring, reversing the gates.

I knelt, forcing my fellow travelers to crowd back against the far window in astonishment; reaching up over the doors, I released the emergency locking lever. With both hands, I chalked up from the pouch, and then pulled the doors apart. My feet and legs hung out the open door.

"What are you doing?" The woman's voice spoke panic. The wind swirled through the car, raising chalk. I put the white powder away in the pack along with my Stetson hat. The treetops seemed close now, sliding quickly past, without the benefit of the Plexiglas and tin barriers to muffle the effect.

"Research for my next book," I said, reaching out the door and clipping a carabineer on the flange above my head, installed for exactly this purpose. It was my own design modification as a safety feature to the Swiss product. Every car had one. It allowed Ski Patrol rescuers to descend and evacuate stranded passengers with climbing gear in case of a mechanical failure. I clipped an end of the rope through the gate and began pulling until I found the middle mark of the rope in black magic marker.

"Please, excuse me." I smiled and winked, shoving my arms through the straps of the pack, clipping the chest and waist harnesses with a loud snap. I flaked the rope out in two equal strands, clipped a rolling eight into my harness, pulled tight, and swung out the door. My feet dangled in open air, I held tension with one hand around the rope and against my chest. I gave a little Errol Flynn salute, triggering the doors to close with a flourished swipe at the outside tripping lever. I dropped away in a free repel to the ski run below. Hitting the ground running, I quickly let go an end and pulled the rope clean through the carabineer on the car. Not a bad exit after a two-year hiatus from the drill.

I was coiling the rope into my pack as the next car passed over. I saw the Deputy Sheriff's face, nose to the glass and a frown on his face, as he continued up the mountain. I refrained from waving.

I got underway as quickly as I could. It was a good twenty-five minutes to the trailside entrance to West Egg. I knew exactly what kind of shape I was in. This was likely a real stupid idea.

≈

"Mrs. Singer won't see you." The woman with the British accent was a true disappointment. She was plump as a dumpling, piercing black dots for eyes, and a road map of veins in her cheeks. Her attitude was that of a judge handing down a life sentence. We stood in the entrance foyer on marble. The expanse of the tooled leather main floor stretched towards the glassed wall that overlooked the entire set of spires that make up the Sneffels Mountain Range. The Valley Floor in its entire green undeveloped splendor spread out at our feet. The house was the proverbial castle on the hill over the rolling pastoral fields dotted with black and white cows.

"And I told you I must insist."

"The cook has been asked to call the police unless you are off the property in two minutes."

"Please don't do that. Your boss would be put in a very bad position. I want to explain to the lady of the house about the limitations of client privilege and the legal issues she will face concerning the murder of her husband, and what I may be forced to repeat from our discussion prior to his death. Her own words could be used against her."

The Brit opened her mouth to begin another litany of clipped denial.

"Send him up," said a voice, stern and cold. It came from an intercom system in the walls.

My Limy friend turned without another word and huffed across the floor, pointing to the wide stairway, as she left me alone, and disappeared.

"Bitch," the intercom spoke again in a hoarse whisper. The denunciation for the help echoed through the house.

I climbed the stairway. The view was again getting better as I gained height. I found Agnes Singer on the outside balcony in the very same cabana chair, next to the simmering hot tub, where I had first seen her husband three days before. She wore only a small black thong. Arms folded behind her head, breasts and rigid violet nipples rose above the stretched, parchment skin. The vintage body was a monument to an iron will, vanity, and constant medical attention. Tinted oval glasses, with brown herringbone frames, hid her brutal blue eyes from the October sun.

"We have a problem," I began.

"Correction," she said, "you have a problem. My feckless husband is dead, and his boyfriends evicted permanently from my father's house. Your job is finished, Thorpe. I have no more problems. And, I don't want any."

I stared at her meticulously waxed armpits. She hadn't broken a sweat. "Without a retainer, or a signed contract, I'll be forced to share the content of our discussions."

"Tell them how much I hated the bastard? That's a secret?"

"I don't want to have to drag you in on this unless I have to." I really needed this money, I told myself. I groveled.

"You actually think I am going to write you a check for killing my husband? Not that I don't feel gratitude, I do." She licked her glistening ruby lips.

"I didn't kill him." I repeated the truth for the tenth time today. "And, lady, if it's not you and it isn't me, then who? I'd be worried. Any joint enemies with your deceased husband?"

She didn't have a quick comeback. When in doubt, my handbook says always go for fear of life and self-interest. I had finally connected with a nerve. There weren't many in this woman.

"Maybe his sex guru might be worth chatting with," she said, taking up a Turkish towel, covering her chest.

"Singer had a sex teacher?"

"The Church of Compassionate Caring."

"Yeah, it was in the paper. Doctor Wolfsmith or something from the Arizona bible group. The ones trying to buy up the Valley Floor?" I asked.

"Wolfscheim."

"That's the one."

"I call him Meyer and he isn't a doctor."

"You know him?"

"I should." She gave an exasperated sigh for my ignorance. "He was my third husband; two before Singer."

≈

I sat in a leather couch at the Great Room at the Peaks Resort Bar. A double Bushmills on ice on the table in front of me. I didn't want to go back down the Gondola and face the wrath of the Sheriff's office just yet.

Agnes Singer was not going to give away anything. She was tough as a cockroach. The fact that two of her husbands were involved with the church group rumored to already have an option on the purchase of the Valley Floor was an interesting bit of news.

"Murder for a view?" I sniggered. "Sounds like another bad detective novel."

I pulled a pen from my pocket, steadied the yellow legal pad on my thigh and tried to sort out the confusion I was facing and found only the deep primal fear I selfishly felt about a life in prison for something I didn't do.

≈

The redheaded woman eventually found her way back to Berlin, New York. The town around the hospital was a quaint little community, east of the Hudson, way out on the end of the commuter train line, with clapboard shacks and wonderful little roadside restaurants to wile away the afternoon with a glass of red wine and finger foods from the Negro kitchens.

Gatsby was still alive in her dreams. She felt his weight on her in the night and she awoke sweating and in agony from being alone. Why couldn't she put him out of her mind like all the others? Why did he still torture her so? She finally lapsed into a deep depression, turned to bootlegged gin, ending with laudanum in order to forget and sleep. A week later a doctor was called to her room. She was placed for the eighth time in two years at Craig House Sanitarium in Beacon to regain her strength.

That was where Fitzgerald found her. She had come full circle back to the beginning once again. The hospital staff was embarrassed anew by her dangerous and reckless behavior. Her father had been a great benefactor and supporter of the institution, and a room would always be hers. She was almost the last of her father's family. The staff disapproved of her pathological lying and her trips to nowhere to engage in reckless sex with strange men. It was patently unwholesome behavior. The spicy stories she shared in therapy of killing her sex partners at the height of their passion were common gossip along the wards.

"Dishonesty in a woman is a thing you never blame deeply," F. Scott Fitzgerald was later to write about her. The author had known of this woman for months, ever since her latest escape. Her legend grew with each retelling of her exploits. The private detectives he had used to try and find her had pointed the way, but always a step behind. Obsessed was the term his editor's publicist used for the extravagance of the effort. He carried a black and white picture of her from her medical file in a locket around his neck; in it a cool insolent smile expressed a constant sexual challenge under gray sun-strained eyes. The windblown hair seemed blood red even in the washed out photo.

She had come home, back to where she had captured his soul, just as he always knew she would, this rarest of flowers, a deviant Venus Fly Trap among vapid roses.

He stood above her. She slept. He appeared in delightful rapture standing alone beside the bed in the shadows. The strikingly handsome features, full mouth, his high uncreased forehead and slicked blonde hair were posed in a state of spiritual bliss. His mind was full of words, the first in months. He could feel the drought over. The spring of ideas flowed once again. This fragile delicate thing with the cold murderous heart and a deceitful, lying nature was the reason for his joy. He took up her long delicate hand. It weighed the same as a bird's wing. The milk white skin and blue mottled veins smelled of baby oil and talcum.

Fitzgerald brought her fingers to his lips, kissing the tips tenderly. Gently suckling on the longest two, using his tongue to separate a space between them. His mind wandered, lost in delicious prose. The instantaneous erection startled him.

The woman shifted and moaned in her pill-induced coma. Fitzgerald slowly placed the hand back on the spread, smoothing it carefully, and turned smartly away. He had to see someone in charge. This woman would be released at once to his care. His care alone.

~

Darkness was a gentle hue away as the Gondola crested the ridge and exited the artificial brightness of the midway terminal. Telluride's lights sparkled below, setting the borders of boxed grids in the busy streets of town to the east of the pitch black Valley Floor. I was heading home. My thoughts were very depressed, lonely, and worried.

Agnes Singer had, for her own purposes and not my welfare, pointed me towards her former husband, a "shake down artist and con man" who was now Doctor Wolfscheim, head of the Church of Compassionate

Caring that had assets estimated by her at close to a hundred-million dollars. Some of that money was Agnes', and it was a sore subject.

Acrimonious as she was, even the wronged wife couldn't imagine Meyer being able to put a gun to Singer's head and pull the trigger. But, he could hire it done. Or have his motorcycle thugs handle it. Wolfscheim's spiritual awakening, according to his former wife, was based on greed, not eternal salvation. His grandfather had probably rigged the 1919 World Series. The big swindle was in his blood.

I decided, before I off-loaded into the waiting arms and handcuffs of a brace of Deputy Sheriffs, I was definitely more maudlin than morose.

Nineteen

Where's The Money?

"Wit," she said, "I don't want to talk to you."
Click.

I tried my home number again from the phone in my office.

She hung up. The Sheriff had set me free twenty minutes ago with a stern warning not to lose my tail again. Bueller had started the session by shouting about, "not being able to discern if I had remained in the confines of Telluride proper." He was trying like hell to yank my bail. My wife's cooler head prevailed. The Sheriff would actually have to catch me in violation of bail, not simply conclude I might have been guilty of it. Her assistant passed this along to the arresting officer. Everyone saved face but me.

The couple from Detroit had also made a statement that I had given them an alias, had physically intimidated them, and endangered their very lives by my fool stunt. The ski mountain management was considering their own complaint for recklessly frightening gondola passengers. First the murder, and now this. I was to be banned from using the "G" for the rest of my life.

I had called to thank my wife as soon as I got back to my office. She didn't want my thanks. I was lucky I wasn't still in jail. It was implied that if Mrs. Singer gave me up for talking with her today, she would tell them personally to throw away the key.

But that wasn't my biggest problem at the moment. I couldn't send Ernie to Sodoma, Utah. He wasn't the man for this particular job. I was the one who was eternally expendable. Besides I wasn't sure he really believed I was actually innocent. And, my barber was pragmatic.

"If what you say is even half true, someone who shoots people in the head as a solution to a problem is hiding out there. This person is likely in Sodoma, and isn't going to appreciate anyone trying to find them." Ernie stated the obvious in clear certain terms. "It's your murder charge, you take the risks."

"Thanks for the help," I said.

"Hey, I'm always here for you, old cod," Ernie said with a melodious Bronx accent.

≈

How was I going to be out of town, keep a tail happy, and not be caught? My Mustang couldn't make the drive. Ernie's Bentley would be the same as forming a parade committee to get me to Arizona on the QT.

Who owed me? After a moment's reflection, I admitted that no one owed me anything. I had tapped out all my favors at least two years ago. I had some bad red ink in the karma department. It was about to get worse.

My eyes had settled on the one thing of value I had in my possession. The problem I faced was an ethical one. Personally, I often find private snooping and ethics a hard blend. For me, the human vat was just the brown sludge of every primary color of crazy emotion and blackmail mixed together. I was not above sacrificing ethics for a greater good, especially my own greater good.

I popped the videotape into the combo VCR/TV. I was immediately assaulted with groans and slaps as two heaving bodies, doggy style, tried to shake the headboard of the huge bed free. This was exactly what I needed. Why couldn't I make things up in my stories that were this good?

I never have a problem driving a hard bargain with an adult male who is as guilty as sin. It was the basic bully in me. I would have Jeffrey Breene's Z3 and someone to cover my ass while I was away. Also needed was some cash, and my contrite perp would definitely want to cover all my expenses.

What a guy. My ethics, however, would not let me also continue to bill the wife for coming up with nothing conclusive on her husband. I guess I do draw the line somewhere. I use a pencil with a large eraser.

≈

The hallway was dark beyond the bedroom, and I sat on Cody's bed listening to her sleep. Her head was on a pillow on my lap as I sat with my back to the wall. A night-light cast shadows. My daughter was still a little afraid of the dark. She had talked until she started snoring, chattering away brightly between yawns, as if she was trying to keep my mind off of my problems.

She had, of course, come through again, and I had copies of everything in my wife's briefcase. I moved my Xerox machine from my office and put it in her closet so that she could make copies with the door closed. It had worked like a charm. I had a half-inch thick stack of reading to do before morning. I needed to get some perusing done before I met with Jeffrey Breene at midnight.

But I didn't want to move. It was the first time today I had been able to stop and just think instead of react to the growing panic in my gut. I had no idea how to solve this case.

I stroked Cody's hair and mused about times when things were better. What had gone so wrong? When had this particular unhappy ending been a foregone conclusion? I was let go from the mountain job because I couldn't take orders. After twelve years, I was fired as soon as the successful bidder for the ski area put the new management team together. No one to coddle or run interference for me simply because I was good at what I did.

I was labeled in my personnel file as a recalcitrant misfit. The discovery sent me on a six-month bender. I hadn't drank really seriously since then, but, from my wife's perspective, the results of that time were still shaping my life.

The infamous hot tub joke shared with Ernie about "being what you write about," had turned me into an unemployable, self-indulgent lug. I talked about writing as if it were a four hundred pound pet I kept in my office. I tried to make ends meet by being an opportunistic snoop and put myself in situations with clients where only the worst things could happen.

My wife had finally given up trying to reason with me.

I left the bed and the house after I had beaten myself up a little more about being a bad father and husband. I would need to see Ernie and coordinate things before I left for the desert. Luckily, I knew right where he was.

≈

"Ernie's not here?" I stared incredulously at Aimless Ed and Rasta Joey as they sat on their respective stools at the Sheridan Bar.

"Been through a couple of times," Rasta shook his dreads with a clatter of beads. "Wouldn't even stop to have a drink. In one door, out the other. All the time."

"Never seen nothing like it," said Ed McMullen.

"I saw him do the same thing down at the Last Dollar twenty minutes ago." A neighbor at the bar spoke up.

My brain trust associates at the Sheridan Hotel Bar bought me a beer and filled in the gaps of the story about the dead man in my trunk. I got all the particulars from the street gossips. Singer's wife controlled the money and kept him on a short leash. He had appeared to be an okay guy except that he had his hair dressed instead of cut. Of course that was before he "got some balls, left his wife, and went off to Arizona to become gay." Ed offered the quick Cliff Notes' rendition to put it all out there on the table.

I waited for almost a half hour, discussing the nuances of hair dressing preferences and the subtleties of sexual orientation of otherwise okay guys. No sign of Ernie.

"It's spooky," said Digger, the bartender.

The mob agreed.

It was almost midnight, and Ernie's current behavior was odd even for him. I headed for my office. The streets were mostly empty; everything closed up and put to bed. Was it only a week until Halloween? Where did the summer go?

A shadow ducked back into darkness on the deserted street, just catching the corner of my eye. Someone was in the shadows in the open passageway across the street that led down towards the rows of condos along the San Miguel River. The bells and whistles started going off as I thought of Singer's autopsy report and how much blood a head wound can spread around.

I moved as quickly as I could across the street, jogging towards the opening, turning the corner sharply, expecting to see a fleeing suspect and awkwardly stumbling into a person hiding there. We both went down, and I raised my right fist to strike when I heard the man speak.

"Easy old cod," Ernie said. I groaned and dropped my fist to help him up.

"What are you doing?" I said without sympathy. Spit was hard to come by.

Ernie brushed himself off, rearranging the thick camel hair coat that covered him to his knees. A matching hat, trimmed rakishly, hid his eyes, a spitting image of Mr. Price in "Murders at The Rue Morgue."

"Destiny hates a laggard," Ernie said.

"Pardon?"

"There is always an earlier crime," he said. "Find the earlier crime, find the murderer."

"Okay," I agreed rubbing the funny bone at my elbow.

"Follow the money. Most crimes involve money. Or, maybe, passion. I am really crazy for both, but I always bet on avarice first." His mind wandered, and then he caught himself. "Passion is a simpering sister next to the power of cold hard cash."

"You on to something?"

"Where is the money?" Ernie continued needing no encouragement from me.

I shrugged my shoulders. Ernie raised his eyebrows.

"Jeffrey Breene?" Ernie said to himself. "The only guy I know who has more money than God. The truth is I saw him sneaking around my barbershop window about an hour ago. Suspiciously, I might add."

"He seemed pretty fed up with me a couple of nights ago in front of the Excelsior." I was, for want of a better idea, trying to follow my partner's reasoning. "He dropped me on the sidewalk."

"Listen, old cod, dropping you on your head has occurred to a lot of your friends and neighbors down through the years. It would hardly warrant a second look without the coincidence of the Singer tryst."

"What has Breene got to do with it?" I said.

Ernie kept his mind to himself.

"I'll call you later," I said, needing to get to my office.

"Yes, my boy, that will do nicely."

I watched him scramble gracefully around the Sheriff Department's Bronco that was parked at the curb, cross the street, and disappear into the shadows on Pine. I wondered if my barber was finally cracking under the strain. Squeezing bread and now this? Maybe it was better if he didn't know I was gone. I should keep the growing litany of my own lawbreaking to myself.

I looked to my late and never sorry tail, waved. He had pulled up to the curb just as Ernie and I were getting to our feet. If someone had meant to do me harm, I would be dead meat.

I crossed in his headlights and went to my office. I entered the building using my key and, while out of sight from the street, dropped down a flight of stairs to the basement and let Jeffrey Breene in the alleyway door. Ernie would be searching in vain for this particular shadow for the rest of the night.

I felt a pang of guilt as I went about the dirty business of a shakedown. We went up to my office and discussed my needs. He only balked at the un-negotiable caveat that he remain here in the office, behind locked doors, indicating to the Sheriff's car below that I was working at my desk all night.

I was forced to put the videotape in the set for the second time and turned up the volume. I hit play. He raised his hand in surrender before I counted three non-conjugal flaps. I was covered. He had brought twenty-five hundred, divided into two separate envelopes with him, expecting a payoff would be necessary to solve his problems. Smart boy. I took it all.

Twenty

Sodoma In The Caboose

There are only the pursued, the pursuing, the busy, and the tired," F. Scott Fitzgerald had written in 1925. I fit all four categories as I idled the Z3 down the main commercial street of Sodoma. The newly constructed Arizona town was a perfect movie set replica of a real fifty-year-old southwestern Texas town. The two-story storefronts, perfectly matched in a 1950s montage, stretched for two crowded blocks in four directions from the central intersection in town. The corner was densely built, with a stoplight and cross walks; empty high plains desert stretched from the last clapboard wall for as far as you could see.

The car was already moving out of Sodoma proper before I knew it. The two lane black top rifled straight ahead until it disappeared in the distance over a red sandstone butte. I began to look for a place to turn around. It was only by chance that I turned behind a sagebrush barrier on the far side of a double telephone pole and noticed "Maggie's Caboose" hidden by scrub from the road.

The Caboose was the final relic of the last legitimate use the canyon rim had seen during the hectic railroad days when a spur down to the heart of southern California had run for two hundred miles through the red desert. The railroad car was now a traditional western dinner for the few ranchers and desperadoes who hadn't migrated to the higher-class eateries in town. It was exactly the type of place I needed. Being careful to park the Z3 out of sight behind a rusting tanker truck in the far corner of the rutted lot, I set out the goals I needed to accomplish before hightailing it back to Telluride. I wanted to arrive before the Sheriff knows I'm gone. My final stop here in Sodoma, I decided, would be to talk with a redheaded lady.

"Coffee?"

I nodded as I took a seat at the long vinyl topped counter that ran the full twenty-five feet of the Caboose. Booths lined the wall in front of the windows to the lot. Six or seven customers were yammering away at each other from across the empty space. Two stout women with aprons leaned against the freezers, sandwich board and such, behind the counter. The crowd was scattered, and I looked around under my Double-X Stetson from the first stool near the door.

"Ain't got nothing to do with the cost of feed." A patron continued the conversation interrupted by my barging in.

"The hell it don't."

"We is drying up here. The water is all going to the damn golf courses. When it's gone, it's gone."

"You're doing fine, *compadre*. Sittin' here all day collecting money from them for simply grazing your herd in the low pastures. Didn't they just paint your barn for you? Jeezus."

"Yeah, but how many of us is left? Your spread, mine, maybe half dozen others along the road from town to the canyon rim. That's it. Down from fifty, sixty working ranches, ten years ago. Them fellas only paint my barn because their people see it as they drive in to the big trophy homes with the view of the golf courses. It's damn disgusting, I say."

"Didn't turn 'em down though."

"No sirree, I didn't turn 'em down. I'm an ornery old coot, but I ain't crazy."

The whole crowd laughed. I ordered hash and eggs, sunny side up, wheat toast and a side patty sausage. I turned in the stool with my coffee cup and faced the two tanned cowmen in a far booth and a threesome beyond them; a couple of singles were spread around the rest of the dinner. It was a sure fire invitation for conversation, coming from a perfect stranger.

"Where you from, fella?" The ornery old coot seated in a booth by himself spoke with his mouth around a toothpick.

"Colorado, the mountains," I said with a smile.

"Come to see the canyons?"

"Are they worth it?"

"Can't say, born here myself," he said, "never thought about it. People like you seem to like 'em enough."

"People like me?"

"City folk, modern people, no insult intended."

"None taken. A lot of city folk here abouts?"

"Sure, ever since that cock-a-may-me church bought up all the available land around the rim and put up this here pretend town." His eyes narrowed as the entire dinner hushed and everyone froze in place. "You ain't one of them church fellas are you?"

It was the deadly silence of public places before an insult spoken is taken or left in the air.

"No, I don't go in much for churches myself."

The tension left the diner with an audible flutter. I was immediately welcomed to town as one of the chosen few willing to lament the past, wile away the present, and worry with words incessantly for the future. Within the next five cups of weak cowpoke coffee, I was fed and stuffed full of ideas and information on how to get a chance to talk with the Church. The last thing the ornery old coot said stuck with me.

"Steer clear of those motorcycle hombres," he said. "They been taking to roughing up locals and church members alike over the past couple of months. You wonder who's paying 'em."

"Bad, ass fucking, dudes," the waitress named Mabel said, and I was sure I got the punctuation right.

$$\approx$$

"See ya Mabel."

"See ya Wit," she said with a knowing wink. "Keep your topknot and your butt plug intact."

I smiled and gave a salute. They had wheedled it all out of me. "Maggie's" crew were all diner gossip professionals. The whole story of Lambis, Singer, my wife, the bail jumping, had all tumbled out onto their breakfast plates. They, in turn, shared with me the death of their town at the hands of the Church of Compassionate Caring.

"The cock-kuh-kuh-suckers, we call 'em," said Mabel. She spelled out the initials of the Church of Compassionate Caring.

I left the caboose and my new friends with a firm agenda and a gnawing suspicion that I was on the trail of some weird and dangerous folks with an awful lot to lose. My normal operating procedure of checking the amount of gas in the tank with a match would likely get me killed. I needed Ernie's brains, and he wasn't answering his phone. Cody was at school and out of contact until recess. I tried to think of every possibility and gave myself a headache.

Mabel and the old coot had at least given me an idea on how best to get a tour of the church grounds and an audience with the head guy. The sure winner was to pose as a journalist wanting to plaster their project all over the front page of a big magazine. I pulled the zippered folder from my duffel bag, opened it and scanned the bogus business cards, arranged alphabetically by occupation on the tabbed pages. Computers and laser printers are wonderful tools of the private detective trade. Being someone else at times was a real asset. I went to "J" for journalist.

I pulled a thin pile of "Teddy Buxby's" colorful and thickly embossed cards. He was an editor for *America's Great West Magazine* in Denver. The phone number was the Last Resort Detective's office in Telluride. I would call and leave the appropriate message on my answering machine to indicate that the number was Teddy's desk. I would forward the number to the car phone in case I had to be Teddy's secretary.

I shoved the Stetson hat and the jean jacket in the duffel bag and pulled out a rumpled brown tweed sport jacket and put it on. I took a left at the light and headed for the church grounds shimmering somewhere off in the red clay hued distance.

Twenty-one

The Fifth Level of Compassion

The only glitch in the steady progress from the front gate to the huge reception center and offices was the fact that I had grown more irritable underneath my clever bon vivant attitude. The two motorcycle thugs at the gate had been downright rude, and pulled me from the car and frisked me without so much as a "may I." The truculent one, as opposed to the adversarial one, led me at a snail's pace along the wide paved roads lined with tall cacti. His fat ass Soft Tail Harley was barely keeping forward momentum. I knew he was jerking my chain, and I didn't like it. We rode along with my bumper six inches from his exhaust pipe.

The desert changed to rolling green grass stretching in wide swaths in every direction. Waving fans of irrigation sprays dotted the landscape, along with swaying palms glistening under the mid-morning sun. A huge canyon opened ahead, dropping six hundred feet to the small red line trickle of a mostly barren creek bed.

The phone on the car's console rang. The screen showed my office number. I waited another ring. I hit the hand's free button.

"*America's Great West Magazine,* can you hold?" I snapped my fingers and turned up the radio. Mr. Truculent pointed me towards an underground parking garage. I gave him a thumbs up that turned to a single finger as I dropped out of sight and shut the radio off.

"How can I direct your call," I tried to put some perky attitude into my voice.

"A Mr. Buxby?" A female voice directed.

"The editor? Mr. P. T. Buxby?"

"Yes?"

"I'm afraid he's on an important assignment in Arizona."

"Sodoma?"

"Beg your pardon?" I giggled in falsetto.

"The assignment?"

"I'm sorry I can't give out that information," I giggled, "but it sounds right. Kinky, too."

"Thank you."

"Would you like to leave a message on his little ol' voice mail, sweetheart?"

"No, thank you."

I pulled down the ramp out of the desert sun feeling rather pleased with myself, laughing at my own jokes, feeling cocky. Confidence and good old fashioned pluck were paving my way straight to the answers I needed.

≈

A press packet was shoved into my hand and an eager twenty-something refugee from "Up With People" tried to overpower me with charisma.

"Dr. Wolfscheim is very busy today," he said with an apology and seemed to mean it. "We can squeeze in five minutes, just before ten, seeing that you want a cover page story." I was assaulted with a billion candlepower of pure blue eyes.

I spent the next forty-five minutes on a golf cart touring the nine-hundred and seventy-eight acres of the church grounds which included three pro tour caliber golf courses by leading designers, seven gourmet restaurants, and a couple of dozen other informal eateries and martini bars. Central shopping malls with the likes of Gucci, Lauren, and Frederick's of Hollywood were scattered inconspicuously across the landscape. A Cineplex, a performance center, outdoor amphitheater, and swimming lagoons were highlighted on the glossy map. We pulled in front of a massive timber and stone house. A slate porch stretched the entire front of the seven thousand square foot trophy home.

I pulled my video camera from my backpack and my driver's face was suddenly crestfallen.

"We don't allow any filming or pictures. You understand."

"Hard to do a cover without some pictures."

The smile was back in full riot.

"We will provide everything you need. We have the very best professional photos of the grounds and everything."

I put the camera away and sulked a bit. The sales pitch went on.

"We have a one-tenth share available in this beautiful vacation home and retreat cottage," my guide said. "Church membership and club house privileges are also included in the price."

I stared at the eight-by-ten glossy of the house front on my lap. I turned it over and read the bottom line at the bottom of the page. It was a seven-figure sum that rhymed with jive.

"Let me get this straight," I said. Maybe it was the wrong word to use and I looked over to see if it registered pain. It hadn't dampened the smile. "I put all this money in your hands. I get to use this house and all the facilities for five weeks a year. I come here, go to church, so to speak, and become a resident of Arizona. In ten years I don't lose my privileges at the church, but I get my money back, plus a solid fifty percent interest that is totally tax-free because it is a home sale in partnership with a church enterprise fund dispersal under the federal and state income tax codes."

"I think so. Some of the financial stuff is way beyond me. But, we even arrange the loans through our own local bank to make it easy for you to join the church." He gave me those puppy dog eyes. I was feeling a little nervous, like a prime cut pork chop in an Italian deli.

"So, if I can afford to put ten thousand dollars a month into this scheme for ten years, my one million two hundred thousand dollar investment turns into two, maybe even three million?"

"It is the tax free profits from our enterprises that are shared. Remember the good Lord said give to Caesar only what is owed. Our church not only saves, but re-invests its revenues wisely."

"But a guarantee of a clear million?"

"Maybe more, depending on how many more folks than church members we can encourage to use the facilities. We are exploring new opportunities all the time at other prime locations. It also encourages us all to recruit new converts. Our numbers are growing all the time. Besides, where else do openly liberated men and women get to hang out in the world's most lovely places, and be exclusively with people who understand God's work and share in the profits?" His hand was on my forearm. I pulled away with a start and looked quickly at my watch.

"Time to see the doctor," I said to this sad, beautiful and hurt face.

"Oh," he said and quickly readjusted the pitch, a little heart broken if I judged his tone. "The fifth level of Compassion and Caring also includes the Vestals if you prefer hetero only."

"Vestals?"

"The virgins," he said. "Only they are far from virginal." He winked his long eyelashes with a knowing look.

"This is all part of the deal?" I was impressed and sounded it.

"You can have it all." He smiled, puffed out his lips, and I knew he was trying one last time.

I wonder if women feel like this when someone comes on to them? Miranda Sterling at the Excelsior? I patted the boy's knee, and he brightened up. Rejection is best served with an inexplicable sigh. The chariot raced down the rolling paved cart paths with reckless abandon, pushing the electric motor to its limit as we hurried to the main offices.

$$\approx$$

"Please don't get up," I said as I entered the church director's huge executive office.

"I already am," he said with a flicker of resentment at my failure to notice. He walked from behind his aircraft carrier sized desk. Doctor Wolfscheim was bald and barely five feet tall in his platform shoes. He bulged out of his tight white linen suit like a bloated sausage. Brushing at his trim lapels with both hands, one of which held Teddy's card, he advanced across the hardwood floor towards me.

Another figure was in one of the tall wingback upholstered chairs facing away from me and towards the desk. My neck hair came to attention. Motorcycle boots and black leather riding pants with silver seam buttons were crossed casually in front of the chair, the figure's identity hidden from view.

I shook the limp and flaccid hand of Doctor Wolfscheim and sighed. It could not have been this man who shot Singer. This man would not dirty a nail with the muzzle flash of a thirty-eight. I had eliminated a suspect. But Agnes had been right about the powerful presence of the man. I speculated that a deep and rigidly controlled mean streak ran just below the surface.

"Mr. Buxby?" he said, as his beady eyes darted over my shoulder.

"Ted, please." I corrected the formality with a hearty smile.

He led me forward to the vacant chair without touching. I took a seat and glanced at my companion while Wolfscheim made the hike around the desk. I started to get back up in haste.

"Sit," Walter said. I did.

"Meyer, baby, this is the Thorpe guy, a private eye, I told you about from Telluride. The one who murdered Singer."

Wolfscheim's hand went to the waddles on his neck with an effeminate squeak.

"Probably came to do you next." Walter leaned forward in his seat and shook his arms in the air and made terrible boogey man noises that echoed off the heavy wood paneling.

Wolfscheim cowered in fright. Liking the reaction, Walter's eyes came back to mine, a cruel smile spreading across his lips.

"What do you want, dead man walking?"

"Answers," I said.

"Fat fucking chance," he said, showing his teeth.

"Who killed Stewart Lambis and Singer?"

"You." He smiled again.

"Not likely," I said. This was getting nowhere fast.

Walter's cell phone chirped from his leather vest pocket. "Yeah?" He listened for ten seconds and hung up.

"Gotta run," he said leaping to his feet. Walter slapped his hand on the desktop loudly and enjoyed the resulting frightened response from across the table. He pointed an accusing finger at the diminutive Doctor of the church. "You tell him anything, any thing, and the deal's off. Got it?"

Wolfscheim slowly nodded.

Walter brought the finger to me. "I'll see you later." His promise sounded sincere. It was a very real threat.

"I'll be looking forward to it," I said, trying to keep my eyes from flinching.

He smiled again and shook his head playfully, breaking eye contact, chuckling to himself. He left with a theatrical slam of the huge oak door.

"What deal?" I said to Wolfscheim with cold intent. His displays of fright vanished when he saw it served him no purpose. Pity was not in my cards today. He looked at my expression and knew his day wasn't going to be getting any better soon. Maybe, I could almost see his mind working, he could cut a deal, and hit two birds with one stone. I was the stone.

It took me twenty minutes to squeeze the prophet dry of useful information. He swore he had given me every last bit of the story. He probably would have done it all in ten minutes, but I think he was amused by my inexperience in such things.

Twenty-two

Beale Street Blues

Kidnapping, blackmail, fraud, extortion, and extensive use of highly illegal drugs, plus steroids, hormones, and prostitution had tumbled from Wolfscheim's mouth. I had hit the proverbial mother lode of secrets if I believed half the stuff now out on the table. Walter, the motorcycle goon, was almost owed thanks for softening up the good doctor. My threats had not taken long to find their mark. The truth was that I hadn't beat up a truly defenseless man in quite a while, but the possibility always existed, and luckily Meyer Wolfscheim was savvy enough to recognize it.

I was back with Mabel at the Caboose for a club sandwich and fries. She was disappointed that I couldn't bring her and the other patrons up to date on the case. I thought I had better keep what I now knew strictly to myself until I could figure out what to do next. The stack of papers and my own notes filled the countertop in the far corner booth.

I had re-read the reports stolen from the ADA. What I found collaborated with at least one element of Wolfscheim's story. Walter's rap sheet listed a long series of assaults and misdemeanors for thug-like behavior. Four of the nine arrests were in Arizona. The counties mentioned in the reports included Sodoma.

The bio sheet on the victim, Robert Forrest Singer, was still a bit sketchy, fingerprints being run, DNA being tested, etc. Yet, the one inexplicable connection, at least from the terse paper facts, was a listed contact in the Arizona State Police Department who would be sending along information available on the "deceased." Walter Silverton and Mr. Singer were perhaps old buddies. And they were obviously deeply involved with Wolfscheim and his church.

Getting a fresh cup of coffee from behind the counter, I sat back down and searched my gut. I was apprehensive. I didn't want to ever know what Walter had in store for me. I didn't want to see the church grounds again, ever. It was just a little too creepy. Maybe apprehensive was not the right word. Circumspect might hit closer to home. I picked up my pen in a state of bewilderment and considered all the unintended and hidden consequences of my life. I also knew I was going to look up a redhead.

~

Fitzgerald sat watching the rise and fall of her breasts tucked securely under the crisp eggshell blue cotton twill sheets. The border was trimmed in white lace. The door to the verandah was open and the morning freshness, full of sounds, wafted into the darkened room from the slanted green lawns and sweet gardens beyond.

"It is invariably saddening to look through new eyes at things upon which you have expended your powers of adjustment," he whispered, tenderly nurturing the line he had written with such insight early this morning. The thrill of it had set him to tears.

It was her, she. She was doing this, stroking the needs of every blank page he faced, giving the magic to the work by some strange proximity of his needs to the vibrations of her very being.

She had stayed drugged for her own good, under the doctor's care, here at the hastily leased rustic house; an old hunting lodge located near the sanitarium. For two days he had written as he hadn't done in years. He couldn't sleep. He sat with her when the exhaustion wouldn't let his eyes focus on the page. Fitzgerald trembled as his body again warned him of its desire to sleep, to shut down.

She moved. A leg twitched and slid loudly up the sheet, falling out towards the edge of the bed. Her hand came slowly to her cheek. Radio music, from the separate kitchen and servant's quarters drifted across the open green space and through the curtains. Saxophones played the Beale Street Blues.

He waited, knowing by hospital ward gossip what was coming next. His anxious vigil was close to being rewarded. He ground his teeth in a bizarre feeling of anticipation, re-crossing his legs, and discreetly adjusting himself in his trousers to relieve some pressure.

Her fingers drifted across her mouth and pulled at her full lower lip, then continued down. Drifting across the pink ribbons of her nightgown, cupping her own beautiful breast, she slid her arm beneath the starched covers. Fitzgerald caught his breath as the rustling bulge of her hand under the sheets continued on a mission down her abdomen and settled at her crotch.

She moaned. Her head turned so that her cheek was trapped on her pillow, the eyes still closed. Her eyes darted about under the deep blue lids. The naturally red lips parted and glistened moist, a nib of a pink tongue appeared. A tangle of lustrous hair fell across her cheek. She churned languidly with her hand at her vagina and clitoris, her breath beginning to start and stop in slight catches as she dreamed on. Her tempo steadily increased.

Fitzgerald finally exhaled, realizing he had been holding his own breath for minutes, hours, and became light headed. His joy was overwhelming and he felt himself swoon. Tears rolled down his cheeks as he watched her bring herself to orgasm with a primal grunting and accompanying convulsions that wound down like a decked Flounder. A shaft of light cascaded brightly on her face as a breeze shifted the curtains.

"Gatsby," she said in a hoarse whisper, a feral smile, she pulled her lips apart and exposed sharp teeth. "Gatsby...

Gatsby..." She groaned with an open mouth as she came again, murmuring in ecstasy his name over and over as the tremors of pleasure washed over her and she went as rigid as a board. She slowly let the tension fade and squirmed deeper into her covers.

Fitzgerald leaned forward, his face in his hands, brushing away the tears from his cheeks. His heart leapt and tore apart at the same time. She was in such torment. There was so much more to this obsession? Her tortures so intricate and complete, beautiful and damned.

Who was this Gatsby? The name alone was a knife in his heart.

≈

Wolfscheim and Agnes had a son named Eric. He had been kidnapped, brainwashed, drugged, addicted, and enlisted as a security gang member by Walter and his motorcycle cronies. The ransom for getting the boy back was shared control of the church and its assets. That was the easy part to understand.

The hard part involved Singer and how events got from extortion to murder. Forrest Singer's strikingly sensitive features, according to Wolfscheim, made you want to call him Ashley, the unrequited love of Scarlet O'Hara. Singer and Doctor Wolfscheim shared everything, including business discussions. Wolfscheim had always longed for a sharp mind to discuss the future. Singer was a charming and well-educated man, unhappy in his heterosexual marriage to a rich crone they both knew so well.

It was, again according to Meyer, Singer who convinced him to hire their old friend Walter Silverton and his culture challenged friends to act as a security force for the Church. It had seemed a good idea at the time considering the rash of anti-gay hate crimes sweeping across the country. This bad mistake had been made sixteen months ago. The Church, according to its founder, now needed protection from its own security force.

Wolfscheim's son had been lured, according to the not so good doctor, into the motorcyclists' world. His son was gay by design, heterosexual by choice, and vulnerable by nature; a fragile self-image from a troubled adolescence, Wolfscheim confessed, he was an easy conquest for the bikers. Now they virtually held Eric prisoner, fed his cocaine and methamphetamine habit, made sex a group activity with Walter's whores at the Vestals' condo and lately wouldn't let Wolfscheim see him alone.

Walter had started calling all the shots three months ago using increased violence as his proxy and had taken personal charge of the Church's latest business deal. Singer had seen the writing on the wall and lent his support. It would mean hundreds of millions of dollars in cash flow over the next five years. Control of the new project and its non-taxable profits were what Walter and Singer wanted in return for turning the kid loose.

"I can't call the police," Wolfscheim had said. "Even a sniff of scandal and the church would suffer catastrophic losses. Exposing the criminals with charges of kidnapping, brainwashing and extortion without tainting the rest of the church's operations is impossible. Besides, the boy is over twenty-one and free to associate with whoever he wants."

"Whomever," I had said, adding, "You want me to storm the biker gang, take them down, and return to you a responsible drug-free son?"

He had answered with a question. "Isn't that what tough guys do?"

I wondered. Looking up from my notes and returning to the present, I saw the herd of black leather missionaries file into the diner. Speaking of the devil. My escort to the thrashing that Walter had promised me arrived. Too many by far to argue with.

"You're wanted to answer some questions out at the Church," a mean looking, grizzle and bone, intensely angry son of a troll, said.

"What if I don't want to go?"

"Then, Tiny here is going to persuade you to come." The same greaser spoke again, indicating with a thumb a massive offensive guard type right behind him.

"Looks like I ought to come along."

I could see that they were all more than a little disappointed that I was being agreeable. I winked at Mabel, paid my bill, and left the Caboose peacefully. She waved good-bye.

"Want I should call the cops?" she said.

"Naw, it would cramp my style," I said.

"You got style alright," she said with a gold toothed smile. "I'll talk about it at the funeral."

≈

On the way back out to the Church of Compassionate Caring's security offices I pondered the literary use of smells and wondered if I should try to flesh out some of my scenes in the unfolding short story with odors. The stench from the burly chunk of meat riding shotgun would argue against inflicting such misery on those who might end up reading the story. He weighed two-seventy and had arms as big around as my waist. He spilled all the way over into my seat in the Z3. The smell was equal parts long dead fish, body odor, stale beer and dirty motor oil. He wore a red-checkered bandanna where his hair ought to be. A dog collar with studs circled his left wrist.

"Have you been saved?" I said.

"Shut, the fuck, up."

"You know what I mean, gone around the world with the church," I said. "Found fulfillment with something up your ass?"

He showed me his right fist clenched and ready for a hammering. It was the size of a soccer ball. I shut up, kept driving, and followed the four other bikes in front of me. They were humming along military style in two-by-two formation. I found the fact that each of the bikes but one was doubled up. Was it flattering to have all these thugs assigned as escort? It wasn't in my nature to let the huge fist be the last word.

"Eight guys for little old me?"

"Naw, they all came along to watch."

"Watch what?"

"Me kick your ass," the biker said, his voice was like the rumble of thunder.

"Oh." I thought it over and reluctantly agreed he was right.

We rolled right through the security gate without a stop and pulled into a small sunken parking lot in front of a windowless bunker. The roof of the in-ground holding cells and security headquarters was level with the desert floor. My mind was working pretty steadily on an escape plan, but none presented itself. Whatever Walter had planned for me, I was pretty sure, I didn't want to be around for.

I was escorted to a cell and pushed roughly into it. The clang of the lock sent a shiver through my body. I'm glad none of them were looking. Bravado is ninety percent showmanship.

Jailed but good this time. It was a dumb move to come here. I felt pretty sorry for myself. Being helpless made me crazy. I pulled out my pen, the receipt from the Caboose, and tried to write the bile down.

≈

That night, before he left his study, Fitzgerald wrote the name he had heard her call out in his notebook. He underlined it twice. He finally wrote after it, for reasons only he knew, "I think he killed a man."

His writer's curiosity was complete. Grabbing the bottle of no-name gin from the table bar outside his door, he walked quickly through the dimly lit house to the woman's bedside. Jealousy raged in his stomach, right alongside the awe and wonder at the richness of his discovery. He must find a way to solve the mystery of this woman and what drives her madness. Someone must find this Gatsby.

He sat and swigged directly from the bottle, raising it again and again. Fitzgerald drank angrily and with a senseless purpose to forget everything else in his life but the story, this woman, and now, this man, this killer: Gatsby. He watched her face as the glow of the alcohol brought forth her features in a shimmering haze.

She was beautiful and flawed in innocence of what she did. Fitzgerald would later write, "Her face was sad and lovely with bright things in it, bright eyes and a bright passionate mouth...a promise that she had done gay, exciting things just a while since and that there were gay, exciting things hovering in the next hour."

Some in the ward claimed she was married, and her husband beat her. She kept running back to him, in spite of it. Getting home to him in New York City was always where she eventually headed when she left the rigid confines of the hospital.

Fitzgerald woke in the morning in the straight-backed chair. His head ached, and he was startled when he slowly pried open his eyes and saw her gazing back at him with a languorous expression. She was not the least bit surprised at her circumstances or questioning about why she was not in the hospital. Her gray eyes silently appraised him as he slouched in stupor. The writer was unable to risk movement that might add pain and nausea to his already debilitated state.

She raised her hand and raked it through her rich red hair, throwing her neck back and arching her spine off the bed. Breasts popped free of the sheet, and she ignored it. Her head settled on the pillow and the face fell back towards him. She smiled. Her hand left her hair and came to her lips. She licked the tips making them moist, a slender tendril of saliva hung for a moment between mouth and finger, and then she slowly plunged her hand beneath the covers that still covered her waist and legs.

"I know all about you," her voice was a velvet fog in the painful drumming of his head.

"You like to watch," she said and smiled knowingly.

Fitzgerald was paralyzed.

"Watch," she said. Her eyes, daring, challenging, and never leaving his. The pink nub of her tongue peeked between her almost clenched teeth. Her eyelids drooped, losing focus, as she applied herself to her wonderful task.

≈

Walter, himself, let me out of the cell an hour later without an explanation. He was as flatly cordial as he had been at West Egg when I had last seen Singer alive, only his eyes sparkled with brutality.

"Your bill for trespassing on Church property has been paid in full." Walter said.

"Who?" I said.

He smiled, and I knew he wasn't going to tell me. "Lets just say that having you out causing trouble might just make my life easier."

"Why are you holding Eric?"

"A favor to his mother."

"His mother?"

"My ex-wife," he said. "Agnes. Don't you worry about Eric. He is being well-supervised."

I looked at him as my mouth dropped open. Agnes Singer is his ex-wife? I was about to make a wise crack concerning the old rich crone and a guy who had to be younger than me.

His finger and his head waved back and forth at the same time discouraging me. He exposed those canines again. I decided against making the remark.

"Best if you high-tailed it back to Telluride, before someone finds out you're gone." He winked, implying a threat.

"Did you kill Singer?" I said.

He smiled coldly, zippering his mouth closed with his thumb and index finger, turned his back and walked away. I started to follow and the one called Tiny, my friend from the smelly drive over, stepped up off the couch and put his massive chest into my face.

"I ain't got my workout in yet today." His breath smelled of fish patty sandwiches. "Want to play?"

I then left. For once, no ill-advised wiseass comments escaped my lips. Who says old dogs can't learn knew tricks? Even a month ago I would have taken the beating as part of what I deserved for being such a schmuck to be caught with my pants down. Two motorcyclists trailed me to the other side of the town limits and turned around.

So did I, just as soon as they were out of sight. A certain redhead needed a visit. I drove to the puce colored storefront and the doorway to the suite of offices on the second and third floors. I was working myself up into just the right mood to have a little heart-to-heart with Miranda Sterling. I thought I understood her so much better now. I continue to make that same mistake about people. I was thinking straight angles when I needed to consider curves through the maze of all of Agnes Singer's ex-husbands.

Twenty-three

A Chunk of Terra Firma

Wit Thorpe," I said through the opaque glass paned door that read, "Sterling Productions." I followed with a hard set of full knuckled knocks. "I need to talk with you. Now."

I thought I heard a muffled response, or at least a noise. It could have been "Come in," or "Go away." I preferred to hear the former and opened the door.

Miranda Sterling slammed the fire door exit hard behind her. I caught only a glimpse, but she looked afraid and was moving quickly. I looked back. The empty space over my shoulder meant I was the boogieman.

I ran to the door and tried to slam it open with my shoulder and forward momentum. I ended up on my *keister* sliding backwards up the hallway. I sprang back to the door, pushing slowly. It opened a few inches and came to a stop. I could see that she had jammed a long broom handle between the door grip and the open weave metal floor of the fire escape landing. I got my weight against the handle and, on the third full-grunt shove, the wood snapped, and I tumbled out onto the balcony of the fire escape.

Miranda had reached the alleyway three stories below and was heading for the driver's door of a red Grand Am convertible. I scrambled to my feet and hightailed it back through the offices and down the front stairs

The Z3 was parked directly across the street. I failed to look both ways. In defense of my stupid, brainless act, I offer that I hadn't seen more than a handful of cars on the street since I rolled into town. The car clipped me just as soon as I stepped into the street and sent me smacking against the windshield. I could hear something shatter. I was pleased when I realized it was the windshield. The next thing I remember is landing hard on the street. My right elbow took the brunt of the fall and it was numb, tingling as I tried to lift the arm. I looked up and watched the red Grand Am that had just mowed me down fishtail on the dusty pavement as it ran the red light and gained speed heading out of town.

I scrambled over to the BMW sports car supporting my elbow with my one working hand. Getting behind the wheel was painful; I hurt everywhere and cursed each part of my aching anatomy that I could think to name in a litany of abuse.

I swung the car into a tire squealing U-turn and finally regained control after a full half block with the gas pedal slammed to the floor. The red dot in the distance stopped pulling away, and as my car smoothly moved past a hundred miles an hour, I started to reel her in. She must have seen me coming and pulled sharply off the road. I watched the rooster tail of red dust trail out behind her as she headed down a county spur. I spun the rack and pinion steering into a controlled skid as I joined her on a jeep trail beelining towards the canyon rim.

I stayed back, out of her dust plume, figuring that she couldn't hide. I didn't know where this road was going, but it stood to reason that she couldn't hop the canyon. I passed a couple of ancient and rusted real estate signs that looked to have been part of the scenery for a decade or more. The cactus got taller as we both slowed to twenty and tried to dodge the worst of the deep ruts.

I was almost past her before I noticed that the road ahead was clear. The Z3 skidded in the red dirt to a stop. I was out of the car before the dust reached its full height. My first instinct was to run towards her as she leaned back against the rear side panel of her car that was pulled just off the single lane road. Her strapless purse folded into her arms across her chest.

Before I closed the distance to ten feet, she moved quickly and drew a pistol from the bag and leveled it at my kidney. Anyone who has faced loaded guns will tell you this choice of target is much more frightening than having the barrel waving at your head. You know this is a person willing to shoot and knows the first bullet does not have to be an immediate matter of life and death. The wise shooter targets only pain, immobility, and internal bleeding. I stopped.

"What's going on here?" I said, again marveling at how she was the virtual image of Fitzgerald's mystery woman in my head. Maybe, I should slap her to get her to like me.

"You tell me," she said calmly. She spoke with a confidence that proved she knew how to use a gun. "This is your meet."

I reconsidered the slapping thing.

Miranda slid and backed away towards the front of the car, motioning me towards the trunk with the barrel of the small caliber Walther PPK. She tossed the purse in the open window.

"Lean against the car with both hands," she ordered.

"Can we talk?" I said, doing what I was told.

"Sure, lean against the car with both hands and..." she said with a cold menace that was unladylike and exciting. "You know the drill."

I put fifty percent of my weight on my arms and leaned forward on the trunk, spreading my legs out behind. I knew the drill.

"Stare straight ahead," she said and slid out of sight behind me.

"Who killed Singer?" I said.

"You did," she said.

"I didn't!" I said, shouting to emphasize the point.

"Then who did?"

"I don't know," I said, "you gotta tell me."

She didn't say a word. I kept my eyes front. No need giving this woman a reason to shoot. I didn't want to bleed if I could help it.

"Wake up," I said. "There is someone in that group of yours that shoots people."

"What group?" she said, her voice a menacing whisper in my ear. I felt the warm gun barrel at the nape of my neck. "I don't have a group."

"Doctor Wolfscheim, his son, you, Agnes, Walter, the church," I said. "Not to mention a dozen or so bad ass bikers."

"Who...?" She stopped abruptly. "Who do you think...?"

"Everyone."

"Me?" Her voice seemed amused. I grunted when the heel of her hand, then the Walther, firmly established contact with my tailbone. Her hand expertly skimmed my belt, pockets, pits, crotch and down both inseams to my knees. The gun barrel ground into my lower back as she squatted and checked my ankles. She backed away again.

"Little old me, a murderer?" she said and grabbed a handful of my gluteus maximus and squeezed. She let go before I could recover from being startled. Miranda was very good at this.

"Nice ass," she said. "Tell me, my private detective, all about our little family of suspects?" Her laugh was far from merry. Was she going to shoot me? Probably was the best answer. I tried to keep talking. My mouth was as dry as the sole of my boot.

"The only ones crossed off my list of possibilities are the dead, odd couple, Lambis and Singer, the Gay Blades," I said. "The rest of them…" I stopped, feeling her tense behind me.

"Maybe not you, of course," I said, remembering the gun and what a bullet felt like. "They are all guilty of something. I just don't know what it is. But I will."

"Stewart Lambis and Sandy?"

"What do you know about it?"

"Never mind." Her voice had lost its humor. "What about Stewart Lambis?"

"The banker who was killed in Telluride with a plastic bag. He and Robert Forrest Singer were reportedly playing ring around each other's May Pole."

"Not that I mind that sort of thing," I added quickly. But it was too late.

They say the journey into unconsciousness for many people is a different path each time. For me oblivion knows only a single road. Unconsciousness always feels as if I have been smashed by a giant fly swatter. The lingering sound of a vulture circling in the sky over my head led me back towards the twilight of stupor. An hour or more had passed.

She was gone, and my head felt sticky and twice its normal size. I had been hit by a rock the size of a brick. This chunk of terra firma, with bits of hair and tissue clinging to its flat end, lay next to my aching head.

The modern drunk's too frequently answered prayer was the only coherent thought in my head as I dropped, barely conscious, behind the wheel of the Z3: "Thank God for the car, I'm too dizzy to walk."

The sun was almost down; shadows of low dunes and flat topped mesas stretched across the barren landscape. I was long past due to be headed back to Telluride. I knew I wasn't going to find Miranda again tonight. My only chance was to somehow preserve my freedom until I could figure this whole damn thing out.

Get back to town before I ended up back in jail. This was my simple mission and, in my present battered and woozy state, one that would require all of my attention for the next five hours. I cleaned the blood from the wound on my head at a gas station about seventy miles down the road in Tuba City. It would be well after midnight before I got back to my office and delivered the videotape into the hands of my benefactor.

I tried, and failed, to keep out of my mind the linkages between Miranda and the woman in the story. Pulling the gun from her purse was just a bit too much. Being able to almost run me over and hit me that hard on the head showed a real mean streak that could lead to murder. This was a hell of a woman. First Walter and now the redhead doing me favors by leaving me breathing just didn't seem right.

Curiosity, and its evil twin vanity, drove me to pull the wrinkled yellow pages of the legal pad from the boot and find an all night truck stop to spew up onto the page the next ingredient for the short story. I had to have a goal in my life besides self-indictment. It was obvious. Follow the clues; find Gatsby.

～

He knew she would leave. He had no way to hold her, except to try and make her understand what enormous stakes she was risking to be the naïve waif. She was adrift in this nutty world. Fitzgerald himself was no stranger to unreasonable craziness in people. His own wife, Zelda, was at a hospital dealing with demons found at the bottom of a bottle in the dark hotel room closets.

The redheaded woman stayed only a month, slowly building back her strength. They did not become lovers on the third night, nor the fifth, or even the seventh after she awoke. She spoke little, despite his endless questions. Her lovely gray eyes simply stared into his with challenge, intimate knowledge, and wonder.

She finally took him less than fully into her bed by making him sit in a chair and caress her maidenhead with his wet fingers until she came. Finally after she saw what it was doing to him she teased him mercilessly, questioning if he would be able to satisfy her, ridiculing his boyish take on manhood.

She finally saw enough of the exquisite pain in his lovely face and allowed him into her bed with a sigh and a single whispered word of encouragement. She then lay inert, disengaged, a flaccid lump while he pushed himself into her, weeping and crying for her to respond. He finally found release with a cascade of inhuman groans that drew a derisive rebuke from her. He ran from her bed in anguish and embarrassment and was drunk for days.

She then changed completely. It was a Sunday. Her compassion appeared, and it suddenly overwhelmed her. She came to him that very night during his drinking and reversed their roles as she nursed him back to sanity. She made love to him tenderly, softly, with an open heart, and he slept exhausted without dreams. They were both frail and unsteady as they walked together in the garden the next afternoon. He had finally been able to rise, with her to lean on. They knew they were back from the very dreadful edge of things.

He had taken to calling her "Daisy," a flower they both admired because of its "pluck-ability." They would play the "love-me-not" game with its petals for hours. He resumed his morning meanderings. The woman's impact on him, expressed in mere words, had replaced the feverish race to finish the novel. He wrote at length of their carnality.

Once awakened, the lustful beast in her would not rest. She screamed, and pleaded, shamelessly calling out her orders to him during their lovemaking, burning the Baptist-bred ears of the help. This went on for a week, until the accumulation of sleepless nights and exhausted days finally satiated the need to devour him in lust whenever they were together in the same room. At times the maids and gardener would run from the spectacle as she would leap from hiding onto him, forcing him to the ground and ripping into his clothes to pull his erection free and mount him by pulling up her dressing gown, even when the servants were present and couldn't help but watch.

One morning she announced at breakfast she would leave the next day and be gone "for a time." He argued. He wept. He threatened, cajoled, and in the end she left as they had both knew she would. The private detectives promised that this time she would not elude their efforts. He prayed that they were right.

Later Fitzgerald wrote about their last afternoon. "He sat with Daisy in his arms. It was a cold fall day, with fire in the room and her cheeks flushed. Now and then she moved and he changed his arm a little, and once he kissed her dark shining hair. The afternoon had made them tranquil for a while, as if to give them a deep memory for the long parting the next day promised. They had never been closer in their month of love, nor communicated more profoundly one with another, than when she brushed silent lips against his coat's shoulder or when he touched the end of her fingers, gently, as though she were asleep."

Fitzgerald's heart was broken, his ego crushed. She was going to Gatsby. Straightaway. Running from him to the arms of another man. The anguish he suffered put a strain on his fish net soul that he had never felt before. A fragment of his mental torment that went from the random notes to the final work says that for days he "tossed half sick between grotesque reality and savage frightening dreams."

Fitzgerald wished in his black heart that Gatsby didn't exist. He wished him dead. He knew in his shattered heart that Gatsby was every man but him.

Twenty-four

Putting the Snipers in Play

The Sheriff in his warm Bronco followed me slowly up the cold streets as I walked against the bitter wind the six blocks home. The entrance door to my house was dead bolted, and I let myself in through the storage door to the basement. I pulled back the blinds and saw the Bronco shut down its headlights and pull to park in the street below, so the driver could watch the steep stairs leading up and away from my house. I couldn't be sure, but I figured it was Bueller himself.

I was busy trying to erase the graphic image that greeted me when I opened the door of my office at 2 a.m. The unclad pair from the videotape were at it again. Patsy Susie was bent at the waist over my desk, hands braced on the windowsill, while Breene moved like he was in the finals of the Grossinger's Catskill Resort hula-hoop competition, thrusting enthusiastically from behind her. He had a very hairy back and rear end. Hers was agitating wildly and milky white. Apologizing, I dropped them the tape and left, figuring even if they didn't lock up when they finished, there was nothing left in the office worth the effort to steal. I backed out and closed the door as they continued uninterrupted.

Cody had left a note taped on the back of the couch for me to wake her when I got home. I went to her door and opened it. Her night-light suddenly began blinking like a strobe, and her eyes opened dreamily.

"Gotcha," she said and stretched under her covers.

Closing the door, the blinking light stopped, and I came and sat on her bed while she rubbed her eyes awake.

"What do you have for me, Q?" she asked with a final yawn.

"Precious little, Bond-San," I said in my best sushi bar accent. "Except a massive headache."

I had to show her my wound, and she fingered it gently, while I told her most of the story. I left out Mabel's one-liners and about how scared I had been.

"She did this?"

I nodded. "How is Telluride taking the whole murder thing?"

"Bad," she said. "People are scared. Mostly of you, at the moment. Nothing new there. It didn't help your murder defense on the Singer thing to have just been caught kissing to death an admitted homosexual in order to get a car loan. Is Seppuku a noun or a verb?"

"That wasn't how it went down," I said, ignoring her reference to a knife in the bowels.

"Easy, dad," she said, uncrossing her hands from behind her head. She propped herself away from the pillow to give me a hug that I returned greedily. "I'm on your side. You just need to know what everybody is saying."

"Besides," she said. "I read that twenty-nine percent of all writers on trial for murder didn't do it."

"You're making up statistics again."

"And why not? Someone makes up statistics. It might as well be me."

I finally let her roll over and close her eyes, and I stretched out beside her with my head on the pillow.

"Was it really gross? One kid says dead people's eyes pop out of their sockets when they suffocate. Is that really true?"

"No."

"Not even a little?" she said again, and I knew it was a rumor she herself had started and was now looking for the collaborative evidence that she was right.

"Anyone thinking anything other than suicide for Lambis?"

"Not really," she said, the cogs churning away until she blurted, "Why?" Her eyes squinted into mine.

"No reason, nothing."

"Give it up."

"Just looking for an earlier crime," I said.

We discussed in slumber party whispers what kind of priority I placed on the needed information from the ongoing investigation into Singer's death. If she was going to get busted boosting her mother's brief case, it had better have more than a chicken salad sandwich in it. She graciously spared me the price, saying she would work it out later. I loved this kid in a lot of ways. I also wanted ten percent of all future earnings.

I was almost snoring when she slipped out of bed. I opened one eye to watch my little spy knock on her mother's door, open it, and whisper, in a small pitiful voice, "Mommy, I'm scared. Can I sleep with you?" She gave me a wink, a cat scratch wave, along with the big smile as she let herself into her mother's room and slowly closed the door.

I wished I was her, sliding in next to my wife. I wished that all of this had never happened, that I had never dreamt up the redheaded woman. I wished for a lot of different things, including a spell checker, as I got up and went to the couch. I lay back and re-read the grease stained yellow pages of the story, looking for ways to ferret out the clues.

$$\approx$$

"Jolt of java?"

I declined the coffee with a raised hand. Ernie and I had been at it for over an hour, ever since I dropped the girls at school and day care. We had re-hashed every word and event of my trip right down to Mabel's quips about butt plugs.

"You are lucky to have gotten away with it, old cod," Ernie said. "I don't want to have to find the real murderer on my own. So shape up."

"So what do you think about Walter also being an ex-husband of Agnes," I said.

"The woman is a marrying machine."

"That's all?"

"I also think she has made some poor choices when it comes to men," Ernie said.

"Three husbands, all in Sodoma, is a mighty rare coincidence," I said.

"The Church of Compassionate Caring is soon coming to Telluride," Ernie said looking up from the Daily Miner. "The funeral of Stewart Lambis, Church Deacon, will be a gathering of the faithful."

"What?"

"Seems your kissing cousin was also saved."

Ernie was challenging me to connect the dots. Church, Singer, Sodoma, bank, Lambis, Walter's new business deal, the bikers, a fabricated resort community in the desert, Telluride, a toy cow, and the Valley Floor. It all had to make sense. Everything needed to fit.

"I don't get it," I said.

"It also says his ex-wife lives here in Telluride."

"Can't be," I said.

"That's right," Ernie took an excited sip from his cup. "Agnes Singer. Is there anyone, besides you and me, who hasn't been married to this woman?"

"How about a bumper sticker: 'Honk if you're not Agnes Singer's ex-husband.'" Ernie coughed, bad humor is far worse than none at all.

Cody's note, written on my palm in red ink, was a welcome intrusion into my headache, confusion and self-pity.

"Can I still use the Bentley for the big to-do tonight?"

"Of course dear fellow. When do you need it?"

"Now?"

"Really? I thought it was dinner and a movie?"

"We added on lunch at Rustico's for six other friends."

"What a father."

I chewed on my expletive retort. Cody drove a hard bargain. If I wanted the complete file as of this morning, I would only get it after the lunch. I only hoped that my daughter would continue to deliver the goods. Besides, I thought, I get to work off my debts and spend time with my daughter. What's wrong with that?

≈

After the lunch chauffeuring was over I spent the rest of the afternoon with a readable copy of the complete transcript on the investigation. It was current as of 6 p.m. last night. Cody and I were a bit amazed at how involved in this case her mom wanted to be, even after she had declared a professional and ethical conflict of interest. This was the same file her counterpart from the neighboring county was using to prepare his case. Was she intent on making sure that nothing got screwed up in the investigation so they would nail me for good this time?

"The funeral's on Saturday." Cody reminded me.

"Time to shoot the crowd," I said.

"Precisely, Q," she said, "You could become competent in this business, given time."

"Time, I ain't got," I said.

"I already got the snipers in play."

"The usual gang?"

"All but Duffy. She has to go to the orthodontist."

"You're way ahead of me, Squirt."

"Exact-a-mundo," she said. "We'll try and get all the living ex-husbands first."

Cody was a realist. She went to answer her phone.

I tried to force myself to concentrate on the now and forget the rest. I scanned the signed statements from many of the cast of characters. Alibis for the time period of Singer's murder were included in the files.

Agnes Singer, according to her staff was still too distraught for a sworn statement. They attested that she prepared for bed at her usual time, around 10 p.m. She retired to her room where she watched a little of David Letterman. She rang for a sleeping pill at 10:45 p.m. The English maid watched her swallow the sedative and left. No further requests came from the room, until Agnes rang for the maid and her breakfast at 7:50 a.m. The news of her husband's murder did not affect her appetite. The English maid was very certain to mention that fact.

Walter Silverton, also known as: Walter Silver, Walt Mint, W. G. Eldorado, and Fiad Silubrha, et al. had no warrants pending at the present time. He had been a model citizen for twenty-two months. On the night in question, he left West Egg at 11 p.m. and took the Gondola down to town, arriving at the base at 11:15 p.m. The lift attendant identified him and the approximate time. He took a room at the New Sheridan Hotel and stated he remained in his room until breakfast.

Doctor Wolfscheim had offered his own statement by phone and explained that he had been in Sodoma at the time of the murder. He had been in the middle of leading a two-week seminar. His whereabouts were confirmed at 10:13 p.m. and again at 6:12 a.m. by staff and clients in attendance. Sodoma was a long five-hour drive away from Telluride. No planes had landed at the airport; no choppers were heard.

The sum total of the facts in the file was that only I could have committed the crime. It was the long list of the circumstantial case against me that held my attention.

My gun was probably linked to the bullet that killed Singer.

The last bit of circumstantial evidence, new to me, was the slippery icing on the cake. A phone call was made from my home phone to West Egg at 11:45 p.m. the evening Singer was killed. Only two phones in my house: kitchen and master bedroom. It was either the ADA or me that made that phone call. Who would you believe?

I now understood what rueful laughter was. It rang in my ears.

Twenty-five

Cold And Fishy

was dressed in a Hawaiian shirt and a plain brown knit tie left over from the polyester days of my high school career in Montrose. Dressing the role of chauffeur was part of the deal according to my daughter. We were on our way to pick up Cody's date, Denver Manz, last. I wound through the mountain road with the Bentley heading towards Ophir and the gateway to the ultra exclusive ranch estates known as The Preserve. All of the girls were "just dying," "way badding," and "I swearing" as they chattered away. Cody was sitting pensively next to me on the front bench seat ignoring their conversation. The other four were sprawled out in the cavernous back seat.

"I can't make up my mind," she said.

"Always pick the fish," I said.

She withered me with the Look. "I mean about 'bases,' you know, on the first date."

"Bases?"

"You know, kissing, tongue, writhing, petting..."

"Stop," I said.

"Sure," she said.

"You know what I'm gonna say, right?"

"Yeah," she said, "save myself for my wedding night, or some such advice you parents can't believe you hear yourself saying."

"That's about it," I said. "Do I have to say it?"

"No," she said, crossed her arms and set her chin just so to discourage further conversation.

I was glad she was so smart, and I didn't have to hear myself say all those things I can't believe I find myself saying to my daughter.

It was a magnificent house, the Manz's estate, known as "See Forever" on the huge bronze sign at the electric security gate. The porches and windows overlooked Illium and the down valley canyons all the way west to Norwood and beyond. Denver's parents met us at the door and as we shook hands, getting the names right, the two girls started out towards the car under the lighted portico in the courtyard. They held hands.

"What a lovely couple," the father said. His wife nodded her head tilted to the side against his shoulder in dazed bliss.

I stepped back and looked at them. He in a rust v-neck, pinstriped shirt, and white khakis; she in a scattered beige L L Bean ensemble that hugged her trim figure. Her hand instinctively sought out his arm, sliding closer for protection. My expression must be portraying my state of conflicting emotions. Her eyes registered the shocking truth that I might not be totally a new age, sensitive, accepting of everything kind of guy.

I turned away without coming to any fundamental conclusion about how to take that innocent enough comment about my daughter being part of an all female couple. Silence is the best defense for a confused state of mind, and I needed all the defense I could muster.

I slid into the driver's seat and looked over at my daughter. Denver's golden tanned and tattooed arm was draped around Cody's thin shoulders. This girl was a full head taller than Cody, two grades older, and looked like a runway model from Eastern Europe. It must be the puffed out lower lip and tongue stud. She wore a see through black mesh blouse. Her Victoria's Secret push up bra created a half inch of forced cleavage. Her purposely uneven page boy cut was at least four colors of the rainbow, four primary colors, and a single delicate silver post, the shape of a human skull, pierced her left nostril. The tattoo on her shoulder was a bloody heart stabbed through with a knife.

Denver had been watching my perusal with a jaundiced expression. The pale blue shark eyes, outlined in raccoon black mascara and devoid of expression, caused me to contemplate panic. I started the car and drove on around the circular driveway and headed back to town. The reservation was for six at seven o'clock.

≈

I parked right in front of La Marmont, the gourmet French restaurant, chosen by my daughter for this particular attack on my credit card. I sat, listening to public radio and a weird, even by Telluride standards, hour-long program of a single cut of modern Sitar music with the DJ breaking in and reading racy segments of the *Karma Sutra* in a bull rider's drawl. The red Grand Am with the Arizona plates was already past the Bentley before I let it register. I noticed that the windshield had been fixed, but the hood still had a permanent wave the shape of my hip.

I jumped from the front seat, running after the vanishing image that turned the corner. I arrived just in time to see its brake lights turn back up towards Colorado Avenue. I ran back to the Bentley and went in pursuit. I watched the red convertible cross the intersection of Pine and Pacific from a parallel street a block away. I eased the rolling shocks of the town car over the speed gullies as I paralleled her track.

She had pulled to a stop in front of a house I was beginning to know well. Stewart Lambis had lived at 345 Aspen, and I watched Miranda swing out of her car with an overnight bag on her shoulder, walk up the walk, use a key from her key chain to open the front door and disappeared inside. A second later, a light went on in the front room and the door closed.

Stewart's funeral was tomorrow. She had come to be at the banker's grave. Why? What was she to Lambis? I would go to my office and call her at Lambis' number. She had a gun and might not like being surprised by a lug like me at the front door. Hadn't I killed Singer? Kissed Lambis to death? The last time I saw this person she had just about knocked my brains out. Homicide by a redhead acting in self-defense was sure to be the next act in this string of bizarre events. I wanted to play it safe and hope to live until the finale.

≈

"Miranda?" I said as she answered the phone.

"Thorpe?"

"Long time."

"Not nearly long enough," she said, "I thought that was you creeping around in the Bentley."

"What brings you to town?"

"Personal," she said. "I'd like to chat, but I was on my way to bed. Besides, I don't think I want to have anything to do with you. Folks in your vicinity get themselves bloody or dead."

"I'm sorry about Stewart," I said and meant it.

She didn't make a comeback that gave any hint to her relationship with the man.

"Can you tell me why someone wanted him dead?" I said.

"No." Her voice was hard. "I can't."

"Miranda, listen, I had no reason to wish Stewart harm." I said.

"What about Sandy?"

"If you mean Singer, him either," I said.

"They both had a lot to live for," she said and hung up.

I had used my cleverest banter to get all of these wonderful answers without a scrap of new information. I admitted that I usually gave away more than I got back in any verbal exchange. It sounded like the self-serving lament of a stupid sleuth to me. Cody brought me half of her dessert squashed in a linen napkin when I picked them up.

≈

We were three bugs in a rug under Katie's down comforter reading "Kianna's Iditarod" by Shelley Gill for the thousandth time. Reaching Nome by dog sled with Danger, the cat was always a thrill. After I had finished, Katie grabbed the book and said she would now read it to us. Using the pictures to cue the lyrics, she did a good job of finding rhymes. Cody and I helped when she got stuck. It was the best time I had experienced all week.

Later as I said goodnight to Cody, I couldn't help but broach the subject.

"First base on the first date?" I said fighting down my embarrassment at being a nosy father.

"Dad?"

"Yeah?"

"How do you know?"

"About?"

"Whether you're gay or not?"

What could I say? I admitted to her that I didn't know how to know.

"That's okay," she said.

I knew I should say something wise and profound. I stood there unable to think of anything. I was knee deep in stupid.

"It felt cold and squishy," she said as a matter of fact, pulling her covers up to her chin. She squirmed to find the most comfortable position. Her breath already growing slower and deeper. She would be asleep in seconds.

I couldn't think of anything left to say, so I softly closed the door. I smiled. A flood of disturbing rationalizations followed. Was I wrong to feel relieved that a first kiss was not an explosion of violins? No, I didn't think so.

The reality in my tiny little world was a fragile and tenuous thing. Shouldn't I find some joy in the moment by moment experience? Life throws you enough curves, why not enjoy the straightforward fastball when it comes? Swing for the fence? I did, and picked up my legal pad, already starting to write and remembering the fear of not knowing how things would ever turn out okay.

~

Fitzgerald sat alone in the cab. The engine was running, it was dark, and a cold rain rattled on the hood. He pulled his long, damp wool coat around him and shivered. Alone, without a drink, his hands shook. He was waiting for the cabby to bring the private detectives down from the room above.

"Daisy" had stopped only once on her way from Berlin to New York City. She stayed in a two-buck room above a bowling alley in Vernon along Route 20. Detectives followed her to a neighborhood speakeasy, she came home with a man, and left on the Gotham bound train the next morning. The man she had been with disappeared. He was a grafter, a hobo, and no one remembered her calling him Gatsby.

"She's there," a thick shouldered Mick in a threadbare trench coat said as he opened the door and slid into the back seat. The driver's door opened and the cabby joined them, out of the rain.

"Him too?"

"Yeah, like I said. I got us the room so you could see down and into where she is. Cost me a sawbuck for a two bit flea bag."

"Take the cab and get something to eat," Fitzgerald said, pushing some money into his hand. "Give me a few hours."

"Sure Mack," he agreed quickly with a wink. "You're paying the bills."

It took the writer ten minutes to find the correct room in the darkened hallways. The numbers were scribbled in graphite pencil on the jams. He burned his thumb twice with his gold lighter. Fitzgerald cursed the incompetence.

He kept the light off as he entered, going directly to the low backed wooden chair by the window. He straightened himself as he sat, smoothed his oiled hair, loosened the belt on his coat. Taking a deep breath, he slowly pulled open the curtain a crack to let in the light from the street.

Across the narrow two lanes of roadway and broken sidewalks, in the second floor apartment above the Woolworth's, the redheaded woman was laying on the single bed of the dingy apartment. It seemed every light was on in all three street-front rooms. The curtains flung back as if inviting the night in. Dark shadows still hid the corners outside the oblong pools of light that spread over the threadbare furniture and dusty, empty shelves. He watched her sleep with keen attention.

At ten p.m. a man walked into the scene with lumbering deliberation, scuttling in haste along the empty sidewalk. He paused to check the street behind him and discreetly let himself into the hallway and went directly up to the room.

She startled awake and ran to the door to met him with a joyous embrace in front of the window. The bear sized man returned the hug and kissed her hard on the mouth. She held the kiss, frantically helping him out of his coat. Her eager hands pulling at the studs and collar of his shirt, his hands pulling her dress up to her hips so that he could wiggle his fingers up under her black corset and cup her buttocks.

Gatsby watched. His own bizarre world rebuilding itself once again, right before his eyes. The man's name according to the detective agency was Vladimir Tostoff, due to perform a premier of his own composition, *Jazz History of the World* at Carnegie Hall in May. Reported in the newspapers as a composer, conductor, genius of New York society, he was her ex-husband.

She currently was the subject of a restraining order in the State of New York that forbade her to be within a hundred feet of this man. She had tried to kill him. Tostoff's recanting testimony, concerning her lack of intent to actually use the Luger, had saved her from going to trial. She had not made any friends downtown according to the detectives.

Fitzgerald, the voyeur, watched each frame of the scene unfold as she stripped the clothes from their bodies and let out the lurid beast he knew so well. Tears fell softly from his blue eyes. He lit a cigarette, ducking behind the curtain to shield the lighter's strike, before cracking the curtain again and resuming his awful post.

Twenty-six

It's A Kidnap

It was Saturday morning, and my normal spy network was unfortunately closed down until the first school bell Monday morning. Once I started the bacon sizzling and mixed the water with the pancake mix, I cracked Cody's door so that she would get up to the heavenly smells and sounds from the kitchen. I needed a favor. I find people more receptive to my self-serving method of begging on a full stomach.

My wife, without a word, entered the kitchen and helped herself to a cup of coffee.

"I didn't do it," I said.

She refused to acknowledge the sound of my voice as she sat down at the counter to re-read last night's local paper. *The Daily Miner* was twelve pages of tabloid format and usually wasn't worth even the first reading. The current issue was all about our town's epidemic of dead bodies.

I hadn't been able to read it all the way through. I got to the part about charges had been filed and a former murder suspect had been accused of the crime. I couldn't go on and read my name in print. The freshly minted, new to town gen-X reporter had dragged up all the well-hashed innuendoes and accusations from the last trial. Noting as an afterthought my being cleared of all charges by writing, "The jury and District Attorney had been unable to find enough evidence to convict Thorpe in the shooting death of his client." This journalist was going places.

"I didn't do it," I said again, pouring four small circular pancakes onto the hot griddle.

She flipped open the paper and picked up a pen. I watched her circle something. Putting the pen back into a drawer, she rose from the stool and walked away, down the hall, coldly closing the door of our bedroom behind her.

Cody walked out of her room clad in an ankle length nightshirt that read, "Danger Zone!" in huge red letters. She yawned and stretched her arms over her head, posing for a second in the follow through of a basketball jumpshot. She took her mother's stool.

"I need your help today," I said setting a glass of orange juice in front of her. Her eyes were already focused on the paper.

"I figured," she said her hand waving at the crackling bacon, the dripping bowls and the smoking griddle. My dishcloth apron added to the scene of Little Miss Homemaker.

"Little Miss Homemaker," she said, reading my thoughts.

"I need to find out more about the redheaded woman staying over at Mr. Lambis' house."

"Miranda," she said with another wide yawn. "She's a documentary film maker, Hollywood, Connecticut, and Sodoma, Arizona."

I am told my blank expression is a classic.

"She is also the daughter of Mr. Lambis and Mrs. Singer."

Cody spun the newspaper around on the counter so it faced me. Circled in pen on page two was a final paragraph under a continued column labeled "Murders from page 1." The article explained that the deceased banker was survived by his only daughter Miranda Lambis Sterling, her business, and her address in Sodoma.

I smelled the flapjacks burning as I read the last sentence. Miranda's mother, and also Stewart Lambis' ex-wife, was a current Mountain Village resident whose own recent tragedy is covered in a related story on the front page. "Mrs. Agnes Singer could not be reached for comment on the murders of her former husbands. Funeral services for Mr. Lambis are today at Grace Brethren, 2 p.m."

≈

Kids in most societies on earth are given license, especially at public rituals. The Last Resort Detective Agency banked heavily on these sacred cows. Three perky pre-teen girls stuck their small Sony camcorders into the faces of the entire crowd that attended Stewart's funeral. This kind of intrusion would have never been allowed if the videographers had been adults. The pictures and recorded conversations were the same regardless of the operator's age and were very informative. The audio portion alone, recording conversations on and off camera, was second only to the bread line at Rose's for obtaining new gossip. The topics, however, were much more specific. The murders and the extent of "Wit Thorpe's involvement" in both, headed the favorite discussion items.

Ernie arrived in a style reserved for cream colored 1947 Bentleys, wearing a black suit with a shiny black silk t-shirt under a maroon tinted heavy wool three-quarter length broad collared jacket. He carried a walking stick with a duck-billed silver handle and wore a short brimmed black Homburg. All the young girls hired by my daughter were sure to waste some time and effort getting some good footage of him. He looked by far the odd ball out.

"Swell showing," he said as he came to stand next to me. We watched from across the street the people in twos and threes file into the rapidly filling church.

"Stewart wasn't a bad guy from all I heard," I said.

"Pity to die so badly then."

"Yes it was."

The two matching white Mercedes pulled to the curb in front of the doors to the church. I wasn't surprised to see Meyer Wolfscheim. I was a bit surprised to see Walter, the motorcycle chieftain, and the blonde haired young man who could only be the son of the Church's founder, Eric, walk arm in arm through the thinning crowd. Three additional refugees from a Gold's Gym paraded their tight fitting suits and blown dry haircuts, getting their guarded bodies from the sidewalk to the church doors, each lackey trying to look mean, competent and busy.

One even tried to shoo away a video camera-laden child, but the young lady ducked away and continued filming. The guy ambled after her. It was a bull moose herding a cat. The girl laughed and did little dances taunting the moose, circling back, laughing, to get full frontal shots of Meyer, Walter, and the wayward son. Another goon soon joined the fray, arms out, two mastodons herding ducks this time, and faired no better.

"Shall we?" Ernie said, clucking at the scene.

"We shall." I took his arm, and we walked across the street and through the Church of Compassionate Caring's gauntlet of overzealous hormones to the doors of Grace Brethren.

"I believe that by simply passing through these portals we will be closer to those who know the truth. The Lord be praised," Ernie said in a nasal Noel Coward.

"Decidedly so," I said in kind. We smiled and waved at the cameras and the red faced, sweating bodyguards.

~

"Stewart Lambis was a kind man, a gentle man. A man of principle and integrity." Doctor Meyer Wolfscheim was a formidable presence the second he ascended to the pulpit. His voice was lotus and honey, rising and falling like waves on a beach. "A good father, husband, and man of the church. He will be missed by all of those who were lucky enough to call him friend."

The amplified voice was oozing compassion. I tuned out and watched the crowd. Cody and the filmmakers had left once the service started, after getting each of these hundred or so faces in their lens. Ernie and I had chosen to stand against the wall with a few empty rows between our perch and the rest of the crowd. Our vantage point offered a good view into the front pew of the church.

"Stewart focused his rare gifts on his work, and his daughter. He was honest and loyal. Some who didn't know him could say he carried his firm ideals to a fault. They would be wrong. Stewart Lambis was simply a good, honest man."

In the front row, from the outside in, sat Walter, the young Eric Wolfscheim, and Miranda. Across the main aisle sat Agnes Singer, alone. The line-up was complete. Ex-husband, son in law, son and brother, daughter, wife, divorcee times three that I know, mother, and widow. With Meyer Wolfscheim at the podium, I added father, ex-husband, stepfather, and church sex guru for starters. The deceased was at least another ex-husband, father, lover, trustee. That was a mouthful of family ties. I don't believe in coincidences. What could possibly be going on in Agnes Singer's extended family that added up to murder?

Miranda Sterling and Eric Wolfscheim sat with their heads down. They held hands. Miranda stroked the long fingers of the boy and spoke softly to him in short whispers. He showed no response. It was a touching scene. I was even more confused.

My eyes wandered and connected with Patsy Susie in the fourth row. She was watching me watch the family. Her blonde hair against the black dress was startling. I wondered how far a broker would go for a sale. I guessed to the moon and back. Maybe I didn't want to know.

Wolfscheim's son suddenly stood up, brushing aside Walter's restraining hand. He barged past the gang leader and out into the aisle. The young man wore a grim expression as he hurried from the church. Tears welled in his eyes. More than a few heads followed his progress towards the rear doors. Wolfscheim's voice faltered at the pulpit then regained its timber, drawing the crowd's attention back from the brink.

I watched Walter reach for his cell phone and punch a single key. He didn't get up in hot pursuit. Figuring this was my chance to talk with the boy, I winked at Walter as he caught my eye and then followed Eric Wolfscheim out through the swinging doors. I blinked in the bright sunlight as I saw two of the well dressed goons from the Church's Mercedes converge on the black leathered young man.

"Leave me alone," he said, pointing a finger at them.

"The boss told us to take you anywhere you wanted to go," the semi-articulate body builder said. His bookend grunted in the affirmative.

"No," the young Wolfscheim said in protest, as he reluctantly let them each grab a skinny bicep in their huge paws and move him back towards the Mercedes.

The third power lifter came at me on a tangent across the lawn. His obvious mission was to stop me from following the two with the boy. He was used to intimidating people with his size and was still pocketing his cell when he came within my space. Even at the ready, most muscled-up body builders can't clap their hands in front of their nose. This one was not ready, and also slower than cold molasses. I didn't break stride as I straight-armed the heel of my right hand, putting momentum and weight behind it, into the bridge of his nose. It was the stroke I used to break boards and impress the female students at Bennie Hanna's Dojo. I felt the cartilage crack. He dropped like a wet towel with tears closing his eyes.

I turned back towards the two white cars at the curb and saw Sheriff Bueller stepping down from his Bronco on the other side of them, across the street.

My first thought was hopeful. I had some back up. Then I noticed he had eyes only for me. The obvious crime going on only ten feet away from him was ignored. The Church thugs pushed Wolfscheim into the back seat, bending him roughly in the process. One bodyguard slid in beside him pushing him across the leather bench seat. The other sprinted around the car for the driver's door.

"Stop them. He doesn't want to go. It's a kidnap," I said and pointed for Bueller's benefit. The Sheriff glanced at the white Mercedes and waved. The two kidnappers waved back. I saw their smiles flash behind the tinted glass. Bueller was unholstering his pistol as he pointed an index finger at me.

"Don't move, Thorpe," he said in a menacing voice, "You're under arrest."

I put my hands on my head. I had always figured Bueller for a shooter, and I wasn't going to give him an excuse to shoot me. He looked disappointed.

≈

The bodyguard I "assaulted" refused to press charges. Between the clinic where they reset his nose and the Sheriff's Office, he had received his marching orders from someone. I was sure Sheriff Bueller worked hard to change the injured goon's mind. The "someone" must have some kind of juice. I usually bet on fear, money, or both as the source of most juice. Walter led my list of candidates. He seemed intent on keeping me on the street while I relentlessly sought enough rope to hang myself.

Ernie met me at the gate to the jail for the third time in as many days.

"Do you get frequent flyer miles from this establishment?" he said.

"Hilarious." I credited him for the flat joke. "A drink seems in order."

"Fabulous, my boy. You are clairvoyant."

"Don't call me Claire."

"Gotcha, how about the marvelous Miss Voyant then?" Ernie said on cue, and gave himself a rim shot on the leather of the steering wheel. "Back in the saddle, old boy."

We drove along the pristine and tranquil Valley Floor back towards town. The herd of cows would soon be taken to lower pastures in Nucla for the winter. The tops of the buildings in town just peaked above the trees a mile away. The backdrop of the multi-leveled rooftops were the vertical walls of the box canyon. Bridal Veil Falls sent a cascading bloom of mist, just off center in the perfect picture, as it dropped over a few hundred feet down sheer granite. I felt an unexpected tug of attachment to this place, such a beautiful and rare chunk of real estate.

"Who wants you out of jail and causing trouble?" Ernie said, his rhetorical question interrupting my pensive moment. "It remains the pivotal question that won't go away."

"You mean, who runs Walter?"

"Precisely."

"How do we find out?" I said hoping Ernie had thought of an answer. He had.

"Split the young and weak from the herd," said my barber.

I thought about it for a second or two. Only one thought came to mind. "Rescue Eric Wolfscheim?"

"You gleam like a forty watt bulb," Ernie said.

I pondered the difference between an insult and a compliment for the rest of the drive. In the end I figured it made no difference. Both are based on the premise that you care what someone else thinks of you. That's why Ernie and I get along so well. We don't spend too much time worrying about what someone else thinks.

≈

"Cody," I said. "I need your help and I don't have time to negotiate."

"I just love blank checks."

I gave my daughter the skeptical look she deserved, and she gave it right back to me. I shivered. What was this worth to me? My life?

"I need to find those two white Mercedes from Arizona. Can you do that?"

Cody gave me a "puh-lease" look. "How soon do you need to know?"

"Ten minutes ago?"

"Right," she said and went to her room and closed the door.

My wife walked in from the steps down to the house with our daughter Katie in tow. She ran into my arms, my daughter that is. My wife ignored me and went to the refrigerator.

"Daddio." My four year old squeezed my neck and it felt good. She then headed for the front room, the television and Sesame Street.

"I didn't do it," I said as I watched my wife twist the top from a juice container.

"That seems to be your life's mantra, Wit." she said. "What specifically didn't you do this time?"

"Call West Egg the night of the murder."

Her green eyes flashed coldly at me. The implication by process of elimination was that the call had come from her room. The sounds of The Count Muppet naming his numbers came from the television.

"I didn't do it," I said again. "Any of it."

Cody appeared at the door of her room and wiggled her finger for me to come. I did, leaving my wife with her thoughts and suspicions.

～

Cody's phone tree of her classmates, older siblings who drove, and gossiping parents had led me to an estate off of Fox Farm Road in the Ski Ranches subdivision above Mountain Village. Ernie was AWOL on some mission, absent from home and the bar at the Sheridan, and I couldn't track him down to cross-reference the owner's name within his social circles of the town's elite second home entrepreneurs. It would have saved me the shock of seeing my recent ride, the silver Z3, parked behind the two white Mercedes under the portico.

The large main house and separate guest cottage were visible from the road through the tall aspens. A "For Sale" sign was at the entrance to the drive. The broker's name was a familiar one: Patsy Susie Blaze. I had seen her nude, banging uglies with Jeffrey Breene, owner of the very same Z3, twice within the last week. Once again, I didn't believe in coincidence. What did either of them have to do with the Church?

In my writing, as in real life, it is always better to be lucky than smart. I had just shut off the Mustang and settled in for a long wait for some one, anyone, to leave the Fox Farm compound, when the door from the main house opened and Eric Wolfscheim came out into the courtyard between the two buildings and lit a cigarette. My recent dance partner at the funeral followed him. The thug was sporting a huge white gauze and tape bandage bridging his broken nose. Both stood outside, hunching their shoulders to keep warm without coats, while Eric ingested his nicotine.

I started the Mustang quickly and figured the only thing to do was the obvious. I turned down the entry road and pulled into the courtyard amidst a cloud of unmuffled black smoke.

"Hey Eric, need a lift?" I said above the sound of the engine and pushed the passenger door open.

The thin blond man didn't hesitate. He chucked his cigarette and was around the hood of the car before the bodyguard could react. The Sodom's Devils' black and blue eyes helplessly watched me back into a spinning one-eighty in the gravel and accelerate back out of the drive towards Fox Farm Road. In the rear view mirror, I watched him scramble back towards the front door that opened wide before he reached it. Walter was staring after us with a wide sardonic smile I could see even at a distance in the rear view mirror. He was an orthodontist's dream.

"You're him, right?" Eric said in a squeak as we fishtailed onto the pavement and began rocking our way through the tight curves.

"Who?"

"The one who killed Sandy?"

"Who?"

"The one they're always talking about?"

"Who?"

"The dead man walking," he said and gripped the door handle as we slid all four wheels around a sharp corner and dropped down a steep incline towards the exit from Ski Ranches.

I expected them to chase us, and I had about a zero chance of outrunning a Mercedes on mountain roads. I put an end to further conversation by not responding and concentrated on a place to hide me, Eric, plus the car within the next quarter mile.

Bradley Yates's barn came suddenly to mind, and I took a hard left on Sunshine Loop and doubled back up into the winding maze of the Ski Ranches' roads. I pulled into a field, through an open gate, and around back of the weathered and abandoned barn. The transplanted building was perfectly set in a small pasture that gave a spectacular view of Sunshine Peak. Eric sat in the car while I threw open the tall double doors of the defunct dude ranch operation and raced to move the car inside and get the doors closed behind us.

In a matter of seconds we sat in the deafening silence in the semi-darkness of the barn. I could hear my heavy breathing as soon as I shut the engine off.

"You've got to help my father," Eric said in a soft voice. "He's next. They want him dead, too."

"Who?"

"Maybe you should probably just kill him, too. Just like Sandy. It would be mercy. If you don't, they will."

"Who?"

Eric looked up at me from under his blonde bangs. He was perplexed.

"Is that all you know how to say?" he said. "Do you speak English?" He followed the insult with an ethnic injury.

The expression on his face in the dim light indicated a first impression that he thought I was probably a couple of cans short of a six-pack. Luckily it wasn't my first such flattering assessment of the day. I took it better than usual.

Twenty-seven

A Bear Attack

Stewart Lambis and Robert Forrest Singer were not lovers at the time of their deaths. It was the only useful bit of real information that Eric would part with after his initial outburst. The sun went down quickly, and we snuck back into town on the only road available without seeing anyone, which I pointed out to Eric was different than not being seen. He asked to be dropped at Miranda's. Luckily, I knew what he meant.

Eric Wolfscheim's half-sister gave him a frantic hug on the porch and then barred my way from following them inside.

"We have to talk," I said to her.

"No," she said, "we don't."

"It's a murder."

"Exactly." she said. "Your murders."

"I didn't do it."

"I saw you stalking Sandy at the Peaks."

"I wasn't stalking him. I was on another case."

"Hardly. I don't believe in coincidences." She was obviously my kind of thinker.

She continually pushed the door closed until only my foot kept it open. Her eyes told me not to force the issue. "Don't make me call Sheriff Bueller."

I nodded and withdrew my foot. The door closed. I couldn't help but hear the open handed slap, the surprised cry, and the muffled sobbing before I forced myself to leave the porch. I guess that's why they call us snoops.

I read the girls to sleep, and my wife spent the entire evening in her room working. I was in a sour mood as I walked out onto the back porch and noticed the crime scene. Spread twenty yards down the cleared slope that we called our "front" yard were the remnants of my life. Tissue paper, a milk carton, coffee filters and grounds, butcher's wax paper, cellophane wrapping and aluminum foil were all the discarded viscera of a black bear attack on our bear-proof garbage bin.

The rake and pail were in the same place I had left them the last time this had happened, a week ago. In the semi-darkness, with only the lights from inside the house giving any illumination, I could barely make out the bits and pieces of garbage. I was raking in the shadows when I first saw the darkly clothed prowler step down from the steep stairway to the road above. The figure hugged the shadows next to the corner away from me that led to the deck that ran the entire width of my house.

I froze, gripping the rake and wondering if the shadow had a better weapon. An arm reached into the circle of light and knocked softly on the sliding glass panel. The door glided open as if someone had been waiting for a signal. The shadow quickly rounded the corner and passed through the parted drapes into my wife's bedroom.

I was stunned, and my knees buckled as I knelt down on the scrabble, still holding the rake. I tried to convince myself that staying hidden was the reason I was on the ground in a pile of garbage. It was Bueller. Bueller and my wife were… what? My reality took another tumble.

≈

An hour later I am still sitting alone and trying to pinpoint my emotion. I run through the seven deadly sins for help. I find plenty. It finally dawns on me that what I am feeling isn't simply an emotion. It is painful and frightening. I wrote on the yellow pad about the pain, sitting at my kitchen counter, looking down the hall at the barred door to my own bedroom.

≈

After her night of debauchery, the redheaded woman had waited two days for Vladimir Tostoff to come back. She had neither eaten nor drank, sleeping only in exhausted spasm, fainting into unconsciousness, her dreams marked by continuous wailing and despair. Fitzgerald watched in two-hour shifts with the detectives, sleeping in catnaps on the lumpy bed.

"Sir?"

"What is it?" Fitzgerald, startled from a black hole of release, sat up in a bolt from the bed. It was pitch dark. A voice spoke again and helped him locate the window and its sliver of light.

"She's leaving."

Fitzgerald was shaken, drifting, unsure of himself and lost in self-loathing. He felt "the rock of the world was founded securely on a fairy's wing." His entire dark obsession with the woman was based on an illusion of gigantic proportions. A muse was devouring him whole. He now knew that the pompous Catholic priests he hated so much were right about one thing. Corruption dwells in beauty; evil hides itself there. Pretty words, wonderful places, swell people were all choked with the dust of past sins. Escape was impossible. He was doomed, so was Daisy, so was everyone.

The two detectives bundled him into a car in the alley. It was late night, the damp streets deserted. At the corner they parked in the shadows and watched her stumble along the street. Fitzgerald sat in the back and watched her, framed by the broad shoulders and heads of his men. She scrapped the sidewalk in her high heels; the dress hung from her shoulders, the back zipper hanging open. She dragged her purse and her coat on the ground as she wearily forced herself in small halting steps towards some distant destination.

A cab stopped. She got in. They followed the cab across town and out of the city. Fitzgerald was caught by surprise as they traced the roads back to the very home in Great Neck he had given up only a month before.

The cab dropped her off at the gate. She let herself in and disappeared up the drive. Fitzgerald directed the driver down a small side lane just beyond the estate and the car bounced on the cart path until the hedge had a break in it and the house was visible. Every light was ablaze in all three stories.

On the lawn, in a lounge chair, the woman sat and a man reclined. She leaned forward and placed her hands on his chest, lowering her lips to his. They kissed tenderly. The reaction was immediate, as if someone had cut a marionette's strings; she collapsed onto him in a dead faint.

Fitzgerald watched as the man gathered her up into his arms and strode into the house. Through the open windows Fitzgerald watched him carry her limp body up the wide staircase he knew so well. Soon, one by one, the lights went out. The cicadas twirped loudly in the tall hedges.

The thick-necked detective scooped the handful of mail from the mailbox as they headed back towards the city. Fitzgerald stared at the strange name above his former address. The detectives were ordered to find out everything they could about the man in the house named Sandy Gatz, Esquire.

≈

Ernie's hand was a bit shaky as he scraped the six-inch long razor across my Adam's Apple. I wasn't going to mention my case until he was done. He also smelled of bourbon. It was 8:43 a.m.

"How goes my case?" I said as he finally handed me a warm hand towel with a tong.

"What case," he said.

"That good?"

"I won't apologize," he said letting the pressure he was feeling out, "I didn't ask for this. I got half a mind..."

"That's why I need you," I said, handing him a twenty. "That half of a mind is twice what I got." I gave him my most sincere smile.

I could see he was touched.

"I came here to get away from the law."

"So did Butch Cassidy and Sundance." I kept up the smile. I couldn't afford a real lawyer. Ernie was all I had.

"Nice analogy."

"What do you need me to say, Ernie?"

"Plea bargain."

"I didn't do it."

"Tell me one thing," Ernie said as he one armed the cash register.

"Sure."

"Why did you jerk the guy off before you shot him?"

The other three shop regulars seated at the foot of the barber chair started to chuckle and look sideways, gauging each other's embarrassment level. It was an old guy thing. Droopy Drawers Hal led the chorus of old males who repeated the question.

"Screw you," I said, unhappy with my lawyer and his humorous take on confidential consultations regarding my case.

"Not in this life time, Percy," Hal quipped as I left the barbershop. I bound up the stairs three at a time to put the laughter behind me.

The door to my office was open and Miranda Sterling was waiting inside, thumbing through a file folder. She wasn't startled when I knocked on my own open door. She was her mother's daughter. I wondered if her armpits were waxed.

"Can I help you find something?" I tried to be sardonic.

She wore a tight fitting dark blue pin stripe suit. The skirt cut her thighs in half. Black fishnet nylons disappeared into her black platform heels. The sight of a woman in anything but jeans was still a shock in Telluride.

"What did my brother tell you?"

"That he was scared."

"Of what? Of me?"

I shrugged, taking the open folder from her hands and tossing it back into the mess on my desk. I stood next to her, definitely in her space, and could smell the scent of her shampoo through the subtle perfume. It had honey in it. She kept her eyes on my chest. Sexual tension hung in the air.

"I want to hire you." Her voice was throaty and breathless. Either she was a great actress, or I made her sweat.

"To do what, exactly." I tried not to appear flattered or surprised.

"Protect Eric."

"From who?"

"Does it matter?"

"Only my daughter gets blank checks," I said.

She moved away the two feet the office allowed and faced out the window.

"Walter could want him dead."

"Why?"

"Money," she said, "Inheritance."

"What does that have to do with Walter?"

"He wants it all. And he'll probably get it."

"You know that for sure?"

"I should know what he is capable of," she said and turned back towards me. Her eyes finding mine. "He's my husband."

I couldn't readily explain why the thought clanged in my brain and made my stomach revolt. I am not by nature a trusting sort. I can sometimes spot a pile of bullshit from a blimp in a fog storm. My meter must be shorted out by her red hair. Just when I thought I had found a safe clearing in the jungle, the hungry tiger arrived.

"Will you help me protect Eric?"

"I'll do what I can."

"Watch out for Walter. He likes hurting people."

"He killed Singer?"

Her eyes flashed. "No," she said, "you did."

"I didn't," I said it as sincerely as I could. She faltered. I could see the relevant new fact strike home and explode into uncertainty. It was over in a blink of her lightly green tinted lids, and then she smiled a flirtatious and cruel smile. Her gray eyes went cold.

"Hello darling," she said, her gaze going past my shoulder to the still open door. I could only guess that her attack dog had joined us. They were a couple? Married? I was in the middle.

"Aren't you supposed to say, 'Honey, I'm home,'" he said.

"Honey, I'm home," she said.

"That's my girl."

She slid past me into his arms. He grinned that full white toothed smile at me and winked as he led her down the stairs with an arm around her waist. They laughed as they turned at the first landing and looked back up at me to let me know I was the butt of the joke. I watched them go.

Honey, I'm home? Were they both reading my story?

Twenty-eight

Doing the Horizontal Tango

Sterling is not Walter's last name," I said to Ernie, trying to convince him I was less stupid than I knew I was. My partner held up the photocopy of the motorcycle gang leader's rap sheet.

"Silverton, Silver, Mint, Eldorado, Silubrha are all aliases linked to the precious metal," Ernie said sipping coffee. "Sterling, my boy, was an obvious clue."

"Okay, I'm stupid."

"Decidedly so." Ernie heartily agreed.

I grunted.

"Was he shagging her?" Ernie said.

"When?"

"At the time of Singer's demise you dolt." Ernie momentarily lost his patience. He found it quickly at the bottom of his glass of Scotch. "Are they each other's best alibis? Can we check them off the lists of people who want you locked up, dead, on the one hand; or free to cause trouble, on the other."

"Probably," I said, not really wanting to know if someone was sleeping with my fictitious redhead.

"Assuming makes an ass of you and me," Ernie said. He was right. The other right answer to his questions about their alibis could help us continue to divide the herd. The trick was in knowing whom to ask.

It pays to have a large family every day of the year but Christmas. Grace Mankiller was my cousin. Ute and Shawnee blood mixed with some fine Spanish ancestors gave her the face and regal bearing of a Castilian noble woman. She was the chief housekeeper at the New Sheridan Hotel. She was often the only one on duty during the off seasons. I found her in the laundry room at 9 a.m. pulling crisp white sheets from the dryer and folding them. We hugged.

She remembered the night Singer died. She remembered the bearded man in black leather. She had not seen any attractive redhead. The bed was pretty well used up when she cleaned it in the morning. Seemed reasonable that the man was there in the room all night.

I was disappointed. We had already hugged good-by, and I was leaving when I found my culture slapping me in my face. If you don't ask the question, you won't know the answer. My people are not chatterboxes or natural gossips unless they are encouraged. It is the way. I was forgetting who I was and where truth comes from.

"Did you see any one else in the hotel that seemed strange?"

"Yes."

"Well?"

"Coming down from the second floor a little after midnight was someone."

"Who?"

"The wife."

"Miranda Sterling?" I said.

"Who?"

"Who...What wife?"

"Singer's wife, the dead guy's."

"Agnes?"

"You know her so well?" Grace gave me a suspicious look out of habit.

"Not well enough, it seems."

"She was in the sack with Walter?"

Grace Mankiller gave the fluid up-down-up, side-to-side head movement of my people that carried so many hidden meanings while leaving the obvious alone.

≈

Patsy Susie Blaze made more money each time she brokered a single family trophy home than I had so far earned in my entire life. Her full-page advertisements in every published bit of media had her long Jodhpur covered legs straddling a wooden pole fence in a field with the San Juan Mountain Range as a backdrop. A cowboy hat was held over her blonde head in a howdy-all pose. The thin cowboy shirt was purposefully stretched tight over her ripe twin blossoms of female anatomy.

Susie had gained twenty pounds since that photo was taken, now built for comfort not speed, but she was still a fine looking woman with a taste in expensive clothes to hide the fluid hips and accent those perky breasts.

If ninety percent of sex appeal is attitude, Susie had it in spades. She wasn't above sleeping with a client in the newly acquired master suite to celebrate a deal and keeping the perk a secret from the buyer's wife. It was Telluride Style, she would giggle seductively, flashing her wide mischievous blue eyes.

Ernie and I had a 10 a.m. appointment to meet with Ms. Blaze for coffee at Cafe Vienna on Colorado Avenue. We were all on time and met on the street. Patsy Susie was getting out of my favorite Z3.

"New wheels," I said, running my hand along the front fender.

"Something for my embarrassment," she said, looking back with pride of ownership at the sleek silver sports car. Her handshake was firm and her eyes, squinting in the bright sun, held no embarrassment or hint of humor. It was remarkable, considering the fact that I had seen her naked, both on tape and in the raw, within the last seventy-two hours.

The waitress brought the designer coffees. We had short-handed our way through the pleasantries when Ernie got to the point.

"Susie, who's renting the house with your sign on it up on Fox Farm Road? The old Howell place."

"Doctor Wolfscheim, why?"

"Let me be candid. No secret that Wit here is accused of a murder he didn't do. Trust me."

Susie Patsy wasn't the trusting sort but the smile let us know she was amused by the possibility.

" The Church of the good doctor, Meyer Wolfscheim, is connected to Singer, Lambis and their deaths. We need your help to get to the bottom of it. What's going on? Go off the record, no breach of professional confidence exposed, and let us find out who killed Singer. Please, my dear?"

Susie gave us a gunfighter's stare.

"And we'll give you the other copy of the tape," Ernie said. I gave him a hard look.

"Other copy?" Patsy Susie's back went rigid.

"Yeah, Wit's personal library." Ernie was struggling, keeping the conversation light. "Besides, it's just between us mountain rats, right? It'll all stay off the record."

"Way off record," I said for emphasis with my best smile. Business ethics are different than personal ones; they go directly to the bottom line. Patsy Susie had seven figure deal ethics. Helping me was not in the business plan.

"And I don't have another tape," I said.

Ernie smiled. She glared at him. We weren't getting anywhere with blackmail. So I reached for another deadly personal sin.

"Doesn't it bother you that Lambis and Singer got popped by one of your little friends? Do you trust each of them that much? What if you got on the wrong side of the wrong one?"

"What?" Susie said quickly, jarred from a moment's reverie.

"A lot of money at stake here with a killer in the middle somewhere. You want someone like that around for the next twenty years? A partner you trust, waiting until it serves their purpose to have you dead."

"Off the record?" she said, biting her lip.

"Someone should know your side," Ernie said. "In case something happens."

It struck a dangling synapse in her blonde head that the bottom line wasn't worth a diddle if you weren't around to spend it. "What do you want to know?"

"Everything," I said.

"It'll cost you."

I nodded.

Her eyes bore into mine. I was giving away another blank check. She wanted me to know that she was going to collect. Idiot was proving to be more than a middle name.

Patsy Susie was really a talker at heart. The annotated version, and she was proud to tell us all the dirt, gave the framework to hang the events of the past week on.

The Church of Compassionate Caring, through its executive officers, had entered into a land acquisition strategy that, when completed, would leave them the largest, by acreage, landowner in San Juan County.

Singer and Lambis had both been executive board members. They were the trustees, along with Meyer and Walter, of the soon-to-be acquired church assets. All trustees were officers of the Church. Every ex-husband of Agnes Singer was on the governing board.

It got stranger.

Leveraging a half billion dollars in real estate with a scant ten percent cash down payment through the Telluride Savings and Loan managed by Stewart Lambis was a cinch. The final negotiations on the deal had been held up by the need for an extra five million that the original partners could not, in good faith or bad, borrow to meet the minimum bank requirement.

Singer had been insured, as a matter of his position on the Board of Trustees, for exactly two-point-five million. The same recompense to the Church was also true for Stewart Lambis. The five million insurance pay-outs would push the deal to completion.

The meeting yesterday afternoon that I had rudely interrupted by snatching Eric was for the purpose of setting up a process for passing proxies to the heirs and pledging the insurance money to closing the deal. Telluride, if the church had its way, would soon be spiritual home base to the ten thousand potential members of the Church of Compassionate Caring's retirement program.

Patsy Susie was lead broker on the purchase of the Valley Floor, the single largest contract, to the tune of fifty million dollars. Six percent commission was a staggering sum.

"I want to see this deal go through," she said with a voice that would grind millet. "I'm moving to Maui."

I was learning to appreciate people stating the obvious. I resolved to do it more myself. Miranda, according to the chronology from Patsy Susie, had just become a full stakeholder on a hundred million dollars in real estate if she inherited her father's shares. Agnes would surely acquire a full share by her husband's murder. All of the survivors had benefited by both Singer's and Lambis' deaths through the bonded insurance money. Motive was again firmly placed in the frontcourt of every member of the church's cartel. Where to begin?

Talking with Miranda alone was of prime importance. For my own peace of mind, if not for the case. My heart pounded loudly. It was embarrassing how hormones still run my life. I wondered what she had in mind, setting me up between her thug of a husband and her half brother. It was probably going to be painful for me to find out.

I was also wondering what this new information would ultimately cost me. Patsy Susie winked hard when she left, sporting a Mona Lisa smile that had me worried.

～

"Agnes," I said, "you were not in bed asleep on the night of your husband's murder."

"No?" The cold voice on the phone responded. I shivered.

"You and Walter Silva, now Silverton, both your ex-husband and son-in-law, were doing the horizontal tango in his room at the New Sheridan."

"Doing the what?"

"Making whoopee," I said.

"Really." She sounded bored.

"You were seen coming from his hotel room after midnight. Did you then stop off and give your husband a parting shot?"

"Very clever," she said, but didn't mean it.

"You know I always bet on sex, jealousy or lust when it comes to murder, but I got a partner who swears that avarice trumps fornication in this case."

Silence.

"He is dead set on some trail of huge money. As far as I know now, your husband was broke, no assets, zippo. You said so. Why would someone want to kill him if greed was the motive? Who stood to gain the most if he died? Insurance maybe?"

The muted buzz on the phone meant something.

"But, don't worry Mrs. Singer, Ernie is tenacious and knows everybody. He'll get a whiff of the truth and run down the scent like a rabid bloodhound."

The phone went dead. I hadn't lost my knack for stirring up the hornets' nest. It wasn't the first time I wished I had my gun back. Adolescence is a hard habit to kick.

~

Cody jumped into the Mustang, leaned over the space between the bucket seats and gave me a two-armed hug. It felt wonderful.

"Why the squeeze, Bond-San?" I said, always looking gift horses in the mouth.

"Emotional support."

"Do I look that bad?"

"No, Stump, emotional support for me."

"Oh." I didn't understand. "Why?"

"We broke up."

"You broke up?"

"Denver and me."

I thought about all the possible fatherly responses. "Are you okay?" I asked, figuring it was the only question that really mattered. Even I get one right once in a while.

"Oh sure." She flashed me an honest big smile. "Denver needs a grip."

A grip?

"She is totally letting her parents run her life," my fifth grader said. "They said she couldn't be tied up with me, now that my father is being charged as a murderer. But, she goes, 'maybe after the trial if your dad proves himself innocent we could try again.' Like sure, I said, fine, end of story. Besides..." Cody paused to wave at one of her friends and her mom in a huge suburban assault vehicle.

"Besides?"

"Besides, I'm PHAT, not some body's POMOD."

"POMOD?"

"Piece Of Meat On Display."

"Right," I said. My head went numb with random thought overload. Luckily, I was driving and able to keep my slack-jawed expression to myself.

Twenty-nine

Icing the Wrong John Doe

Later in the day, Digger, the bartender at the New Sheridan, was polite enough to serve Ernie and me a happy hour drink before he slapped the *Daily Miner* down in front of us. Bushmills for me, Kettle One for my barber.

"It's the Grand Jury," he said, "next week."

It did not prove that Digger could read, just because his statement was close to what occupied the front page 136 pica bold headline. I was in a judicious frame of mind and getting use to cutting hairs.

"Never seen the system move so fast," Ernie said. "They want you bad, old cod."

"At least someone does." I was moving towards morose.

"Wit," Ernie said, "whining is one of the most unbecoming things you do. Snap out of it, before I am forced to slap you around."

"I need to be slapped."

"Pitiful."

"Even my wife thinks I did it."

"She's a smart ADA," said Ernie.

"Ship my damn carcass off to the big house to make room for the next lard ass in her life."

"Disgusting," said Ernie with a wink and a smile for Digger.

"I don't deserve it."

"What makes you think that?" Ernie said.

I shrugged, holding up my glass for Digger's attention.

"No wonder you're alone." A big passionate voice boomed from the business side of the bar. "You're a bully and a drunk with no respect for the opposite sex," said Digger suddenly having a lucid thought, and parting with it on the spot. "The way you treat your woman is a rotten shame. She's a fox, man. Deserves better. You got no friggin' sense."

I thought he was going to cry. He turned and walked away. He pulled a dirty, red checked bandanna from his hip pocket and blew his nose. Digger, it seems, also had a thing for my wife.

"What the hell was that?" I was peevish.

"The truth," Ernie said.

For the hundredth time today, I watched Bueller slide through the glass door into my wife's bedroom. Maybe I should just plead guilty to murder. Go and hide away from these kinds of soul-wrenching discoveries in prison. I wouldn't be missed. Angst immediately replaced moral anguish when the redhead walked in.

≈

"Mr. Sampesee," she said offering her hand, "I'm Miranda Sterling."

"Indeed, you are," said Ernie helping her to sit in my seat. It didn't matter I was still in it. I moved a stool down the line. She kept her back to me and her charm focused on my barber.

"Thank you for the flowers at my father's funeral," she said, pulling from the blue leather clutch purse a thin gold case for her unfiltered cigarettes. Of course there was a matching lighter. She pulled an exotic bright white cigarette out, tapped it lightly on the case, and put it to her lips. Ernie took the lighter from her slender, light blue tinted nails. He held it to the tip. She exhaled.

I knew she would dab at the tobacco bit on the end of her tongue with her little finger. She did.

"Stewart Lambis was a fine man. I'm sorry I didn't know him better. I am deeply troubled by his death," Ernie said, his own prodigious New

England falsetto charm oozing. He paused a delicate moment and then added, "Perhaps you could ease our confusion by sharing your opinion on why he died."

"Love."

"Pardon?" I said over her shoulder. She turned to me and her eyes drilled into mine with a strange challenge. I, of course, took it sexually. I was still running true to form as a Neanderthal.

"Love, Mr. Thorpe," she put sweet smelling eastern European smoke into each word. "An emotion that controls more human tragedies than you think."

"In love with who? Whom?" I was never sure.

"Sandy," she said.

"Stewart died because he loved Singer?" Ernie piped in, unable to contain himself.

"Precisely," said Miranda.

"Precisely?" asked Ernie before I could open my mouth.

"Sandy had broken up with my father five years before he married my mother. It was ancient history. Love isn't always about being consumed by jealousy and possession. Big studs like you should know that. It'll help you score with the ladies."

We two were silent.

"But murder?" Ernie said.

Miranda shrugged.

"Who did it?" I said, trying to keep my mouth from falling open in surprise.

"Isn't that what you are supposed to find out," she said, "Mr. Private Eye."

Ernie and I looked at each other in confusion.

"Gentleman." Miranda adjusted herself in the stool, crossing her black nylon legs under the mid-thigh hem of her skirt, then commanded our attention back from her anatomy, by changing the subject. "Are you going to provide some kind of security for my brother?"

"From who? Whom?" I said. This questioning a question was getting embarrassing.

"I told you before. I don't think that should matter."

"I think it does matter," I said. "I want to know whose gun is going to fire the bullet I'm supposed to step in front of. Call me old fashioned."

"My husband, then, maybe others."

I could almost hear Ernie's brain cranking along so I followed up. "Where were you the night Singer was murdered?"

"You can't suspect..." she said. I kept my eyes on hers.

"You weren't with your husband." I said.

"No?"

"No."

"I was with my step brother," she finally said, tentatively, without focusing on what the words meant. "How do you know I wasn't with Walter?"

"I know where he was."

"Where was that?"

"Why don't you ask him?" It was something Philip Marlowe, a real fictional detective would say, but I didn't mean it. I wanted to tell her everything just to see her flavor of reaction. She remained silent, knowing I desperately wanted to spill it and had no self discipline. She waited, not blinking, coolly appraising my retreat from the high ground. I finally couldn't stop myself and gave it up. I was truly one of the most honest men I know, when it serves my own shortsighted purpose.

"He was with the grieving widow, your mother, in a room together at the Sheridan Hotel."

Her eyes went hard. They flashed at me for the lie, then looked away recognizing the truth. She excused herself without glancing at me again, threw a folded check from her purse to the bar, and left quickly without turning back. Ernie's good-bye went unacknowledged. I look at the check from Sterling Productions, Incorporated. Two things surprised me. The return address under the company name is now Telluride, and the check has more zeros to the left of the decimal point than I have ever seen before in my life.

"What do you make of this?"

"A bribe my boy," Ernie said, scanned the check and whistled. "Cash it quickly before she figures out we aren't the bribing kind." Sound advice from my lawyer.

I tried to agree. Downstream was a little muddy. I already felt dirty, seamy. Self-pity and confusion will do that to a man. I left the bar soon after, and went back to the office to write down the bones.

≈

Fitzgerald felt the trapdoor fall from beneath his feet. Her brother? Sandy Gatz, Esq. was the red haired woman's half brother? A wealthy industrialist had a single child with a Boston socialite before growing tired of her, divorcing, and finding a southern woman to marry. St. Paul's, Andover, Brown, were all part of the sibling's checkered dossier. He was also a failed lawyer, an injured movie stunt man, and currently a small time bootlegger.

Fitzgerald remained perplexed in his troubled dreams as he slept the sleep of sedated exhaustion. The doctor, summoned by Scribner's Publishing, had responded to the call from the nurse on duty in the suite at the Plaza. He administered to the noted author another sedative after Fitzgerald had re-read the reports from the private detectives. They were all worried about his state of mind. He admitted that he felt like he was slipping backwards in time. A psychiatrist was suggested, consulted, an appointment made.

When he awoke his mind was made up. The drug induced grogginess left as the hurriedly hired car drove out of the city speeding along at fifty miles an hour on the small winding roads. Each four-corner intersection held a tight cluster of homes, shops, or farm buildings. He had already cautioned the gruff, threatening driver once about speeding and now labored to keep his mouth shut and tried not worry. Once he felt a thump and heard the dying squawk of a chicken that was quickly drowned out by the rumbling of the engine and the loud rolling of the sedan's tires. He smoked.

Fitzgerald dismissed the car at the gate of the house in Westport. The gravel stung his cheek as the angry driver departed in a cloud of road dust. The former tenant strolled past the imposing gate and went directly to the front door. It hung open, exposing the broad length of hallway through the dining room and wide glassed doors to a glimpse of the pool and hedges beyond. He called her name, knocked his knuckles languidly against the sill.

The white flowing curtains, strummed by the light afternoon wind, framed the "fresh green breast of a new world." Birds chirped, music came from a Victrola somewhere out of sight, and the curtains swayed in a sinuous dance, seductively, in the light breeze.

No stranger to this house, he walked right in. In a moment Fitzgerald was looking down from the rear porch into the pool. Gatz sat at the edge of the kidney shaped lagoon, his feet dangling in the water. Both of them were naked, and she stood chest deep in the aquamarine water, her shoulder touching Gatz's knee.

"The bard," Gatz said recognizing him instantly, and a gloating smile lit his boyish face. "I'd ask you to come in, but you already are. Rudeness becomes you, my dear."

Fitzgerald disliked him immediately; the feeling was a flash fire emotion and it consumed him. The man was swine, bred in a meat yard in the Midwest. The author pegged him as a bully and a schemer who enjoyed getting the best of everybody. Fitzgerald's eyes remained focused on hers. She smiled in a silent, warm, inclusive greeting and spoke. Her hand went to her brother's bare knee.

"Join us," she said. "The water's fine."

~

One of the pieces of information that I was giving undivided attention was the autopsy report on Stewart Lambis. The new info was courtesy of my daughter Cody early this morning. Sperm was found in the shaft and crown of the penis indicating that the deceased had also ejaculated within three to eight hours of his death.

"Miranda said her father died because of love," I said for the third time.

"Lambis and Singer were also ancient history according to the dear young lady," Ernie said. "Who was the banker diddling?"

"You're the one who put Lambis, Singer and love together," I said. "I think she gave the right answer to two different questions."

"What are you talking about?" Ernie jumped to his feet from the barber chair so that he could pace and think at the same time. "You sure you're not a lawyer?"

Ernie scoffed at himself over my double talk and wiped his sweaty brow. This whole idea of practicing law again was very frightening for him, and he looked a mess. In thirty years before the bar, he had never presented to a Grand Jury. He seldom saw the inside of a courtroom.

I was worried too.

"She told us her father and Singer were a couple," I said. "But not now, the past. She also said her father died for love. That is the present, up-to-date part we have to go on."

"Stewart and Singer both married to the same woman? Two decades apart? I don't like it. Something is rotting in Denmark, my boy, besides the love thing. Follow the money, find the previous crime, catch the bad guy."

I agreed. Could this get any more complicated?

The phone rang, and Ernie handed the receiver to me. It was as if I were humming a show tune and turned on the radio to find it playing.

"Daddio?"

"What's up?"

"Singer isn't Singer," Cody said.

"What does that mean?"

"Mortuary back East opened the casket. The family, Singer's family, says the stiff isn't their son. Their son disappeared at least eight years ago, out West somewhere. Some cult or something. Prints are in the works now, trying to find out who the dead guy is."

I was stunned.

"Daddio?"

"Yeah?"

"You iced the wrong John Doe."

"I didn't do it."

"Yeah, like, whatever," Cody said. "What are we having for dinner?"

~

Agnes Singer made a statement to the Sheriff that the body she had identified, and Telluride Mortuary had placed in that casket, was the very same man she had married six years before. She only knew him as Robert Forrest Singer or "Sandy." They had met at a fundraiser for the Joffre Ballet at the Convention Hall in Mountain Village. He knew a *glissando* from an *entrechat*, and they got on famously. She did not know his family, except by reputation. The business the Singer family wallowed in was not sewing machines, but pharmaceuticals. Her husband had claimed the clan and he were permanently estranged. He had been disinherited. It happened in the best of families. She had seen no reason to doubt him. Until now.

The second sheet of paper I was purloining from my wife's briefcase, while she took the girls out to get a video movie to celebrate surviving my attempt at vegetarian lasagna, was the FBI report on the fingerprints. Three paragraphs of disclaimers and hedges on probable certainty led to the meat of the search. The sixty-five percent match had turned up a man arrested in 1974 in Arizona for running a bordello without a license out of the back of his gas station and auto repair shop. He pled guilty, paid a fine and was let go. The man's name was George B. Wilson. One of his aliases was "Sandy."

I sat down on the couch as I read the last paragraph. Wilson's partners, also charged, in running the illegal operation were Meyer Wolfscheim, Robert Forrest Singer, and a juvenile offender remanded to social services. The boys name had been purged from the record with a magic marker. In pencil above the black line was the name Walter Silva. The town was Sodoma. I got up, replaced the paper in my wife's file, and helped myself to a tumbler of Bushmills. What kind of rabbit hole had I fallen into? Who the hell was George "Sandy" Wilson? And why was he only now truly dead?

Thirty

It's My Middle Name

Ernie, my erudite corporate tax attorney, had talked with me at great length about the Grand Jury process. Having been through it all before, I gave him the lowdown on what to expect. He took notes.

My lawyer started to have an anxiety attack when I told him he had to make an opening argument, convincing the jury of my innocence and making bunkum of all the evidence against me. I was worried and was very careful to remind him that "premeditate" means to "plot, arrange, or plan in advance." When you add that word to murder in the State of Colorado it equals the death penalty. He took notes.

I shaved myself in the mirror of the barbershop with the straight edge razor. I was practicing to live dangerously.

"Cody is on to that other thing?" Ernie said.

"I guess. Boy, I don't even want to know who she cons to get that stuff off the Internet. It spooks me sometimes. Especially when it has all those warnings and consequences stamped all over it." My daughter's two favorite places are the semi-secure U. S. Justice Department public information databases and Raymond Chandler's Home Page.

"Best to look the other way and let her have her fun." Ernie said, "Kids will be kids." Ernie appreciated results, regardless of the means. Easy to be sage when it's not your child.

"Precisely," I said as I tempted fate with a last close scrape of my Adam's apple. Cody would get us what we needed on anything, even the moldy goods on Wilson's Auto and Bordello. We would pay, of course. Homage is a very dear and valuable commodity when extracted by children from fully-grown men.

"Stay away from all of these rich people, Wit. They will eat us for lunch if they have something over us," my lawyer said, as I wiped my face with a warm, moist towel from the steam caldron. I threw a twenty on the register for luck, promised to meet Ernie for lunch, and left.

Men of my temperament don't always take advice, even good advice. I had to give Miranda back her check, personally. I might look after Eric, but I would do it on my own time, for my own reasons. I hoped my lawyer, who advised me to take the money to pay for my growing legal bills, listened to me better than I listened to him.

The Mustang wouldn't start, a battery as flat as my prospects for acquittal. I let myself into my neighbor's garage and pulled out the beat-up electric battery charger, popped the hood, and turned on the juice. I walked up to Prospect and down three blocks on Aspen to the Lambis house. A white Mercedes was parked in the driveway at number 345. Miranda's red convertible was nowhere to be seen.

Clearing my throat and not giving myself any time to think about alternative plans, I knocked at the front door. To my surprise, Walter, the wayward husband and thug, opened up and backed away with a flourish of his arm.

"Come right in, Thorpe, make yourself at home."

I did, putting my hat back on, and noting again that this guy out-weighed me by twenty pounds of muscle. Forewarned is forearmed. If it came to a gouging match, I reminded myself to bite, scratch, knee the groin, and go for the eyes with my thumbs.

"You got balls, man. *Grande testiculos.*" Walter walked past me into the parlor and sat down in a high-backed recliner against the front windows. He put his legs up. An embroidered doily was a halo around his head.

"You got to hold some kind of record for pissing off the most people in a twenty-four hour period."

I looked around the corner into the kitchen to see if Eric or Miranda were waiting to pounce. The house felt empty. It was. When my attention came back to Walter, I decided I liked him even less than before. His attempt at sounding Tex-Mex galled me in particular. My brown face read "Spic" to him.

"I thought we needed a quiet time," Walter said making a steeple on his chest with his Bratwurst sized fingers as he watched my facial antics. "Get it all out there on the table. Maybe convince you that no one is going to line up and take the fall for your killing the old fart."

"I didn't do it."

"Now that's going to be a novel concept behind bars." Walter laughed goodheartedly. "Listen, Thorpe, you must have done Sandy. No one else had much to gain, or, for that matter, cared very much if the old queen lived or died. Why not let it go? Take what you got coming. Why you got such a hard-on for the rest of us?"

"Sandy who? Singer, maybe, maybe Sandy Wilson?"

"Does it matter?" Walter's voice was silk.

I had hoped it would matter. Obviously my hard won information on the body switcheroo didn't impress this guy.

"You gained," I said, "and Meyer and Miranda, and the rest who get the insurance money to seal the land deal."

He shrugged and smiled at me, letting me know I was a mile behind in a hundred yard dash to the end.

"Listen to me, Thorpe. This is a big fat deal. Don't try and spoil it just because you got caught. Let it be, man. It could be worth something to you, your kids, your wife, maybe."

"What?"

"*Dinero, hombre,*" Walter dropped his voice. "Big time *pesos, chico.*"

I crossed my arms and gave him another quizzical expression. I could get by in four local languages around the Four Corners area, including his elementary Spanish, but I was being obstinate. Walter's eyes lost their humor. I watched the darkness of violence sweep over his face. His jaw muscles clenched tight.

He reached inside the zipper of his leather jacket, jerked his hand out and pointed it in my direction. My brain yelled, "Gun!" I winced. My squinting eyes saw a folded check. I took it.

"More where that came from, buddy. Don't be an idiot."

"It's my middle name," I said.

"What?"

"Never mind," I said.

Walter then stood, smiling again, having accomplished his mission, turned and walked out of the front door without another word. He left the door open.

This check squashed the last recently established record for the most zeros to the left of the decimal point I had ever seen. I counted to six again. My name was stamped in clear blue ink on the pay-to-the-order-of line. I was tempted to rip it to shreds and leave it on the floor. Luckily, sanity returned, and I thought better of so rash an act. I tucked the money in the back pocket of my jeans and left.

Judge "Hang 'em High" Annie Cromwell presided over the Grand Jury that was being convened in the old courthouse on Colorado Avenue. The huge square whitewashed clock tower, visible from anywhere along the main street of Telluride, marked the historic stone and brick landmark.

Inside the classroom-sized courtroom, twelve of my peers were taking their seats on the folding chairs in the small jury box. The young ADA from neighboring San Juan County was arranging the stacks of files and affidavits on the polished mahogany of the prosecutor's desk.

Ernie sipped at a paper coffee cup while the public seats filled with all the usual suspects. The gang of inquisitive denizens of a small town who turn up to witness disasters, fires, high school graduations, and murder trials showed up, one-by-one..

My wife sat at the back near the door, her face absent any trace of emotion. When was the last time I saw her smile? Guilt grabbed me by the lapels and sat me down. This must be the feeling men get when they know they are going to die. I didn't, at this low ebb, even have the energy left to hope things might turn out okay.

We stood when Annie came in, decked out in her black robe. We waited while she gave the jury a swearing in and instructions on what they should listen for and what they should try to ignore. She thanked them in advance.

While this wasn't a full-fledged trial, a Grand Jury fields witnesses and hears arguments. My fate certainly rested in the hands of these twelve people. They would judge if the prosecution had enough evidence on me to go to trial. These folks would decide about reasonable doubt. I knew most of them. It didn't make me feel any more confident because I could put names with their faces. These people would bend over backwards to do the right thing. According to my daughter Cody the prevailing opinion on what the right thing was involved me doing hard time until she was grown up and married with grandkids of her own.

Ernie had on a shimmering fog gray Armani suit and shiny Italian black shoes. I was in faded blue jeans, a hand beaded belt, courtesy of my maternal grandmother, and a flannel cowboy shirt with faded and cracked polished pearl buttons partially hidden by a black leather vest. We both seem to have missed the mark on our choice of apparel. Our opposition at the prosecution table was in muted earth shades of corduroy with patches on his sport jacket elbows and a bright tie blazoned with smiling kids' faces.

The jury was calm, eager to get underway, staring straight ahead. No one was smiling. I fidgeted, knowing I must look guilty. It was a well worn habit. I hadn't been really innocent since I was seven.

"Mr. Sampesee."

"Yes, your honor."

"Is your client aware of the charges made against him, and are you prepared to proceed?"

"Yes, your honor."

The hearing began with the prosecution. Opening remarks took until lunch. Ernie took four minutes of that time; stating our belief that maybe I didn't do it. He apologized to the jury for wasting their time before he said it.

≈

Cody was trying to cheer me up.

"I hear they scagged all over you in court today."

"Scagged?"

"Like, totally wasted you."

"Not, well, totally."

"I heard the barber was lame."

"Ernie did okay." I was defensive.

"'All dare evidence is circumstant-eye-able,'" she mimicked Ernie's mannerism and speech pattern. "Like, no one has ever been convicted unless there was a witness?" She held her arms up in a pleading gesture.

"Were."

"What?'

"Never mind," I said knowing full well I had been scagged but good. Ernie wasn't up to it. I was a cooked goose. My lawyer's cheery advice at the end of the morning was that I could definitely file an appeal after I was convicted because I had been the victim of incompetent representation. He would testify on my behalf. I bought him a drink on the way home. We were a pair.

"I got something on the Wilson deal in Arizona." My daughter interrupted my thoughts.

"What's it gonna cost me?"

My daughter got up from her stool where we sat at our kitchen counter and gave me a big hug. I needed it. I was acting and sounding so damn pathetic. I gave the hug back.

"We'll talk about that later," she said with a bright smile, patting my hand as she resumed her seat. There is no such thing as a free hug. Good to know there are some constants in this topsy-turvy world. I loved her to death.

"Wilson had taken out a hundred thousand in life insurance eight months before he croaked. It was a lot back then, ten years ago this December, before I was even born." Her voice made the fact incredible. "The beneficiary on the policy was the Church of Compassionate Caring. Wolfscheim, Silverton, who was barely an adult and calling himself Silva, Lambis and Singer, who we now know was actually Wilson, all bought the canyon rim from starving cattle ranchers with the insurance money."

"And they began recruiting members to finance the development. Each conversion to the scheme built up the infrastructure, the number of sand traps, and the bottom line," I added the obvious, trying to prove I wasn't so dumb.

"Golfers," I finally spat out the word with more vehemence then I intended. Cody gave me the Look. Her body language told me to focus.

"They must have pawned Singer's body off as Wilson to get the loot, to build up a fortune, to dodge paying income and property taxes, and, finally, growing old and evil, covering up their greed and hatred of free grazing cows and open green space until now." Cody stopped to take a breath. "All this in order to frame you."

"Seems obvious to me." I finally smiled without humor, letting her make fun of me. What else can a dad on trial for murder do?

"To some twisted minds it could make sense," she said. "Our problem is finding a twisted mind on that Grand Jury."

We laughed. I needed that as much as the hug. I made toasted cheese sandwiches for a snack while we waited for Angelina, the caregiver, to bring Katie back from pre-pre-school. We discussed how to get those untracked, fertile minds on the jury to become twisted like us. It seemed my only hope.

"Don't worry," she said. "I'm writing it all down. It'll make a great story."

I gave her my best hairy eyeball. Was that such a good idea? Almost nothing I had done up until now was above board. I'd hate to have to answer for all my screw-ups while trying to get the evidence I needed. True confessions were some time way off in the future. The full story would probably add exponentially to my hundred plus years of jail time already in the works. If, I was lucky enough to get jail time.

"I even got an interview with Patsy Susie," Cody gave me an eyeball right back. "I told her she might just be named the fifth grade's Woman of the Year if she did good."

"How did she take it?"

"I was afraid for her heart." Cody smiled and raised her eyebrows. "I swear."

Thirty-one

Three Women In The Pool

I was back knocking on Miranda's door. The door cracked a sliver. I saw Eric's tousled blonde hair and a single bloodshot eye peering out at me. He groaned and tried to close the door. My foot was in the way.

"I've got to talk to you."

"No way," he said, quickly giving up on a shoving match and backed away from the door. I pushed into the narrow hallway and followed the skeleton of a retreating figure out into the kitchen. He turned, unsteady, with a hand for support on the table. He was stoned. Maybe more.

"So, I'm supposed to try and keep you alive."

He tried to focus eyes that looked like radishes in my general direction. He wasn't having much luck.

"Why does your sister think you need protection?" I said.

"She ain't my sister."

"No?"

"No. No fucking way, man. That would make me guilty of incest. I ain't guilty of nothing." The smile he gave was lopsided and cruel.

"I'll go for that."

"Fuck you," he said.

"Not likely."

"Oh, that's right, you're the homophobic one, the bigot red neck who won't go on tape and be exposed." Eric seemed to be enjoying this.

"Where were you the night of the murder?"

"Kidnapped by my half-sister," he said and tilted his head trying to look winsome. "Why?"

"Witnesses?"

"At least half a dozen leather clad motorcycle freaks." He slurred his words. "All probably with a hard on, anxious to cooperate with the authorities to see good old Sandy avenged."

"I'm sure," I said. "Who in particular would want to hurt you?"

"Only those I ask to." He winked.

"Asked anybody lately?"

"Not since Miranda, last night," he said cupping his testicles and giving them a firm grope. He laughed, but it wasn't funny.

"Wishful thinking?" I said with an edge in my voice.

Eric laughed again and narrowed his eyes at me. "She's got to you too, hasn't she." The laughter smacked off the thick ceiling coamings. "The little bitch just can't help herself. Trust me, she ain't all she's cracked up to be." He went hysterical for a few seconds, recovered, said, "cracked ...she ...her crack...Jesus."

"That right?" The haze in his mind cleared when he looked into the grim lines of my face. I clenched my teeth.

"You fucking dope. Can't you see she pussy whips every man she can?" His voice was rising, the laughter gone. "You're following her around like a lovesick bull." He made a mooing sound. He made it again.

I did what I do best. I was on him in a split second, backhanded his jaw, keeping contact, spinning him around. I had him in a full Nelson, the side of his head made a sharp smack as it hit the Formica of the 1950's style kitchen table. He groaned. His hips and ass ground backwards into my crotch. He groaned again in an enjoyable tone. I let go of him like a scalded cat.

"That's the way I like it, dark meat," he said to me with his face still on the table. "Rough and tumble." He wiggled his bottom at me again and patted it with both his hands.

"We had you all wrong," he said. "You know all the moves, *Chico*. Old Stu Lambis had a thing for handcuffs. I'm sure there are some around here if that's how you like it. You can always say you couldn't get away."

I didn't know what to say. Usually, when that happens I resort to beating someone up. The only good reason I could think of not to leave him busted up and bleeding would be that it would be too damn easy. And he might enjoy it. Instead, I tucked his sister's check in his back hip pocket, turned and left. I wasn't suddenly becoming a sensitive guy or, for heavens sake, a mature human. I was due back in court. It was almost two.

Minutes later, I was in the back room waiting to be brought out to the defense table by the bailiff. I scribbled down all the lightning crashing around in my head.

～

Fitzgerald was embarrassed as the cool water sloshed between them in soft, sucking sounds and her ass suggestively ground backwards into him. Sandy Gatz, Esq. watched from a lounge chair where he reclined with a martini glass held aloft. Two green olives rolled in the empty basin. The steady afternoon wind rippled the water of the pool and rustled loudly in the barrier of trees.

"Let me pour another," he spoke slowly, softly, not making a move towards accomplishing what he had announced. His eyes and Fitzgerald's locked. It made the writer uneasy.

Her eyes were half-closed and she writhed, pushing backwards until she had trapped Fitzgerald into the corner of the pool. She spread her arms to both sides and began swaying more sinuously as the water sloshed to a rhythm of music, possibly Latin, she heard in her head. He felt used.

The doorbell rang.

"The Woolseys," Gatz said.

"So soon," her voice cracked as she rode against Fitzgerald with sexual frustration and increased urgency. She made primal grunts under her breath.

"It's two, snookums."

"So soon," she said wistfully, stopping, hopping up out of the pool in a fluid motion, leaving her suddenly untrapped partner in a state of sexual arousal. The Woolseys came around through the side lawn, and introductions were made with Fitzgerald not leaving the water for obvious reasons. No one thought it the least bit strange. The party had simply begun again, for the fifth day in a row.

Ernie was watching the slow progression of prosecution witnesses and the court stenographer read depositions as if he were home in his barber's chair watching *People's Court* on television. I would say he was exhibiting dispassionate ease. It worried me.

I looked up from my legal pad, and the fictional predicament Fitzgerald had found himself in, and tried to pay attention to the witnesses. It was a long series of talking heads that pinpointed motive, opportunity, and means.

"That's all, your honor," the boyish ADA finally said, smiling shyly at the jury, apologizing in mime for making it so simple for them to reach a verdict. The last witness in his case was about to step down from the stand. It was the young woman from the bakery who had discovered the body in the trunk of the Mustang.

"Mr. Sampesee?"

Ernie stood up and walked quickly to the center of the open floor between our table and the Judge's bench. Every eye was on him. Startled by this flurry of activity from the defense table, a hush fell over the Jury and crowd. It was the first time he had spoken since his five sentence opening argument. He unbuttoned his suit coat with great deliberation. He extracted a pencil from his inside vest pocket and then tapped it into his open hand. The seconds dragged by.

"Could anyone else," he said, and then repeated it with his hands up in surrender on either side of his head, "any one else, but my client have done it?"

Ernie looked at the witness, the jury and then at the judge. He looked contrite and sorry when everyone in the courtroom remained silent, and the blurting confession he was hoping for did not come forward. The witness was too stunned to mutter a word. I started to make an objection, but held myself in check, barely. I wasn't even that much of an idiot. Someone behind me groaned.

"That's all I have for today your honor," Ernie said re-buttoning his suit, brushing it flat with both hands, and sitting down, visibly pleased with himself that he had pulled off such a coup. Imagine, questioning a witness in a murder case before a Grand Jury.

With a friend like this representing you, who needs enemies? I tried to file my roller coaster emotions as fodder for future writing.

~

Judge Annie had mercifully let us go at 4 p.m. No more damage to our defense strategy could be done today. Or that's what I foolishly thought. I was sitting at the New Sheridan Bar, nursing a headache and a glass of poor well scotch.

The chief reason for drinking is the desire to behave exactly how you feel and then be able to blame it on the alcohol. I felt as if it was me against the world. My attitude was lower than quail crap, and then the bottom dropped out.

"Hello Wit," she said sliding up onto the vacant bar stool to my right. People were avoiding sitting anywhere near me lately. Must be they felt being considered guilty of murder in the first degree was an impediment to lively bar conversation. I glanced at her, held my face from registering my confusion, and turned back to my drink.

"Are you and Ernie going to call any witnesses?"

"Not that I know of," I said.

"You might want to, you know."

"Advice from the other side?"

"If I have to watch you roll over and play dead anymore, I'll gag." My wife knew how to make me pay attention.

"Any ideas?" I said.

"Maybe the Sheriff's dispatcher working the night of the murder," she said, and gently waved away Digger's non-verbal offer of getting her a drink. He backed off as if she were royalty.

"Your point is?"

"The phone call from our house," she said. "If it wasn't you, and it wasn't me..."

"Bueller?"

"The call from Eagle's Lair was a male voice. 'Hurry, he's going to kill himself,' was all that was recorded. The Sheriff was notified immediately of the call by radio."

"Bueller called the Singer house from my bedroom?" I asked.

She stiffened. I guess she had hoped I wouldn't bring out the truth about her and the Sheriff until she wasn't around. Why was she getting an attitude? Wasn't I the cuckold?

"Just, check it out," she said and slipped out of the stool and walked away, out the door. I knew every eye in the place had watched and listened to the whole exchange and sided instinctively with my wife. I was left alone with my random, brutal thoughts. I couldn't even find a way in my head to silently thank her for the tip. If you're all set to suffer, nothing is going to get in the way, least of all, good advice.

$$\approx$$

"Hello Wit," she said sliding up onto the vacant bar stool to my left. I had barely stopped hyperventilating in repressed rage and self-pity from my last visitor.

"Hello," I said, grinding my teeth.

"Not going so well?" she said.

"What was your first clue?"

"The fact you haven't been returning my phone calls." She smiled and motioned Digger to re-fill my glass. She declined to join me.

"Haven't had much time to think about anything but this little trial thing," I said as the amber liquid swirled amidst new ice cubes. "Murder, you know."

"Don't be so maudlin. I could take your mind off the trial." Her voice was throaty and confident. The invitation was blatant.

"No doubt," I said feeling a shade uncomfortable. This woman seemed to enjoy going through life with her horn stuck on.

"I haven't asked you for my favor yet," she said, as the pocket on her short fashionable Range Coat chirped. She dug out the phone. "Patsy Susie here, how can I help?" She listened. Her voice was perky. Her eyes were dead.

"What do you mean they are short?"

Her teeth clenched

"Fuck the insurance company."

She meant it.

"I'll be right there," she said.

"Gotta run?" I said, trying to keep the hope out of my voice.

The real estate business had called its star, and she was gone with a look that could freeze a cobra and a bit of advice. I listened closely. When hope is hungry, everything feeds it.

"I'd be worried about Meyer Wolfscheim if I were you." she said. "He doesn't play fair. And he doesn't like his ex-wife today."

As she left, with that hip grinding sway, she drew the whole bar's attention. Her hands were pushing that natural wave back into her long blonde hair. I wondered what it would be like for a moment, and pulled myself back from the brink. I wasn't about to go there.

Why would I worry about the good doctor? Another church related murder in the making? My only job was to keep score.

≈

I was still pondering the possibilities when a third female in as many drinks joined me at the bar.

"Hello, Thorpe," she said sliding up onto the vacant bar stool to my right. The redheaded Miranda made the greeting sound like a death sentence.

I kept quiet.

"I don't like people who back out of deals with me. I don't like it one, little, bit." As a person who cultivates his own edginess on occasion, I could hear Miranda struggling to keep her voice low and even. Eric had obviously spread the news.

"Get used to disappointment," I said taking a teeth-shattering drink. I felt like a kid getting even. For what, I wasn't sure.

"You asshole."

"Precisely." I smiled.

"Did that mother of mine tell you the truth about Sandy not being the man I thought he was?"

"Indirectly."

"Make any sense?"

"Yeah, seems he was a brothel owner who switched bodies to collect an insurance policy. Funny thing is that he was listed as partners with your dad, your husband, and Wolfscheim on the land deal that started the Church in Sodoma. Is that gonna make it into your little documentary?"

"Hardly." Her voice sounded unsure.

"I'm gonna give it all up to the ADA just as soon as I find out who killed Sandy and probably made your father suck plastic," I said.

"My father killed himself. Simple as that sounds."

"Why would he kill himself?"

She waited.

"It wasn't for love, sweetheart," I said.

"You would know?"

"It couldn't be suicide," I said, "no way."

"Give it up Thorpe," she said smiling sweetly. "You haven't a clue about what's going on here."

"You're saying these two deaths should both be looked at as suicide? One suffocates and then handcuffs himself to a chair? And one shoots himself in the head and then loads himself into my trunk?"

"You are as dumb as a box of rocks," she said with the same sweet smile.

"Maybe," I said and ordered another drink.

"You need to get off those bizarre conspiracy theories if you want to get anything out of this. Plea bargain. Take the money. When they figure out it really was something else you'll be free and rich."

"So, I take the fall and wait for you to save me with your theory of the day. I don't think that gets me any closer to the truth."

"The simple truth," she said in a low voice, "is that they probably both really wanted to die. They were hopelessly caught up in something. They couldn't face what was coming at them from out of the past, and they wouldn't even tell me what it was."

"Maybe a hundred million smackers?" I said, acting as a humorless skeptic. She shrugged.

"A ten year old murder," I said.

"Yeah, probably," she said. "My father and Sandy were both pretty depressed."

"Enough to kill themselves?"

"They were very sensitive and private men."

"They were scam artists about to get caught. But that doesn't seem enough to off yourself over."

"Your theory stinks. It's too much of a coincidence to think someone was trying to kill them off before they could do it to themselves. I would bet a million dollars that my father wanted to commit suicide, and Sandy was also a bad day away from following suit."

"How about five million in dead men insurance that closes the big land deal?" I said.

"The money comes to the Church, suicides or not. They all had a "Key Man" insurance policy. All the trustees were vested. It just takes longer if suicide is the cause of death. The deal is made and recorded when the money is paid. Maybe it was my father's last brave act, all for the good of others?"

"And Sandy?"

"Still looks like you had an ax to grind, and you ground it."

"Something else is going on here besides me or settling old scores. Even the crime scenes match up. Both men got it off just before they died. I know it sounds crazy, but either both are suicides, or both are murders. But, I didn't do any of it."

"Got a light bulb going off, Thorpe?" she asked with a smirk. "Who else could it be but you?"

"Get a clue, Miranda." I was also getting angry. She wasn't helping. I needed answers, not speculations that confused the issues even more. Who was she to tell me what I know?

"Reality is what is, not what you want it to be," I said nursing my foul mood.

"Want a bit of advice?" she said.

"Seems to be in order today."

"Don't underestimate the power of all those big dollars," she said. "This deal will go through, over your dead carcass if need be. You got my word on it."

"I'll never see it coming," I said knowing she was right, but I don't like being threatened. I can't stop myself from doing something about it. I was building up for a venting. I should display a sign on my back: *Don't bring a bad attitude*. My teeth were clenched trying to choke it off.

"Why don't you want to help my brother stay alive?" She changed the subject and made it an accusation. "You got something against bi-sexual and gay members of our free society?"

"He ain't your brother," I said coldly, warning myself not to go any further. Yet, in my dark, ridiculous, anger at her, the world, everything, it was too good a set up to ignore. I went on. "If he really happened to be your brother, what you two do together would be incest, and it is punishable by jail time in most states, including Colorado."

She took a deep breath. It escaped in a steaming hiss. She stood, and when I looked up to see how much I had scored, she slapped me solidly along the left check. It was a roundhouse right, and her hand was in a fist. My bar stool teetered, my neck snapped, and I saw stars. It stung, a lot. She gathered herself, stomped her high heel sharply to reinsert her foot, and strode from the bar holding the numb fist tight against her flat abdomen with her other hand.

Attention was drawn a third time from all six of the bar's occupants. Miranda walked from the New Sheridan with a marked condescension, a stride oblivious of others, her mouth set in an unspoken sneer, a challenge to anything in her way. She vanished out the door. The bar let out a collective held breath. I suppose we all long for total self-confidence, until we look at someone who has it.

Digger took my glass away with an angry swipe. It was half full. I left the bar before I really got into trouble. I was still rubbing my jaw when I saw Ernie's window light on at the Barber Shop.

~

Ernie was reluctant to call a witness, a counter expert, a character witness, a friendly face, anything. We sat in his barber's shop discussing my defense. I was betting that he didn't know how to call a witness or anything else before a Grand Jury and was embarrassed to ask anyone. He was trying to explain in lay terms his end-game strategy.

"I was banking on you explaining away the whole thing," he said with a sage expression. "Like you did for me that time."

"But, Ernie, even you don't believe me."

"Not my job," he said. "The blind eyes of justice." He poked a victory "v" at his eyelids as his foot moved his barber chair back and forth on its swivel.

"Blind ain't gonna get me off the hook, Ernie."

"Can't help that. We put up the best defense we got. Gotta take the cards where they fall. It's jurisprudence." He was being fatalistic and grabbing his lapels like William Jennings Bryan. His first murder case. So, he goes 0 for one. I could see his mind working. I didn't like what I saw.

"Ernie, you're not giving me a lot here."

"Now you want a nursemaid?"

"It's my life on the line."

"Let me explain something to you, Wit. Once a thing happens it is no longer one thing. It's three things: itself, history, and God's will. You can't change that." Ernie sounded like a Baptist preacher measuring me for a pine box. He was not the religious type.

"But shouldn't we try to put some doubts in the Jury's mind?" I asked the question with a definite whine in my voice. "I got a feeling we are losing here."

"So, what can I say, you shouldn't have shot him." He stuck his chin out, finally getting defensive. "Simple as that."

"I didn't do it."

"Prove," he said, "it."

"Isn't that what we have been trying to do?"

"Smart boy," Ernie said. "But, my being a blind eye of justice, I can't help too much on your end. You're the detective. I'm the lawyer. Bring me the proof. I'll get you off."

Ernie had a point. Everyone had a point. The three crones at the bar, and now Falstaff were giving me some sort of strange cosmic sign. I had to fill in the blanks. Time was running out.

Thirty-two

A Business Gonnegtion

I read once that the first-rate mind is always curious, creative, original, and pessimistic. The last one was the only attribute I was feeling as I drove through Ski Ranches on my way to West Egg.

The people I seem to admire most are those I don't know very well. I admired Agnes Singer for her iron toughness, arrogance, plain talk, and for not caring about anybody else, especially her gang of ex-husbands. I decided to get to know her better in order to cure myself of that affliction. It was 9 p.m. at West Egg. I hadn't seen today's paper yet. That jolt still waited just over the horizon.

I was surprised the English maid led me from the front door right into the library without any strong-arming.

"What were you doing with your daughter's husband, Walter Silverton, in his room at the New Sheridan the night your own husband was murdered?" I asked to break the ice. The look I expected was the one I got, and it still chilled me to the marrow of my bones.

"You are a sick man."

"But, I'm not a killer."

"What difference does it make?" she said

"Who do you think shot your husband?"

"You," she said staring back hard into my eyes. "My dear boy, don't you think I would love to pin a murder on one of those parasitic leeches I am forced to call my family? If I could, I would. It isn't Walter. Wolfscheim hasn't the balls and was conveniently in Sodoma. Miranda was with her brother. End of story."

"Tell me about Eric."

"That poor boy was under the influence of those bikers. They don't let him out of their sight for a minute. If they did, I would stop paying them their ransom." She said in contempt. "That leaves only you."

I again commented to myself that the skin complexion of really rich people is totally different than that of the rest of us. It glows from within and seems to be made of an exotic new material not found elsewhere. Who wants skin that doesn't move when you talk? It's creepy.

"Ransom?"

"I pay the bikers ransom to keep him safe while he finds himself."

"I'd call it something else. A jailer's fee maybe?"

"Such a clever boy. As if it matters to you." She yawned. "Eric is a drug addict. The bike gang keeps him off heroin. Who are you to judge things? Get out."

"You know, lady, all your ex's have some big deal going on to buy the Valley Floor for their church?"

"You don't say." She smiled a Cheshire smile. She wasn't surprised by the news. Why was I the last to know everything?

"What do you know about it?" I was groveling for a clue.

"All I need to, dear boy." Her bearing was haughty. I wished I could think of something to say that would rattle her. I knew instinctively there was a long line of us waiting for the same thing.

"So you think you know all about it?" I said.

"Knowing all about everything those fools were up to has been my passion for many years. I know more about their little scheme than they do." She checked her ruby nails. "Even more than what's in the newspapers."

I gave her my sharpest stump look and she handed me the anemic daily paper. The headlines were "Murder To Save The Valley Floor" and "Thorpe Labeled Eco-Vigilante."

"What is this?"

"Looks like the whole story about Sandy and Lambis, Wolfscheim and the damn Church. You're a hero, smart boy. A Merry Prankster, a Monkey Wrencher, a 'live by your own law' cowboy."

"I ain't no damn cowboy," I said thumbing my Stetson around in a circle as it dangled between my knees. My tooled boots were muddy.

"Touchy, aren't we?" Agnes was being deliberately nasty. "You kill a deviant old man and suddenly you're the most popular criminal since Robin Hood. People are such cattle."

"It's going to happen, Agnes. The front door of your father's memorial house here is going to be an adult theme Disneyland. They've won. Your precious pastoral view is definitely history."

"One shouldn't stand in the way of progress," she said with a yawn, "especially if you are going to get even filthier rich by the outcome. But don't you worry; I'm running this show now. While plotting their revenge, the fools uncovered a great new take on the oldest profession, a sex business, a tax scam sex club, all legal and above board. Pure dumb luck on their parts, so I just took it away from them. Just like that." She snapped her fingers under my nose.

"Did you kill your husband?" I was flustered and confused by her handing me this new angle.

"I'm afraid you'll never know." She stood and pointed to the stairway. "Go."

"I'd watch your back, old woman." I launched back the only attack I could manage, playing the age card like a cheap trick. "You're sleeping with your daughter's husband; the guy's a criminal, a controlling partner in the action with agendas of his own. Miranda isn't happy about the relationship between you two, and she's good with a gun. People are dying all over the mountain, and no one seems to care. A business deal is going down worth mega millions a year, and I'm determined to find the killer and the whole damn story with or without your consent." I stood up.

"Get out," she said.

"If you think you know what Miranda, or your main squeeze, Walter, or even your boy Eric, are possibly capable of, I've got news for you lady: You don't," I said and strode towards the huge main door. "You got no clue. Somebody you know is capable of murder."

"And vice versa, dear heart, vice versa."

Her voice was shrapnel as the English maid closed the door to West Egg with a condescending, "tah."

≈

I drove up on the mountain and kept climbing towards Alta Lakes and Prospect Bowl in the dark until I found the house in Ski Ranches from whose portals I had snatched Eric. I pulled down into the patio driveway. The front door opened almost immediately, and the huge motorcycle enforcer named Tiny was framed in the bright doorway in a "wife beater" undershirt, exposed tattoos, and a fully functioning shoulder holster. I sat in the car, the engine idling loudly. Tiny yelled something over his shoulder.

Meyer Wolfscheim scuttled under Tiny's arm that was holding the door open. The bowling ball shaped figure shoved the hips of the towering man out of the way. He waved for me to come in. I figured in for a penny, in for a pound, and got out of the car.

Tiny towered behind me as I followed the church leader into the vast sunken living room of the house. A fire was roaring in the river rock fireplace that stretched thirty feet to the vaulted ceiling. The varnished wainscoting overhead shone like veins of gold in the flickering light.

"I understand you're looking for a business 'gonnegtion'?"

"Pardon me?" I said.

"I beg your pardon," said Mr. Wolfscheim, "I had a wrong man."

"Excuse me?" I was very slow on the uptake and by the time I realized he was quoting from his fictional namesake in *The Great Gatsby*, it was almost better to be stupid than slow. I changed the subject. "Do you mind if I ask you a few questions?"

"He turned around in the door and says: 'Don't let the waiter take away my coffee.' Then he went out on the sidewalk, and they shot him three times in his full belly and drove away."

"Enough with *The Great Gatsby* already," I said, "I just got done talking with your ex-wife. She wanted me to tell you that the last alimony check was late."

"My dear boy," Meyer said, "I look at the paying of alimony like feeding of hay to a dead horse. She'll get hers when the time comes." It sounded a double threat.

"I have these questions."

"You want to know who did it."

My heart leapt. I sat down in the plush armchair facing his. My face was an expectant flush.

"Nick Caraway," Wolfscheim said. "He was a god damn snotty nosed, anti-Semitic little prick from nowhere out west of Chicago. What right had he to play with other people's stories? Other people's names?" He straightened up trying to contain his anger.

"Asshole," he said, and finally let it go. His pale eyes re-focusing on me. I got to the point because he wasn't about to.

"Did you kill Singer?" I ask.

"Whoa, hoss," Meyer said with a nervous cough, sitting up and re-arranging himself in his chair. His feet couldn't touch the floor and stuck out slightly forward like a pudgy eight-year-old.

"You got a problem with answering that?"

"I don't kill people."

"Anymore," I said. He looked up, startled, I winked.

"What?" A nervous edge had replaced the soothing public tones of his practiced delivery.

"Does the name George P. Wilson mean anything to you? Sandy?" I felt Tiny's huge mitt grip my shoulder. The truth always hurts. It usually always hurts me.

"Who? What?""

"A brothel owner, alias of Sandy, wanted for insurance fraud." I quickly hammered the message home.

"How…"

"Right," I said. "How are you going to get the money for your big deal if the insurance will be tied up for years in the cases of a suicide and an unsolved murder?"

"Get out of here." Wolfscheim's face had screwed itself up into a real puss. Blood vessels throbbed in his forehead. "Blood sucking little…"

It was over just like that. Charm had exited the building with the flick of a light switch. I was jerked to my feet and led with a stiff arm the twenty feet to the door. It slammed shut behind me. I sat down in my car and thought about what I had just learned. Not much. Wolfscheim was certainly a fan of F. Scott Fitzgerald. Why that peculiar coincidence? What had he told me about my sorry case with his reaction to the news that I knew about Wilson? Did it make any sense?

Nothing he said made any sense. Nick Caraway, the fictitious narrator in *The Great Gatsby* did it? Did what? The questions kept piling up and I wrote them all down, without an answer in sight.

≈

Cody was still waiting up when I got home from my encounters up-mountain. I told her what had happened in my day. All except the part where Agnes had made me scared. I knew she guessed it anyway. Miranda's punch wasn't mentioned either. I had made it a point to compliment Tiny on his having smelled much better than the first time we had met. I didn't want to always be so negative.

"Nice article in the paper," I said.

"They changed most of it," she said with a sigh. "I certainly didn't make you the hero executioner of Telluride. You got a big enough ego as it is."

"I didn't murder anyone."

"Do you really buy the double suicide thing?" she said.

"I don't see the prosecution folding their tents and going home if I simply mention it."

Cody stared at me without a reaction.

"Lambis handcuffed himself to his chair and Wilson, neigh Singer, plopped himself dead in my trunk because they were both going to get filthy rich?"

Sarcasm is so hard to get right. I didn't even try. "Golly, I'd like to go with the theory, but, gee honey, a ton of physical and psychic evidence says otherwise."

Cody said, "You're always telling me to take a tough question apart. Break it down. You got to take this one down right to the bones. Put it back together in a different way to help understand things. Right?"

"Maybe." I was struggling to keep positive.

"Something else pretty weird is going on," she said in a whisper as we sat together eating Oreo's on the couch. She was a twist, separate, and licker; I was a divide and scrap man who devoured the filling first.

"Weird? You mean like your father being the target of a murder trial, or his being afraid of rich older women, or maybe having fictional characters turning up in his real life?" I asked.

"No, like, Mom's going crazy."

"What?"

"She's being totally forgetful. Leaving important notes on your case and files all over the place. She's making it too easy for me to get everything you need. It's like, duh, here, take this surprise piece of incriminating evidence. I'm almost embarrassed enough to cut my fees."

"Really?"

"No, not really."

I waited. She had something else to say.

"What's going on?" She prompted me. "What's happening?"

"Maybe she hopes I'll prove myself innocent?" I said softly, trying to make it sound true. My throat went scratchy, my eyes stung a bit.

"Sharp as a stump, Sherlock." My daughter kissed my forehead with a sticky white frosting kiss and headed off to bed.

"Can I wear the cow costume tomorrow?" she said over her shoulder. The cow costume was a prop from an old ski patrol comedy event as part of the AIDS Benefit weekend. I hammed it up in black and white dots for years.

"How come?"

"Big rally on the court steps in the morning."

"Rally?" I said.

"Half the town is going to be there to support our own number one celebrity. You are the 'Save the Cows Vigilante.' I swear. 'Night."

I smiled. She had to be joking. Thinking about that would make me nervous. The first comment about her mother doing what she could to help kept me smiling, and was the single best news I had received in weeks. Cody didn't even charge me for it. I smiled, and added, at least not yet.

Despair is anger plus paranoia with no place to go. I had a hard time sleeping. I lay awake going over the players in my head. It was all very murky. No matter how I sliced things, it seems everybody involved knew more about what was going on than I did.

I tried to think what someone like Sam Spade would do in a situation like this. I wasn't having any blinding insights. When "Sandy" Singer/Wilson was shot, Agnes and Walter were probably doing the hanky-panky in the sack; Miranda was having a chat with her brother; Meyer was still in Sodoma at a seminar. It all sounded solid, except no one outside of the Agnes Singer's ex-family club could vouch that any of it was true.

Why had Singer called police and claimed he was ready to commit suicide? Wouldn't the whole scam to get the money for the Valley Floor work better if he made his suicide look like a murder? Or, if you were not Sandy and out to kill your insured partners, why would you let anything in the murder look like a suicide?

I was getting a headache, and I hadn't even got to the tough questions. Why had Bueller made the phone call to West Egg from my house? Why did my wife think it was so important to find out about that call? Pillow talk between her and the Sheriff? I clenched my teeth to put that thought away. It didn't go away easy. It is almost impossible to stop the poison of jealousy from entering your system. My mind seldom bounces back from the intrusion of a self-demeaning thought.

I got up, went to the kitchen counter to get away from those thoughts and wrote. I was angry and confused and fighting to hold in check my deep and growing certainty that I was going to be rotting in jail for a long time.

≈

When Fat Louis Armstrong's drummer fell into the pool after tripping over the small dog that was allowed to run between the guest's legs by Sandy Gatz's mistress, the party was already well along. The hyperactive little dog had been a drunken present from Gatz to her when he had shown up late for their afternoon soiree on Wednesday. A slightly drunken Fitzgerald had been in tow on the late train back from New York City. It wasn't until later in the party that the nasty little dog took a dunking herself.

Gatz's arrogant eyes roamed the crowd.

"Perhaps you know that lady," Gatz said to Fitzgerald who sat next to him on one of the two cabana chairs at pool side watching through an alcohol haze the hundred or so people mill about the house and its grounds. In the green shadows under the trees figures posed and trolled. The host's hand extended towards a woman sitting alone under a white-plum tree.

Fitzgerald would later remember he "stared with that peculiar unreal feeling that accompanies the recognition of a hitherto ghostly celebrity of the movies."

"She's lovely."

"The man bending over her is her director and her lover."

"You don't say."

"But I do, I do say, chappie." Gatz's voice was cold. His eyes watched his mistress Myrtle flit from group to group, using the dog chasing bit to get over that pregnant shock of first encounter with everyone here. She was flashy and cheap, big busted and thin hipped; her social skills fractured. Her voice was a ghastly shriek. She dominated the scene. Gatz seemed to enjoy the conflict and revulsion she brought out in people.

Two young women had taken off their summer dresses and were swimming languidly in bras and low slung support garters in the cool olive waters of the pool. Fitzgerald watched them listlessly, their heads bobbing and arms paddling. He was well towards being drunk. He resented them their easy shedding of social mores, watching their faces for clues to what kind of creatures they really were.

His "Daisy" caught his eyes as she walked from the house. She wore only a vaporous white silk shift that hung from her shoulders on string thongs and stopped at mid-thigh. Her violet nipples pressed their tiny buds through the translucent fabric. She wore nothing underneath. Conversations ceased, whispers were Adders, as she walked past the clusters of mesmerized onlookers on her way to the pool.

It was a moment they had all waited for. Even Myrtle, who gave no one a second glance, pushed forward to watch. The redhead swam every afternoon. It was why the parties started so early.

She stood at the pool's edge. Her eyes looking across the water to where Gatz and Fitzgerald were reclining. She waited. The two women, reacting to the growing silence of over a hundred people, scrambled from the pool, snatching up their piles of clothes like thieves. The wind blew, pressing the flowing folds of the silk against her skin, and a gasp was heard from more than one open mouth as the rib cage below her uplifted breast became almost visible.

Her arms finally crossed as they slid down her stomach and gripped the tailing edges of the garment, lifted it clean over her head in one feral moment. The body exposed was nothing short of perfection. She raised her hands above her shoulders, and her legs spread slightly, falling open naturally, as she dove into the water, a brief glimpse of bright red hair amidst milk white skin. People, mostly men, and a few brave feminists, applauded.

Fitzgerald staggered under the blow as her hands parted the water, and the glimpse was gone. Sweet death pervaded his nostrils. The smells of climax. The world stopped, and every detail was frozen in a caricature within the blink of a writer's eye. This was indeed the spoiled edge of things.

F. Scott Fitzgerald knew with a ghastly certainty that he had been looking for this place his whole life.

Thirty-three

A Tongue In The Dark

I dropped Cody off fifteen minutes early. I was adamant about not letting her skip school to rally at the courthouse. Also, I was thinking, I didn't want my daughter to be the only one there. I was embarrassed enough by all this. What if those damn spoiled cows couldn't even draw people over to my side?

I had to be at court by eight. As I turned out onto Colorado Avenue, I spotted a car leaving a space right in front of the courthouse. This was my lucky day. I remember thinking that very hopeful thought before I noticed that it was a white Mercedes and a squat figure, which could only be Meyer Wolfscheim sitting behind the wheel. The car stopped dead, half in and half out of the space.

On the steps of the courthouse were a herd of black and white spotted costumes. My stomach clenched. What the hell was this? I stopped behind the soon to be empty space with my blinker on and stared. Maybe thirty people were holding forth. Half were in full bovine regalia, including horns, and a few carried signs. "Stop the Vestal Virgins, Vigilantes For Open Space, Save the Cows" were the general themes.

"Free Wit," was being chanted. Rasta Joey and Digger were leading the chorus. Ed was in Bovine black and whites and already weaving drunk. The rubber teats swaying over his stomach. "Free Wit," sounded ominous, like thunder over a high ridge line, coming from this odd assembly of fanatic and practiced malcontents.

Beyond the white car in my way, the tall lanky figure of Eric Wolfscheim was crossing the extravagantly wide 19th century street. The scarecrow-like witness had already cleared the two lanes of east bound 15 mph traffic and was walking out from behind a Fed Ex delivery truck parked on the median to continue his awkward meander to the courthouse. His walk was all chicken wings and toe scrapping. Stoned was the very next thought I had.

"Wait until his short circuited mind registers the hallucination of the protesting cows," I thought aloud. "He'll freak."

Meyer accelerated quickly, tires squealing, aiming three tons of European metal straight for his son. A loud scream from a young woman leaving the court house, heard above my offending muffler, woke Eric from his stupor and he stumbled back just in time to disappear behind the rear end of the chocolate brown Fed Ex delivery van.

The white Mercedes tried to slide into the place where Eric had been, smashing the left rear panel of the sedan into the wrap-around extension to the truck's bumper. The crunch was loud and blended quickly into the squealing of tires as the rear wheel drive Mercedes spun across the four open lanes in a wide arcing power slide to turn the car back towards the spot where Eric was sprawled flat on the black macadam of the road.

Without thinking of anything except stopping bloodshed, I jammed the gas pedal to the floor. The Mustang was never a quick mover, and I wondered if I was going to arrive a few yards too late. Luckily for Eric, the Mercedes side-swiped a parked Toyota Land Cruiser as it reached the end of its spin and Meyer paused to pull himself up erect behind the wheel in order to see over the hood and circular ornament to locate his son lying in the road.

I barely missed Eric's outstretched legs as I pulled sharply around the back of the Fed Ex truck and lined up the Mercedes emblem on my hood. The impact of the two charging cars sounded like lightning on a mountaintop.

My chest dislodged the top half of the Ford's steering wheel, snapping the charging horse logo in half, and my head slammed with a thud against the windshield. I should have buckled up. My left arm went numb, and I knew I had probably dislocated my shoulder again. The car still idled and rocked as the engine skipped. Steam hissed from broken radiators.

Even knocked senseless, I noticed that the Mercedes somehow managed to get in gear and back away from my inert car, the white hood crumbled up so badly I couldn't see the short driver; a front fender hung down to the road, scrapping along on the driver's side.

All I could think of was that he was getting away. I pushed down on the gas pedal, aching from every bone in my body, and the Mustang lurched forward, the right wheel wobbling badly. I couldn't raise my left arm and I sawed frantically with the right one on the half-broken steering wheel. It was painful work to keep the car on the wide road.

The speed limit is 15 mph, but, by the time I saw the white Mercedes again, as I passed the High School roundabout and headed out along the Valley Floor, we were both doing sixty, and the wheel on the Mustang was vibrating less as the wind whipped at my face from the dislodged windshield. The spreading web of cracks was shutting down my visibility. Tears ran from my eyes. I tried to treat these last developments as good news. I wasted time hoping that the wobbling wheel wasn't about to just fly off, and that I wasn't hurt all that bad.

The Mercedes was still putting distance between us. He disappeared out of sight over the slight rise and sweeping curve at Hillside. I plugged along, and by the time I limped into the intersection at Society Turn I could see, even through the opaque windshield, the black smoke and ball of flame down the road, billowing in a puffball cloud over the rise just ahead.

The right side of the mountain road heading down valley was vertical cut rock, and a fifty-foot long black line of automobile scrapping at eye level was just now flickering out with the last bit of gasoline driven flames. The car must have caught fire, slammed into the rock cliff and then careened over the edge. The guardrail on the other side of the road fifty yards ahead was split open, and the four hundred foot drop into the Illium Valley lay beyond. Smoke, black and oily, rose up from below my line of sight. I pulled over and managed to get out of the car feeling woozy, my legs about to give way.

Staring at the burning white Mercedes halfway down the slope I felt a twinge of regret. Did Meyer Wolfscheim deserve to die? I didn't know for sure. Who could ever know for sure? I put my first gut reaction down to the sad fact that the world had one less F. Scott Fitzgerald fan in it.

My car suddenly wheezed, coughed and died for once and all in a blue haze of bubbling antifreeze. The second Sheriff on the scene took me to the clinic for some bandages and a sling. Judge Annie had postponed the trial until after lunch when I had failed to show up at the courthouse on time. I had summarily forfeited my right to bail, and become involved in yet another violent death. Where was the being innocent until proven guilty part in all of that?

≈

"My witness at the Zia Sun has it that you sideswiped the kid and tried to kill his father by smashing into him head-on with your piece of shit Ford," Sheriff Bueller said as I sat on a wheeled gurney in a curtained cubicle at the Telluride's Clinic emergency room.

"It wasn't like that," I said, feeling the insult to my dead Mustang a shade callous. I knew it was certainly no time to be telling the truth. I tugged at the webbed, full elbow sling on my left arm, and hummed the "Battle Hymn of the Republic." The painkillers were already kicking in.

"You expect us to believe the hero bit you've been trying to feed the ADA? You been reading too much of your own press, Bucko."

"It's what happened," I said. "Find the screaming woman in the cow suit. Ask Eric Wolfscheim. A dozen people must have seen what happened."

"There ain't no screaming woman, dipshit, and those cows on the steps scattered like dried up turds in a twister at the first sign of trouble. You had better tell those dressed up freaks of yours that I don't want them back at the courthouse, never."

"You're udderly ridiculous," I said under my breath and smugged appropriately.

"Another church guy is dead. What have you got against these people, Thorpe? The national media is picking it up as a hate crime thing. You're gonna' be famous for all the wrong reasons."

"Don't you get it that all three of these deaths are connected, and it isn't about salvation?"

"Yeah, all connected by you, Thorpe," Bueller said, "you're all over each of the dead guys. Your gonna' fit right in with the social life in prison. Give it up, why don't ya? You're wife might not ask for the death sentence."

"I didn't do any of it."

"All I got to do is nail you for Singer. The rest just muddies up the water. I got you good, Bucko."

I was unlikely to make my point with this guy. At that moment, I didn't have a plan B. My mind was drifting away, and I appreciated the fact that I didn't hurt all over.

"Young Wolfscheim is sedated. I'll get him to issue the charge against you as soon as I can. I hear he's recovering with his sister. You know the one," Bueller sniggered. "I hear she decked you again at the Sheridan. Zero for two with the little lady. You just can't seem to keep a woman happy. "

"Fuck you."

"Tsk, tsk, ladies man, I get to throw you in jail as soon as we're done here. Judge's orders." Bueller smiled with pleasure. He took out his handcuffs, jangled them in my face, and eyed the sling.

"Just give me the cuffs. I'll do it."

Bueller dropped them into my open palm.

"Can I wait till we're done here?" The doctor on call had gone to see about getting me discharged. I still had to struggle into my shirt.

"Be my guest," he said, looking down at his belt-clipped beeper. "I got to make a call." He walked around the corner and out of sight.

I stared at the manacles. Bracelets were going to be part of my life for a long time. The cuffs in my hand were the final nudge over the edge into a snap decision and a call to action. Plan B was spontaneously stupid, but it was all I had.

Shuffling like an eighty-year-old speed walker, I left the cold comfort of the gurney. I had struggled all last night taking apart the crime scenes, looking for questions. The biggest one staring me in the face was my only hope to turn this case around. Did Lambis or Sandy kill himself? I let myself out the employee's entrance into the bright sunshine. My hat was down, the brim hid my face. I got my good arm in a sleeve and was buttoning the sling awkwardly inside the shirt as I forced myself to walk quickly up the crowded sidewalk towards Colorado Avenue. I was on a straight line mission and ignoring that fact, I was less than incognito.

I got to the Telluride Savings and Loan after having everyone I met on the street for eight blocks stop walking and stare after me. The wake of gawkers in my passing was twenty yards long. A few clapped and said, "Way to go Wit." They were usually the ones with their pants hanging off their asses exposing their underwear for the sake of fashion. I had taken one detour to ACE Hardware and bought a roll of gray duct tape. I had the clerk put it into a thin plastic shopping bag and on my tab.

Only one elderly male customer was at a teller's window and the rest of the female staff were clustered around a desk at the far corner of the bank. I took a hard right just inside the doors and went straight towards Stewart Lambis' office. I heard someone call loudly from across the room as I shouldered the door to the office open. I locked the door behind me and dropped the louvered shades and spun the shutters closed on both the door and the full view windows.

I had made up my mind. Off the deep end was where I was heading. I couldn't pause to think, or it wouldn't happen and then, I was a cooked goose. I sat quickly in the chair behind the desk. Nothing had been disturbed since they removed Lambis' body and probably wouldn't be until after the Grand Jury had made their decision. I grabbed one of the remaining cows from the desk and placed it in my lap. I took the tape from the bag and managed to use my fingers to start the roll. I placed the plastic bag over my head. I dug my finger through the thin plastic and into my mouth to tear out a good sized breathing hole. Sharp pounding hit the frame and glass of the locked door. The shades rattled.

It was hard with one hand, but I managed to get the tape started, and by bending forward in the chair, tried to duplicate the wrapped turban Stewart Lambis had on his head. Around and around, I was careful to leave the breathing hole clear. I did the best I could, and with the final wraps, I couldn't see anything at all, totally black. The sounds of the bank clerks at the door were muted and distant. I was breathing hard and the torn plastic ends rattled loudly as my mouth sucked in the thin air through my parted teeth.

I pulled the Sheriff's cuffs from my pocket grabbed the cow in my slung hand, slotted on a handcuff, tore the Velcro free, and pulled my arm out of the restraint. It was like electric eels running down my entire left side as I let the almost useless arm fall back behind me. I grabbed the dangling cuff with my good hand and pulled it through the wrought iron swivel frame at the base of the chair, duplicating exactly how Stewart Lambis had been found. I transferred the cow to my numb hand and cuffed myself into a no-escape position.

Something had kept bothering me about Lambis' death. All the pieces just didn't fit together. I didn't have new pieces; I just wanted to find the answer to the one big question. Could Lambis have done this to himself? I couldn't think of any other way to get inside Lambis' head. My own breath rattled the plastic bag.

My plan was to pull this stunt and get my theory in front of the jury and the whole town that these two crimes really could be suicide. Either they were both suicides, or they were both done by the same killer. How else was it going to happen? My lawyer wouldn't even call a witness. Desperation brings foolish choices and self-destructive behavior.

In the dark, in pain, I finally felt like my namesake, a complete and total idiot. What the hell was I doing? This was going to prove nothing and no divine insights were coming. I tugged on the cuffs and the pain was awful. I did it again beginning to feel the first warning bugles of what could only be claustrophobia.

My shoulder cramped, and the cow fell to the floor. I knew it had fallen in the exact same place as before, just as Lambis let his life slip away. I know what his last thought was. He had probably at the very last had only thought himself as stupid. The dice rolled twice. I was spooked. My heart rate accelerated rapidly.

"Help," I said with a deep breath.

I then heard a sharp click that penetrated the wrapped plastic and duct tape. The rear door to Stewart's office opened. I could feel the rush of cool mountain air from the alleyway beyond. This was beginning to feel like the other end of my particular rabbit hole.

"Hurry up," I said to my rescuer. "This is getting real old." I tried to sound calmer than I was.

Instead of cutting away the head wrappings, the person came and spun the swivel chair around with a sharp force, and I almost blacked out as the hyper-extension of my injured shoulder and arm stopped the momentum of the seat, dead.

"What the f..." I was stopped in mid-expletive as the person in the room roughly straddled my legs, stuck a tongue through my breathing hole and pressed my head back into the seat. The tongue swirled and mated with mine in sticky, wet saliva. The lips and membranes of the open, greedy mouth slid on the plastic entrails of the shredded opening. I was beginning to panic. I couldn't breathe. I thought better of trying to bite the flesh in my mouth. In a flick of a second, the tongue was gone. I bucked in the seat; the intruder rode me like a snakeskin. The lips remaining locked to mine. I needed to breathe. My nose sucked the plastic into my nostrils and scared the hell out of me. I tried to twist my head but the mouth was agile and kept pace with every twist. I felt the warning bells of unconsciousness.

Suddenly the pressure on my mouth was gone. Gasping, I heard the distinctive rip and tear from the roll of duct tape. I took a deep breath trying to fill my lungs as panic ripped through me and the new tape closed off my only air hole. I strained against the cuffs. They dug into my wrists as I tried to scream. The air trickled out my nostrils and rattled the plastic. I grunted in fear. I realized I was going to die in under sixty seconds, and the tinges of the blackout began to wash in from the edges of oblivion.

Then without warning, hands were all over me, tearing at the tape pulling my head roughly in every direction. I gasped for the sweet free air, wretched and gagged a bit of phlegm towards my lap, coming up short against the handcuffs. My knees came up as I doubled over in paroxysms. Hands slapped at my back as someone pulled free the last snagged bits of the plastic and tape from my hair. I couldn't tell them to stop. I couldn't catch my breath from the pounding. Life isn't fair.

≈

Bueller was a jackass once again. He felt he had the right to treat me like a criminal when I had just handed him the entire case on a platter. He yanked me this way and that with my hurt shoulder making sure everyone could see he was in charge as we departed the bank. Lucky for him, I was still cuffed behind my back. I was trying to keep from having tears of pain roll down my cheeks. My shirt hung from my tethered hands, the sling from my bare neck. I was a sorry looking wreck.

"Thorpe, you capped a load this time. Do you want to confess to also killing the banker for the record or just let your attempted suicide speak for you?"

"I wasn't trying to kill myself, but he did."

"Didn't look that way to the folks who found you alone, choking to death, and handcuffed in a locked room."

"I left a place to breathe."

"Like you were saying."

"I didn't try to kill myself."

"Tell it to the shrink," the Sheriff said. "I sure as hell hope you aren't trying to plead insanity to avoid the death penalty. The whole town would probably support the fact you are a certifiable loony. But it's a little late, Bucko. Lets go."

Nellie, the newspaper photographer, asked Sheriff Bueller to pose with his catch and snapped a whole roll. Another Deputy Sheriff was videotaping the entire arrest. It was a parade, the four Sheriff's Department Broncos with lights flashing, all proceeding at 15 miles an hour on their way out to the jail.

$\approx$

"What kind of fool stunt was that?" The Assistant District Attorney, who happened to be my wife, slapped me as soon as we walked into the intake room. It was the same area that was still recovering from Miranda's fist. I rotated the jaw painfully to make sure I still could.

Bueller took the lead to manhandle me into a chair. My wife looked like she was going to slap me again.

"You could have killed yourself," she said. "Twice in the same damn day."

"That's my point." I thought I managed to pronounce every syllable, but I couldn't be sure. "It was just the way Lambis did it, but he could have saved himself. It wasn't suicide. He was killed by the same person who tried to murder me. Even the cow landed right."

"Bullshit," said Bueller.

"Listen, you moron, I don't think building a murder defense that claims another ongoing homicide Investigation was a suicide, so your own murder charge must have also been a suicide is going to fly. This kind of fantasy at the last minute is not going to win you a lot of support with the jury." She collected herself, barely. "Why the hell is Wolfscheim dead?"

"I guess," trying to pick my words and be tactfully truthful, "he might have reacted to something I might have said, about something I thought I knew, last night at his house in Ski Ranches."

"What did you 'might have' said about something?" she asked.

"I told him I thought he and his partners had probably murdered the real Singer maybe ten years ago and switched his body for Sandy Wilson's insurance money. The body was cremated in Las Vegas where the death occurred."

"How do you know that?" Bueller butted in, indignant.

"I saw Agnes Singer last night too," I said. My wife and I traded stares. I finally looked away.

"A social little butterfly." Bueller said. "That's against court orders. We'll tag another five years on for that."

"Why would Meyer want to run over his son?" my wife said.

"I think Eric had been blackmailing all three of them for a while about Singer or Wilson. I let the cat out of the bag that he had blabbed."

"But he didn't blab," she said.

"Right."

"So now Meyer Wolfscheim is dead too, so we'll never know the whole story.

"It's what happened. What can I say?"

"Something that's a little more plausible," she said.

"Answering for that decade-old crime could have been a pretty heavy factor in each of their deaths," I said.

"Because Miranda Sterling says so?" the ADA said. Her hands were on her hips, back in her no nonsense stance. "You're pathetic."

My wife was in a state she calls exasperated. "The damn horse is dead, get the hell off." She mocked me.

"I got tongued." You could have heard a gnat fart in the silence of the interrogation room.

"You what?" She gave me the Look while rocking back on her heels.

"The one who tried to kill me, also stuck a tongue in my mouth," I said quickly, before I refused to admit it.

My wife continued to stare at me as if I were offal.

"Whoever," I said, blushing, "they kept it in there until I almost passed out. Then they put the last bit of tape over my mouth and left through the alleyway."

"And you don't know who it was?" Her voice was a whisper.

"Please." I pleaded with her.

"This pornographic fantasy world you're living in is not healthy, Wit." My wife stated the obvious.

"What can I say?" I said. "It happened."

"So who was it?" Bueller asked with skepticism dripping from his berry colored lips. "A man, a woman, what?"

I hesitated. I didn't know. I couldn't say. My head shook left to right.

"You're sicker than I thought, little fella." Bueller picked up on the hesitation, and then said, looking over at my wife, "You might just get that insanity plea yet, Wit. I'll do all I can to help you out. Believe you me. You need help. As long as they put you away for the rest of your damn life."

My wife turned her back on me.

"Anyhow, little brother, rest assured I'm also working a vehicular homicide case against you for Wolfscheim," said Bueller, "and Lambis, however he died, has now got your name all over it again, too. I got you every way but Sunday."

"Give it a rest," my wife said to Bueller softly, glared at me again and walked out.

He laughed and left the room on the heels of my wife. I was still handcuffed. I tried getting used to it.

Thirty-four

The Spoiled Edge of Things

The Grand Jury was reconvened at 2 p.m. I took a pasting, along with a few snide comments, from Judge Annie and managed to keep my mouth shut. The fact that one of the witnesses to be called in the proceedings was now deceased and in route to the Medical Examiner's Office and morgue in Montrose was not lost on the members of the jury. The whole town was on fire with the latest in a trail of dead bodies associated with me and the Church of Compassionate Caring.

"Another suicide?" Ernie said. Skepticism seemed the order of the day.

"How the hell should I know? It looked like attempted murder to me." I was testy. He hadn't come to visit me in the jail over lunch. He picked his teeth with a peppermint-flavored toothpick while my stomach growled.

I was sporting my arm sling with a flannel shirt drape. My spiked hair still had sticky threads of gray glue from the duct tape sticking to the most pointed parts. I was pretty beat up and woozy from the codeine, and my eyes must look like the devil's. I vowed to keep them closed for the whole afternoon. Mrs. Robert Forrest Smythe Lambis Wolfscheim Silva Singer was sworn in, and I refused to look at her until the District Attorney asked her a question.

"Do you know the defendant, Wilfred Thorpe?"

"You mean the murderer sitting right over there?" Agnes pointed at me.

I jammed Ernie with my elbow just a little too hard and he squeaked. The judge, Agnes, the DA, and the jurors all swung their eyes to look at my barber. I whispered the word "objection" to him at the top of my range so that everyone in the courtroom heard.

"Objection?" Ernie added the question mark.

"Mr. Sampesee," Judge Annie said," welcome back to our little world. You have an objection?"

"I do?" I was scribbling quickly on my legal pad and shoved it in front of him.

"What is your objection?"

Ernie stalled as he leaned down, straightened back up, opened his coat, extracted his glasses and put them on.

"Counselor." A sharp rebuke came from the bench at the lengthy delay.

"Strike the remark from the record. It is heresy and conjunctive?" Ernie took off his glasses and looked apprehensively at the judge.

"You should learn to ask, not order the court, Mr. Sampesee." The Judge sighed. "Heresy and what?"

I pulled Ernie down and whispered loudly in his ear. He straightened up and said, "Hearsay and conjecture on the part of the witness, your Honor. I am kind of new at this."

"You don't say, Mr. Sampesee. The court sustains the objection. The jury will discount the use of the term 'murderer,' and the witness will not attempt to pass judgment or state opinion unless instructed to do so. Just answer the questions as they are asked. No more, no less. Okay?" She got a begrudging nod from Agnes. "Go ahead counselor."

I glared at the old woman, and she gave it right back.

The young ADA from Durango led Mrs. Singer through the sequence of events beginning with my phone call and our meeting at the Franz Klammer. Agnes told the court that she simply wanted me to pass along a message to her estranged husband that she wished him to vacate her father's house that was held in trust by her alone. Everything that happened after that initial talk was done by me on my own initiative and in response to a growing animosity between me and the deceased.

She had not spoken with me at any other time prior to the single meeting before the murder. No money for my alleged services ever exchanged hands. She had spent the evening of the murder with a friend in downtown Telluride. Her whereabouts have been substantiated.

"Did you know Mr. Robert Forrest Singer was in fact Mr. George W. Wilson of Sodoma?"

"I did not."

"Did you want your husband dead?"

"I did not. I wanted a divorce. It is a much different thing." Agnes glared at me again. "You didn't have to kill him." The Jury was eating it up. The ADA quickly sat down on a very high note.

"Cross?" the judge asked politely.

"No questions at this time, your honor," Sampesee said in a low baritone, standing at the table with his palm on the flat surface, a thumb tucked up under the opposite lapel. I closed my eyes and put my face in my hands.

～

Walter Silverton was in the hall during the afternoon's twenty-minute recess. He was going to be next up on the stand. He saw me from twenty feet away, raised his hand, made it into a gun, and pulled the trigger. The recoil sent the arm over his head. An inappropriate greeting for a man accused of 1st degree murder with a pistol was my first thought.

I was handcuffed to a Deputy Sheriff and had just come out of the men's room as he walked up. He punched me solidly, a short jab into my slinged shoulder. I almost fainted; my knees sagged a bit. I jerked the Deputy's arm up as I went for the cleaned up biker. My cuff mate didn't like that and jammed the point of his nightstick into my already sore ribs.

"Hey, Darryl," Walter said with a smile to my escort.

"Hey, Mr. Silverton," Darryl said as the tailored charcoal gray suit moved down the hall with a wave over its shoulder. I was threatened with mace if I tried anything like that again.

Mister Silverton? It sounded pretty cozy between a habitual criminal and the law. What had I missed here? Now my head also hurt with the new possibilities. Maybe Darryll had been promised a high-end security job when the church came to town. Maybe this was the *Invasion of the Body Snatchers*.

Back in the courtroom Walter spoke in a steady monologue about how they had disarmed and detained me after I had willfully trespassed on private property with the intention to intimidate and threaten the legal tenant. He was hired to protect his employer, Mr. Singer, who was living on the premises. I was painted as an armed and motivated intruder. The incident was immediately reported to the Sheriff's Office. I had escaped with my handgun before the Sheriff arrived. A complaint was sworn to.

"And then the very next morning?" the DA prompted.

"He shows up again," Walter said, "with a posse of armed cowboys who proceed to shoot the place up. Firing hundreds of bullets over our heads and into the surrounding countryside. Trying to scare us into leaving the house."

"I'd like to enter as evidence exhibit A, a collection of ninety-two shell casings left at the scene by the Cowboy Action Shooters that Mr. Thorpe brought to West Egg for the sole purpose of intimidating the murder victim."

The Judge agreed and after parading the plastic bag past the jurors, he went back in front of the witness chair.

"And then the defendant did what, exactly?"

"He approached Mr. Singer, and from my perspective went to head butt the much older man. Mr. Singer raised his hand," Walter demonstrated what he meant, "to protect himself, and sustained a sprained wrist during the encounter."

"Were there other witnesses to this violent assault?"

Ernie yelped. I shoved him to his feet.

"Objection," he said.

"Mr. Sampesee."

Ernie looked down at me. I made my index and tall finger walk down the table.

"Walking, your honor," Ernie said.

"Walking, Mr. Sampesee?" The laughter rippled through the courtroom.

Ernie heard my whisper over the growing din. "Leading, your honor, sorry, I'm new at this." He got a laugh. "Isn't there something about calling something a crime that isn't proven within a question?"

"Yes there is something, Mr. Sampesee."

The laughter erupted again and drowned out the Judge calling for order. The judge's "sustained" brought a round of applause, and she had to threaten to clear the courtroom to restore quiet. My Grand Jury was a crowd pleaser all right.

~

"And Sheriff Bueller, you also witnessed the physical exchange between the defendant and the deceased, did you not?"

"I did. As I stated a few minutes ago for the District Attorney. Cut and dried." Bueller was in full dress blues, his stiff brimmed service hat perched on the stand beside him. He didn't get to dress up much was my guess.

I had run out of paper on my legal pad and was now writing on the blank backs of my short story and passing them to Ernie. I had scrambled to come up with a series of questions that could challenge Bueller on the phone call to 911 from West Egg and his return call from my house. It was the only lifeline I had left. And I didn't know where it would go.

"Wouldn't this kind of incident, regardless of who started the altercation, raise your level of response in the future, in case of a call for assistance, for example?"

"Usually."

"But not this time?" Ernie said.

"Not this time," Bueller said and smiled.

"Where were you when you received the call on your radio from dispatch concerning a possible crime up at West Egg in Mountain Village?" Ernie asked.

"It was a suicide report, not a reported crime."

"It turned out to be exactly the opposite though didn't it?"

"I suppose you could say that," Bueller squeaked leather adjusting himself in the chair and acknowledged the fact enthusiastically.

"Why didn't you take the threat seriously?"

"In assessing the danger, I felt I had good reason to believe that I knew the whereabouts of Mr. Thorpe. He was under close observation." Bueller's gaze sought out my wife standing by the doors at the far back of the room. I turned and followed his eyes. Of course everyone else in the courtroom followed my lead.

"I was distracted. It happens on stakeouts. It turned out bad for Mr. Singer. I'm sorry. I couldn't help myself."

Her face was unreadable, and she just held his stare. Her arms were casually folded and she was leaning her back against the wall. My heart ached.

Bueller coughed and chuckled under his hand as he readjusted himself in his chair. The leathers of his holster and utility belt squeaked again.

"How were you distracted? Where were you staked out?"

"Do I have to answer that judge?"

"Do you have a legal reason or some confidential conflict in context of another case to withhold that information?"

"No." Bueller smiled in an aw-shucks way. "Not really."

The doors to the courtroom slammed, and we all turned as one. My wife was gone. The whispers started like a steam engine in downtown Durango.

"Quiet," the judge ordered with a shout that silenced the room. "Answer the question."

"At Assistant District Attorney Thorpe's house."

"But the defendant claims to have not seen you, and he was also in the home. His wife went to her room at 8:30. The call came to your office at 9:23. An empty message was on the answering machine at West Egg at 9:25. It was, according to previous testimony, made from the phone in District Attorney Thorpe's bedroom. Did you make that call?"

"I may have."

"Don't be coy," Ernie said.

"I'm never coy," Bueller said with a shit-eating grin. He was enjoying telling this. He wanted people to assume he was there for sex. Just because I couldn't even imagine it, did not make it not so. He was almost winking, the jack-booted, leather cropped bastard.

"You left the house. When?"

"Later." He winked at the jury. I swear. "I couldn't be sure."

"And you went home." Ernie read from the Sheriff's statement. "Do you sleep on the couch, Sheriff Bueller?"

"Objection," the young DA was on his feet. "Immaterial. Line of questioning, your honor?"

"Where are you going with this Mr. Sampesee?"

Ernie looked up at her with a dazed expression on his face. It was obvious; he was fishing and actually enjoying himself being center stage. No explanation was forthcoming.

"Sustained. Next question?"

I scribbled frantically. I ripped it jaggedly from the yellow pad and flung it across the defense table. It fell off the table to the floor and Ernie picked it up. He read it carefully. He read it again. We all waited.

"Mr. Sampesee?"

The minutes dragged on.

"Mr. Sampesee?" Judge Annie asked again.

"Sheriff Bueller, ahem, what do you know about the spoiled edge of things?" Ernie rattled the yellow papers in his hand violently at the Sheriff. My barber was trembling. His face was suddenly flushed and his voice rang from the moldings.

My heart sank. I looked down at the pad. Ernie was trying to make sense out of the last paragraphs of the Fitzgerald story. My question for Bueller was on the other side. How could anything else go wrong? I waved to get his attention, but his back was to me as he faced the jury. Judge Annie pointed at my chest; I stopped jumping up, and sat back down.

"I beg your pardon?" Bueller lost his smile.

"The spoiled part, where your lewd fantasies get out of hand. And you dive right in, naked. Isn't that what happened the night of Mr. Singer's murder?"

"What?" The smirk was off the Sheriff's face.

"You don't answer my question." Ernie let his voice rise. He was on some moral high ground from what I had written. He was tossing spears and sounding like William Jennings Bryant.

"Are you sick in the head or something?" Ernie said with a rumble in his throat.

"Mr. Sampesee," Judge Annie tried to caution my lawyer. He was ignoring her body language, having none of it.

"You have some sick way of thinking about things, Sheriff Bueller." A sprinkling of claps followed. The judge rapped the gavel.

"What about the pool, Sheriff Bueller?" Ernie was now almost waving the yellow paper in his face. His voice booming. Bueller's face was pale. "Sweet death? What about that damn pool?"

"How..." Bueller said, stopped, stammered. "How could you...no...know ...the hot tub?"

"Indeed," Ernie said. "A very, very hot, tub, wasn't it Sheriff Bueller." Ernie turned to his audience. His embarrassed indignation plain for all to see.

Bueller had grabbed tight to the railings in front of the witness chair, his hat was brushed onto the floor where it bounced and skidded to a stop at Ernie's feet. The Sheriff was stunned. He looked like he was about to explode. He had a gun. I was worried.

"What about the pool?" Ernie said as he picked up the hat, waved it in Bueller's face. "The horrible things in that pool have caught up with you."

"How?"

"Sex, Sheriff. Did you have sex in that pool?"

"There weren't no damn sex. He was already dead."

"Who was already dead?" Ernie asked in falsetto the single question on every one's lips. Bueller's silence was the key for everyone in the room to reach the same conclusion: Sandy "Wilson" Singer was already dead.

"I want to talk to a lawyer." Sheriff Bueller barked his answer back at Ernie. He had been skewered with this bit of fictional nonsense from my story. "You fucking little jerk. I ain't saying one more thing. I want a damn lawyer."

"Sheriff," Judge Annie said into the trapped silence, "you'll watch your God damn language in my court, or I'll have you jailed for contempt."

Ernie smiled, turned his back on Bueller, probably the bravest thing I have ever seen anyone ever do, and walked slowly over to the ADA's table. He softly set the hat down.

"No further questions at this time your honor, but I request the right to call this witness back at a later time."

"I want to see both counsels in my cubicle right now. Court is adjourned until 9 a.m. in the morning." Judge Annie was pissed. "I want to emphasize with the jurors not to discuss this matter with anyone, even among yourselves. Anyone, do you hear?"

"Sherriff Bueller, you call one of your deputies and have him take you home. You stay there until I decide what to do with you."

We all rose with judge. Bueller remained sitting, his arms frozen in a grip, his head shaking back and forth. The whole jury had filed out, each taking a long curious look at him before passing through the doorway. He then stood up quickly as some of the locals began to sit back down in their seats to see what developed next.

The Sheriff retrieved his hat and the crowd parted to let him through. He was almost running when he hit the doors. What had caused that kind of reaction? What had Ernie said? What was wrong with the hot tub the night of the murder? I didn't even have a hot tub.

≈

I was escorted back to the holding cell at the jail. Ernie came by as soon as he got out of the judge's chambers. He had a very long face.

"The judge isn't going to let me call Bueller back up on the stand. She says we have to show a substantiated reason to pursue this line of questioning. Bueller has now claimed official confidentiality problems with ongoing cases. He also has a lawyer from Grand Junction."

"What was that about? All that crap in reaction to my story?" I asked.

"You write that shit?" Ernie asked. I glared at him and he found another subject to stay away from. "It was something about a hot tub that set him off. I can't believe I did that." Ernie smiled shyly begging for a compliment. I wasn't in the mood.

"Get me out of here," I said.

"I tried."

"Try harder."

"Lets see, how exactly did Judge Annie put it? 'Seems people die when he is free to roam the streets.' She couldn't have been any clearer."

Ernie handed me the local paper. "Attempted Suicide by Murder Suspect," was the headline, and the only good news was the headline. In the article I was mentioned as either a nut case with a death wish, or the eco-terrorist killer, or both. An editorial called for me to be summarily charged with another 1st degree murder immediately for Stewart Lambis' death, plus a vehicular manslaughter charge for chasing Wolfscheim off a cliff. A letter to the editor from Digger called for the whole community to band together and seek a full pardon from the Governor on my behalf because I acted "on behalf of the cows and in the best interest of Telluride's threatened ambiance."

Ernie and I agreed to meet here at the jail for breakfast. I wasn't likely to miss the date. The more I thought about it, pessimism is the same as optimism without the silly ritual of cheering one's self up getting in the way. Both perceptions are based on self-delusion. I wrote by the dim light of the emergency lights.

≈

The dog ended up in the pool when the gun arrived. It was late. All of the lights in the house were ablaze, and torches on slender bamboo stilts lighted the gardens and grounds all the way to the hedgerows. The air was quiet and thick with the humidity that promises a summer rain. Heat lightning flickered out on Long Island Sound. Cicadas were loud, busily trying to drum up their mates before the deluge came in the morning.

Fitzgerald still lay sprawled in the cabana chair in a tangled layer of white poolside towels. He was drinking gin from a bottle at his side, his eyes half closed, near his limit. Gatz had walked into the house to clean out the last of the hangers on, asking loudly who needed a cab. Myrtle Wilson, his local mistress, was recovering from passing out in the den with her head in the lap of a snoring impresario from a recent musical show on Broadway. She was now whimpering upstairs in a guest room bath between bouts of nausea.

George Wilson, the cuckold and gas station owner from the town of Great Neck, walked through the long slashes of light amidst the dark shadows and around to the back of the house. He stood at the end of the pool and saw Fitzgerald sprawled in the chair, a revolver raised in his hand and aimed at the seated figure.

"You bastard," he yelled. The grasshoppers hushed. The dog came running at a familiar voice, barking its little yaps, and circled Wilson's legs jumping and snarling for attention. A sharp kick sent it arching into the pool where it landing with a small splash. Spurred on, Wilson began to walk towards Fitzgerald with the gun waving at him. The man was sobbing, shoulders heaving.

"You bastard," he said again as the dog began yipping for its life.

Fitzgerald was trying desperately to swim back to lucidity as the adrenaline rushed through his body. His heart hammered with an awkward rhythm in his chest. He wanted to speak, but couldn't. Nothing was following his orders.

Wilson came to stand over the writer. His hand was shaking now in spasms and his sobbing growing more desperate. Wilson sank to his knees and aimed the huge pistol up between Fitzgerald's own arched knees towards his head. A fetal position was to be the final pose.

"Myrtle's my wife, you bastard," he yelled over the screeching of the terrified dog in the pool.

Fitzgerald closed his eyes. He knew he was going to die. How long, he thought, and time stretched out in pale landscapes, the kind you see in Europe. Spain from train windows. The gun went off. He counted five shots, and then the heavy hammer hit loudly on metal for six more pulls. Fitzgerald opened his eyes.

Wilson stood at the end of the pool, aiming the eight-inch barrel at the water. The small white dog that had managed to avoid the hail of bullets finally pulled itself from the shallow end at the stairs and looked back at Wilson like a drowned rat. Wilson threw the gun at the dog that yelped and ran for the house. The pistol landed in the pool.

"Myrtle," Wilson cried. His voice keening.

Fitzgerald had actually died with each explosion. He had wet himself, lost all hold, and now he tumbled off the chair to the hard granite slate of the pool's rim and vomited. This was too much, too much.

A hand closed on his shoulder. It was her, she. His Daisy woken from a stupor. She was still naked. They left Wilson, eyes down, sprawled at the edge of the grass crying softly, and she led them in a drunken haze, staggering towards the pool house. Fitzgerald's eyes tried to swim with the little white dog that could dodge death. The taste of vomit was in his mouth.

Thirty-five

Ain't We Got Fun

At 10:30 p.m., in the half-light of the security monitors, I woke up to the heavy lock on my cell door clanking open. I was painfully sitting up when Darryl and a female Deputy named Christine boosted me to my feet. I had to struggle to reach back and grab my yellow pad. They brought me through a labyrinth of hallways back to the interrogation room. They threw my clothes and effects on the desk and ordered me to get dressed. I did, and was still buttoning my shirt over my sling when the outside door to the jail smacked me in the backside. It locked behind me.

"Thanks for letting me call a cab, assholes," I said knowing the entrance security cameras would pick it up.

I didn't have a jacket, and the temperature must be in the low thirties. I rubbed my aching shoulder and tried to decide what to do. It would have been too easy if I had my cell phone. It was all I could do to keep from gnashing my teeth. Almost four miles to town, I started walking.

A hundred yards down the road I noticed headlights, and I looked behind to hold up my thumb. The car came to a stop on the gravel at my side with a short controlled slide. It was the Z3. The window oozed down.

It was Miranda. Her beautiful red hair, swept back at shoulder plus length, looking as if it had just been done, her face aglow with the best cosmetics money can buy. The smell was sensual ambrosia.

"I was coming in from Ophir and thought I'd take the Illium road. So this is where the jail is? Lucky you. Get in."

Hardly, I thought. Flying saucers and laser fried homework assignments made a more believable story. But, I needed a ride. She had something to say. I needed to listen. I'd work on the non-coincidence part later.

"Patsy Susie's?" I said pulling open the car's door.

"Yes. Patsy Susie and I are like sisters," she said.

"Lucky you," I said.

"Pardon? Have I said something?"

"Not yet." I smiled back. A dark cloud ripped across her face. She smiled again, instead.

"This is fortunate. Quite a coincidence really. I needed to talk with you," she gunned the car and we fishtailed quickly up to fifty. The G-forces when we pulled into the sharp right hand turn to the stop sign at Highway 62 had our shoulders pressed together. It sent an electric shock through me. I tried to tell myself it was the injury.

"Am I gonna get slapped around again?" I was a bit miffed that she imagined I was such a cretin as to believe she had just happened to be here. She really did think I was as dumb as a stump.

"Depends on you, tough guy," she said as the car squealed away from the intersection and was soon doing seventy uphill through the tight, unforgiving turns that yesterday took Meyer Wolfscheim's life. We could follow suit in a matter of seconds with a miscalculation of inches. The yellow crime scene tape marking the broken guardrail flashed by my window.

Miranda downshifted, and the engine moaned as we crested the top of the hill. We were at a legal forty-five when we went through Society Corners.

"So what do you have to say to me that made this brilliant coincidence happen?" I was trying to show her I was a sharper stump than she thought I was.

"I thought we'd get a drink, talk about old times." Her eyes summed up my attitude with a smirk. I had never thought seriously about slapping a woman before.

"I'm particular about who I drink with," I said, and added, "whom."

"What?"

"Nothing, I just don't want to be seen with you," I said. "I've got standards, as low as they are. You understand?"

She gave me a sideways look and a low snarl.

"Listen boy scout, I'm sick to death of you too, and I'm not alone in that department," she said. "I came to tell you that Eric knows more about this than he is saying. And, now he is jeopardizing the whole damn deal by not coming forward. That simply can't happen."

"The deal's the thing isn't it?"

"Of course. Aren't you supposed to be a detective or something? Eric is staying up at West Egg in the guesthouse. It's his residence of choice and convenience. He was living there the night Singer died. He must have seen something."

"I thought he was with you having a family moment all evening."

"So I lied," she said. "He made me."

"Even I'm not that stupid. Your mother claims he's in a drug rehabilitation program with a gang of gay bikers."

"You believe half what that old woman tells you? Why would she tell you the truth? This is all about her. You're not as smart as folks say, but maybe you're not an idiot, right?"

I wasn't sure how to answer, so I just kept quiet.

"Eric runs his own damn show in that security outfit when he isn't stoned, drunk, or wrecked. He's the brains; Walter, is just the meanness. They got a good scam going pretending they don't like each other. Often wonder if they aren't doing each other on the side as well."

"All I know is that it seems you screw around with some pretty screwed up people," I said, passing a quick judgment to hide my confusion. It was my last stand against the thought that she was actually trying to help me. Help me what?

"Loser," she said. I didn't have an appropriate response given my present situation.

We didn't talk again. She dropped me at the Sheridan Bar. I didn't go in as she laid a squeak of rubber leaving the curb. I turned right, limped down through Rotary Town Park and headed for the Gondola terminal.

I stopped at Honga's Restaurant and helped myself to a nice warm parka hung on the hooks in the entrance by an unlucky diner. I'd return it tomorrow with an apology. I was stiffening up fast and needed it more than the owner.

I had to track down a certain hot tub, one that had Bueller worried, and I thought I should start with the one at West Egg.

$\approx$

I had dispensed with the sling on the ride over to Mountain Village. Crunching down two more Vicadin on the trip, I was walking as if I needed to find sanctuary at Notre Dame. It seemed everything hurt more than before. I took another pill. In twenty minutes I'd probably be swimming through clouds.

I only hoped the golf cart shuttle for the convenience of the hikers and shoppers staying at the Peaks Hotel was left plugged in and charging in the usual space behind the ski school building. It was.

I crossed the red and blue ignition wires and was off on a battery-assisted ride up the mountain roads to West Egg. Two cars passed me along the way and kept on going. I wasn't their business, and golf carts were common. It took twenty minutes rather than an hour of walking. I was feeling mighty pleased with myself as I turned into the huge pillared stone entrance and parked on the lawn outside of the security gate. I was feeling no pain as I awkwardly climbed the fence and trekked up the entry drive.

Architecturally appropriate lighting pinpointed the towering eaves and glass walls of the house. I saw no movement inside, and I crossed the courtyard and went up the sweeping iron stairway to the hot tub balcony. Having an eclectic work history as a caretaker for a number of wealthy people and their houses, I knew the simplest way to detach and lift clear of the water the fine mesh aluminum filtering screen at the exhaust port. I was busy holding it to the dim lights of the house reflecting out onto the deck, or I wouldn't have been such a target.

The first explosion sent a studio chair flopping over behind me. The next pistol shot splintered the cedar planking just in front of my knees. The shard of lumber scrapped across my cheek, and I almost dropped the filter. The third shot clanged off the metal railing of the staircase leading back down to the courtyard, and that's where I headed in a running crouch. The next bullet went off behind me, and I launched myself head first for the stairs. I felt a cold edge of pain rake across my buttocks.

I sprawled down the first ten or so stairs on my stomach before coming up against the curved rail. It was a full face plant. I kept swimming, arms working hard, around that corner. The gun went off again. I reached the bottom and scrambled to my feet without the help of the railing. Looking up, I saw Agnes taking aim from ten feet above and ten yards away. The silver pistol, a small lady's purse affair, had pearl handles.

A brilliant shaft of light spilled out onto the courtyard, and Eric with his hand messing up his own hair walked out of the guesthouse front door. My eyes went back to the matron of the house as I tried to hide behind the skimpy wrought iron of the stairs. I was close to two hundred pounds, and the railing an inch wide. I felt exposed.

Inexplicably Agnes raised the gun and began firing at Eric. Luckily, she was not a good shot. A piece of slate exploded in the retaining wall. The door jerked on its hinges. Eric had hit the ground with his hands over his head and was now an easy, exposed target. In four more shots, exhausting her nine, she couldn't even come close at the fifty-yard range.

I heard her swear as she went back inside to reload. I was planning on being gone before she came back. Eric was stumbling along on my heels as I threaded through the woods heading for the golf cart. We saved our breath, glad each of us still had something to save. I was so unnerved I wasn't sure which of us had enough of a grip on reality to begin to explain what happened back there. Neither of us tried to talk. At a top speed of 18 mph on the flats, we raced back towards the Gondola.

～

Before we reached Wapitti Drive, the law was on to us, the flashing lights silently speeding up the hill from town. Instinctively I didn't want to talk with Bueller or any of his goons right now. I wanted to talk with my wife, the Assistant District Attorney. I was going home, and I was pretty sure Bueller was not going to make that easy or convenient. Bullets have a way of bringing on tremendous clarity. I was suddenly clear on where I was going and what I needed to do.

I took a sharp right and almost lost Eric out of the cart.

"Where the fuck?" he said.

"Golf course, slick, we'll go the road less traveled." In the dark, I felt the grass give way to a black ribbon of tarvia. Shutting down the headlight actually helped, as the stars, unnaturally brilliant in the clean night air at two miles high, lit the landscape like a half moon. I knew the way. Eric was wise to shut up and hold on. I crested the ridge and left the cart path, see-sawing violently through the ruts. From the ski runs of Misty Maiden to Telluride Trail the cart held together. We rode the machine like the Grinch's sled, down twenty-three-hundred vertical feet on the bumpy, winding gravel road with the clutch pushed in and the cart reaching forty on the rough straight-aways.

We raced at a crawl through the deserted town. I pulled to a stop at the curb a block from my house. I jumped out and started limping towards home.

"What the fuck am I supposed to do, man?" Eric said.

"Go see your sister."

"She's with him."

"Walter?"

"No, Breene."

"The bread squeezer?"

"Huh?"

"Jeffrey Breene, the billionaire?"

"Yeah, she likes 'em old and rich. Found him at Rose's hangin' near the deli in a false beard. A fruitcake if you ask me," he said, paused, "She and me never did, you know, nothing. Sex, nothing..."

I just stared.

He then asked, "What went on back there?"

"Your mother seems to want you and me in the same place as her three ex-husbands. Why would she want that? You got any ideas?"

Eric shrugged, keeping it to himself.

"Your sister is also putting the finger on you for being alone up at the house the night Sandy died. Why did you lie?"

Eric was trying hard to use his fried sunny-side-up brain.

"You were also shaking down your father and the rest because you knew about the Wilson switcheroo."

Eric shrugged.

"I'd be getting a little worried right now if I were you," I said.

"What should I do?"

"Tell the truth."

"The truth?"

"The whole thing, the whole story from beginning to end. Once it's all out there on the table the reason to want you dead sort of disappears. Right?"

Eric looked at me with his rummy eyes. He waved me off. I wanted to slap him around and make him do what I needed, but it was time to hurry before Bueller showed up. I wondered what was going through Eric's head. What if my own mother had just tried to kill me?

I looked at his mouth wondering if he was the one that tongue attacked me in Lambis' office. I hawked and spat on the ground, knowing I couldn't be sure it wasn't.

"You know I can kill the deal for the land?" Eric said. "I got twenty-five percent now that my father died. I can make the whole thing not happen. I think that's maybe what I'm going to do. It would serve them all right."

"Your mother knows this?"

He shrugged. She knew everything. Could that be why she was trying to kill him? Wouldn't it make more sense to keep him alive to kill the deal if she wanted to protect her precious Valley Floor?

"Your half sister says you are way smarter than I give you credit for. Prove to me she's right. If I were in your boots, I'd want what I know out there, said in public, so killing you makes no sense. But that's just me, slick. You could want to be dead for all I know. See you in court." I turned and shuffled off as fast as I could down the street.

≈

I climbed up through the neighbor's landscaping and into my own yard. The bears had been at it again, and the thin trail of garbage disappeared into the scrub bushes at the edge of the property. The thought of Miranda and the hairy-backed Breene doing the hootchie-kootchie was more than I could handle right now. I tried not to think about soapsuds and the rest.

It was almost midnight, and I wasn't surprised that the lights were off as I let myself in the entryway door. The voice from the dark startled me.

"What are you doing here?"

"They let me out. We have to talk."

"Who let you out?"

I thought about it. I didn't know. My wife was sitting on the couch in the dark. I couldn't see her, but sensed the tears.

"You were supposed to stay in jail. Annie did it for your own protection, knucklehead. What are you doing here?" Her voice sounded desperate. "Don't you get how serious this all is?"

"I went to the hot tub. Old lady Singer tried to shoot me. And, she tried to off Eric too," I said.

Silence. My wife struggled to believe a word of it.

"Agnes Singer?" she said.

"You got to believe me."

"Why would she want to shoot you?"

"Maybe I'm getting too close to the truth," I said.

"Fat fucking chance, scum bag. You are under arrest."

Bueller had walked down the hall from my wife's bedroom. He was still in the dress blues from court today. His gun, a Glock 9mm, was drawn and supported with two hands. Its barrel zeroed in on my heart. His eyes were wild, full of hate.

"I have proof."

"What?" Both Bueller and my wife asked the same question at the same time.

"I have the straining screen from the hot tub. It's got something in it that looks like Sandy Singer's brains."

"Move against the wall. Hands on top of your head. Spread 'em." I was shoved towards the closed door behind me and frisked roughly. He came away with the hastily folded screen from my front pocket. "Whose to say you didn't rig this?"

"I'll take that," my wife, the Assistant District Attorney said. She was standing behind Bueller. He stretched his arm up out of her reach, the gun in the small of my back. She held her ground.

"I'll take the evidence," she repeated.

"You don't want none of this," Bueller said. His words held an implied double meaning. Had he lost his mind? You don't threaten the Iron Maiden. I waited for it to start.

My wife, the Assistant District Attorney, put her hands on her hips and took a step forward to occupy the space between herself and the Sheriff, who easily outweighed her by a hundred pounds and had a gun in my back. The darkness seemed to crackle with static electricity.

The lights in the kitchen suddenly came on and Cody stood at the hallway light switch. She had on her pink daisy nightshirt, in her hand was a video camera. The red light was glowing as she watched the flip out digital screen.

"Mom could you back up one step so I can get a close up of the barrel of the Sheriff's gun in dad's back?" Her voice was in the exasperated tone of an over worked, second unit director. She waved her hand from the wrist to underscore the order.

Bueller let out a held breath like a bellows and dropped the handful of metal screen into the Assistant District Attorney's hands. "Come along, Thorpe," he said in barely repressed anger, handcuffing my hands roughly behind my back. "It was some stupid clerical foul up. You are still supposed to be in jail."

"How could that happen?" my wife said.

"Idiots," Bueller said, "like our boy here."

"Defecate yourself," I said and smiled for the camera. This home movie would definitely make my all time highlight reel, if I didn't end up in the electric chair. Cody gave a circular motion of her hand, "stir it up," and a big grin.

I told Bueller he was a fat, ignorant, impotent slob in both Ute and Spanish. I smiled for the camera knowing my daughter got it all. Bueller didn't have a clue what I was saying, but on principle he shook me hard and my shoulder just about came out of its socket again. I couldn't hide all the fun I was having from my face.

"Sheriff, I think it's wise if I tag along," my wife said with authority, "just to be sure Mr. Thorpe is not the victim of any further, how do we say, clerical errors?"

Bueller growled, and I looked puzzled. Did she mean she wanted me locked up for good? Or could she think Bueller might do something else to me on the way to the jail? I certainly could imagine that. Would she care? I waved good-bye to the camera with my eyebrows while my wife woke up Katie. I guess we're back to "get one Thorpe, you get the tribe" I was down right proud to be one of the tribe.

In twenty minutes I was right back where I was supposed to be. The lyrics of the old flapper tune "Ain't We Got Fun" kept running through my head. Bueller hadn't said another word, but kept banging his forehead on the steering wheel on the way here. I took it as a sign he was perturbed, and I had best keep quiet if I knew what was good for me.

"Hey Bueller, did you do Lambis too?" I asked the question politely as soon as I could take a breath. His fist banged back against the Plexiglas barrier between the seats. I tried to think of something else to say, but couldn't. The pain pills were finally finding their home.

I didn't sleep much, but I smiled each time I thought of my wife stepping forward and cowering that big lughead. If anything had been happening between them before, it certainly wasn't any more. I stayed up and thought some about that. I lost my good mood in moronic circular reasonings that have no purpose and no end.

Thirty-six

Snatching Defeat From The Jaws Of Victory

Ernie and I had been warned by the judge in her cubicle that any further note passing shenanigans would result in a contempt of court citation and Ernie joining me in jail. If I wanted to represent myself, I would have to dismiss my lawyer. We tried to argue, and she gave the "zip-it" motion and sent us on our way.

Downstairs at the courthouse we were sequestered in a small office usually occupied by the county assessor with a Deputy Sheriff in the hall guarding the door. I hadn't seen Bueller this morning. I hadn't seen my wife either. The Deputy opened the door and handed me a legal envelope with a round object the size of a rubber ball in it. The envelope had been inspected.

"From the little girl," he said.

I knew what it was. I hoped it was my answer to Ernie's problems. He watched me pocket the object without opening the envelope.

"Something?" he said.

"Yeah, something," I said. "Remember, the kid is stoned, don't get him riled up. Just calmly try to get him to tell you what happened the night of Sandy's death. Call the stiff, Sandy, on purpose, remember? Not Singer, not Wilson, just Sandy. You know what we talked about?"

Ernie wriggled in his seat. "I'm gonna do my very best old cod, it's all I can do."

"Stop trying to be the lawyer. Stop being anything." I raised my voice and it got his attention. "Just be a god damned barber, and get people to tell you everything they know."

"It isn't that simple," he said.

"You can do it," I said.

≈

Eric was sworn in. He looked like hell. He still wore the leather clothes from the night before, grass stains, scuff marks and all. His eyes were hardly able to stay open and couldn't quite focus. He seemed happy enough, dreamy almost. I was sure that if he was frisked he would be holding heroin and a means of putting it into his veins. He was our first defense witness. The jury appeared unimpressed and stared with open hostility at our star. Eric leered back in a lopsided grin at a matronly plump rancher's wife who looked as if she had just cracked a bad egg.

This was my last hope. If Eric stayed taciturn, the Grand Jury would hand down an indictment in spite of Bueller's meltdown and incriminating comments. Those are the facts. I have too many years that I hope I will never be cross examined for because I don't have any alibis or excuses, but I hated to go down for something I didn't do. The fairness quotient on this rap sucked. It all hinged on this burned out addict, what state of chemical imbalance he was experiencing, and if Ernie could coax the truth out of him.

"Mr. Sampesee?" Judge Annie started the proceedings.

Ernie started to get to his feet, and I passed the object from Cody into his hand, keeping it above the table so it wouldn't be mistaken for a note. He sat back down and looked at it in his lap. He smiled. He lifted the shaving soap brush to his nose, its short bristles reeked of old lather. The smell of the barbershop. The familiar round porcelain knob seemed to tenderly fit his long thin hand.

Ernie stood up straight, and before he had even left our table the words were flowing like gelatin. The soft fluid tones were wrapping everyone in the courtroom up in the empathy and goodwill of a family picnic. Ernie genuinely felt compassion for Eric Wolfscheim; a boy who had just lost his dad. How was he holding up? Apologizing to him for having to be here.

Thankful that he was still alive despite those awful attempts on his life. Eric was a good citizen, here to set things straight and help get the truth out.

The young man on the stand relaxed under the attention and sat slouched in his straight-backed wooden seat. It was a tableau of Ernie, the silver tongued mongoose, and the leather-clad sleepy cobra on the stand. Every eye in the place followed the barber. Ernie established the family connections, all of them. It took five minutes. He then stated that Eric presently lives at West Egg and had also been there the night in question.

"You cared for Sandy?"

Eric nodded, his face turned sad.

"He was your friend? Your lover? Like a brother?"

Eric nodded again. I thought he might cry.

"Did you see him dead that night?"

"Yeah."

"In the Mustang?"

Eric looked puzzled; then a brain synapse fired, and he shook his head.

"But you saw Sandy after he was shot?"

Eric nodded. His blonde hair covering most of his eyes.

"At Eagle's Lair?"

"Objection. Leading."

"Sustained. Restate your question, Mr. Sampesee."

"Sorry Judge," Ernie said, "But..."

"You're new at this," Judge Annie loudly completed for him. "Get on with it." She got a ripple of appreciative laughter.

"Your Honor, objection, the whereabouts of the body has already been established. I challenge the credibility of the witness. He appears to be under the influence of some inebriate." The young prosecutor was trying to look aggrieved.

"And you have every right, counselor, but you'll do it under cross," Judge Annie said back. Her voice was a willow switch. I berated myself as a chauvinist as I considered the ups and downs of lunar cycles.

"Please, Eric, take your time, and in your own words, don't hurry. Just tell us what you saw that night," Ernie said and stepped one foot up onto the flooring of the witness stand and leaned in next to Eric. It was them, together, against those who wouldn't believe the truth. Support in the room was palpable. The young biker began to talk in a voice that was hard to hear at first. Even Judge Annie pressed forward to make out the words.

Eric had seen Sandy's dead body at West Egg. He had looked up at it from the courtyard. His former lover was dead, shot, sprawled next to the hot tub. His head and shoulders leaning over the edge of the cedar planked deck, the skull wrapped tightly in a white towel, turban style. A dark red stain on the towel covered the side of his head visible to Eric.

"I panicked and ran into the house to call 911," Eric said in agitated defense of his actions. "I said that he was going to kill himself…myself. I got scared. I didn't want to be there no more. I wasn't going to be a witness to nothing. It was just too much. I was shaking. Needed a fix. Sick, man, what could I do?"

The jury and the crowd were stunned.

"Did you see the Sheriff?"

"Yeah. He passed me going towards the house when I was about halfway into town."

"Did he have his flashing lights on?"

"Objection your honor. Leading."

"I'll allow it." Judge Annie wanted to know the answer.

"Yeah, I pulled over onto the shoulder and slowed down."

"That's all, your honor," said Ernie and put the brush in his suit's breast pocket where the bristles popped up like a decorative kerchief.

The cross from the prosecutor was brutal. A litany of arrests for possession, assault, public drunkenness, and a juvenile record that warranted two years in reform school was paraded before the jury. Eric had been known to accept "gifts" from the three church trustees so that he would not talk about the murder and insurance scam that seems to have founded the church all those years ago. He was also known to take the money his mother was sending to the motorcycle gang. It bought the drugs they were trying to keep him off.

"The old woman could afford it," Eric said with a shy smile.

But the story was the story, and although Eric admitted to being high that night, his memories were intact. He looked to Ernie for support and approval. In the end, the story hung together because it corroborated Bueller's melt down.

Ernie called back to the stand the 911 dispatcher who got word to the Sheriff over the radio to call Eagle's Lair, and the logs showed that no other situation was in progress that would have necessitated lights and sirens during that time period. A traffic stop would have been called in with a plate number as per procedure. No such request was made from the Sheriff.

Lois Miller, Maggie's baker had been driving home from a night shift and also saw the Sheriff pass her at the Norwood turn doing a good clip with lights blazing.

My wife's secretary testified to the results of the preliminary analysis of the filter screen. It was skull fragments, skin and brain tissue, and hair. DNA analysis had been ordered. The decomposition was hard to determine, but roughly fit the time of the death concerned in the trial.

We broke for lunch. I went to a cell in the basement. It didn't seem fair. Hadn't we just proved that there was no murder? Everything had happened somewhere other than my Mustang, and I was still in jail. Maybe every wish really is that old black pudding, and it was all over my nose. I wrote with despair to pass the time.

~

She forcefully shoved him backwards into the pile of towels on the floor in the pool house and was on top of him immediately. His heart was still hammering from the gun in his face and the sounds of his own death screams.

The buttons on his shirt popped and skidded under the lockers. His starched collar still hung off his neck as she ripped the shirt from his chest and pulled it down his back, trapping his arms behind him, pinning his wrists at his sides. A shiver of fear surged through him as her mouth kissed him roughly, biting away at his upper lip as she straddled his thighs, both hands to his shoulders to hold him down.

Her face was mad, over the top. Deep depravity tore at him through her eyes. She was insane. She bent her head and bit his chest. The pain caused him to yelp and try to pull away. She bit harder. He lay still.

"That's better," she said, her mouth pressed against his skin. She playful nipped down the soft rise of his stomach. He quivered. The resignation in the movement forced a hoarse laugh from her. His breath was shorter now, shallow. She bit harder for an exclamation point.

Her hands went to the buttons on his pants with an audible growl. He tried to squirm and rise, but a single hand slammed into his chest, forcing him back down. Red nails dug into the skin.

"Stay," she said, "still." She expertly completed the job of exposing him. She began to pull on his penis, churning the flesh, watching his face with an overt challenge and excited expectation.

Over her shoulder Fitzgerald suddenly saw Sandy Gatz leaning with a graceful ease against the doorsill. A lighted cigarette dangling from his pouting lips, a single tendril of smoke rising, almost closing his right eye

"Started without me?" Sandy asked. "Shame on you two. Save some honey for Sugar."

She grunted like an animal and came up off of Fitzgerald's legs to wave her bare behind at her half brother. Her mouth crashed into Fitzgerald's, splitting his lip. Blood taste lingered as her tongue swam against his gums.

"I'm all the honey you both need. Take me with your stinger, my little Gatz Bee," she says over her shoulder, her breath hot in Fitzgerald's face.

The author knew in that very instant as the night closed in around them that he had found an open doorway to the mezzanine in hell.

～

The judge called the trial back to order and then was interrupted by a messenger. She left the courtroom and called the counsels and me to her office. It really was only a cubicle. With the prosecutor present, she showed us a letter from Sheriff Bueller's attorney. It stated that the Sheriff had gone to West Egg and disturbed the crime scene described by Mr. Eric Wolfscheim.

The Sheriff had re-created another crime scene in the Mustang with the body found at the hot tub. It was with the express purpose of implicating Mr. Thorpe. Bueller cited job stress, a military discharge for "combat fatigue," and an ongoing emotional obsession with a co-worker as mitigating factors in his actions. He was immediately seeking professional psychiatric help while awaiting the court's pleasure.

Ernie started to object, to say this was all too sudden, and the Judge yelled, "You won, you moron, your client's free to go. Is winning also a new thing for you?"

"Hardly, your honor."

Once she had also said the same thing in court, and dismissed the Grand Jury, it was official. I was a free man. The crowd and the jury took it hard. This was the best show in town, and they were sorry to see it over. Ernie and I hugged. No one shook my hand as we left the courtroom. People still sat quietly in their seats hoping it was all a big mistake. "Free Wit," was a rally slogan that didn't play as well in a victory celebration.

Patsy Susie was waiting in the hall, real tears in her eyes, a smile on her dark red lips, and gave me a full hug, shoving those perky breasts hard into my stomach. My wife watched in disgust from the entry to her office before turning and slamming the door. My mouth dropped open as defeat was snatched from the jaws of victory. Patsy Susie pushed me away and was gone in a rush of some exotic vinegar-based scent.

"You still owe me," she said over her shoulder. "More than you know, *Chico*. I'll catch up with you later."

I didn't like the sound of that.

Thirty-seven

Caressing The Divine Details

Ernie and I bought our own drinks at the New Sheridan Bar. We bought Digger a shot for telling the truth, so help us God. I enjoyed the first one almost a little too much. I would have to watch myself tonight.

Some of the patrons even congratulated us on my getting off the hook, again. Others asked what the fuss was all about as if they had never heard about the murder that wasn't. The cow costumes could now be put back away. It was almost as if people were disappointed that I wasn't an eco-terrorist with a bovine bent. We were yesterday's news, and it was only 2 p.m.

"I don't usually believe in coincidences," I said. "But this time it made sense. Who would have thought this stuff up? Here's to Goddamn coincidences."

"Here's to Bueller, the codfish prick, for being such a complete airhead," Ernie said.

"Don't talk about pricks and head in public," she said in a mock conspirator's whisper that echoed through the bar. "Don't you know people are already talking about you two?"

Patsy Susie hopped up on the stool beside Ernie and gave a limp wristed wave in our horrified faces.

"Next you'll be wanting to go off together for a seminar at the church in Sodoma." Patsy Susie laughed and took cigarettes and a lighter from her coat pocket and put them on the bar. She was settling in. Digger brought her the usual. She took a long pull on the bourbon before speaking again.

"I'm a happy lady. Yes-indeedy-do, talk about a sleigh ride," she exclaimed. "I even had to up front a hundred thousand of my own as a binder. We go the extra mile."

"Congratulations," I said. "Binder?"

"The deal's going through in spite of your best attempts to screw it up, Thorpe. A local investor is going to put up the rest of the money for the poor old church, God bless 'em, because the damn insurance company will now go even slower paying for suicides, thank you very much. Can't let a few dollars hold up all the rest. I just need to get the signatures of the surviving members of the original church and the new trustees. Fifty-five million at six percent. Bingo, fat city, I'm buying. Want another drink?"

We both said no, too quickly, and in perfect unison.

She eyed us suspiciously. "Got other plans?" she said, finally, lighting the cigarette. "I was hoping we could discuss my favor, Wit. I got an itch."

Ernie and I both looked at our watches. I stepped out of my stool before she could reach across Ernie and grab me.

"Dinner," I said. "I'm cooking a celebration macaroni and cheese feast for my kids."

"Got to go park the Bentley," said Ernie.

Her steel blue eyes were no longer warm and full of ripe suggestions. Imagine, leaving her sitting at the bar all alone. Like, she didn't own this town and everyone in it? The hard stare sent the same kind of shiver through me that Agnes Singer's did. I would definitely let this lady sell my house.

Ernie and I slinked away. She watched until we were out of sight.

~

I got a big hug from Katie as I walked through the front door, a crooked smile from Angelina. Cody came running from her room and threw herself into my lap as I sat down exhausted on the couch.

"We done it." She was proud.

"*Muchos Gracias, Senorita* Bond." I tried to match her enthusiasm. A vague apprehension was putting a crimp on my normal full-tilt enjoyment of dodging a murder charge. Even imagining the shitload of trouble Bueller was in didn't help me levitate to a really good mood.

It's said that God is in the details of life. My raging egomaniac and literary hero Vladimir Nabokov said that good writing, "caresses the divine details." The details of Sandy and Lambis were far from divine, in spite of the church 'gonnegtion' with Wolfscheim. The details didn't add up.

"You worried?" she said.

"Kind'a."

"You think the murderer will do it again?"

"What?" How had she slipped inside my head?

"It wasn't suicide, Sherlock?" I said.

"Please," she said. "Someone tried to almost kill you in Lambis' office. Agnes Singer tried to shoot both you and Eric. Why? Wolfscheim tried to kill his own son? Walter is the only surviving member of the original church trustees and seems to be in bed with his ex-wife Mrs. Singer who stands to gain back her view with the church going under. And, don't forget, the stuff in their pants."

The stuff in their pants? My face flushed. I wondered if Cody and her mother had already discussed the birds and the bees.

"Dad," she changed the subject, "are you at all worried about how the story's going to end?"

Story? I gave her a blank stare.

"The Fitzgerald thing." Cody looked into my eyes.

"How? When?"

"What do you think I was trading Mom for all those documents from her office?"

"You've read it?" I was immediately embarrassed. Your kids should not read your writing, especially if its about mysterious sexual fantasies and troubled men and women.

"No, I haven't read it yet. Mom won't let me, but she has told me the whole story, each segment, leaving out the racy stuff," Cody said without a trace of embarrassment.

"And I know what it's about."

"What is it about?" I didn't know what it was about. I was just writing down the words. I held my breath.

"Temptation and redemption." The words were hard for her to form and I knew they were both her mother's words.

"Oh, yeah?" I wanted to smirk, but couldn't. She was probably right. Why hadn't I seen it?

"You worried about how to finish it?"

"Maybe."

"Don't be," she said, giving me another big hug, "it will end itself. Just don't stop writing until it does. Trust me. It's how the big boys do it."

I did trust this midget, and felt better.

"Besides, I think I got you an agent."

"Huh?"

"Been working with Harriet Ober at Creative Artists since last week. We're going for *Rolling Stone* or *PlayMiss*. She figures five figures and a cover lead is 'do-able darling' now that you actually beat the rap and all the publicity is going national. Deadline this Monday. So get on it." Her words tumbled out. "She thinks we could also go for a book by Spring Lists if you would just tell what happened to Mr. Singer; I mean Wilson, uh, you know, Sandy."

My anxiety went through the roof as my daughter responded with a headlong rush to answer a "Yankee Doodle Dandy" chime from her room. I looked after her in awe and amazement. My story, about to be looked at by someone I don't know? I felt sick. Deadline?

"I think we should call it *Gatsby's Last Resort*," she said. "What do you think? "Why, hello Denver. It is great news about my innocent dad."

She giggled

"Friday?"

I wasn't thinking any more today.

≈

"What's with you and Patsy Susie?"

"*D'nada*," I said. My wife and I had avoided each other all evening. We were now in the kitchen putting away the dishes from the dishwasher.

"Those perky little breasts were giving your stomach a pretty good working over after the trial."

"Forget it," I said.

"Why? Cause she's not a redhead?"

I flinched.

"Wit, I don't need to know all about the self destructive things you do. But I'm not gonna be in a marriage that's all one sided. It's not fair to the girls."

"I'm not a good dad?" I said.

"When you're all here, you're great. It doesn't happen as often as they need it."

"What about you and Bueller?" I was always one to figure a good offensive remark is better than a defensive one. It is not a strategy I recommend to anyone with my half a brain.

"Bueller brought me the stuff you had Cody sneak off and copy. That's all. What could you be thinking?"

"In your bedroom?"

"Where else? In my office? Don't go there, Wit," she said. "Bueller was and is a bonehead. One who was doing me a favor. Give me a break."

She was right, and she never told a lie.

"In a marriage," she said, "you don't settle for anything except what you need from your partner. I need you to be honest with me about what you want. Dump yourself here, in this family, or get off the pot and let us get on with our life."

"I'm trying."

"Trying what? Dumping us or getting off the pot?"

"I love you," I said not knowing what else to say. Once I started apologizing I would never stop.

"Gotta do better than that," she said. "Way better."

"I was wrong," I said.

"That's a start," she said folding her arms and leaning back against the white porcelain sink with the trace of a welcoming smile.

"No, I mean about the suicides."

"What?"

"Lambis and Sandy were both murdered. I know it; you'd know it too, if you let yourself add it all together. They might have even wanted to die, but someone killed them both. I'm dead sure of it. I can't let them get away with it."

"Wit, the trial's over. Sandy is almost officially dead by his own hand. Let it go. Anything else and you're back as the prime suspect. I'm the District Attorney and I'm satisfied. What do you care about the damn Church? Don't you get it? Bury the bone. The case is closed."

"I can't let it go," I said in a tone that surprised me. I even believed myself. My wife was not buying it. She had heard the "I'll finish it no matter what" speech before. She didn't find it ironic that I now wanted to finally finish something when it was better to leave well enough alone.

"You're an idiot," she said and walked down the hall to the bedroom.

"It's my middle name," I said under my breath as the door slammed shut. I knew I was on the couch again tonight and possibly forever.

How was I going to put this thing right once and for all? Should I simply forget it? Not be the designated village idiot?

Stubbornness comes from both sides of my nature. I had to see it through, just to prove to myself that I could actually get to the end of something that mattered. Respect for myself had been in the toilet bowl for too damn long.

It was "*galgenhumor*," gallows humor. It overwhelmed me as I picked up a pen and decided to put an ending to at least a big part the story.

≈

Fitzgerald, unfulfilled, stumbled from the pool house in shaking disgust. He staggered forward to the edge of the freshly mowed grass and vomited, again, retching until his insides ached. Minutes were spent rocking on all fours like a dog.

He took the Pierce-Arrow from Gatz's garage and made it back to the city. He bolted from the car at the Algonquin Hotel leaving it running for the doorman. Rushing across the empty lobby he heard the deskman calling after him. The button for the Penthouse was pressed and the door closed and jerked upwards before his mission could be interrupted.

At her bedside he held her hand as she slept. Zelda was sedated in sleep and immersed in the wild territories of her own frightful dreams. Fitzgerald would later write that he "wanted to recover something, some idea of himself, perhaps, that had gone into loving her. His life had been confused and disordered since then, but if he could only return to a certain starting place, and go over it all slowly, he would find out what that thing was."

Fitzgerald went and looked out from the balcony that eyed Central Park. Cars passed with the splash of tires in shallow puddles. In the deep shadows of the blank windows of the empty skyscrapers he saw the people who ate at his insides every day. He forced himself to remember the clear voices of little girls, gathered like crickets on the grass in the park singing:

"I'm the Sheik of Araby.

Your love belongs to me.

At night when you're asleep

Into your tent I'll creep..."

He smoothed his hair, put his face in his hands and wept.

He would leave this town, this city and its limitless arrogance. It was a rotten place really, a place without a soul. They would sail on the first boat to Europe, Paris, yes, Paris. He could stay with the Murphys. They would be happy there at Villa America. It would be swell. He would write, Zelda would heal, Scotty would keep them together; they would be a family. He would forget about the things he had seen and done in the name of living life's alleyways.

Words would come. He would write about the places very important people see when they have gone too far in this vast heedless universe. The spoiled edge of things was where the real thunder and lightning was, a place a writer in debt to himself could work. He would create a world in his next work where even his own darkest ghosts could drive endlessly, "on toward death through the cooling twilight."

finis

Thirty-eight

Last One Standing

I walked. It was midnight. I was busy shaking my firm belief that something bad was still going on. It was getting harder to do by the minute. The only place to go was the place I least wanted to be. Isn't that always the case? I turned up the collar of my Carhart jacket against the night air, jammed my hands in the pockets. The pit in my stomach gurgled. I turned onto Cordova Street.

Patsy Susie had converted one of the turn-of-the-century small clapboard miner's houses into her real estate office and lived on the second floor. The impeccable little property had gingerbread trim and five hues of pastel paint to highlight the gabled roof. I could see that lights, a lot of lights, were on from a half block away. One of the church's white Mercedes was parked in the drive in front of the diminutive one-car garage. The fact barely registered as I forced myself forward.

Get on with it, I kept urging myself along, dreading each footfall. It was only when I turned down the sidewalk to the porch that I noticed the front door standing open. I knocked, but could feel the stillness and quiet of the inner office. Calling out, I let myself in and closed the door behind me. It was then I smelled the blood. A copper scent laced with a hint of spoiled cabbage. A leg stuck out from behind the receptionist's desk. I stretched over the counter and peaked. It was a body all right. Chest wounds, two to be exact, had ceased draining blood from the cold corpse.

I never understand people in the movies or on television who run to a dead body and touch it. I had no such impulse. Actually, I wanted to bolt for the door. Instead, I forced myself to go and open the door to Patsy Susie's private office. I needed to call the police, right after I called my wife the Assistant District Attorney to tell her I was still turning up stiffs. And, of course, in recognition of my new commitment to our marriage, to say, "I told you so."

The desk was strewn with papers. It is amazing how the simple swipe of an orange highlighter will draw attention from a pile of meaningless black and white. Three faxes were marked up.

The first was a typed note without a signature. It read: "Regret to inform you that unless the purchase agreement is signed by tomorrow at noon, Mountain Standard Time, and all moneys deposited to my account, Geneva, I will withdraw my offer of the Valley Floor and seek a buyer elsewhere. Inform me, soonest. I will keep 100K earnest money for my trouble if deal fails." An international business number was noted.

The second was handwritten almost illegibly in a large angry scrawl. "I am not signing the land deal. No way. Fuck off. You can all die. I mean it. Eric Wolfscheim."

The third was also written, but in a flowery female hand. "Sending Walter, as the surviving Trustee, to pick up the paperwork and deposit into my account your escrow check. We're calling the whole thing off." It was signed, Agnes Singer.

All three single-page faxes had a wide oval circle in orange in the upper right hand corner. It circled a coded number from the sender's fax. All three came from the same machine. It was penciled on one sheet that the machine's number was at West Egg. Agnes Singer was caught acting as both one of the buyers and the mysterious seller of the Valley Floor. Once the murders became suicides and the insurance money was to be glacially slow in coming, there was no sense in going through with the charade. Walter and Agnes now controlled the church in Sodoma, its assets, and Eric and Miranda get a quarter full of nothing. The insurance money, years down the line might ease the pain in time, but the party was over. The only other one screwed in the transaction was the broker who had told us she was to be out a cool hundred grand if the deal fell through, not that any amount of money mattered now. The players were getting dead one by one. I noticed for the record how fresh blood fills a room and permanently stains the air. I decided I hated the smell.

I had to get up to West Egg pretty quick. The real murderer was probably already at the house, and I might have a chance to put this thing to rest once and for all. I'll call my wife and the police from there. I was sick of keeping one eye on the dead body, expecting it to get up like a dazed zombie. I forced myself to reach into the pocket of the finely fashioned, but bloody coat to extract the car keys. As I closed the door, I noticed the bullet hole clean through the recessed panel of the front door. I was shivering all over as I eased through town heading for Mountain Village in the Mercedes waiting for the heater to drive away the cold. Whoever left that bloody mess back there was not a marksman, but eventually, shooting until something hit home, they found a way to be effective.

 ≈

I saw the crumpled figure in the courtyard as soon as I crested the hill at a jog. I had to leave the borrowed car at the security gate because the code had been changed again. I was winded, but forced myself to keep running towards the open doorway of the huge round-log guesthouse. It was Eric Wolfscheim. He was busy as hell bleeding to death. I got him over on to his back. A gaping hole in his chest oozed dark black blood. His dreamy eyes stared blankly at the stars in the night sky. Only the dim security lights on the stone bunkers lit the compound.

"Why?" he said and coughed. The blood pulsed out of his ruptured sternum.

"I'll get an ambulance, help," I said, "hold on."

Eric wobbled his head on the flagstone. "Walked right up and shot me... surprise." His voice was weak. "I'm dead already."

I couldn't argue the fact.

"Inside," he said. "Be careful..."

I looked towards the main house. The massive front door was standing open, dark shadows beyond. Fear surged through me. What was I going to do? End up dead probably, bleeding like this poor guy. What a...

"Bitch," he said. It was the last breath Eric had to give, and it fit into my thoughts perfectly.

≈

I used the stone bunkers to hide behind as I tried to edge nearer to the door. Maybe I could use a lamp or something else heavy, and crack the killer in the head. I made myself try to believe it. That kind of stuff doesn't actually ever happen in real life. I was sneaking inside to get myself shot. Probably shot dead. What an idiot. At least I had called 911 from the guesthouse. It would probably take them fifteen minutes to get here. Maybe I could stay hidden that long? I hated myself for thinking like a coward. I made sure not to talk my thoughts out loud.

Voices were faint, coming from somewhere beyond the door. An argument was taking place. It was hard to make out all the words.

"Shut up...managing to...go ahead!...I will... Anyhow...it was just personal... Money?...fuck you!" Major parts of the conversation were unintelligible. The voices shrill against their own echoes in the huge room.

I was now crawling inside and up the four wide stairs to the leather floor of the main room. Silhouetted against the tall wide windows, framed under a bright shaft of starlight, sat Agnes Singer in a straight backed Victorian chair. In the shadows by a tall stone pillar was another figure. An ember burned, and cigarette smoke curled out into the shafts of light in the comparative brightness by the windows.

"You haven't a clue what really went on here do you?" Agnes said with a sharp tone of dismissal. "If it wasn't for Thorpe putting this whole thing back to a couple of suicides and delaying payment, I would have even had those poor slobs' insurance money already. Everything they had was going into that five million down payment. Every last cent. What a lost moment. Now those two ungrateful whelps will probably get the insurance in a couple of years. Damn it all to hell anyway."

"Only one will," the voice from the shadow said.

"What do you mean?" Agnes' haughty tone lost a few thousand feet.

"Thorpe shot Eric before he came to get you."

I could now see Agnes was tied tightly to the chair. The news of her son's death seemed to not affect her one bit. She tried to straighten up in order to puff out her chest in pride at what she had almost pulled off. The fact she'd probably get Wolfscheim's insurance money now was all that showed in her face. She refused to accept that she wouldn't be around to gloat over it.

"I wasn't going to lose my view. I've got the votes on the City Council to claim the land for the town by eminent domain. Condemn it. Tie that bloody church up in the courts for decades while I hold all their money. It almost worked. Who would have thought those two spineless bastards really had the guts to kill themselves? I didn't know they had it in them. Usually when I break one, they stay broke." Agnes laughed a wicked laugh.

"It wasn't suicide," the voice from the shadows said. "I killed them both."

I just about blurted I told you so.

"Even gave them both a last orgasm before they knew I was going to be the end they had in mind all along. You trained them well to obey orders, I have to give you that, you old battleaxe. Sex for them was always about bondage, pain and finally letting go. They didn't have the guts to kill themselves. It was all histrionics and hissy fits of despair. I was the one who had to help them find their way to where they needed to be."

Patsy Susie slowly stepped from the shadows and pointed a gun at Agnes. "Just the same, it doesn't really matter. I'm not going to worry about you having a final tickle."

"You haven't the balls," said Agnes.

"I suffocated Stuart and shot Sandy. I think balls are banging around in my court," Patsy Susie said.

Patsy Susie paused to take a drag from her cigarette. "Why were they all so afraid of you?"

"They knew I'd get them in the end. Do I still have to explain who is in charge here?" Agnes said.

"Don't think I won't kill you." Patsy Susie held up a check. I had a feeling it was signed by her to Agnes and was made out for a hundred thousand dollars. "It's your last rodeo, you cold-skinned bitch. New rules: Don't fuck with a broker on commission."

"You are such a toad."

I could see Patsy Susie come back to the moment, stiffen and tense her arm out straight in front of her. She was going to shoot. Agnes was defiant, but dead meat.

"Aw, shit," I said standing up. "Patsy Susie, I still owe you that favor."

The movement in the dark startled her. The gun swung to me. I put my hands on my head and began to cover in a long slow trudge the forty feet to the two women. I had known the killer was Patsy Susie as soon as I found Walter shot dead in her office. The bagman had gotten himself bagged. By now I had accepted the fact I was almost right about everything. I was also, to put it mildly, confused.

"So, I got to tell you, I called the police and they are already on their way. If you need to make an escape, you better do it now. It's the best favor I can give you. We're even."

Patsy Susie, looked a real mess up close. Mascara running down her cheeks, hair in tangles, and Walter's blood still flecked on her smart little range coat. She was pointing my own gun at me. I was never so unhappy to see an old friend.

"Better get going," I said.

"I have to kill her," Patsy Susie said. "The bitch has ruined me, my plans. I can still pull this whole thing together when Miranda inherits it all." The gun swung back to Agnes who finally flinched a twitch in spite of herself. This old woman was certifiably immune to duress.

"That's my gun."

"Of course it's your gun. I took it in the bowling alley before you were bowled. How do you think I am going to pin all this on you without your gun? That's the favor I need, Wit. I just have to get rid of one final witness, before I kill you in a justifiable rage of self defense."

"You can have it," I said. My eyes never left the gun in her hand. The hammer was cocked. A twitch would drop the hammer.

"Pity how you hunted each of us down, Thorpe. Got Walter at my office, chased me up here when I came to warn poor Agnes. All of us, the ones who got in the way of your crusade to save those damn stupid cows. Even poor Eric. Shame, shame. You are one sick eco-terrorist, Wilfred Thorpe."

The barrel came up to point at my shadow coming towards her.

"Don't make me go out of sequence here, first things first," she said, and although I hadn't really met someone totally insane before, I was pretty sure I could spot this one without professional help.

"You're out of bullets." I dropped my hands to my side and walked towards her quickly with a confident stride.

"What?" Patsy Susie pulled the gun close to her face and then swung it back up to my chest stopping me at the end of her outstretched arm.

"Count 'em," I said, pressing forward against the barrel for affect. "Sandy, one. Two in Walter, three. One in the door at your office, four. One in Eric outside. The gun holds six, hence it's called a six-shooter. I never load one under the hammer. Five in, five out. You've shot your wad, so to speak. Your shootin' days are over, Annie Oakley. So, like I said, my favor to you is that you better start running for the border. I got a few minutes work here. You can make the getaway."

I began to concentrate at untying the thin Venetian blind rope that was wrapped in childlike endless swirls around the old woman and the chair. Patsy Susie's eyes were wild, not quite registering what the hell I was talking about. I turned my back getting between her and the struggling old woman in the chair. Agnes was not shocked, stunned, or speechless, and she was swearing at me to hurry the hell up. I didn't figure to tell her I was banking our lives on Patsy Susie not being someone who was going to bother to go and buy shells to reload a stolen murder weapon. She could chip a nail.

Out of the corner of my eye, I watched Patsy Susie look at the gun in her hand again, closely, and then let it drop back to her side. Then frustration and rage at letting the deal of her life slip through her fingers, Patsy Susie exploded in an anguished guttural scream. She swung the gun up over her head and pulled the trigger. I hit the deck at the loud report and pushed Agnes' chair over onto its side away from the windows as the forty-foot tall pane of glass shattered and collapsed in a cascading waterfall of irregular marbles.

I scrambled to my feet, crackling glass that had spilled forward onto the floor after the initial straight-down cascade. I quickly finished untying Agnes who was breathing in raspy gulps. I helped her to her feet, and then she slapped my hand away.

"Leave me alone, you stupid goat," she said, walking directly to where Patsy Susie stood with fragments of sparkling glass dust in her disheveled blonde hair. She seemed to have slipped over into another world, and her chest heaved in slow motion.

"I lied. I always load one under the trigger," I said.

Patsy Susie pointed the thirty-eight at Agnes and the hammer struck home a few times metal to metal.

"Sorry," I said. It was an unkind thought as I apologized to the world for not having one bullet left over for Agnes.

Mrs. Robert Forrest Lambis Wolfscheim Silva Singer knocked the gun aside and laid an open hand to Patsy Susie's face that sounded like another gunshot. The Realtor staggered backwards and then stood her ground in a punch drunk daze. I looked at the dropped pistol on the leather floor amidst the glass shards and left it where it fell. It was an old friend, but I was going to leave it behind. Too many ghosts were connected with that hunk of iron. The siren and red flashing lights of the Deputy Sheriff's Bronco pulled into the courtyard. Five seconds later Darryl called from the door for us to come out. Hands up.

"Eric's dead, Walter too," I said.

"Last man standing," Agnes said. "I win."

"This was all your game," I said. "Everything?"

"I had this little real estate whore pegged to a post." Agnes put her hands on her hips adjusting her thick bathrobe and turned to the dazed Patsy Susie.

"Oh sure, I forgot," I said. "I could see that you had Patsy Susie right where you wanted her when I walked in." I registered a sharp flashlight beam quickly scanning the open main doorway a flight of stairs below. I waited for a thank you for saving her life.

"I'm coming in. I'm armed, and I will shoot," Officer Darryl said. His voice broke on shoot.

"Why would this bimbo go off the deep end and start killing everyone for losing a token hundred grand when she was playing to make such easy, quick millions. Low life moron. A deal is a deal," Agnes said.

I wasn't going to get a thank you.

"Pegged?"

"My brain-challenged gang of ex-husbands needed money to swing the big deal for the Valley Floor, and they had their patented quick, insurance scam solution that had always worked before. All I needed was a broker with balls enough to seal the deal and another real patsy to take the blame."

"You knew?"

"I put the pieces together and waited."

I didn't want to ask. Agnes answered anyway.

"You weren't exactly one surprise after another."

"Predictable. especially after I got a chance to see that trivial bit of writing."

"Gatsby?"

"So presumptuous, you hack. It was sad and predictable."

"Glad I kept up," I said.

"You ran like a rogue elephant, Mr. Thorpe. Single minded in ignoring everyone else's best interests but your own. Never a dull moment."

"You planned all of it?"

"Every wrong headed mistake was a pretty sure bet."

"Why, Hello Officer," Agnes said. She smiled forcibly. Arcing that chrome plated brow, the sharp chin jutted forward and the cowl on the soft black cotton robe framed her head. It was the face of Norma Desmond, the shriveled silent film star from *Sunset Boulevard* clutching the staircase and declaring she is finally ready for Mr. DeMille and her close up.

I looked at her with what I hoped passed as open disdain instead of simply plain ordinary disgust. She stared back at me, down her nose, with eyes that appeared dead. She was going to win the staring contest, so I tipped my nonexistent Stetson, hoping that the real thing was still in the driveway and not roadkill under the patrol car. I backed away and walked over to the phone.

The Sheriff's deputy led Patsy Susie away to his car. I called Ernie and asked if he could meet me at the Sheriff's Office. I told him no. I didn't need bail. What a guy, even to ask.

Thirty-nine

Green Eggs And Spam

I have decided that all celebrations should be held over until breakfast. It is a hopeful meal, and the whole day with its endless promise spreads out ahead of you. My wife sat close to me on the bench at Sofio's Restaurant. The coffee was hot. My two daughters, my cousin Angelina, and Ernie rounded out the table.

My wife and I had shared our bed for the first time in months. I had missed her and did my best to show it. She was sporting a bright red road rash on her cheeks from my two-day growth of a beard. I was walking proud. She let me. We decided that people have only their own special kind of love to give, and it's often not our kind. We would learn to live with the challenge of that.

Katie and I had both ordered green eggs and Spam. The kitchen was laughing and seeing what they could do for us. Cody was on the cell phone again with Bailey giving her friends the blow-by-blow account of last night.

"Totally. Yes, way. I never trusted blondes, anyhow," she said, adding quickly, "except you, of course."

Miranda and Jeffrey Breene surprised us and came out of the back room, hand in hand. They stopped at our table where Miranda and my wife eyed each other coolly. Miranda showed no outward sign that both her half-brother and husband had died the night before.

"Where are you two love birds headed, Commissioner Breene?" Ernie said finally breaking the silence, not really wanting to know.

"Thailand," Miranda said, beaming.

"Permanently?" my wife said.

"Till next month." Miranda ignored the slight. "I'll then be in town permanently, thank you very much, running Patsy Susie's real estate office while she is gone away."

She made it sound like a summer on the Riviera rather than life in the "big house." I didn't speculate about my little town's need for another ambitious real estate broker, especially one with a grudge against me who knew how to use a gun. I tried to sound brave.

"Want to take along a video camera and save me some work later on?" I said to Jeffrey Breene. I remembered I still had a retainer from his wife.

"Did you know Jeffrey had a passion for warm buns and Italian loaf?" I asked Miranda.

"Nice way to talk in front of the kids," Miranda said. "Did God miss you in handing out class?"

"Naw, she just has a ribald sense of humor," I responded wishing they would move along. I had better things to do. Crazy billionaires and femme fatales still give me the willies. Cody gave me a pinky grip across the table for the "ribald."

"We'll see," she said and glared at me. She had her mother's eyes.

Breene belched once, picked his teeth with a toothpick. You could tell he was already half snockered, and tried to drag her away. She was a foot taller, three feet skinnier, and a hundred IQ points smarter than he was. They would soon deserve each other.

"See you on the rebound, Wit," she said winking at me.

"Not in this lifetime," I said back as she left. She walked ahead of Breene with that determined take-no-prisoners stride.

My wife's hand went to my thigh, and I knew I had said the right thing. I should practice doing that more.

When we had all finished breakfast and Ernie paid the bill, I stepped out into the sunlight on Colorado Avenue and looked up at the high mountains framing our perfect little post card town. As Ernie often said, Telluride is an asylum for the reality-challenged and the "Lost Boys of Pandemonium" are running the whole place. I had to remember that snippet for a future bit of writing. It was a pretty sure thing that there would be further bits of writing. I had found a certain hump, the right emotional pain and edge while working. I would write about that.

Ernie and I strolled along together, sucking in the marrow of the morning. It was cold and clear, and our breath clouded at our chins. The mountains had a new light dusting of snow at their peaks, termination dust for the weak of heart who can't brave a winter two miles up in the Rockies.

"Seems we aren't half as worthless as some might have believed," said Ernie.

"No where near half," I said.

"Shall we crow over our success?"

"Like screaming banshees."

"That's the spirit, old cod."

We had laugh at our own expense.

I adjusted my hat and thought about how lucky I was. Down the street, ahead, I watched my three women tease Ernie about how he had taken to holding his lapels with two hands now that he had won a murder case. All of them laughing and imitating his puffed out chest and tucked in chin. Katie was the best. Angelina walked in the street with a tolerant smile, away from these crazy, almost white children and their destined to be a saint of a mother. The astonishingly bright red hair of all three members of my family glimmering from their shaking heads like splotches of wildflowers in the shafts of light and shade.

I put a thumb to my Stetson hat for F. Scott and the mysterious woman conjured up in my story. Then again, maybe she wasn't so mysterious and strange as I had thought.

Isn't it funny where stories come from? What detritus of memory writers throw together to make it right? Where the characters finally take you? The different ways they can save your life? It reminded me how, in the Land of

Oz the people are all the same folks you knew back home. All of the dialogue meant to teach you a specific lesson and move the story along.

I swore to myself that very moment, if a genie showed up and I had three wishes, I would give one to each of my family. Let them wish for their own black pudding. I had wished all the wishes I wanted, and here's hoping they don't all come true; at least not all at once. Things were really starting to look up. Optimism coursed through me like bottled lightning. I always make that same old mistake.

Author Biography

R. J. Rubadeau has honed his life view and communication skills in various shore-side occupations: professional yacht captain, school teacher, race car driver, university lecturer, grant writer, fund raiser, newspaper columnist, politician, speech-writer for an Alaskan governor (No, not that one!), public policy wonk, and twenty years as a professional political campaign strategist. He is a frequent contributor to many magazines and periodicals, especially the sailing magazines, his autobiography Bound For Roque Island: Sailing Maine and the World was published in 2010, the writer is also an award winning poet. Rubadeau and his wife Mary, best friends and partners since their teens, live with their horses and a menagerie of animals at ten-thousand feet in the Rocky Mountains near the town of Telluride, Colorado. They base Dog Star, their family's historic eighty year old ketch, and primary summer preoccupation, on Mt. Desert Island, Maine.

ON THE BOOKSHELVES
JUNE 2011

Announcing the second in the Telluride Murder Mystery
Series New from award winning mystery author

R. J. Rubadeau

The Fat Man
A Telluride Murder Mystery

Register at BeaconHillPublishers.com for a special advanced discount
price and a publication notification with ordering instructions via Email
(Read an excerpt)

"There were plots and counterplots, kidnappings, murders, prisonbreakings, forgeries and burglaries, diamonds large as hats...It sounds dizzy here, but in the book it was as real as a dime."

Dashiell Hammett, 1926

One

A Chica With Sharp Spurs

I fully expected the wolf's jaws to crunch. My extremities were frozen like a scared rabbit. It was no advertisement for a private detective who still thinks he's full of pickles. My hand won't complete the simple act of inserting a key into my mailbox at the Telluride, Colorado Post Office 81435. People are shuffling past averting their eyes. I ignore their embarrassed hellos, trying to muster the discipline necessary to handle rejection without caterwauling. My courage this sunny afternoon is as thin as mountain air two miles high.

"Howdy Thorpe," Judge McCarty whispers in my ear.

"Hal," I answer softly, without looking up.

"If this is a stake out, you aren't doing so hot on the inconspicuous part."

"Pretend I'm not here."

"Is that how it works," Hal hitched up loose-fitting pants on his bony hips. "Pee eyes," he said under his breath as he moved away.

"Merry Christmas," I said in return and continue to focus on the key slot to my post office box.

The old saw states that there are only two openings for a successful story, either someone new comes to town, or someone takes a trip. I had put both, plus a murder or two, an offbeat villain from a favorite novel, plot twists and turns, and a flawed private eye into twenty odd pages of ideas. The post office sent it off to an uncertain fate over a month ago.

"Wit," Digger said over my shoulder, straining on tiptoes to see exactly what held my undivided attention. "Your bar bill hit four figures yesterday. You wanted me to let you know."

"I wasn't drinking yesterday."

"The crew, especially Dolores, thought you would want to buy us all a cocktail on account of the holiday season and all." Digger was the bartender at the New Sheridan Hotel on Colorado Avenue. I spend a lot of time there.

"Dolores claimed you owed big money because of the pick-up."

I moaned a cat-sized mew.

"It was a big crew," he added around a gap toothed, nicotine stained smile.

"Merry Christmas," I said, wondering where the extra money was going to come from. I forced the key an inch closer to the lock. My present bank account could crawl under a duck, and the two twenties folded against my kidney felt very thin indeed. I gave a mental credit on the apt description to Dash Hammett, my idol of the moment.

The targeted Hollywood producer of my mailing is a total stranger by the name of Rosewater; a cold voice over the phone. He had read the only short story I have ever published, and invited a submission of a treatment for a screenplay based on my experiences as a private investigator. Specifically, the agent confided, "the producer wanted a bizarre story of murder, mayhem, and red herrings, just like the old movies of the thirties." In reality, the quick to capitalize moneymen wanted a disguised fictional account, to avoid liability, of my recent murder charges and all of the strange circumstances surrounding the highly publicized capitol crimes among the cesspool of celebrities and the clawing glitz of Telluride.

A scrapple of ideas entitled THE NOT SO THIN MAN is now, obviously, sitting under a slush pile in a production assistant's office at the aptly named Miracle Productions. The envelope was quietly gathering dust along with all the other bad ideas from equally famous-for-a-minute people. I expect a form rejection letter any day. You don't want to be around when I open it.

"Do you need an ambulance to get back up straight?" Officer Guild said. He actually thought the comment was funny and shared a laugh with himself. "Getting older and slower every day, aren't we?"

I noted the glee in his voice but refused to straighten up. Guild worked out at Benny Hanna's Dojo. He was current top dog. His unkind remark referenced my hand speed.

"You should see a shrink, Thorpe. The whole town knows you're a certifiable looney," his voice had lost its humor. "You should do us all a favor and lock yourself up. You're a menace."

"Merry Christmas," I said and edged the key another full inch closer to the lock. Three feet to go. Guild lost interest, sauntered away, hands on his Glock 9mm pistol grip and his mace. His leather creaked.

It is a good thing I don't carry a gun anymore. I would have it out in my free hand fondling it, hoping its deadly reason for existing would give me the moxie to face what waits behind the mouse sized door.

The facts were that my concealed weapon had, in the distant and recent past, been used against me. Also, I was more likely to hit a target by throwing the two pounds of steel at someone rather than pulling the trigger. The problem was stubbornness. I had nurtured for years an adolescent-sized strong opinion that a private detective had to carry a gun.

Having strong opinions and being indecisive is a double handicap in my line of work. Trying to forge a living as a professional sleuth on the western slope of the Rocky Mountains with these twin curses of character has almost gotten me dead a number of times. It is why I gave up guns. Since I had taken the cure, I wasn't getting shot as much.

"Wit Thorpe?" A young woman's voice tried to get my attention.

Asta, my dog, again jerked on the leash I have trapped under my foot. Asta is a mottled white Pomeranian, Chihuahua, and Terrier. The pedigrees are pureed. She is a fidgety genetic disaster. Her attempts to double paw every passer-by while standing on her hind legs at the extreme length of her tether are neither cute, nor threatening. The mutt stood ten inches tall at full stretch, ugly as a deformed Pug.

"Spitz?" the woman asked.

"No she just growls and slobbers once in a while," I said without losing my focus or concentration and giving the old joke all the enthusiasm of cold mutton.

My daughter, Cody, currently waiting in the still to be paid for pick-up truck, had rescued the football-sized canine from the pound. I thought a private eye should have a Pit Bull or Doberman, maybe even a German Shepherd. I am often not mature enough to see embarrassment as a waste of time.

"Wit Thorpe?" she asked again.

My eyes left the unopened postal box. Whether you looked at her face or at her body in that powder blue one-piece ski suit the results were satisfactory.

"I'm sorry," I said, skipping right to the chase and apologizing. I always end up there with tall, self-assured, beautiful women so I thought I would try working backwards for a change.

"We do know each other."

"We've known each other for years," I played along. She knew I was treading water.

"Monica Charalambides," she said holding out her hand.

"No," I said, making a ridiculous chopping gesture somewhere around my navel that indicated how tall she had been when I had last seen her. I took the offered hand and it melted into my nervous, sweaty grasp. She pulled free and wiped her palm on her thigh.

"Mother's just back from Tahiti." Her voice was light and warmed my ears. "My brother Gilbert and I flew out from the coast this morning. We had hoped to see my father."

Monica's eyes were bright blue and fixed on mine in a predatory survey. Blonde hair tumbled around her shoulders. Her delicately framed cheeks, blushed with a morning of skiing on the mountain, glowed. Her full mouth glistened with a warm shade of sun block. She flirted. My tongue stuck to the roof of my mouth.

"I read your story," she said, *Gatsby's Last Resort?*

I felt as if my strings had been cut. *PlayMiss Magazine* had bought and printed the short piece of fiction because it was full of old taboos, F. Scott Fitzgerald's sexual fantasies, and some bizarre anti-social behavior of the ultra rich. It also included murder. The kind of stuff that happens when Telluride locals have a first rate view at stake. *PlayMiss* is chock full of bare-naked women with a few fluff fillers thrown in. My story had helped fill last month's issue.

"You read *Play Miss*?" I asked.

"Mother made it mandatory for our trip here," she said and winked, "now I'm a big fan."

"I'm glad ...," I stopped, thinking.

"I'm glad you read the story," I said instead.

"Got to hand it to you, Mr. Thorpe. You followed up your quarter hour in the spotlight with a flare. I suppose somebody's got to make a buck from all those juicy celebrity murders here in Telluride," she said.

"The story I wrote had nothing to do with the murders," I said. I am a chronologically challenged adolescent and don't take teasing all that well.

"You predict the future?"

"I just write what comes in to my head," I said.

"You got four out of five-and-a-half erect penises in the contents. Not bad," she said.

"It was meant to be fun," I whispered defensively.

"Sinfully so, have you checked out the Gatsby's Last Resort Fan Club's web site? They got you pegged, for certain, mister I-didn't-know-the-words-were-loaded."

My face formed a question.

"GASTBYRULES.com." claims that one forty-two specific references turn up in your story, Fitzgerald's book, and transcripts of the trial. Most folks think you were writing about your own experiences and, definitely, after the fact of the verdict. It's all a literary publicity scam. The story just sums up what happened, plays on the bizarre twists at the trial, and ties it all together. Good con to say it was precognition. Got folk's attention, all right."

"My story was only about Fitzgerald," I said. "And it wasn't a trial."

She kept it up. "Inquiring minds spend hours chatting."

"I wrote the story segments before the murders," I said. "I didn't make that part up. My imagination just got away from me. Then things happened."

"Just coincidence?" she asked. "The real killer naked in a hot tub with F. Scott Fitzgerald? Now, that could trick a chicken."

"Trick a chicken?" I thought, recognizing a "Roscoe" when I heard one.

"It's amazing what you can hallucinate under stress," I said. "I was in front of a Grand Jury at the time, for a murder I didn't commit."

"Hallucinations don't usually walk around on the streets saying hello," she laughed, "even here in Telluride."

"The next time you try to pull the same kind of scam with your writing. You'll be crucified," she said with a disarming smile.

I must have switched from a dumb stare to a guilty one. Her blue eyes were the answer after a tumble with a guillotine

"Working on anything?" she asked coyly, trying to read my face.

"A screenplay," I confessed.

"Murders, and plots, and more sex, oh my," she chanted. "I have a permanent boyfriend but, oh, you kid."

"Oh, you kid?" It blurted out.

She looked at me like I was a center cut pork chop in an Italian deli. I pulled my Stetson from my head and dropped my eyes to check if my cowboy boots were tied.

"I'm probably already under contract," I said. "Can't talk about it." I never learn that lying is always the start of something bad.

"Scrutiny is always awkward?" she said.

"Beastly," I tried for humor. "I'm best ridden on a pretty loose rein."

"You just need a good *Chica* with sharp spurs," she tilted my head up with a pointer finger under my chin. Her blue eyes were milky in a surge of sexual challenge above a deliciously cruel smile.

"You're going to whip me into shape?" I asked, thinking it had an outside chance of being construed as a witty repartee' on the horse theme.

"Better be careful what you wish for," she said, leaning in close to my ear. I felt her breath against my lobe, a lip brushed my neck, and I shivered. She smelled like bee honey, musk, and wild flowers.

"Be careful," she repeated. "Whips I got."

"I hear the whip thing is over rated," I said, pulling back just in time to catch hold of my runaway libido, as it galloped west alongside my lust laden heart. I couldn't meet her eyes, again.

"Your picture in *Play Miss* made you look like a *Chicano* choir boy on steroids," she said. "Quite a mug shot."

It could have been worse. I had kept my clothes on. Leather loin clothes and woven ponchos were out, and I wouldn't wear their brand new cowboy hat with an Eagle feather, or even the fancy rhinestone studded shirt. I wore my own battered tan Stetson, with sweat stains around the hand beaded medicine band at the crown. I did look over my shoulder when I smiled. They opted for the full page.

"You had the best ass in the whole issue," she said. The teasing was back in her voice.

My mind suddenly shuddered to a halt with the thought of her unfolding the November centerfold. It was a waterfall scene in Cuba with suds, a brunette, and an AK-47.

"Great sex advice, kinky, yummy," she said and dropped unexpectedly into a squat at my feet. She gave Asta a double handed scratch behind her pointy little ears. The dog swooned, rolled on her back, and let her hind legs fall open. My reaction would have been the same. When Monica looked back up at me with a playful look, I coughed, felt a twitch from "mister frisky," and noticed my left hand still held the key locked in the ready to insert position. I let it fall.

"Do you know where my father is?" she said, gliding up slowly to her full height of five-ten with athletic ease. Her eyes were almost level with mine and she invaded my space with a purpose. I could feel her breath on my chin. Monica reveled in my discomfort over the directness of her stare. Her powder suit sighed again as the nylon stretched and settled tightly around her body. Nubile was the word that entered my head.

I shook my thoughts into submission, not trusting a verbal answer.

"It seems he's taken a trip or something," she said, "No one seems to know where. We would really like to see him. It's been so long. Almost ten years. Any ideas?"

"Ernie Sampesee," I said, "used to be your dad's local lawyer, I think. Maybe still is."

"Really." Her eyes wouldn't stop with the humor and I was the joke. "And where would I find Mr. Sampesee?"

"At the barber shop," I said as Asta, wanting more attention than she was getting, wrapped her two front paws around my leg and began to hump my shin. I blushed, which is hard to notice because of my equal parts Ute Indian and Spanish blood, which normally carries double the volatile octane as Black Irish. Monica noticed. Her laugh was shattering glass on my maleness.

"He's the Ernie's Barber Shop on Colorado," I said with my teeth clenched, shaking my lower leg discreetly to dislodge the amorous canine. My old tattered Stetson dropped lower over my eyes from the leg twitching.

"A lawyer, a barber, and a leg-humping dog?" she giggled. "My, my."

"It's Telluride," I said as if that explained everything. It didn't if you were a stranger. I pushed my brim back with a thumb.

"Mother would love to see you," she said with a slow wink that fluttered my stomach. "We're at the Peaks Resort. Her name is Price now."

"Sure."

"You're not what I expected."

How was I supposed to answer that? What did she mean?

"Tah," she said and walked away. I watched every tug of silky fabric until she rounded the corner and left me flustered with a no look wave over her shoulder.

I waved back to an empty hall.

My determination to face unpleasant facts left the building. Why did she have to mention her mother?

Two

The Last Resort

W ho's the dame?" my daughter said.
"What are you chinning about?"
"The one with the mile long legs who was trying to climb into your lap while you were still standing."
"You're on the boil this morning," I said.
"She's pretty," Cody said as I handed her the five-pound humping dog and slid into the bench seat of the aged Ford F-250 pick-up truck. The near wreck was a gaudy aquamarine and black. You could still read the peeled off towing service logos on both doors. Cody had seen the whole encounter through the wide windows of the new Post Office ten feet away.
"If you like them like that," I said.
"You mean young, rich, sexy, and looking like a super model?"
"She's not my type."
"You got types?"
"Only you, pip-squeak," I said, "midgets with wicked jaws." I gave her another modified stock phrase from Dashiell Hammett. We had both been devouring his work this past month. Learning our favorite lines by heart. Cody was helping me read the classics of the detective genre in order to

improve my writing. She patiently explains the parts of the intricate plots that confuse me. She was in the fifth grade at Telluride Elementary School.

"And how about that petite red head you wandered off with at the school concert last night?"

"That's beside the point," I said. "She just wanted to show me some French etchings. Besides, she was no lady, she was my wife."

"Precisely," my ten year old said. I received a Look in the process.

"What's that got to do with what?"

"Everything," she said, scratching the belly of the thoroughly excited dog in her lap. "So, who's the dame?"

"A kid I used to know. I did some work for her father a long time ago."

"How long?"

"Before you were born. Before I was married."

"She have a crush on you?"

"She was a kid."

"And you're a thirty-five year old Peter Pan," Cody said with a certainty that was disconcerting for a child of almost ten. "What about the crush thing?"

"Thirty-four and a half."

"C'mon shylock, spill the beans."

I was used to being interrogated by all the women in my house and although her mother was the Assistant District Attorney for San Miguel County, Cody was by far the best at getting answers I didn't want to give up.

"How should I know?" I said.

"She's crushing you now," Cody said.

"Get out," I said. She had me dead to rights, if wishes were horses. I forced myself to not even think about the possibilities.

Cody shrugged her shoulders. "No mail?" she asked trying to stifle a smile, knowing the question was a dagger in my heart. I hadn't been able to put the key in the lock.

I started the truck and the rattling fan motor for the lukewarm heater discouraged further conversation. Twelve years ago, in the prime of my male ego, I thought everybody had a crush on me. That personal delusion included a Cody-sized Monica Charalambides, and, of course, her mother.

Join Wit Thorpe as once again his desire to write classic noire fiction steps off the page and decorates the Rocky Mountain town of Telluride's holiday season with dead bodies, kidnapping, extortion, red herrings, blackmail, puppy-love missing implants, and a tall blonde with a story to tell. Join our whole gang of Telluride irregulars as they tackle another bizarre case with their usual wisecracking incompetence. Its Murder served Telluride style.

Log on at BeaconHillPublishers.com for ordering information.